the two of us

of us

ANDY JONES

**SIMON &
SCHUSTER**

London · New York · Sydney · Toronto · New Delhi

A CBS COMPANY

First published in Great Britain by Simon & Schuster UK Ltd, 2015
A CBS COMPANY

1 3 5 7 9 10 8 6 4 2

Simon & Schuster UK Ltd
1st Floor
222 Gray's Inn Road
London WC1X 8HB

www.simonandschuster.co.uk

Simon & Schuster Australia, Sydney
Simon & Schuster India, New Delhi

A CIP catalogue record for this book
is available from the British Library

PB ISBN: 978-1-4711-4244-4
EBOOK ISBN: 978-1-4711-4919-1
TPB ISBN: 978-1-4711-4294-9

Typeset by M Rules
Printed and bound in Australia by Griffin Press

Andy Jones lives in London with his wife and two little girls. During the day he works in an advertising agency; at weekends and horribly early in the mornings, he writes fiction. Follow Andy on twitter: @andyjonesauthor

27.6.15

For Chris and Dorothy, my parents.
For everything.

the two
of us

Prologue

People ask: *How long have you been together? How did you meet?*

You're sitting at a table, fizzing with the defiant ostentation of new love (is that what it is? Is it love already?), laughing too loud and kissing more enthusiastically than is *de rigueur* in a quiet country pub, and someone will say, *Put her down! Get a room! You make a lovely couple*, or some variation on the theme.

You're surreptitiously nibbling your new girlfriend's earlobe when a voice says, *They serve crisps at the bar, you know. If you're hungry.* You turn and apologize to the large middle-aged lady at the adjacent table. She laughs good-naturedly, then shuffles her chair sideways so she is now sitting at your table. And here it comes . . .

So, she says, *How did you two lovebirds meet?*

1

In the last week, we must have been questioned about the particulars of our romance on half a dozen separate occasions. On other nights and afternoons we have told increasingly pale shades of the truth: *We work together; Blind date; I cut his hair; Book club.* But now, emboldened by wine and routine, Ivy leans forward and says in a conspiratorial voice: *It's awful; I'm best friends with his wife.* But . . . she places her hand on top of mine . . . *you're a woman of the world, you know what it's like. When you* have *to have something?*

The woman – ruddy-faced and emanating a warm aroma of cheese and onion – she nods, says, *Aye, well, yes, you have a nice . . . you know . . . night*, and shuffles back to her own table.

Because the truth is, the truth is too long a story to tell a stranger in a country pub when all you want to do is finish your drink and get upstairs to your room. And anyway, *how* we met is academic – you don't ask how the rain began, you simply appreciate the rainbow.

People talk about chemistry, and perhaps it was – something molecular, something transmitted, something genetic. Whatever the mechanism, there was something about Ivy that immediately made me want to *not* sleep with her. And what higher compliment can a scoundrel pay a lady? Not that it matters, but at the time I was going through a phase where I wasn't looking for any kind of commitment beyond those to personal hygiene and discretion. I had broken up with my girlfriend six months earlier, I was young, I was free, I was . . . well, let's just say I was being generous with my affections. Then along came Ivy with her handsome, uncontrived beauty, trailing pheromones, nonchalance and easy humour.

Not that any of that matters. What matters is that we met. And what matters most is what happens next.

Chapter 1

It's the last week in August and my sunburn prickles as Ivy steers the car into the street I grew up in, towards the house I came home to the day I was born.

When the radio is on Ivy sings; when it's off she whistles, and she whistles badly. I almost recognize the tune, but can't quite grasp it. The left side of her face is scarred from a childhood accident – the lines are white now, but the grooves and misalignments are stark – and when she whistles the scars pinch and deepen. Whether this affects her whistling or not, I don't know, but if her singing is any indication, she's simply tone deaf and entirely oblivious of the fact. We've been together less than three weeks so it's a little too early to be drawing up a list of 'things I like most about my new girlfriend' but if I were so inclined, Ivy's careless tuneless whistling would be up there in the top eleven. And whilst we're on the subject of sequencing, it's also a bit premature for *meet the family*. But here we are, about one minute from lift-off.

'Brace yourself,' I say.

Ivy turns to me: 'Hnn?'

'The family,' I say. 'They're a bit . . . you know.'

'Don't worry,' she says. 'I've done this before. Loads of times, hundreds of times.' And she smiles to herself.

'Funny. Anyway, it's not you I'm worried about.'

We round a corner and Dad's house comes into view.

I've never paid attention to the way my childhood home looks; it's been there as long as I've been alive and I scrutinize it no more than I do my feet – probably less. But today, with Ivy beside me, I'm aware of its ordinariness, banality, of everything it isn't. Victorian houses – like the one I live in in London – age improves them, bestows character and integrity; but houses like this, built in the sixties and seventies, they age like old factory workers made ugly with time and effort and smoke and disappointment. Maybe it's not my sunburn prickling; perhaps it's my inner snob. I look at Ivy and she glances back, raises her eyebrows as she pulls up in front of number 9 Rose Park.

And forget the house, wait till she gets a load of the family.

They must have been lying in wait because before Ivy has a chance to kill the engine, my father, sister, brother-in-law and twin nieces pour out of the front door. I wave, grin, mouth 'Hiya' through the windscreen, but no one is looking in my direction. They line up in the middle of the road, faces lit with excitement as Dad opens Ivy's door as if she's some kind of dignitary. The twins, Imogen and Rosalind, are only ten years old, so I can forgive them dancing impatiently on the spot and jostling to get a better look at my girlfriend (it does feel good to say: *girlfriend*), but my sister and Dad have a combined age of almost one hundred and they're behaving like imbeciles. And then it comes to me what Ivy was whistling: 'It Must Be Love'. She climbs out of the car and straight into a bear hug from my dad. I grimace an apology as he lifts her off her feet and Ivy either winks or winces in return – but with her face squashed against my old man's neck, it's hard to tell which.

As I slip unnoticed from the car, it occurs to me that I may have misidentified Ivy's whistling. The more I think about it, the more I am convinced it was 'House of Fun' or possibly even 'Embarrassment'. Whatever it was, it's definitely Madness.

By the time the welcoming party gets off the road and into the house, I've hauled the bags out of the boot and upstairs, taken a pee, boiled a kettle and made a pot of tea.

'Tea's in the pot,' I say as everyone troops into the kitchen.

'Have we got any wine?' asks Maria.

'I assume *champagne* will be okay?' says Dad, opening the fridge with an excruciating flourish.

'Wow,' says Ivy.

'Well,' says Dad, 'special occasion, isn't it. Get the glasses, son.' And he steers Ivy into the living room.

Maria hangs back to help me rinse the dust from five champagne glasses. 'Seems nice,' she says, smirking.

'She is. No Hermione?' I say, heading off the inevitable (*what does she see in you?*) sarcasm from my big sister.

Maria wasn't quite sixteen when she gave birth to my eldest niece. Mum had been dead less than a year, and baby Herms played a big part in our collective healing. For the first six years of her life (until Maria met and married Hector) I was, I suppose, more like a father than an uncle to Hermione. And more than a decade later, I continue to think of her more as a daughter than a niece.

'Hot date,' Maria says.

'You're kidding! What's he like?'

Maria shrugs. 'Better than the last shit-bag.'

'That's not hard. I was hoping she'd be here.'

'You're no match for new love,' Maria says.

'Some might beg to differ,' I say. 'Come on, let's save Ivy from Dad.'

When we get through to the living room, Dad has already got the family albums out. This is the first time I have ever brought a girl – let alone a woman – home, and I guess everyone has been waiting too long to do all the things you do in these situations. So I sip my champagne and take my humiliation like a man as they laugh at my hair, clothes and bare backside through the ages. My girl-friend of nineteen days tilts her glass in my direction, smiles a coy smile and winks.

Both Ivy and I work in film production (commercials in my case, everything you can think of in hers), which means we are essentially freelance. For our first four days together we didn't leave Ivy's flat. Nothing was explicitly said, but we seemed to arrive at a psychic agreement not to venture outdoors until it became unavoidable. Because we under-stood (and understood that each other understood) that after the bubble bursts there's no returning to the intimate stupid collusion of the First Days. When provisions ran low we drank our coffee black, picked mould from the last of the bread and ate toast with holes. We dined on eggs and biscuits, aubergine and mayonnaise sandwiches and pasta in chicken-soup sauce. Ivy read while I watched American detective shows on her crappy portable TV; we played Monopoly, Scrabble and Snap, and got drunk on wine then vodka and finally a bottle of semi-crystallized booze of unknown origin. We resisted anything more practical than ordering pizza, instinctively knowing that delivery men fit the romantic script only if they drive mopeds and not supermarket lorries. The pin came in the form of a job, with Ivy booked to work on a pop promo all day Friday. On her way to the shoot she dropped me – and a bagful of her clothes – at my flat, and we kissed goodbye with the kind of fervour normally reserved for airports. Work took up most of the following week, but we spent every night together, sometimes meeting in a restaurant, other times in bed. On our second Saturday we packed my Fiat 126 and drove with no specific agenda or destination, spending nights in the New Forest, Cotswolds, Yorkshire Dales and Peak District. We walked, ate, drove, drank and missed breakfast every morning. Yesterday I realized we were less than a two-hour drive from my dad's house and I was in too good a mood not to visit. Ivy and I must have driven more than five hundred miles in the last week – singing to the radio, Ivy feeding me M&Ms from the passenger seat, me feeding her Skittles when we switched – but there was something different on the drive here today. I can even identify the point at which the atmosphere changed.

We stopped at a small village for a snack and a walk around the shops; Ivy went to Boots for 'toothpaste and stuff' while I paid a visit to the local Co-op. We met back at the car, Ivy with a bagful of toiletries, me with a bagful of ingredients and clinking bottles. And from that point forward something was … off. Nothing glaringly obvious, but Ivy was definitely more subdued. She sang with less gusto, didn't play I spy, didn't squeeze my knee with the absent-minded affection I have come to crave. Maybe she was apprehensive about meeting the family. And, witnessing the current inquisition, who could blame her?

Dad wants to know where Ivy's parents live, what their names are, do they go to church; Hector asks if make-up artists earn a lot of money, does she have an accountant, does she have a website, has she ever met Madonna; the twins want to know does she have any sisters, any brothers, any pets, does she prefer cats or dogs, would she rather be a mermaid, a fairy or a princess; Maria wants to know where Ivy bought her cufflinks, where she has her hair cut, has she always worn it long, what does she see in me?

'Make yourself useful,' Maria says, waving an empty glass in the air.

I throw my head back and sigh. 'I just sat down.'

'You've been sitting down for three hours,' Dad says. 'Go on, stretch your legs.'

I make a big show of hauling myself to my feet and out of the room, huffing and muttering under my breath. It's not that I begrudge my family another drink or an audience with my girlfriend, but the truth is I know very little about the woman I'm very much in love with and I'm as eager for answers as the rest of my family. I know she prefers cider to beer, her favourite pie is chicken and leek, and she snores when she drinks too much; I know her hair smells of coconuts, and her breath smells like hell in the morning; I know she fell through a glass coffee table when she was eight years old and her favourite sweets are Skittles. But there is so much I don't know – her favourite Beatle; the name of her first pet, boyfriend or record; I don't even know her middle name, for God's sake. And for some reason, I'm particularly interested in where she stands (so to speak) on fairies versus mermaids.

When I return with a bottle of wine everyone (Dad and Hector included) are listening with rapt attention as Ivy describes the best way to shape the tip of an eyeliner pencil.

'What time we eating?' asks Maria.

'I'm starved,' says Hector.

'What we having?' ask the twins.

Everyone turns to me, and I shuffle again from the room, grumbling about slavery, presumption and ingratitude.

I've chopped four chicken breasts, three onions, two chillies, six red peppers, half a bulb of garlic, and eaten at least a third of a smoked chorizo when Dad walks into the kitchen.

'Need any help?'

'I'm nearly done,' I tell him.

'So,' Dad says from the fridge doorway, 'this is unexpected.'

'I'll say.'

'Here,' he says, placing a glass of wine beside the chopping board.

'Cheers.' I take a sip, and then nod in the direction of the living room. 'And?'

'You could have done worse,' he says, smiling.

'Oh, I have,' I say. 'Christ, have I.'

Dad rolls his eyes with resigned, long-suffering affection. He teaches RE in the school I went to almost twenty years ago, and attends Mass anywhere between two and five times a week – he's the next worst thing to a priest.

'Sorry,' I say.

'Do it again and I'll pray for you.'

We're elbow to elbow around the small dining table, but it's a cosy, intimate squash as we cycle through the old anecdotes and make our way through several bottles of

13

wine. I've been separated from Ivy, who is now flanked by Dad and my sister. And whilst I would rather have Ivy at my side than across the table, it does give me the opportunity to observe her as she entertains and indulges my family – laughing at their jokes, listening to their stories and jumping firmly aboard the let's-take-the-piss-out-of-William bandwagon. And my family are giddy with doting affection, competing for Ivy's attention, attempting to trump each other's gags, boasts and revelations. I extend my leg beneath the table and run it up the inside of what I assume is Ivy's shin. Maria flinches, striking the underside of the table with her knee and making the cutlery jump.

'What the hell are you playing at!'

'Cramp,' I say, and Maria looks at me like I've come unhinged.

'What are you up to?' Ivy says.

'Nothing. Stretching.'

Ivy narrows her eyes at me. 'Were you . . .' she turns to Maria '. . . was he playing . . . *footsy*?'

Reflexively I glance in my dad's direction, but he is apparently fascinated by the pattern on his plate.

'What's footsy?' asks Imogen, the elder of the twins by twenty minutes and always the most inquisitive.

'Never you mind,' says Maria.

'Something naughty boys do,' says Ivy, earning a chuckle from the twins.

'I was stretching!'

'Stretching credibility,' Ivy says, and Hector all but claps at this display of Wildean wit.

I keep my feet to myself for the remainder of the meal. And I come within a forkful of making it through to coffee without further incident.

We're eating dessert (the room is silent for a rare moment as everyone savours their cheesecake) when Dad announces: 'By the ways, William, I'll take your old room tonight, you and Ivy can use my bed.'

It's probably less than the five thousand years it feels like, but there is definitely a long awkward pause where my father's words – in particular the word 'use' – hang above the table. Ivy, fork still held between her lips, looks at my dad, smiles, hum-mumbles the twin syllables of *Thank you*. Or maybe it's *Blimey*.

Maria glances across at Ivy and smirks. Hector looks at me and winces. I look at my cheesecake and feel my cheeks flush.

On the drive down I had wondered about the sleeping arrangements. Dad's as Catholic as guilt and the only double bed in the house is his, which had me resigned to spending my first night sleeping alone since Ivy and I got together. On the one hand it would be a shame; on the other it was bound to happen sooner or later and, to be perfectly honest, I'm exhausted. Plus, it would avoid any embarrassing conversations with my father.

'Changed the sheets,' says Dad. And when I make the mistake of making eye contact, the silly bastard winks. It's not a lascivious wink by any means; if I had to guess, I'd say it was self-congratulatory at being so modern and god-damned organized. But a wink is a wink and, if I had to put a flag in the ground, that would be the moment my sex life died.

The awkwardness as we undress for bed is tangible; I stumble removing my jeans, embarrassed by my pale, dangling nakedness; and Ivy, for the first time in our time together, climbs into bed wearing pants and a T-shirt. I was in all likelihood conceived in this bed, and whilst I have no desire for anything more risqué than a kiss on the lips, I am a little affronted by Ivy's assumption that the games are over. Also, I've drunk a bottle and a half of wine, so my mouth comments before my brain has a chance to edit.

'You're shy all of a sudden,' I say, slurring the s's slightly.
'I'm tired,' says Ivy. 'If that's okay?'
If that's okay?
Maybe I've drunk more than I realize, because I hear

myself saying: 'Fine. Whatever.' And the weight of the two words pulls at the corners of my mouth.

And while nothing gets thrown, neither ornaments nor accusations, this is the closest thing we've had to an argument and there is no affection in the room when I turn out the light and climb into my dad's bed.

I locate Ivy's head with my hands and it's turned away from me. 'G'night,' I say, kissing her hair.

Ivy sighs. 'Night,' she says, and she says it very very quietly.

We kiss in the morning, but it's lost something during the night – urgency, electricity, promise . . . something. It doesn't help that I have a pig of a hangover, although Ivy seems to have escaped any ill effects.

She spends a long time in the en suite shower, emerging from the steaming room dry, dressed and with her hair turbaned in a towel. And this sudden absence of casual nakedness, it jars. Besides the scars on the left side of her face, throat and neck, Ivy has scars on her belly, hip, right forearm, right thigh and right breast. And still she will pad about the flat naked or nearly so; feeding the fish, making coffee, eating her Bran Flakes. We must have spent half of our waking time together without a stitch on. So, yeah, when she steps out of the bathroom in jeans, shirt and a cardigan, it jars.

In the time it takes me to step in and out of the shower, Ivy is gone. I find her downstairs, talking to Dad, who has inelegantly heaped three cartons of juice, every box of cereal and every jar and tub of spreadable substance he owns on the kitchen table. He is now trying to make tea and butter toast at the same time and is making a woeful mess of both.

'Are you sure I can't do something?' Ivy asks.

'All under control,' Dad says, putting the lid on the teapot after two attempts. 'Now, how'd you take your tea— damn! You said coffee, didn't you?'

'Tea's fine.'

And instead of just leaving the tea to brew, Dad pours the pot down the sink.

'Scatterbrain,' he says, palming his forehead. 'No, you said coffee, you get coffee. Instant okay?'

Ivy is a confirmed coffee snob and I know she would rather drink nothing than drink instant, so when she tells Dad, 'Instant's perfect,' I feel a fresh pang of affection for her.

As Dad begins refilling the kettle, the kitchen smoke alarm starts emitting a jagged high-pitched beep, and my nagging headache mutates instantly into a snarling monster with very sharp teeth. Black smoke is issuing from the toaster and Dad stands frozen, looking from the toaster to the alarm, trying to decide which one to tackle first. Still clutching the kettle, Dad snatches up a mop from beside the fridge and whacks the smoke alarm three times until it falls to the floor in two separate pieces, one of which is somehow still beeping (albeit less enthusiastically). He stamps on it once and it dies. The toaster pops.

Dad smiles at Ivy like a lunatic. 'Needed a new one anyway,' he says.

I pick up the fragments of smoke detector as Dad retrieves the charred toast and proceeds to scrape the burnt slices over the sink.

'Dig in,' says Dad, brandishing a blackened knife at the stacked boxes of cereal in a manner that suggests he won't be happy until we've eaten all of it. And so we eat a breakfast of burnt toast, powdery muesli and instant coffee, while Dad picks up where he left off last night, questioning Ivy and humiliating me.

Mercifully, Ivy has work tomorrow – a two-day shoot for a German car manufacturer – and we're on the road before ten o'clock and before Dad can inflict any further damage to the domestic appliances or my relationship with Ivy. He insists on making us a packed lunch and sends us on our way with enough brown bananas, soft pears and thick, Clingfilm-wrapped cheese sandwiches to keep us going for a week. There's a significant possibility that I'm still over the limit, so Ivy drives and I press my head against the cool glass of the passenger-side window in an attempt to take some of the heat out of my hangover.

The Fiat came courtesy of my best friend, El; he gave it to me when he became too severely affected by Huntington's disease to drive. One bumper sticker invites fellow road users to honk if they're horny, whilst the other ('bummer sticker', El calls it) declares: 'I'm so gay I can't even drive straight'. And so, as we proceed south on the M6, we are honked and hooted and air-horned by car after car after van after eighteen-wheeled juggernaut. It was kind of amusing last week. Today, less so.

'I wonder if they think I'm a woman,' I say as a Ford Galaxy passes us, parping its horn, three gleeful children waving from the rear window.

'Why would they think that?' says Ivy, not smiling.

'You know ... the bumper stickers.' Ivy frowns. 'Well, you're obviously not a man.' I wait for a smile of acknowledgement; don't get one. 'So presumably, if we're a gay couple, I'm a woman.' I rub my hand over my shorn auburn hair. 'The manly one.'

'Maybe they think we're just friends,' says Ivy.

I spend the next several miles fretting over whether or not I have offended Ivy. Maybe some of her best friends are lesbians. Or an aunty. She's never mentioned it and the subject didn't come up during last night's interrogation, but anything is possible.

A new song starts on the radio: 'Could It Be Magic'.

'So who's your favourite Beatle?' I ask.

Ivy flicks her eyes in my direction. 'You do know this is Take That?'

To be honest, I thought it was Boyzone, but I nod anyway. 'Of course.'

Ivy says nothing.

'Well?' I venture.

'What?'

There's an impatient sharpness to Ivy's response, and now I'm certain she's being pissy. Probably because I was being insensitive or something last night.

'The Beatles,' I say brightly, deciding that rather than apologizing for (and, therefore, reminding Ivy of) last night's behaviour, the best policy is to gloss over all this silliness with a bright coat of chirpy good humour. 'John, Paul, Ringo or the other one,' I say.

'The other one,' says my beloved.

'Mick or Keef?' I persist.

'Didn't we do twenty questions last night?'

'Yes, we did. Well, you lot did; I was cooking. Thing is, it made me realize how much we still don't know about each other. That's all.'

Ivy pulls into the outside lane to overtake a convoy of cars that are doing around three miles an hour under the speed limit. It's hard going on the Fiat, and it rattles as we creep past several cars and vans slowly enough that I could reach through my window and shake hands with every one of the drivers. We pull back into the middle lane and I start breathing again.

'Sorry about last night,' I say, abandoning my policy of dumb ignorance.

'It's fine. They're lovely.'

'I meant me . . . I'm sorry about me.'

'It's fine.'

And I wait for thirty seconds, but Ivy doesn't say I'm lovely too.

And of course I'm in no hurry to know Ivy's favourite Take That song; and I don't *really* care what GCSEs she sat, or what her first cat was called. But there are other details – trivial, too, in their own way – that it feels almost negligent not to know.

'I don't even know when your birthday is.'

'October twenty-ninth,' she says.

There's a beat of silence. Ivy glances sideways, holds my gaze for a second, cocks an eyebrow incrementally. Something resembling a smile tugs the corner of her mouth. 'I'll be forty-one,' she says, turning her attention back to the road.

Eight cars, two vans and two wagons pass us before I formulate a response.

'Cool,' I say. As if, instead of her age, Ivy has just non-chalantly disclosed some impressive talent or skill: *I used to play guitar in a heavy metal band, I ran the marathon in 2:58, I can assemble an AK47 blindfolded.* 'Cool.'

But this information has thrown me (not that it would take a great deal to upset my precarious equilibrium this morning) and neither of us says another word for the next thirty miles or so.

Ivy will be forty-one on her next birthday, making her over nine years older than me. When she was my age, I was twenty-two. When she was twenty-two, I was thir-teen. And, moving in the opposite direction, when I'm the age she is now, Ivy will be fifty – and cut that cake any way you like, that's old. I don't want to think about how old Ivy will be when I turn fifty – fifty is a good age for men: a time of distinguished grey highlights, and not so much wrinkles as lines of hard-won wisdom. How old Ivy will be when I hit my half-century gives me the heebie-crawling-jeebies. She doesn't look old; her body is firm and her skin, where it's not crisscrossed with scars, is smooth. I am fighting a strong urge, now, to turn and inspect the corners of her eyes for nascent crow's-feet. Things will even out, I imagine, when I turn eighty. Also, women tend to live longer than men, so Ivy being almost a decade older than me improves the chances of us dying together, holding hands on the sofa in front of a slowly fading log fire in our retirement cottage on the coast. So there's that.

We stop at the services for a pee, and Ivy takes so long to pay her visit that I begin to worry she has either been abducted or simply taken a lift from a handsome stranger. When she does get back to the car she looks, if anything, more dejected than she has all morning. I've bought her a massive bag of Skittles, which I now present with a chimp-like grin, but Ivy says she's feeling lousy and asks will I drive. She makes an improvised pillow from a folded jumper, reclines her seat as far as it will go – which isn't far – and closes her eyes. And so we put more miles behind us, cars and motorbikes and vans honking their horns and pulling goon faces from the windows as they tear past.

Where did it all go wrong? is the question I keep coming back to. Surely our little spat last night, if it even qualifies as a spat, can't be responsible for Ivy's sudden withdrawal. We have just spent the most romantic, loved-up, slightly sickeningly blissed-out three weeks of my life together. We have not left each other's side, we started calling each other 'babe' without feeling completely silly about it, we made love every day, we made toast in the nude. And now . . .

just nothing. The paranoid snob inside wonders can it be the peeling paint on Dad's front door, the Formica kitchen units, the loose loo seat; but I know it's not. And if it is, then Ivy isn't the person I thought she was. Maybe she feels awkward about her age. Maybe I simply annoy the hell out of her and she's only just realized it. Maybe she looked at my dad buffooning around the kitchen and saw the future me. Or maybe she is simply premenstrual – and I'm so desperate to know what's bugging her, I'm sorely tempted to ask. But I suspect the question would be unlikely to reverse Ivy's current funk.

By the time we cross the M25 and re-enter London's gravity, I've eaten the entire bag of Skittles and I feel sick. And without any prompting, like she hasn't been sleeping at all but simply sitting still with her eyes closed, Ivy straightens in her seat and cricks her neck from side to side.

'Morning,' I say, more brightly than I feel.

'Hey,' says Ivy. She smiles, but there isn't much behind it.

'Your place or mine?' I say, but I already know I'm not going to like the answer.

Ivy has work tomorrow, she tells me, she's tired, she needs to do laundry, take a bath, feed her goldfish, etc.

Her flat is opposite the fourth lamppost on the left,

down a tree-lined street in Wimbledon. We had our first kiss right here, in this car, beside this lamppost. But whatever *frisson* crackled about us then, it's been replaced with a glutinous awkwardness. I get out of the car and remove Ivy's bags from the boot. She takes her suitcase, declining my offer of help, and we stand clumsily on the pavement, Ivy not inviting me in, and me not asking. A wave of indignation surges through me, sweeping away the introspection and doubt, and leaving in its wake annoyance, disappointment and scraps of broken ego.

'Right then,' I say. 'Suppose I'll be off.'

Ivy puts her suitcase down, gives me a silent hug and kisses the side of my neck. She holds it for a count of seconds, for about as long as you'd hold a final goodbye. She puts a hand to my cheek, smiles with her mouth but not with her eyes, says: 'I had a nice time. Thank you.'

'Sure,' I tell her. 'Enjoy your bath.'

We kiss once more, Ivy turns to cross the road and I'm gone before she gets her key in the door.

Chapter 2

'Get r. . . get rid that pi. . . pnapple.'

El can't always access the words he needs; and when he can, he can't always get them out of his mouth. It's much more than a stammer. The effort shows on his face as he attempts to force a word out against the kind of resistance you might encounter trying to blow syrup through a straw. Even so, manners cost nothing.

'Magic word?' I say.

'P. . . p. . . fuckig pronto.'

'That's better,' I tell him, plucking the chunks of pineapple from his slice of pizza.

El opens wide and I feed the tip of the folded slice into his mouth. His head wobbles but he succeeds in taking a bite without getting any more tomato sauce on his already smeared face. Beneath the sauce he has a deep tan, but it's

not enough to create even an illusion of health. El and his
partner, Phil, returned from a holiday in San Francisco two
days ago. It's unlikely El has deteriorated significantly
while he's been away, but his twitches and wobbles and
speech do seem worse.

'Wh... wh... wh...'

'Who?' I try, and El shakes his head. 'What?'

El shakes his head again. 'Lass one,' he says.

'Why?'

El nods. 'Why? Why would you p... put pnapple on a
p...' He points a trembling finger at the pizza sitting
between us.

'It's a Hawaiian,' I tell him. 'You ordered it.'

El shrugs. 'Like the name.'

Like all best friends living within ten miles of each other
in London, El and I used to see each other about three
times a year. But there's nothing quite like terminal illness
to cure apathy. So around two years ago, when the
Huntington's disease began to sink its teeth into him, we
got into a routine of meeting every Tuesday. Initially we'd
go to the pub, but as El's condition progressed he lost his
tolerance for drink along with his inhibitions and grasp of
social niceties. We changed venue to the local curry house,
arriving early in the evening when the place was empty
and El could swear, twitch, stammer and drop his glass

without an audience. But in the last few months, even that has become too difficult. So now it's pizza and alcohol-free beer in El's own living room.

I suppose that somewhere in my mind he exists as the ten-year-old boy I rode my bike with, the teenager that I bought stolen pornography from, and the man who used to make me cry with laughter; and it's as if all the decline El has endured in the last few years – the constant twitch-ing and jerking; lack of co-ordination, balance, and empathy; the weight loss, the loss, in fact, of all the sub-tleties and nuances that make El *El* – it feels today as if all the damage has been compacted into the three weeks he's been away. And whilst I know it hasn't, his speech is unde-niably worse. Before he left for the pub, Phil told me he's finding it increasingly necessary to help El find his words, form his thoughts and understand what other people are saying to him.

I help myself to a slice of Quattro Formaggi, fold it in half, take a bite.

'Still f... fuckig that g... woman,' El says, looking at me, amused, waiting for a reaction.

'I don't remember saying anything about fucking.'

'P... P... Pippa, wasn' it? Bounthy bounthy!'

'Ivy,' I say, wincing inwardly. 'Her name is Ivy.'

'G... g... grows on you,' he says, and although, like so

many others, he said it the first time he heard Ivy's name, it makes me laugh because it's evidence that the old El is still – at least partially – with us.

'Wh. . . wh. . . wh. . .'

'Who? What? When? W—'

'When! When d'I get to meet her?'

Good question.

After my last girlfriend, Kate, walked out on me, I did what any recently humiliated idiot would do. I slept with the receptionist at work. Pippa had an endearing but amusing habit of lisping 'Bounthy bounthy' whenever she went on top. Which was quite often. Which . . . I told El. I know, *I know* – but he's my oldest friend and I couldn't resist. Well, the indiscretion has come back to punish me, because her name has lodged where so little else will – firmly in El's head. Unless my next girlfriend is a trampolinist called Pippa, it would probably be a mistake to introduce her to him.

El looks at me: *Well?*

'Soon,' I say.

El narrows his eyes. 'Sh. . . she d. . . d. . . d. . .'

'Can you spell it?' I ask, remembering what Phil told me about how to tease the words from El with various 'cueing' techniques. 'Or spell how it sounds?'

The tendons on El's skinny neck stand taut with effort as

he galvanizes himself for another attempt. 'Duh... d... u...'

'D–U?'

El nods. 'Mmm...' He twists his neck far to the left, his lips working mutely as if trying to snatch the next letter from the air, 'P ... D ...'

'D–U–M–P–D?'

El swings his hands together, connecting just enough to consider it a clap. 'She d... dumped you... f... figured y'out. Ha ha ha.'

'How's that funny?'

'S'pose it's not really,' he says, suddenly straight-faced. 'Sad, tragic, pred... pred...'

'Predictable?'

El jabs a finger at me like a game-show host pointing out a winning contestant.

'I hate to burst your miserable bubble,' I say, 'but Ivy has not dumped me.'

'Ye... ye... y...'

I know what the bastard's driving at, but I'm damned if I'm going to make it any easier for him.

'Fuck it,' says El. 'D'you think you cn carry me?'

I doubt El ever achieved his teenage goal of reaching five-foot-six, and he was skinny before the Huntington's began eroding him. He can't weigh much more than one of my 10-year-old nieces.

'I'm pretty sure I could throw you clean out of the window,' I tell him.

El contemplates this. 'B... be quicker,' he says.

The house El shares with Phil ranges over five floors. The front door sits atop a short flight of tiled steps leading to the drive and the busy road that runs past the house. El wants 'f... fresh air', so I pick him up, carry him down three dozen steps and set him gently down on the threshold. It turns out he's lighter than he looks, but the effort has my arms tingling.

After some initial difficulty, El removes a packet of cigarettes and a lighter from his pocket. 'L... light one f'me,' he says.

I do as I'm asked and pass the burning Marlboro to El. 'You don't smoke,' I tell him.

El holds up evidence to the contrary and blows smoke in my direction. The traffic here is relentless, so the face full of smoke amounts to little more than an insult in the cloud of pollution that surrounds us on this balmy August evening.

'Well, you didn't three weeks ago.'

El inhales deeply, holds the full-tar smoke in his lungs, widens and then crosses his eyes. I wait for him to turn green, cough, splutter – like they do in the movies – but El merely opens his mouth and lets the smoke slowly escape his lungs. 'W... wan' one?'

'No, thank you, filthy habit.'

'Thass what Phil says,' he grins. 'But they do make y'look c. . . f. . . cool as f. . . fuck.'

'That they do,' I tell him.

Pollution aside, it's pleasant sitting on the steps and watching the folk and traffic move by at approximately the same pace. El is on his third fag when we see Phil shuffling back to the flat. He shakes his head when he sees us, then flicks me a small wave.

'Boys,' he says, mounting the steps. 'Having a party?' And he tuts as he collects El's butts and folds them into a paper tissue.

'Thank you, d. . . darling,' says El.

'You're most unwelcome,' says Phil, sitting between us and plucking the cigarette from El's fingers. He takes a drag and passes the cigarette back to El. 'Filthy fucking habit.'

'All the b. . . b. . . bess ones are,' says El, winking at me.

'True enough,' says Phil.

'What's brought all this' – I waft cigarette smoke away from my face – 'on, anyway?'

Phil looks at the ground and shakes his head again.

'Member that S. . . Smiths song?' says El.

'"Please, Please, Please, Let Me Get What I Want"?' offers Phil with a sly smile.

'"Bigmouth Strikes Again"?' I try.

'Pair of f... fuckig jokers. N... no. "What D... Di...
Diff... fuckit!'

'I know,' says Phil, gently. He takes the Marlboro from
El and takes a deep pull before passing it back. '"What
Difference Does It Make?".'

And, God, do I wish I smoked. 'So,' I say. 'How was the
pub?'

'Crowded, noisy and yet somehow still bereft of atmosphere,' says Phil.

'Sh... sh... shoulda gone t... to the p... b... p... puff
pub.'

'I did,' says Phil.

'S... s... s...'

'Good God,' says Phil. 'It's bad enough having the pip-
squeak take the piss with every other breath. But waiting
for him to spit it out like this ... I swear to God, it's like
waiting for a bloody firing squad to pull the trigger.'

'S... s...' and the mischievous look in El's eye would
appear to confirm that whatever he is struggling (although
you really never know with El) to say, it's got a barb on it.
'Suck any cock?'

'I hate to disappoint you, dear heart, but the only thing
to pass my lips was a rather thin Merlot.'

El shrugs petulantly. Earlier this year he invested a con-
siderable amount of breath and effort in trying to convince

Phil to find a new boyfriend. As well as the physical symptoms, Huntington's disease subtracts character and personality, it wears down logic and reason and social inhibition in its victims. Add to this that El has always revelled in the inappropriate, and the result can be sad, funny and deeply confusing. But there was more to El's dispassionate matchmaking than his disease or his devilment. He understands that he is dying, and that before the end comes he will be diminished beyond recognition. The problem, as El sees it, is that he could last another ten years, by which time Phil will be well into his fifties – hence various nonsense like El 'dumping' Phil and enrolling him on dating websites 'w... w... while he's still y... young 'nough to find som'ne else.' As romantic gestures go, it's about the best I have ever witnessed.

'F... Fisher got dumped,' says El.

Phil cocks an eyebrow.

'No Fisher did not,' I say.

'Yet,' says El, without even a hint of difficulty.

Chapter 3

I'm half asleep on Esther's sofa when my mobile rings and snaps me rudely back to reality – well, to *Columbo*: *Sex and the Married Detective*, which is as near to life as I'm in the mood for this Thursday.

I haven't organized my friends into a strict hierarchy since I was in the second year of high school, but if I were inclined to it's hard to imagine Esther anywhere outside of the top three. We've lived above and below each other for over five years, we exchange Christmas, birthday and Easter presents, and we share the same taste in daytime television, which, considering my job means a lot of free daytime, is no small consideration. My 63-year-old downstairs neighbour is not really one for going to the pub, drinking eight pints and chatting up the girls, but she always has a good selection of biscuits. Esther's husband,

Nino, retires in November, and soon after that they are exchanging the noises, smells and threats of Brixton for the serenity of the Italian countryside. I don't imagine they will miss Brixton one bit. But I'll miss them, Esther in particular, and I will miss her deeply. Without her I'd have gone crazy this past week.

It's been around ninety-six hours since I last saw Ivy. We've talked briefly and sent occasional texts establishing little more than we were either recently awake, or soon to be asleep. I tell Ivy I miss her, and she tells me 'you too', but it seems more like a courtesy than an actual fact. She was working Monday and Tuesday, but when I suggested we meet up on Wednesday, Ivy was 'catching up with friends'. Today she has 'things to do'. More important and appealing things than me, it seems. Esther has supplied hot drinks and sage-ish advice, from suggesting Ivy is married, to Ivy is on her period. Her latest theory (we'd been watching reruns of *Spooks*) is that Ivy works for MI6 ('Well, sweetheart, someone has to').

I pull my still-ringing phone from my pocket. And somehow I knew it would be Ivy, just as surely as I know this is the call where she tells me it's over. I mouth the word 'Ivy' to Esther, even though I have yet to answer the phone so there is no good reason to whisper. Esther hits pause on the remote, and begins the process of extracting herself from the sofa. It's a slow process and I'm worried Ivy will get bored and hang up, so I place the flat of my foot against Esther's broad backside and push her to a full stand. 'Thank you, love,' she says. 'And good luck.'

I answer the call.

'Hiya,' I say with a drummed-up lightness that sounds as manufactured as the phone I'm speaking into. 'Happy Thursday!' I add, stupidly.

'Hey,' says Ivy.

This is the first time she has initiated contact in the last four days, and to judge by the enthusiasm in her voice, it's about the last thing she wanted to do today.

'How's things?' I ask.

'Oh . . . you know.'

No, I don't, I have no sodding clue whatsoever. Or maybe I do and I'm just too thick-headed to get the message. Ivy doesn't clarify, so I dive into the silence. 'Well, it's rock 'n' roll in Brixton,' I chirp.

'Rock 'n' roll?'

'Me and Esther,' I say. '*Columbo*, *Murder She Wrote*, *Quincy* and a packet of custard creams.'

'Right,' says Ivy.

'We must have drunk five pints of Earl Grey,' I say, and the sound of my voice makes me want to bite my tongue out.

'What you doing tomorrow?'

'Nothing, nothing at all.'

'Want to do breakfast?' says Ivy.

And my heart swells, it blooms, it does a cheeky little jig. 'Yes,' I say. 'Yes, definitely, you bet. Your place or mine? Ha, that sounds a bit . . . mind you, I can be there in under an hour if I leave now. I could pick up some saus—'

'No,' says Ivy. 'I mean breakfast, I mean tomorrow.'

'Right . . . yes, of course.'

'We . . . we need to talk,' she says, and inside my chest someone snips the strings that keep my heart suspended behind my ribs. Cut loose, the organ drops and rolls into a place just behind my belly button where it lies heavy like a stone.

'Yeah,' I say. 'I know.'

We arrange to meet at a café in Wimbledon at ten thirty tomorrow morning. I feel sick.

Esther invites me to stay for supper, but I'd be lousy company and I have zero appetite. Instead I drift about my flat, moving from room to room, periodically finding myself staring from a window, looking through the television, regarding my reflection and various other acts of pathetic melancholia. For the last five minutes I've been sitting on the foot of my bed, staring at a framed James Bond poster

(*For Your Eyes Only*). Despite my protestations that it was a Christmas present from Esther, Ivy gave me a pretty good ribbing about it. At the time I took it as a light-hearted, 'aren't you just adorable' teasing. But maybe she simply found it sad. Unless, of course, Ivy really does work for the Intelligence Service, in which case she almost certainly found it highly amusing. The thing is, someone does have to work for MI6, and being a make-up artist is perfect — *perfect* — cover: you work irregular hours so no one questions your erratic schedule; you frequently need to work abroad; you have close access to the rich and famous; you can easily collect hair for DNA sampling. Added to that, Ivy is super keen on yoga, which probably comes in handy for negotiating those laser beam things that are used to protect Fabergé eggs, big diamonds and microfilm. And let's not forget her scars — Ivy says she fell through a coffee table, but who knows the real story?

But even if Ivy is a spy, it still doesn't mean I'm not getting dumped, does it, Commander Bond?

Oh, you're dumped, all right, says 007. *Your licence is well and truly revoked.*

Whatever happens tomorrow at breakfast, at least we'll reach a conclusion and I can be done with this pitiful moping.

*

I sleep badly.

It takes for ever to drop off, and when I do, I dream that various Bond villains – Scaramanga, Odd Job, Blofeld, Jaws – are pursuing me through the maze from *The Shining*. That shrill harridan with the knife in her shoe, she closes to within lethal kicking distance and I wake up, heart banging. I go for a pee, drink approximately the same volume of water that I've just expelled, then return to bed, toss and turn for twenty minutes, then find myself once again in the dream maze trying to escape the inevitable.

At six forty-four I give up, get out of bed and inspect my face in the bathroom mirror. The sun is already up and it is not pulling its punches. Purple shadows have pooled beneath my eyes, the left of which has developed an intermittent twitch. About six weeks ago I had a misunderstanding with a barber who ended up clippering my hair down to the wood; it is now just long enough to stick up at five different angles, which is, of course, exactly what it's doing this morning. Added to all of this I seem to have grown a new forehead wrinkle. I look like shit.

I spend a long time in the shower; I floss, brush my teeth, exfoliate, shave, moisturize, clip my finger- and toe-nails, and trim the hairs from my nostrils.

It's still only seven thirty-two and I am drooped with

fatigue. The phrase 'polished turd' comes to mind as I catch my distorted reflection on the side of the kettle. I've never had a problem with instant coffee, it delivers on all it promises, but after spending only two nights here, Ivy marched down to the local department store to buy a cafetiere and a bag of 'proper coffee'. By eight fifteen, I've drunk an entire pot of the stuff and it's done nothing but supercharge the butterflies in my belly. I try on sixteen combinations of what is essentially the same outfit and end up wearing the first shirt and the first pair of jeans I chose. I wear my best socks and boxer shorts because, hey, I'm an optimist. Also, after three weeks of more sex than I could wish for, I have now had six days of nothing, and if there is even an outside chance of getting lucky, I don't want to compromise that possibility with a pair of baggy underpants.

As the pigeon flies, Ivy lives about five miles west-south-west. By tube, however, the journey takes around twenty-five minutes and three different trains, travelling first north, then west, then south. And as William Fisher flies, you can add on another fifteen minutes for overshooting your stop at Earl's Court and then having to double back because you were so engrossed in cleaning your fingernails with a corner of your tube ticket. A ticket that is now so creased and bent out of shape that it gets jammed in the turnstile at Wimbledon and I have to plead with the surly fucking guard to let me through. It's all very metaphoric.

I'm still forty-five minutes early, so I grab an espresso at the coffee shop outside the station, which kills all of three and a half minutes. The café where I'm meeting Ivy is in Wimbledon Village, a brisk ten-minute walk from the station up a steep hill. And over the course of those ten minutes, it's as if you have left the city and strolled into an exclusive enclave deep in the stockbroker belt. The average house price in 'The Village' must be somewhere in the seven-figure bracket, plus there is a collection of ostentatious-bordering-on-obscene mansions that must – in addition to their gyms, swimming pools, studies, libraries, cellars, triple garages, conservatories and endless en suite bathrooms – have an additional nought on the end of the price tag. Aside from the residential properties, there are a handful of expensive clothes shops, a couple of art galleries, a stable, a smattering of jewellers and chichi knick-knack mongers, a few delis, and a disproportionate number of expensive restaurants and coffee shops. It may be only five miles from Brixton, but it's in a different universe.

It's been a miserable summer, raining more often than not, and the pavements are wet and puddled with last night's downpour. It's cloudy but hot today, humid as hell and pregnant with the threat of thunder. When I mount the summit of Wimbledon Hill Road, I'm hot, bedraggled and sweat-soaked. And one thing is clear, if I am going to reclaim Ivy's heart I'm not going to do it in this shirt with spreading sweat stains at the armpits.

I veer into a designer clothes shop that is so achingly cool even the mannequins appear to sneer at me. The guy – I'm pretty sure he's a guy – behind the counter raises his head from an iPad. There is an almost imperceptible nod, a muttered syllable that could be 'hey', a hint of a smile. It's possible he's being friendly, but it's hard to be sure. I need to get out of here fast; it's as clear as the sweat at my armpits that I don't belong and the fact is aggravating my already jangling nerves.

'Shirt,' I say, then I pull at the fabric of my own as if the concept of a shirt is one that might require clarification.

The guy rotates his head in the direction of a rail hung with said items.

I select the least gaudy shirt from the rail and ask the shop assistant for permission to try it on. The changing 'room' has the same dimensions and as much light as the inside of a wardrobe, so I am forced back into the glare of the shop proper to look at myself in a mirror. The shirt is pinker than I'd like, and – I see now for the first time – is shot through with fine silvery threads that catch the light as I stand squinting at my reflection. I can imagine this shirt looking good on someone else, someone in a band maybe, or presenting an arts show on BBC2, or maybe on someone standing behind the counter of an achingly cool clothes shop. But – despite standing in front of a perfectly good mirror – I can't quite see it on me.

'Looks nice,' says the shop assistant. He purses his lips appraisingly, nods. 'Suits ya.'

I look at my watch and I'm meeting Ivy in fifteen minutes.

'Great,' I say. 'I'll take it.'

In the confines of the changing cupboard, I remove the new shirt and use my old one to mop the sweat from my face, back and armpits. Before redressing I remove the price tag from my new acquisition, but the figure is written in dark ink on dark card and is impossible to discern. I present myself at the counter and pass the price tag to the sales assistant without looking at it – not because I'm not interested, but because it doesn't feel like the done thing in this part of town.

'One-eighty,' says the guy, his voice betraying nothing: no irony, amusement or pity.

Maybe the threads in my new shirt are silver, after all. I start sweating again as I hand over my plastic, praying to God it won't combust in the card reader.

Outside the shop, the best part of two hundred quid (and maybe another two pounds in lost bodily fluids) lighter, I give my face a final wipe down with my old shirt and drop it into the nearest bin.

I arrive at the café one minute before the allotted time, order a coffee and take a seat at an outside table. My system is so full of caffeine and adrenaline by now that my hands are shaking, and it takes a tremendous effort not to slop cappuccino down the front of my brand-new, very expensive shirt.

I'm making inroads into my second cup when I spot Ivy – maybe one hundred yards away – walking towards the café. I make a wave-cum-salute, and Ivy returns the gesture. I can see her legs moving, but she doesn't appear to be closing the distance between us. I pick up my phone and pretend to do something with it, take a leisurely sip of coffee, inspect the menu ... and when I glance back in Ivy's direction she is still more than fifty yards away. I straighten my shirt, act like something across the street catches my eye, fiddle with the sachets of sugar.

'Hey,' says Ivy and I look up, apparently surprised to find her there so quickly.

'Hey,' I say, and as I stand to meet her I bump the table with my hip and slop cappuccino with chocolate sprinkles onto the front of my shirt. Ivy doesn't seem to notice. For some reason I kiss Ivy on the cheek. A week ago we were at it like, well, not exactly porn stars, but there was nothing coy about it, and here I am kissing her on the cheek.

She wears no make-up and her hair is half tied back, half falling about her shoulders. She is dressed in loose-fitting jeans, a checked shirt with enamelled cufflinks in the shape of tiny burlesque girls, and a plain grey jumper. And now that I think of it, in the two months since we were introduced, I've yet to see Ivy in a skirt, dress or one of those jumpers with puffy sleeves that girls seem to like. My guess is that Ivy's style is a by-product of her childhood accident. She can't hide the scars on her face, but those on her body . . . she can conceal these completely. Or maybe I'm over analysing it; maybe her clothes simply reflect the fact that she grew up with three brothers and is an honest-to-goodness tomboy. Either way, she looks beautiful.

'You look beautiful,' I tell her.

Ivy smiles but it fades pretty damn fast.

A waitress comes to our table and Ivy orders tea.

'So,' I say. 'How've you been?'

'Oh,' says Ivy, apparently unable to hold eye contact with me for more than three-quarters of a second, 'good . . . busy . . . you know . . .'

When I was . . . I don't know exactly, maybe seven, my teacher Mrs 'Fatty' Kincaid called me to her desk at the front of the class. I remember that the gouged wooden surface was belly-high as I stood before her, and I remember the fear.

'You've done something naughty,' Mrs Kincaid told me. 'Do you know what it is?'

I didn't.

'Your dad tells me you've been naughty,' said Mrs Kincaid.

My mother and father were both intelligent people, and Dad was (still is) a teacher, used to dealing with errant children. Why he thought to approach my indiscretion via a third party, I have no idea. I haven't thought about it for over twenty years, and I guess you don't need a degree in psychology to understand why this scene has just this minute dropped into my consciousness like a brick into an algae-choked pond.

'What did you do?' asked Mrs Kincaid.

Occasionally I fantasize that I could revisit some past childhood event, equipped with my adult understanding and intellect. If I could answer now for my confused and frightened 7-year-old self, I'd say, 'God only knows. You're the one with all the info, you tell me.' Or something along those lines. Because instead of cutting to the chase she chose to draw it out – to pull the plaster slowly.

What I said, I don't recall, but I didn't know the answer.

Maybe I shrugged. But Kincaid wasn't letting me off the hook. 'What did you do?' she pushed.

So I told her every single transgression I could think of. That I had pulled the heads from three of my sister's Barbies; that me and Simon Henderson had found a tattered porn mag under a hedge and transferred it to another hedge; I stole penny sweets from Randall's newsagents; I often lied when I said I'd brushed my teeth; I read comics with a torch after bedtime; I found twenty-three pence down the side of the sofa and kept it; I didn't always say my prayers; I farted in class; I burped the names of Jesus, Mary and Joseph; and had once removed two legs from a spider (I'd reasoned he'd be more than fine with six legs, and had taken care to de-limb the creature symmetrically).

'And what else?' said Kincaid.

If anything, I think of her fondly; she was pneumatically fat in a robust yet reassuring fashion, and I associate that physical heft with warmth and the promise of a hug, although I don't recall ever being hugged by her. She was, nevertheless, an intimidating woman – and not merely as a product of her mass. Mrs Kincaid was an unyielding and unsympathetic authoritarian, who showed no compunction in humiliating her students with the teacher's standard repertoire of insults: birdbrain, thicky, dunce and dummy; plus a couple of more idiosyncratic slurs like fat-head, divbong and dough-brain. Not that I hold it against her; casual verbal bullying was all part of the job description back in those old schooldays. 'And what else?' she pressed.

'Nothing else,' I said sincerely.

'Really? Your father tells me you called your sister a bad name. Do you remember what you called your sister?'

'No.'

'Try,' my teacher urged.

'Smelly?'

'Worse.'

'Pig face?'

A slow shake of the head.

'I don't know,' I pleaded.

Actually, I had a good idea, but I was particularly reluctant to disclose it to 'Fatty' Kincaid.

'Your father has already told me, so why don't you just be a good little boy and tell me yourself.'

'Fat pig,' I said.

And I do remember Kincaid wincing a little at that. She shook her head. 'No,' she said. 'You called your sister a "dildo".'

'Did I?' I said, genuinely baffled.

'Where did you hear that word?' she asked.

Thinking about it now, I must have heard it somewhere on the playground and – being naïve of its potency – taken it home with me. But twenty-four years ago, staring into Kincaid's implacable eyes, I came up with a different solution to the conundrum.

'I heard it from you,' I said sincerely.

Within her colourful classroom lexicon, Mrs Kincaid's favourite putdown was – *surely her own invention* – 'dimlow'. If you got a question wrong, you were a dimlow; if you talked during class you were a dimlow; if you didn't answer your name during the reading of the register, 'dimlow' was inserted between Christian and surnames. And, well, 'dimlow' sounds an awful lot like 'dildo', don't you think?

'You call us dildos all the time,' I added.

I can only assume Mrs Kincaid registered my sincerity and guilelessness and understood how precarious her own employment had suddenly become, because she turned a deep red, told me never to say it again and sent me back to my chair. I never heard another word about it.

And I haven't thought about it for as long as I can remember. Until now, sitting opposite Ivy as she bites her lip, fiddles with her cufflinks and looks everywhere except at me. But I'm not about to repeat the mistake I made twenty-something years ago; I am not going to start apologizing, justifying or grovelling for one thing when I might be in the doghouse for another. That tactic is more likely to make things worse than better.

'I'm sorry about Dad's,' my mouth says. 'I was a bit of a berk.'

Ivy crinkles her brow. 'Were you?'

Idiot.

'You said you were tired,' I remind her. 'And I said "whatever".'

She nods and the left side of her mouth draws inward and upwards in what could be an expression of resignation, recollection or disappointment. Whatever it is, it's not a smile.

The waitress brings Ivy's tea in a small pot with a miniature jug of milk and bowl of sugar cubes. Ivy lifts the lid off the pot, stirs the tea through half a dozen revolutions, replaces the lid. She doesn't pour yet.

'I've been thinking,' I say, and Ivy looks up as if just remembering that I'm sitting opposite her. 'We should date more,' I say.

Ivy frowns, but she appears to be faintly amused.

'I mean, we've, you know … *seen* a lot of each other, obviously.' Ivy smiles at this, nods in tacit agreement. 'But we haven't really *dated*. Don't get me wrong, I enjoyed it, but it wasn't like … you know, dating.'

Ivy cocks an eyebrow.

'What I mean is, we should go to … I dunno, the theatre, wine bars, Madame Tussauds, the zoo.'

'The zoo?'

'Yeah, I love the zoo. Monkeys, elephants, giraffes, all that kind of stuff.'

'Animals?' says Ivy.

'Yes, exactly.'

'Sounds like fun.'

And this is hope, this is a ray of light, this is not, *Forget it, Fisher, we're finished*, this is, *Sounds like fun!*

'Really?' I say. 'Amazing. We could go today, it might rain but, hey, we'll just get those ponchos the tourists wear. What's your favour—'

'I have some news.'

And she chooses this moment to pour her tea; it takes forever.

'News?'

'You know how we've been – how did you put it? – *seeing* a lot of each other.'

'Ivy,' I say, 'whatever I've done—'

'Please,' she says, 'this is difficult.'

I take a breath, hold it, nod, exhale.

'We've been having sex,' Ivy qualifies, she half laughs. 'A lot of sex.'

My mind rifles through the possibilities: I'm bad in bed, she is married, she has an STD, or . . .

Sometimes I can be so stupid it's almost impressive.

Ivy and I have absolutely not talked about having a baby,

but we have not exactly not talked about it, either. The first time we made love I asked Ivy (not, of course, with a full coherent sentence, but rather a combination of facial gestures, eye movements and 'do you have any ... *you know . . .?*') if it was safe to proceed.

And Ivy looked at me and said: 'It's okay.'

'You're on the . . .?'

Ivy shook her head, smiled. 'It's okay,' she repeated.

It wasn't a trivial thing. And, naked and enraptured as I was, I was also fully aware of the potential consequences – 'potential' being a significant qualifier. Maybe Ivy knew she was at a safe point in her cycle, maybe she can't have kids full stop, or maybe when she said, 'It's okay,' she meant, *Hey, we love each other, don't we? I want kids, I love kids, and I think you'd make an amazing father, so let's allow nature to take its course.* And while this rapid inventory of possibilities was blurring through my brain, we were naked, aroused, Ivy's hands were clasped at the back of my head, she was kissing my neck, pulling me to her, raising her hips to meet mine and grinding herself against me – which kind of skews the decision-making process. And, yes, I do love her – not to be confused with the more frivolous *being in love*; that too, obviously, but something more fundamental than that. My dad, romantic poet that he is, calls it 'running as fast as you can' – the certain knowledge, deep inside yourself, that you are operating at maximum capacity in the love department. I've seen Ivy around children, the way she engages, listens and responds to them, the way she smiles when she's with them and the way that smile doesn't fade after they've left the room. She adores children; they sense it and then bounce it back. She makes them feel special, because to her they are. It's a part of what I love about her. And she is sexy and beautiful and we're naked and hot and sweaty and ... well, what the hell. It seemed like a good idea at the time.

We made love, twice, and (rather appropriately, it seems) I slept like a baby. It wasn't until maybe three and a half minutes after I woke the following morning that I experienced, if such a thing is possible, a minor panic. I'd known this woman, in a professional capacity, for a little over a month. Beyond that, and before our biologically blasé lovemaking, we had probably spent a total of two hours absolutely alone with each other. So honestly, William Fisher, what the hell were you thinking, having unprotected sex with someone that amounts to little more than a complete bloody stranger?

Ivy stirred beside me, rolled over, smiled, stroked my face and we made love again. Our relationship proper was approximately twelve hours old at this point and, cuddling on the crumpled sheets, it seemed churlish, presumptuous and extremely unromantic to bring up the subject of children.

I placed the potential consequences into a small box and placed the box, locked now, in a closet in a room in a poorly lit corner of my mind. That was twenty-five days ago, and in the hundreds of hours I have spent with Ivy since then, not one single thing caused me to doubt the wisdom of my foolishness. Once or twice or maybe a handful of times, I've found myself walking towards the room in the corner of my mind, but I never lingered and I never opened the door. Because what would that achieve? Of course, in the five days since we drove back from Dad's, it's been apparent that something was off, but the worst-case scenario my inner pessimist came up with was not gaining a baby, it was losing an Ivy.

Sitting outside the artisan coffee house in Wimbledon, Ivy still hasn't shared her 'news'. And maybe, after all that, she is simply searching for the right words to tell me that as a lover I'm about as much fun as a week-old courgette.

'I've been to the doctor,' she says, which, when you think about the options – bad in bed, an STD, married, pregnant – only narrows things down to two.

A waiter appears, as they tend to at moments like this. He asks if he can get us anything and we both tell him, No.

Ivy places her hand on her stomach. 'I'm … you …
you're … we …' and she bursts into tears. She's smiling,
though; she's smiling so much, in fact, that it makes me
cry, too. I get up from the table and squat beside Ivy's
chair, putting one arm around her shoulders and one
around her waist – as embraces go, it's a clumsy effort and
I have to put one knee down to steady myself. My knee
feels suddenly cold and wet, and a downward glance confirms that I am kneeling in a dirty great puddle. There are
a lot of people milling about in Wimbledon Village at ten
forty-five on a Friday morning, and most of them seem to
be walking past our table. Maybe it looks like I'm proposing; I don't know and don't care. I kiss Ivy's jumper where
it lies against her belly, and when she places a hand against
the back of my head it feels like electricity.

'I love you,' I say, but as I do Ivy pulls my head tight
against her stomach, crushing my face against her body
and turning my declaration into nothing more than three
muffled, squashed-together syllables. But I mean every
single one of them.

Chapter 4

Appleseed.
Garden pea.
Blueberry.
Kidney bean.
Olive . . .

Chapter 5

Ivy is puking in my bathroom; the sound carries as clearly as birdsong in an open meadow on a still summer's day. 'Fuck,' she says, her voice echoing and resonating from inside the porcelain bowl, and floating from bathroom to bedroom like a vapour. She spits, retches, spit, spit, spits. And flush. Ivy is an expansive and prolific puker, and before I leave for the office I will now have to clean vomit from under the seat, off the tiles and wherever the hell else it has splashed. And I'm fine with it; she gets the morning sickness, I get the Toilet Duck – it's only fair.

'You okay?' I shout.

'No,' Ivy shouts back. 'But I think it's pas— oh, oh Jesus Chrargbeluurgh . . .'

Me, I'm a door shutter; I mean, that's kind of the point of doors, isn't it? And don't try telling me they're there for opening; I have no time for that line of logic. We could debate cause, effect, form, function all day long, but the simple truth is this – doors exist to keep some stuff in and other stuff out. You want stuff like wild animals, burglars, serial killers, rain, noise and terrible smells on the outside. You want stuff like heat, romance, privacy and quiet on the inside. Well, I certainly do. Ivy doesn't close doors, not internal ones, not bathroom ones. And I suppose it's quaint in an open, uninhibited, it's-just-the-human-body kind of way, but there's nothing quaint about watching the love of your life sit through a nine-minute bowel movement – not that I actually watch, but it's all on show through the open door if I choose to.

It's been quiet in the bathroom for a full minute, the toilet flushes and Ivy moves through to the kitchen, muttering various expletives and curses against nature.

It's been a month since Ivy told me she is pregnant. The way they date these things (from the day of your last period instead of from the date of conception) means that Ivy is close to ten weeks pregnant. Which, bizarrely, is around ten days longer than Ivy and I have been together. Our pregnancy is older than our relationship. The way they measure these things, if you look at any book or website – the baby's development is measured in terms of food: poppyseed, blueberry, kumquat, apple, avocado, mango, cabbage, coconut, ruddy great watermelon. Right now, ours is the size of a green olive.

'Weird, huh?' I say to James Bond.

James doesn't answer, it's not even eight o'clock and cads never rise before eleven unless their lives, or King and country depend upon it. Neither of these things applies to me, but I do have a meeting this morning with Joe, my producer at the company I shoot commercials for. So I get up, open the curtains, and shuffle off to the bathroom to clean up Ivy's vomit and do what needs to be done behind closed doors.

Ivy is propped up in bed when I get back to the bedroom, holding a mug of coffee with one hand, a book with the other. She's reading a novel by someone I've never heard of, a wad of pages held back behind her left thumb.

The cafetiere is standing on a tray on top of the chest of drawers, along with a mug and a small jug of milk. I pour myself a coffee and, as I'm ahead of schedule, I climb back into bed.

'How's the book?'

Ivy rotates it in her hand, looking at the cover (Bohemian plaza, sunset, shadows, silhouettes) as if the answer to the question is printed there. 'Well, it won all kinds of prizes, apparently. But if it wasn't for book club I'd probably ditch it.'

'You totally should,' I say. 'Swap it out for something with vampires.'

Ivy laughs. 'It's not that I never have – quit a book – but I dunno . . . it's a bad habit to get into.'

'Seriously? There was a woman on the tube last week clipping her fingernails.'

'Ugh, you're joking?'

'Not joking. Just letting them ping off all over the carriage.'

Ivy puts a hand to her mouth. 'Stop, you're going to make me barf again.'

'Exactly. I'll take a book-quitter over a public nail-clipper any day of the week.'

Ivy nods as if considering the wisdom of this. 'You're probably right, but I don't want to disappoint Cora – it was her choice.'

'Will she even remember?'

'You never know with Cora. She doesn't know what day it is, but she can quote Dickens down to the dot and comma.'

'Bah, humbug.'

'Exactly,' says Ivy, turning her attention back to the book.

'So, how's the sickness?' I ask. 'Feeling any better?'

'I won't miss this when it passes,' she says. 'You hear

about it, but God, it's dismal. A hangover every morning, without any of the upfront fun.'

'Sorry,' I say.

'I should think so. You have a lot to answer for.'

After Ivy told me she was pregnant, and after I knelt in a puddle and mumbled the words 'I love you' into her jumper, we spent the rest of the day in a state of happy, excited perplexity. Ivy explained her silence over the previous several days – a mixture of anxiety, confusion, and uncertainty. She worried that I would be unhappy, that she'd misled me, that I would want out of this relationship. And I explained that none of this could be further from the truth. We finished our coffee and our relationship slipped smoothly onto the next cog – we walked to the deli, bought falafels, bread, humus, meat, sparkling fruit juice and cheesecake; we went back to Ivy's, picnicked on the sofa, then Ivy passed out in front of the TV. We didn't make love.

We have not, in fact, made love one single solitary time since the day before my dad gave us his bed and jinxed everything. I worked it out; it's been forty days and forty nights – that's an abstinence of biblical proportions.

I put my coffee cup down and place my hand on Ivy's thigh.

'You poor thing,' I say. 'You know what I've always found works wonders for a hangover?'

Ivy lowers her book, looks at me over the top of invisible spectacles. 'You are kidding, right?'

'No,' I say, moving my hand further up her thigh.

Ivy places her hand on top of mine, halting its progress. 'You do know that I don't have an actual hangover?'

'Yeah, but the princi—'

'I have a foetus the size of an olive in my uterus, and it is flooding my body with hormones that make me *feel like* I'm hungover.'

'Of course,' I whisper, 'of course ...' my hand still on Ivy's thigh. 'But it might also work on olive-sized, hormone-squeezing foetuses.'

'I have sick in my hair.'

'I don't mind.'

'I mind. Shut up and drink your coffee.'

I have cash in the bank, equity in the flat, two functioning kidneys inside my body. But for all of the above to remain exactly where they are, I need to make some money and make it soon.

Joe wants to discuss an 'exciting script'. And whilst I've learnt to treat Joe's enthusiasm with suspicion, it's hard not to get my hopes up. I've pitched for two jobs since we wrapped my last production a little over two months ago. I got neither. Two months with no income is worrying enough, but with an imminent extra mouth to feed, it's costing me sleep. Joe and I have worked together for several years and have become close friends, so how I dress this morning should be of no consequence. Particularly as Joe only ever shops at Primark and only then when his wife drags him there. However, I am not Joe's only director and he is not the only producer at the Sprocket Hole, so it does no harm to remind everyone what a cool, go-getter William Fisher really is. So I put on my second-oldest jeans and my newest shirt – the pink article I bought in Wimbledon Village a month ago. I'm still not convinced about the shirt, but Ivy seems to like it.

'You look nice,' she says.

'I am nice,' I tell her. She's still in bed, still reading. 'Will you be here when I get back?'

Ivy shakes her head. She widens her eyes in silent enquiry.

'What?' I say.

'I'll be at home, in my own flat.'

'Oh, okay.'

'Because . . .?'

'You need to feed Ernest?'

'The bloody goldfish is the least of my worries.'

'Oh, right, I . . . Shit! The *mid*wife, of course. Sorry, babes, what time?'

'I can't believe you forgot,' Ivy says, and she seems genuinely pissed off.

'I didn't, I was just thinking about work. I was—'

'I can't do this on my own, Fisher.'

'I know, and you won't have to. It's just ... my mind was ...'

Ivy is smiling. It's a small smile, lips rolled slightly in, eyebrows a notch higher than necessary. It's the smile she saves for occasions when she has dropped a hook and I have swum towards it, bitten and taken the entire thing, sinker and all into my gullible mouth.

'I wish you wouldn't,' I say.

Ivy affects innocent incomprehension. 'You wish I wouldn't what?'

'Bait me.'

'I don't bait you.'

'Yes, you do. You're like ... Baitey Davis.'

Ivy laughs, and the sound of it – an uncontrived, childlike chuckle involving nose, tongue and teeth – is like fingers on the back of my neck.

'I'm Ludwig van Baithoven,' she says, clapping her hands together and doubling up at her own joke.

'I know, I know, you're a master*baiter*!'

The gag clangs to the floor, echoing in the sudden absence of laughter. Ivy forces a polite laugh. '*You!*' she

says, shaking her head and finding her page again. '*Ahh . . .
Baitey Davis . . .*'

I'm racking my brains for a Baiter to salvage the
moment even though I know it's gone.

'And anyway,' says Ivy, in a tone heavy with reprehen-
sion, 'it was a shit wish.'

'Sorry. I wish you wouldn't bait me *and* I had a gold-
plated Ferrari.'

And right there: her compulsion to mock me and her
unwavering belief in the Wish Fairy, they're absolutely in
the top ten things I love about the woman who barfs in
my bathroom. I wouldn't claim they entirely compensate
for my enforced chastity, but they certainly take the edge
off.

Besides the sex, two additional things of significance
have not happened in the month since Ivy told me we are
having a baby and I told Ivy's jumper I love her:

I haven't repeated my declaration.

And Ivy has not answered it.

I want to tell her again, but I worry the words will lose
their potency if I say them every time the urge takes me.
And, because Ivy has yet to say those three words back to
me, I'm worried I might come across as needy. There's a
scene in *The Empire Strikes Back* that El and I thought was
just about the coolest thing in the world – in all of outer

space, in fact. Just before Han Solo is frozen into a slab of carbonite, Princess Leia tells him that she loves him. And, as he braces himself for a potentially fatal ordeal, Han looks at Leia and says, simply, 'I know.' As a boy I'd never considered how that nonchalance – *'I know'* – must have made the Princess feel, but as a love-struck father-to-be I can make a pretty good guess. I'd worry about this more, but considering I had a mouthful of wool when I first announced my affections, I'm reasonably confident Ivy never heard me.

Before I leave for the office, I give Ivy a final kiss. And (in spite of the aroma of sick and toothpaste) those three unsaid words are still swirling around inside my head, trying to find their way to my mouth.

'Have a great day,' Ivy says.

'I . . . I know,' I answer, and Ivy looks at me like I've lost my mind.

Chapter 6

'You look niyth,' lisps Pippa, when I step through the door of the Sprocket Hole.

I haven't slept with her since June, almost four months ago now, and it was never more than a frivolous fling. Nevertheless, I always blush when she says anything more friendly than hello.

'Shirt!' says Gaz, our junior director, who also happens to be Pippa's current boyfriend. He mimes tugging at a collar, nods approvingly and returns to his magazine.

Joe looks up from his phone and regards me sardonically. 'Pink?' he says. 'Matches your face.' Then, 'Hold on, has it got glitter in it? Is that fucking glitter?'

'It's thread,' I say.

'Looks like tinsel. Where'd you buy it, Old Compton Street?'

'Yes, Joe, I bought it in Old Compton Street, from a shop that caters to gentlemen of a homosexual persuasion. Is that what you're suggesting?'

'All right,' he says, 'no need to get your leotard in a twist. Come on, you're buying lunch.'

'It's five to eleven.'

'I've been up since five-fucking-thirty. Kids, honestly, they ruin your life.'

Gaz laughs.

'I'm not joking,' Joe says, pointing a finger first to Gaz, then to Pippa. 'I hope you two love kittens are using protection. Ruin your life, they do, mark my fucking words.'

Joe is attacking a plate of pie, chips and peas as if he hasn't eaten for a week.

I'm sipping a bad coffee and watching.

Joe glances up from his food; one eye squinting, the opposite eyebrow officiously cocked. 'So,' he says, 'how's Ivy?'

It was Joe that introduced us. And, according to Joe, it was immediately obvious that I had a thing for our new make-up artist. Ever since that first encounter he has adopted an attitude of vaguely threatening disapproval, as if he somehow doubts my intentions, integrity or reliability. I'd call him on it, except the revelation that Ivy is now pregnant would appear to confirm his misgivings.

'She's . . .' *She's carrying my child!* '. . . she's good,' I say.

'Still at it like a pair of fruit flies?' Joe jabs his knife forward and back in the air for emphasis.

'What do you mean, *still*? I never said anything about fruit flies.'

Joe shrugs. ''swhat you do, innit. First throes of romance an' all that.' He sighs, stabs three chips and shoves them into his mouth.

'How are the wedding plans?'

'Sooner it's over the better. Eight fucking months she's been planning this.' Joe puts down his knife and fork to show me eight fingers. 'Could build a house in that time.'

'How's Sammy?'

'Potty training,' Joe says.

'Cute.'

Joe shakes his head. 'Nothing cute about a pair of shit-smeared Postman Pat underpants.'

'But it's not all bad, is it?'

Joe widens his eyes. 'What is this, you counselling me? Has Jen been talking to you? What's going on?'

'Whoa, nothing's going on, I'm just asking about your bloody son, is all.'

Joe looks at me like he's not entirely convinced. 'She's been going on about having another,' he says.

'Another baby?'

Joe nods. 'After the wedding. Wants to have at least one that's not a bastard, I suppose.'

'That's how she put it?'

'She's not getting any younger, neither,' says Joe.

'She's younger than you.'

'Next stop thirty-eight, mate. And between you and me, having a nipper puts a few extra miles on the body-work, if you know what I mean.'

'And with you being so well preserved and all. So, what are you going to do?'

Joe laughs. 'You can tell you've never held a relationship down for more than five minutes.'

'I went out with Kate for over a year.'

'Yeah, and we all know how that ended.'

Yes, we do: with Kate (in her own carefully chosen words) sucking a co-worker's cock, and then walking out on December the twenty-fourth, one day before Christmas, one day before my birth-day.

'What I am going to do,' says Joe, 'is what I always do.'

'Which is?'

'Whatever Jen tells me.' Joe builds a small pie-and-pea mountain on his fork. 'At least I'll get a shag on me hon-eymoon,' he says, feeding the pile of food into his mouth.

'Lucky Jen,' I tell him.

'So,' says Joe, rubbing his hands together in a now

familiar signal that he is transitioning from hard-nosed friend mode to hard-nosed producer mode.

'Here it comes,' I say.

'What?'

'This is where you tell me how big your mortgage is, how much Jen spends on shoes, how much the wedding costs.'

Joe opens his mouth to speak.

'And then,' I continue, 'you slide a piece-of-shit script across the table and give me the "this isn't art" speech.'

'Finished?'

I nod.

'*This*, dear friend, is where I ask you to do me the very big fucking honour of being my best fucking man.'

'Oh.'

'Exactly. And it's traditional to say thank you.'

'Thank you. This would mean a great deal to me if I thought your wedding meant anything to you.'

'I'll take that as a yes?'

'Yes, it's a yes.' And the truth is it does mean a lot to me, but if I told Joe he'd only take the piss.

'Right,' says Joe, holding up the fingers on one hand; he ticks them off as he speaks: 'You need to organize a stag do – strippers but classy ones, no hookers, no pounds in pint pots. You're in charge of suit hire, Moss Bros, cheapest shit they have. I need you to buy presents for the brides-maids, fifty-quid budget.'

'Each?'

Joe laughs. 'Fuck off! Between the three – get 'em wine, or something to put in their hair. Taxis between the church and the hotel, and a speech. I want it between three and six minutes long, couple of jokes, rude's okay, but not filthy. And nothing about nutters because Jen's aunty's a bit . . .' Joe indicates a loose screw in the region of his temple.

'That it?'

'For now, yes.'

'And you're sure about the no nutter jokes?'

'Maybe just the one, then,' says Joe, proving once and for all that he is immune to sarcasm. 'So long as it's funny as fuck.'

'Got it,' I say. 'Consider me briefed.'

Joe reaches under the table, produces a brown A4 envelope from his bag and slides it across the table.

'I fucking knew it.'

'I'd hate to disappoint,' says Joe, tapping the envelope. 'Go on, open it.'

I slide the script halfway out of the envelope, read the name of the client printed across the top and slide the script back into the envelope. 'It's fucking bog paper.'

'We all shit, William, don't be such an elitist.'

'We don't all shoot films about it, though, do we?'

'Here we go: I'm an award-winning director, I have to think of my showreel, you're only as good as your last ad, blah, blah, bleat.'

I smile; keep my mouth closed.

'I like you, Fisher, I believe in you, I think you're talented and wonderful and handsome, okay? But ... to be truly award-winning, emphasis on the *ing*, you need to win more than one. Plus!' says Joe, holding up a finger and intercepting my wounded outburst before I get past the first plosive *B ...!* 'Plus ... you may be my favourite little director, but you haven't directed anything since July, which, when you think about it, makes you not so much a director as some unemployed ginger bloke.'

It's no one's ambition to direct commercials for a living. No one grows up dreaming of shooting toilet roll ads; the same way no one dreams of writing headlines, composing jingles, photographing burgers or being the face of low-cost car insurance. You want to write novels or anthems, photograph models, play Hamlet, shoot movies, make a million, marry a film star.

That said, there are much harder ways to earn a lot less money.

Joe is still talking: '... pick and choose how they earn

five grand a day. Some of us, William, have mouths to feed besides our own.'

Tell me about it.

'And by the way,' he continues, 'the script isn't shit.'

I can't help but laugh. 'Is that the criteria now? *Not shit.*'

Joe laughs. 'It'll open doors.'

'I know,' I say, 'ones with engaged signs on the front of them.'

'So you'll look at it?'

I don't have to say another word; Joe's instincts are as sharp as broken glass. I hesitate a split-second too long and he knows he has me.

'Excellent,' he says, already scrolling through numbers on his phone. 'I'll set something up. Time is it?'

'Two minutes to twelve.'

'Great,' he says, phone to his ear now. 'It'll be two past by the time we get to the Goose, you can buy me a pint to say thank you.'

'I don't really have time f—'

'Shut up,' he says, 'you're my best man, now; you're obliged. And anyway, what else have you . . .?' Then, into the phone, 'Michael! Let's talk arseholes.'

Joe would have stayed in the pub all afternoon, but after two pints I lied and told him I had to go and meet Ivy. Joe

sulked and played the 'you've changed' card, but I coun-
tered with the 'promise of sex' card, which beats all others
in this vintage game. Even if it is a lie. Better that than
reveal my true hand and the Ace of 'Oh my God we're
having a baby'. Too soon for that.

When I get back to Wimbledon Village I stop off at an
organic grocer's and then the butcher's to buy ingredients for
a boeuf bourguignon. The grocer's is merely expensive; the
butcher, though, is a cleaver-wielding, blood-spattered criminal. What the grinning psychopath behind the counter
charges for a modest-sized fillet of beef is roughly the same
as a meal for two in a Brixton restaurant. And if the mansions, supercars and garish corduroy trousers weren't enough,
the relative cost of our groceries tells you everything about
the difference between mine and Ivy's postcodes. And for
the first time since we've been together, I have to wonder
how a make-up artist (even a good one) can afford a spacious
two-bedroom flat in The Village. Maybe her parents gave
her the deposit; her dad is a retired lawyer so it's possible. Or
maybe she bought twenty years ago before prices became
what they are today; she is, after all, old enough.

However she came by the flat, she's not answering the
door. I've rung the bell four times now and my left arm is
aching from holding a bunch of flowers behind my back.
It's possible Ivy has popped out for some reason – milk,

bread, fresh air – but the bedroom curtains are closed, making me reasonably confident she is simply taking a nap. I call her phone, but of course it goes straight to voicemail. The midwife isn't due for another thirty minutes, so I sit on the wall and eat raw chestnut mushrooms while I wait for some sign of life. After another ten minutes I call her phone again, and when she doesn't answer I try the doorbell, the knocker and shouting through the letterbox. I'm about to knock again when a voice – it sounds like a laryngitic elf – asks if he can help. I turn to see an awkward, red-faced boy, half in and half out of the neighbour's doorway.

Whenever Ivy is away for more than two days her neighbour's teenage son, Harold, feeds Ivy's goldfish, Ernest. I'm guessing this is Harold.

'Harold, right?'

'Who are you?' Harold's cracked, half-broken voice sends the 'you' up, down and back up again.

'Fisher,' I say, extending my hand.

Harold (and who calls a child Harold this side of a world war, anyway?) looks at the bags of groceries and bunch of flowers on Ivy's doorstep. 'Fisher?' he repeats, looking at me suspiciously.

'William Fisher,' I say. 'Ivy's . . . you know, boyfriend, man . . . friend.'

Harold says nothing.

'I'm meant to be meeting her,' I explain. 'But she's not answering.'

'You should come back later,' he says.

'We're meeting somebody in fifteen minutes.'

Harold shrugs, steps back into his house and goes to close the door.

'Wait!' I tell him. 'Wait. You have a key, don't you? Can you let me in?'

Harold looks at me like I've just asked if he has a ski mask and a knife. 'I shouldn't think so,' he says, leaning away from me.

'Listen. Harold. Someone is coming to see us in fifteen minutes and Ivy is asleep. If she misses our visitor, Ivy will be massively pissed.'

Harold mimes swigging from a glass. 'Drunk?'

'No, not drunk. Pissed off. We have a very important meeting.'

'Maybe she's out?' Harold suggests.

'Her curtains are closed.'

'What's it about?'

'What? What's what about?'

'Your meeting.'

'Well, it's not really any of your business, is it, Harold?'

'Fine,' he says, going again to close the door.

'Harold, wait.'

Harold closes the door.

'Git,' I say loud enough for the spotty twerp – and half of the neighbours – to hear.

I try Ivy's phone again, and again it goes straight to voicemail. I'm halfway through a rambling message when Harold reappears, holding a door key.

'Harold!' I say, like we're reunited buddies. 'Mate, thank you.' But as I reach for the key, Harold withdraws it.

'*I'll* check,' he says.

'You'll what? You bloody won't, give me the key.'

Harold holds the key behind his back.

'How do I know you're who you say you are?'

'What? Who else would I be?'

Harold shrugs. 'Burglar. Rapist. Murderer.'

'With a bag of fucking groceries?'

'No need for that,' says Harold, and he looks genuinely offended.

'Harold, listen, sorry, but if Ivy's in her pyjamas and finds you poking your head around her bedroom doorway she'll freak out. And neither of us wants that, do we?'

Harold blushes scarlet, the hand holding the key falls to his side and I make a grab for it. He's a strong little bastard, though, and his arm stays welded to his side like an iron rod.

'Just give me the fucking key, Harold.'

'Get off me,' he says, his cracked voice jumping at least an octave.

I try to pry the swine's fingers open, but he's got the grip of a farmer and his bony fist does not yield one iota.

'Give it to me, you little b—'

'What's going on?'

I spin around to find Ivy standing in the doorway. Her hair is tousled and she's wearing short shorts, a vest and no bra. I can't see my own face but I can see Harold's, and whoever loses this blushing contest, it's not for lack of a damned good effort.

'You were sleeping,' I say.

'Key,' says Harold, holding it up like a talisman.

'He wouldn't let me in,' I say.

'You snatched,' Harold says plaintively. 'I didn't know who you were.'

'I told you! I'm her manfriend, I'm Ivy's . . . manfriend.'

'Christ,' says Ivy in a not-quite-shout. 'Will you two stop squabbling.'

It takes the vast majority of my willpower not to tell Ivy that Harold started it. Even though I'm pretty sure he did.

'Sorry,' says Harold.

'Thank you,' says Ivy. 'We'll be okay now.'

Harold smiles at Ivy, glares at me, and slinks back into his house.

I pick up the flowers and show them to Ivy. 'Flowers,' I explain.

Ivy shakes her head and it dislodges a hint of a smile. I pick up the groceries and follow her up the stairs. And my word, she does look good in those shorts.

While Ivy showers, I put the flowers in a vase and the ingredients in the fridge. The kitchen and living room comprise a single open-plan area, the boundary between the two 'rooms' delineated by a waist-high breakfast counter. A baby could crawl unimpeded from the fireplace to the under-sink cupboard where Ivy keeps cling film, cleaning products, rubber gloves and bleach. From the kitchen the baby has access to the hallway. Crawling past a flight of steep stairs the little bundle of joy will come to a small bedroom (or modest-sized nursery) on the left and a bathroom on the right. The latch on the bathroom door doesn't close, giving easy access to further ground-level cleaning products and a toilet brush. If the infant is lucky enough to survive this treacherous expedition, he or she will arrive at the master bedroom where, as far as I know, there is nothing lethal or spectacularly unhygienic. The floorboards, however, are in a sorry state ('original' an estate agent would tell you) and on more than three occasions I have ripped a bloody great hole in my sock on a Victorian splinter or proud nail.

I'm pondering all of this from the sofa in the living

room when the doorbell rings, and I am suddenly convinced the midwife will take one look around this death-trap and mark us as unfit parents. The bell rings a second time.

'Can you get that?' shouts Ivy from the bedroom.

The midwife, a rotund lady with a thick Caribbean accent, introduces herself as Eunice. I lead her up to the flat, muttering non-sequiturs about the banisters and stair gates and child-proof locks and DIY and floorboard sanders.

'Plenty of time for that, darlin',' says Eunice, smiling, but at the same time casting an appraising glance around the flat. 'Let's worry 'bout mum first. She home?'

Ivy arrives on cue, hair still wet from the shower, no make-up, beautiful. Her skin is slightly flushed from the shower, highlighting the scars on the side of her face. Ivy must be used to them by now, but it's still new to me and I feel embarrassed and protective on her behalf whenever we meet people for the first time.

'Hello, darlin',' says Eunice. 'Don't you look lovely. Not showin' yet?'

Ivy puts a hand to her tummy. 'I don't know,' she says, beaming. 'Maybe a little.'

And it's true, Ivy is beginning to show a hint of a bump behind her tight T-shirt.

Eunice waves a hand in the air dismissively. 'Pshh, I never bin that flat in me life.' And she laughs deep and hearty. 'Come,' she says, sitting on the sofa and patting the cushion beside her, 'sit.'

Ivy looks as bashful as a schoolgirl as she takes a seat next to Eunice.

'How far along are we, sweetheart? Ten, eleven weeks, is it?'

'Nine and a half,' says Ivy, sitting beside the midwife.

'Excitin' time,' says Eunice, widening her eyes. 'Very excitin'.'

Over the next half-hour or so, Eunice asks Ivy questions, she takes samples of blood and urine, and together they fill out various forms. Besides making tea, I'm essentially surplus to requirements.

Before she leaves, Eunice asks if we have any questions. Ivy says, no, they've covered everything she can think of for now.

Eunice turns to me. 'And what 'bout dad?'

It's the first time anyone's called me 'dad', and the effect is astonishing. As if there's a 'dad' gland buried somewhere behind my breastbone and it's been waiting to hear that one special word before it triggers and releases a whole bunch of dad hormones into my bloodstream. The effect of these chemical messengers, it seems, is to raise a small lump in the throat of the soon-to-be father and make him grin like a monkey in a nut factory. Unlike the adrenaline fight-or-flight response, it's unlikely that this biological quirk confers any evolutionary advantage, but it sure does feel good.

'Actually,' I say, still grinning, spurred by this surge of dad hormone, 'I do have one question,' and I glance at Ivy and smile.

It's as if Ivy can read my mind, because her mouth tightens, her eyes narrow by maybe a single millimetre and her head moves fractionally left and right in a minuscule, pleading, head-shake. But it's too late; I'm committed.

'Yes, darlin'?'

'I was wondering if it's okay to, you know … have …' and despite the immediate medical proof that Ivy and I have had sex at least once; despite the fact that that sex and its natural consequences are the very reason Eunice is now sitting on Ivy's sofa, I am too embarrassed to say the word. So instead, I attempt to communicate the *idea* of sex through a series of facial expressions, head movement and gurning innuendo.

'Sex!' shouts Eunice. 'Ha ha, oh my Lord, yes!' And she gives Ivy's knee a squeeze. 'O'course you can 'ave sex, my darlin'. But no vigorous thrustin', okay?'

Eunice winks at me, and Ivy lowers her gaze to the floorboards.

After we say goodbye to Eunice, Ivy is aglow and it seems all the day's transgressions have been forgiven. As we take the stairs back up to the flat, I am again reminded how fine Ivy looks from behind. Ivy talks excitedly as she clears up the coffee cups, takes them into the kitchen and fills the sink with water. But now that we've had a green light from our midwife, I'm finding it hard to concentrate on anything apart from getting Ivy into bed, and pronto. It's as if there's a sex klaxon going off in my head, and as Ivy plunges her hands into the hot, soapy water, I feel the beginnings of an uprising in my underwear. If not exactly battle ready, the old campaigner is certainly getting himself psyched up.

'. . . don't you think?' says Ivy.

I have no idea what she is talking about; the sex klaxon is still blaring inside my skull. 'For sure,' I say, and it seems like this is the right answer, as Ivy nods and starts drying the mugs. Ivy pushes a checked tea towel into the depths of a mug and revolves it deliberately around the inside. From where I'm standing it looks fantastically erotic, and all the primal systems are on full alert. It's been so long since we last made love, though, that the thought of initiating sex outside of the bedroom and during daylight hours makes me itch with self-consciousness. The trick, I reassure myself, is spontaneity.

'You okay?' asks Ivy.

'Fine,' I say.

'Your face is very red.'

'Fancy a shag?'

Ivy regards me for a moment and then laughs. 'God,' she says, 'I know!' And in a bad impersonation of Eunice: 'No vigorous thrustin'!' and she laughs so hard she has to sit down and fan her face.

'Funny,' I say, and my forced laugh is even less convincing than Ivy's Caribbean accent. But she is laughing too much to notice.

By the time she has recovered – and it takes a while – Ivy is exhausted and says she needs to lie down for a nap. If this – laughing Ivy into bed – had been my plan along, I'd be a genius. But it wasn't and I'm not. The moment has now passed, the klaxon is silent, and little Fisher has renounced the cause.

When Ivy gets out of bed, for the third time today, the sun is fading and the boeuf bourguignon is bubbling nicely on the hob. This was the first meal I cooked for Ivy. I like to think of it as our special dish. Maybe it will help rekindle Ivy's former passion.

'What's that smell?' Ivy puts her arms around my waist and kisses me.

'Our special dish,' I say, lifting the lid on the bubbling casserole.

'We have a special dish?'

'Boeuf bourguignon. I cooked it the first night you came to my flat'

'Oh,' says Ivy with an expression that reveals this is a piece of trivia she had not retained. 'It's very sweet of you, babes, but I don't know if I fancy something so . . . *heavy*.'

'It's not *heavy*, it's . . . it's rich. Rich isn't the same as heavy.'

'To be honest, I'm not that hungry.'

'The midwife said you should eat plenty of iron,' I remind her. 'Plenty of iron in beef. Well, there should be the price I paid for it.'

'Would you mind putting a lid on it,' Ivy says. 'The smell's making me feel a bit . . .' She blows out her cheeks to suggest nausea.

'Yeah, 'course. We can have it later.'

Ivy opens a window, letting in a cool breath of autumn air. That's another thing this place has on Brixton – if you open a window in my flat at this time of night, you can get high off what wafts in.

'What I really fancy,' Ivy says, 'is a bit of caesar salad, chicken caesar salad.'

'Got a craving?'

'No, just like caesar salad,' says Ivy.

I open the fridge but we have no chicken, no salad and no dressing.

'Want me to go get the bits?' I say.

'Would you? And some pineapple? Sorry, babe, I'd go myself but I'm zonked.'

It's dark by the time we start eating our supper in front of some romantic comedy on the box. The salad is fine as far as salads go, but it's a poor substitute for boeuf bourguignon and my stomach is not happy about it. Ivy takes the dishes into the kitchen then comes back and curls up with her head in my lap.

'Are you disappointed?' she asks, and whether she's referring to the film, the salad or the celibacy I don't know, but the answer's the same.

'No,' I say. 'Why?'

'You went to all that trouble, cooking.'

'It'll keep.'

'I'll take you for supper,' she says. 'Friday. Anywhere, you choose.'

I kiss the parting in her hair.

'How was Joe?' Ivy asks.

'Good,' I tell her. 'Sends his love.'

'Liar.'

'Well, he asked after you.'

Ivy laughs.

'He asked me to be his best man.'

Ivy swivels her head around so she is facing me. 'That's nice of him. You going to do a speech?'

'Have to,' I say. 'Part of the deal. You're invited, by the way.'

Ivy turns back to the TV. 'Cool,' she says, but it's not very convincing. 'What was the script?'

'Loo roll.'

'Loo roll as in *for* loo roll, or loo roll as in, it's shit.'

'Both,' I tell her.

'So long as you're happy,' Ivy says.

Onscreen, the rom-couple have fallen out due to some hilariously crossed wires, but somehow I think everything will work out in the end. I have nothing against genre for-mula; I love it, in fact. Good wins over evil, love conquers all, the world won't end – and that's all right by me. Wouldn't have it any other way. What I do object to, is some Hollywood director getting paid in the region of a million dollars to do nothing more than stand behind a camera: the set-pieces are clumsy, the editing is crude, the performances predictable; there's no craft or invention or, from where I'm sitting, any evidence of direction whatsoever. I could do that. I could do better than that. But instead, if I'm lucky, I get to shoot thirty seconds of bog roll for less money than this chancer makes on his coffee break.

'You think I should say no?' I say to Ivy.

Ivy doesn't answer.

'Obviously I could hold out for something better,' I tell her. 'But I have you two to think about now, don't I?' And I place my hand on Ivy's tummy.

Ivy makes a noise as if she's about to speak, and then begins to snore.

Chapter 7

Ivy is ten weeks pregnant today, and all of a sudden the pregnancy feels significantly more real than it did when I last saw her thirty-one hours ago. Yesterday and today Ivy is working on a promo for a new band all the hip kids are into. The shoot didn't wrap until late last night and she had an early call today, so we spent a rare night apart. When I woke this morning there was a picture message waiting for me on my phone.

The picture is a close-up shot of soft female stomach – the faint scar travelling from top to bottom of the image confirms that this soft female stomach belongs to Ivy. Using what I'm guessing is a lipstick, she has drawn a voice bubble emerging from her belly button. It contains the message: *10 weeks preg today! Xxx*

And just like that, this thing has approximately ten times

the gravity it had yesterday. I called Ivy straight away, but it went through to voicemail. I wrote and deleted five different responses before settling on a roman numeral joke – *X!* – which surely came off as nothing more than an apathetic kiss. I wrote an explanation, but it seemed hugely patronizing so I deleted that too.

Joe and I just spent an hour and a half discussing the loo roll commercial with the ad agency. I think it went well but I found it hard to concentrate. The ad involves a giant bunny, and the notion kept snapping me back to Ivy's message – *10 weeks preg today*. I found the knowledge heavily isolating. Everybody getting excited about costumes and casting and bad gags, and me wanting to tap the side of my mug with a teaspoon and announce: *Guess what, everyone? I'm having a baby!* But Ivy and I are keeping the news to ourselves until we've had the twelve-week scan a fortnight from now. So I pretended to listen and take notes, and when everyone else laughed, I joined right in. It seemed to do the trick, though, and Joe is convinced we've got the gig. Travelling back to Brixton on the Victoria Line, I'm a mixed sack of emotions. It's a two-day shoot and I'm paid by the day, so it's a good amount of cash for the increasingly-imminent-family fund. On the other hand, it's still a commercial for toilet paper.

More than that, though, something has been scratching

at my subconscious all day and I can't quite get hold of it. I think it has something to do with underwear. Ivy is taking me for supper tonight; she'll bring a bag with a change of clothes in it, and maybe she'll stay for the weekend or maybe we'll decamp to Wimbledon. It seems neither of us goes anywhere lately without a pair of underpants in our pocket – and half of the time those underpants need a wash. It's never occurred to me to ask for a drawer in Ivy's flat or to offer her one in mine – maybe because it feels like a pretty flimsy offer considering our situation.

Walking back to my flat I pass a key-cutters, and all of a sudden I know what I need to do. Or maybe I've known since this morning, when I walked past the same kiosk on my way to the tube.

Next stop is a cheap jewellers where my request to purchase an empty ring box is met with stark incomprehension.

'It's a surprise for my girlfriend,' I explain.

The girl behind the counter wears three gold hoops in one ear, four in the other and a stud through her top lip. 'What, an empty box?'

'Yes, no, I'm going to put something in it.'

'Wot?'

'A key.'

'Wot?'

'For my flat, you see. I want to put it in a box – the key, for a surprise.'

'We don't sell boxes.'

I do my most endearing smile. 'Is there any chance you could just give me one?'

'I shouldn't fink so.'

'Well, what's the cheapest thing you've got?'

The stud in her top lip slides forward and back in its piercing. 'She got her ears pierced?'

'Why, how much are the earrings?'

'Fourteen ninety-nine.'

'Perfect.'

The girl opens a drawer beneath the counter, selects a pair of silver earrings and drops them into a purple, faux-suede, heart-emblazoned pouch.

'Excuse me,' I say with infinite patience and politeness. 'Could I have those in a box?'

'These come in a bag,' she says. ''s got a heart on it.'

I place both my hands on the glass counter. 'Listen, I don't want a bag, I want a b—'

'I'm afraid I'll have to ask you to please remain behind the counter please.'

I spring back to attention. 'I am behind the counter. I was just . . . *Jesus!* I just want a sodding b—'

'Is there a problem?' asks a thinly stretched male voice.

I turn to face a middle-aged man standing behind the till, his right hand poised conspicuously beneath the counter. I look back to the girl. She crosses her arms and waggles her lip stud.

'Fine,' I say. 'I'll go to Argos.'

'Whatevs,' says the girl. 'But their earrings is clappers.'

I have no idea what 'clappers' means, but I'll bet it's not an endorsement.

Standing in the queue at the Argos jewellery counter, it occurs to me that giving Ivy a set of keys to my flat is only marginally more meaningful than giving her a drawer for her knickers. I love Ivy; I love sharing a bed, sofa and bathroom with her even if she doesn't close the door when answering the call of nature. And let's not forget our child, now the size of a kumquat, with ears, nostrils and a heart that beats one hundred and eighty times a minute. The sensible thing to do – the right and romantic thing – would be to ask Ivy to move in with me completely – body, soul and underwear. The only problem I can envisage, however, is that Ivy would be out of her mind to abandon the leaf-dappled serenity of Wimbledon Village for the pungent, threatening cacophony of Brixton. But it's my turn to be served, so I offer up a desperate prayer to the patron saint of idiots, and ask the bored counter assistant for a pair of her cheapest earrings.

I'm drinking, Ivy isn't.

Two glasses of wine cost more than a bottle so I ordered a bottle, but I'm nervous and it's making me drink too fast. We've finished our starters and our main courses, and are now waiting for dessert to arrive. The boxful of keys in my front jeans pocket is too uncomfortable for me to have forgotten its existence for even one second. I've been waiting for an opportune moment to present it, but every time there's been a lull in the conversation, my nerve has gone and hidden beneath the table. Instead, I've lurched from one inane conversational gambit to another, like a teenager on a first date. Fortunately, Ivy is so exhausted she either hasn't noticed or doesn't care. I attempted to initiate a discussion about baby names, but Ivy said it's too early. I asked if she wanted a boy or a girl, and she said all she wanted was a healthy child. I asked did she want a home or a hospital birth and she said could we just change the subject. I talked about the weather. You can tell Ivy would rather be at home, sleeping on the sofa in front of a crappy movie, which, considering her circumstances, is entirely understandable.

'How was your pasta?' I ask.

'Nice. How was your fish?'

'Good.'

'Great.'

'Yeah, I like fish.'

Mercifully, the waitress arrives with our desserts. It isn't an opportunity, exactly, but this date has about ten minutes left to run, so it's do-or-die time. I brace myself, take a deep breath and reach into my pocket . . . and it's only as the box comes into view above the table-top that it occurs to me what normally comes in ring boxes.

'I've been thinking,' I say, and I only wish I'd thought a tiny bit harder.

Ivy all but recoils in her chair.

It's almost certainly my imagination, but the background chatter of the other diners seems to fade out. I am acutely aware of the guitarist in the corner, crooning quietly about – yes, *amore*. In the movie version of my life, all heads would turn towards me expectantly: a fat woman would pause, dessert halfway to her mouth; a lothario waiter winks encouragement; an elderly lady reaches for her husband's hand and gazes into his milky eyes; for comic relief, a balding bespectacled man would glance at his sour-faced wife and shudder. But this isn't a movie, this is real, unscripted unrehearsed life, and the only person looking at me is Ivy. And I have one hundred per cent of her attention – the way I would if I were waving, say, a blood-stained axe in her face.

'No!' I say, and in my haste to reveal not-a-ring, I fumble the box into my tiramisu. 'Fuck!'

And now I have attracted the attention of a couple at the adjacent table. I smile at the gawping woman and she winks in return.

Ivy is clutching her fork like a horror movie starlet attempting to fend off the unfendable.

'It's okay,' I say, finally snapping the stupid box open. 'It's keys.'

Ivy looks at the keys like she's never before seen such an item. The woman at the adjacent table goes back to her meatballs, disappointed.

'For my flat,' I say. 'For you.'

'Keys,' says Ivy, still processing the situation. Her face transitions from fear to confusion to relief and back to confusion.

'Move in with me?' I say, and I hit the question mark harder than necessary. It sounds like I'm pleading.

Ivy takes the keys, inserts her finger through the ring holding them together, realizes what she's doing and puts the bunch down on the table as if they might be dangerous. 'This is a surprise,' she says.

I do a cabaret flourish with my hands. 'Ta-daaa!'

Ivy laughs politely.

'Is that a yes?'

Ivy chews her bottom lip.

'How are your desserts?' asks a waiter.

Ivy's is untouched but melting; mine has a box-shaped indentation in its centre. 'Delicious,' I say, 'but I couldn't eat another thing.'

'Madam?' asks the waiter.

'All done,' says Ivy. 'Thank you.'

'Can I get you coffee?'

'Just the bill,' Ivy and I say in perfect unison.

We don't talk as we walk back to my flat. It's a cold evening with no stars, but I steer us along the scenic route, nevertheless. We stroll arm in arm, taking in the pungent air and watching the fighting drunks, passed-out tramps, strung-out whores and maniacal pimps. It's a beautiful evening. As we turn the corner onto the relative safety of Chaucer Road, Ivy comes to an abrupt halt, pulling on my arm.

'What is it?' I ask, checking up and down the street.

Ivy smiles, takes my hands in hers. 'Will you move in with *me*?' she asks.

I hug her, kiss her.

'Is that a yes?' she says, laughing.

'I thought you'd never ask.'

Ivy frowns. 'Is this . . . did you set me up?'

'That's not a very romantic way of putting it.'

'I dunno,' says Ivy, and she sets off walking again, pulling me along behind her. 'It might just be the most romantic thing anyone's ever done for me.'

Chapter 8

In the six weeks since El came back from San Francisco, his tan has faded and his head appears smaller, although the latter is almost certainly a by-product of his new beard.

'Fuckig itches like a b. . . bastid.'

'Well, let me shave the scraggy thing off, for pity's sake,' says Phil.

'P. . . p. . . you'll prolly kill me,' El says, then laughs. 'Second th. . . thoughts. M. . . maybe should.'

El's twitches and tics have escalated to the point where he can't shave without cutting himself half a dozen or more times. And he's too temperamental, too stubborn, to allow Phil to do it for him.

'Anway, 's. . . 'strendy.'

'You look like a vagabond,' says Phil, who himself looks uncharacteristically dishevelled. He has bruise-coloured bags beneath his eyes and it looks as if he's been crying, not sleeping or both.

El doesn't reply; he's engrossed in his iPad, as he has been for most of the evening. There are two pizzas on the coffee table, but Phil isn't eating and El lost interest halfway through his second slice.

El holds the iPad towards me. 'Here's a g... good 'un.'

'What is it?'

'V... video. One of my g... gang.'

Phil sighs. 'I wish you wouldn't, El. It's terribly morbid.'

I take the iPad and press play. A woman is sprawled on a sofa, her left arm tangled around the back of her head, the hand opening and closing like a spastic crab. Off-screen, a male voice tells us this is someone's wife, she's had Huntington's for eight years and is making this film for her seven-year-old son while she is still able. The woman slurs, gasps, groans her way through a heartfelt message; telling her son she loves him, apologizing for not being there to see him grow up. While the left hand clenches and relaxes, the woman brings the right to and from her forehead as if chastising herself for dying of this disease. At about fifty seconds in she starts crying.

'Cr... cracks me up,' says El, laughing disingenuously.

Phil stands abruptly and walks from the room.

'G... get her,' says El, loudly.

'Give him a break, El.'

When I visit El, Phil invariably disappears to the pub for an hour, so I'm not overly concerned when I hear the front door slam.

El grins. 'We can have a d. . . drink now.'

'I'll put the kettle on,' I tell him.

'S. . . s. . .'

'Save it, El. Whatever it is.'

I take my time making the tea, and when I bring the pot back through to the living room, El has shut off the iPad.

'W. . . was I a w. . . wa. . . ?' He mimes masturbating.

'Yes,' I tell him, 'you were, but he'll get over it.'

El looks genuinely remorseful. 'I d. . . don' wanna be l. . . like that,' he says.

'A wanker?'

El shrugs. 'That too.' He nods at the iPad. 'Don' wanna e. . . end like that.'

El has crumbs and scraps of food in his beard; they've been bothering me for the past five minutes, and I lean across to wipe his face with a napkin.

'Fuck off!' he barks, and the ferocity of it startles me.

'Okay. Sorry.' I sit back and try not to sigh out loud. I know it's his disease and not him, but the thought doesn't settle me – if anything, it makes me angrier.

El clutches at and drops the TV remote. 'Bastid!'

I start clearing the table of pizza, using it as a pretext to get out of my chair and retrieve the dropped remote. Without saying anything or making eye contact, I place the remote on the arm of El's chair. When I get back from the kitchen he's watching what appears to be a cop drama. I sit down quietly.

After several minutes, El turns to me. 'Havn' got a f... fuckig c... clue what's 'appenin in this p... programme.'

'*Blackadder*?' I ask him.

He nods so enthusiastically I have an urge to ruffle his hair, but I'm afraid the bastard might bite me.

El doesn't have the focus or clarity to follow an original plot anymore, but he can still remember most of the scenes and dialogue from the TV shows we watched together fifteen years ago. Phil has bought him box sets of *Red Dwarf*, *Fawlty Towers*, *The Young Ones* and, of course, *Blackadder*.

'Which one?' I ask.

'Anyfink wiv Qu... Qu... Queenie,' he says. 'Hey, h... how's y'woman?'

'I'm moving in.'

''s quick. Dint kn... knock her up, did you?'

'Funny,' I say.

'I kn... know, I'm f... fuckig h... h... 'sterical.'

Phil returns from the pub at a little after ten, by which time El is asleep in his chair and I'm halfway through episode three.

'God, I love Queenie,' he says. Then, nodding at El, 'How's Baldrick?'

I laugh. 'He's fine, sleeping like a baby.'

'Appropriate,' he says. 'Listen, about the melodrama ...'

'Forget it,' I tell him. 'Honestly.'

'How was he?'

'Fine. Told me to fuck off when I tried to clean his beard, but other than that.'

''s... 's rude to talk 'bout someone when they're ... inna room.'

'Ah, it wakes,' says Phil. 'Let me clean your beard, you're like a hairy bloody toddler.'

El holds his chin forward for wiping. 'Toddler?' he laughs. 'J... jus' wait till I start sh... shittin' myself. W... won' be long now.'

'There,' says Phil, brightly, 'all clean.' His teeth are wine-stained and he's beginning to slur his words. He flops onto the sofa and places his hands firmly on his knees, as if composing himself.

An uncomfortable silence fills the room, all the more awkward because it has blossomed from nowhere.

'S... s... spit it out,' says El.

'Now that's the cat calling the monkey hairy-arsed,' says Phil.

'Spit what out?' I ask.

Phil takes a deep breath and rises from the sofa. He crosses to an antique bureau and returns with a stapled A4 document. 'This is an ADRT.'

'Thassa one,' says El, beaming.

Phil goes on: 'It's an advance decision to refuse treatment. It means that if—'

'W... when!'

'... El's condition deteriorates, he will not receive treatment to keep him alive.'

'Good, innit!' says El.

'His idea, I take it?'

Phil takes hold of El's hand. 'Ours,' he says.

'I fuckig f... found it,' says El. 'Don't steal my f... c... th... thunder.'

'And we need you to witness it, please.'

Phil places the document on the coffee table and hands me a biro. I touch neither.

'So what happens if he ... if he hurts himself, if he breaks his leg? What if he chokes on his pizza? You just going to stand and watch?'

I'm not sure Phil buys into my indignation, and I don't know that I do either. I understand what this is about, I get the need, but to sign it without at least some protest would feel like a betrayal.

'Of course not,' says Phil, gently.

'Y. . . y. . . you fuckig will.'

'El, shush a moment. It means El won't ever be hooked up to a machine to keep him breathing. If he has a heart attack he won't receive CPR.'

'Means I can d. . . d. . .'

'El, please,' says Phil.

'K. . . ki. . . killjoy.'

On the doorstep, Phil cries, as he often does. It's different tonight, though; it feels desperate – like he's crying not only for El, but for himself, too.

'You need some time on your own,' I tell him. 'A break.'

'I'm fine,' he says.

'You're obviously not. I've just spent three hours with the bugger and I'm wrecked.'

'I'm seeing the doctor next week.'

'For . . .?'

Phil shrugs, cries afresh.

'Would you like me to look after him for a day? A whole day?'

Phil sniffs, pulls himself together. 'I'll be fine,' he says.

And I wish I believed him.

Chapter 9

I'm having what the French call *jamais vu*. The opposite of the *déjà* variety.

It's a sense of unfamiliarity around a situation you know you have experienced before. And it's weird.

Ivy is asleep with her head in my lap. The chicken caesar dishes are in the sink. There's a romantic comedy on the TV. The difference, I suppose, is that this is now my home. *Our home.*

I found tenants for my Brixton flat two days after I advertised for them. They moved in the following weekend. And just like that you are no longer a bachelor living in a bachelor flat in Brixton. You are a father-to-be, living in a slightly feminine flat in Wimbledon Village.

I run on a common now, instead of in a park; I buy my groceries in a Waitrose rather than a Sainsbury's; the sweet

63-year-old lady downstairs has been replaced with a surly 14-year-old git. Instead of a James Bond poster in my bedroom, there is a Frida Kahlo print in the bathroom.

Everything has changed, but nothing really has.

Esther and Nino helped with the move. Well, Nino helped with the move; Esther sat on the sofa drinking tea with Ivy. And when we'd finished, Nino cooked pizza and we ate dinner together. Ivy, very obviously, wasn't drinking. Esther made a comment about Wimbledon being a lovely area to raise children, but instead of acknowledging the comment I asked about her own children. Esther told the story of giving birth to her first son in her own bed ('destroyed the mattress') in the flat she still lives in forty years later. She cried and told Ivy to look after me for her, Ivy cried, I came close. And thank God for Nino's silent stoicism. Esther continued to get good and drunk, thanked Nino endlessly for living in a foreign country so she didn't have to. 'Your turn now,' he told her, and then Esther cried again at the thought of leaving London and all its memories behind.

In tonight's movie the love-struck couple embark on a two-minute montage of perfect dates: lobster, Ferris wheel, opera, cinema, jet skis. All the things Ivy and I haven't done. Instead of cartwheeling across a beach at sunset, we've leapfrogged the romance and gone straight to starting a family and passing out in front of the telly.

The Two of Us

It's our twelve-week scan first thing tomorrow morning, and in the evening we are driving to Bristol to visit Ivy's parents. But everything is backasswards now, so instead of announcing the news that Ivy is pregnant, I will be introduced as the 'new' boyfriend. Ivy will be wearing baggy jumpers all weekend, giving her folks the chance to get used to the idea that she has a man before she drops the news that she's having a baby. We're going to claim we've been seeing each other since February, and I've just been too busy to visit. According to our cover story we have been an item for eight months; it sounds a little suspect to me, but Ivy assures me we'll work out all the details in the fullness of time. Which is fine in theory, but in practice we only have another twenty-eight weeks before one very major detail makes his or her grand entrance.

Tonight's movie was never going to make my top-one-hundred list, but it's made all the more difficult to enjoy because Ivy's TV is rubbish. She's a reader and her flat is a testament to the fact. There are floor-to-ceiling bookshelves on either side of the fireplace, and another set in our bedroom – all of them heaving with literature. There are piles of books in the kitchen, the bathroom and the hallway cupboard. (Twenty-three of these books – I counted – hold a bookmark in their approximate centre. Further to Ivy's assertion that quitting a book is a bad habit, these are the novels – *Catch-22, Crime and Punishment, Lord of the Rings*, etc. – that she has absolutely not abandoned halfway through: 'If I mark the place I left off, I haven't quit, I just haven't finished yet.') Point being, Ivy would rather read a book than watch TV, and she takes it as a point of pride that her set is practically a museum piece. My TV, on the other hand, is a 42-inch thing of beauty. And it's balanced on top of a chest of drawers in the spare bedroom – no space for it in the living room, apparently. Also in the spare bedroom are my Xbox, leather armchair, Le Creuset pans, bedding, and a shoebox full of photos. How we're going to fit a baby in there is anyone's guess.

I experience a hot flush that might be trepidation; although it's more likely a result of my overheated feet. Ivy gave me a moving-in present of Womble slippers: 'Now that you live in Wimbledon.' I've never been a slipper wearer, and I don't remember watching *The Wombles* on TV – although I suppose I must have done; I've had the damn theme tune rattling round my head all evening. Nevertheless, I am now the proud (and very warm) owner of a pair of size 10 blue-tartan Uncle Bulgarias.

On Ivy's crappy TV the rom-com couple are making love on a beach, going through all the favourite positions, biting their lips, entwining their fingers, gazing into each other's eyes. They come together and fall back onto the golden sand, thoroughly satisfied and with their hair still perfect.

I slide my hand down Ivy's body and onto her growing bump. She shifts position in my lap and begins to snore.

Everything the same; everything different.

Jamais vu.

Chapter 10

The sonographer introduces herself as Valerie.

'This might come as a bit of a shock,' she says, holding up a tube of gel. 'It's cold.'

We're in St George's Hospital in Tooting, where Ivy plans to have our baby. She's lying on her back, the top buttons of her jeans unfastened so that the white scalloping of her pants is visible. Her shirt is rolled up to her breastbone, revealing the smooth, curving dome of her formerly flat belly. The sonographer applies the clear gel to Ivy's stomach and Ivy's grip tightens around my hand. She is wearing a pair of antique-looking cufflinks in the shape of four-leaf clovers. Whether they were a conscious choice or not, I don't know.

The room is bright and friendly; colourful prints on the walls offset the cold clinical greys and whites of the bulky technical equipment. Ivy's palm is hot and clammy in my hand. This morning she puked longer and harder than she has for weeks. I asked if she was excited about seeing her baby for the first time, and Ivy said she was frightened. I sat in the hallway outside the bathroom, and as she brushed her teeth, I asked did she know that the baby was the size of a lime now? Yes, she said. Did she know the baby has fingers, kidneys, muscles, bones? Ivy closed the bathroom door. When she came out she climbed back into bed and opened a book – code, I assume, for leave me alone.

Valerie slides the white probe around Ivy's stomach. 'Here we are,' she says. 'There's the head,' and on a wall-mounted monitor, a round but otherwise indistinct shape comes into view.

Ivy starts to cry. 'My baby?' she says. Asking, rather than declaring, as if she is still reluctant to count this chicken.

'Your baby,' says the sonographer, smiling like she has the best job in the world. She moves the probe to the side of Ivy's belly. And then she frowns – not an expression you want to see in a room like this. Ivy doesn't notice because her eyes have not left the monitor. Valerie turns from the screen and looks at me with an expression that is impossible to read. 'Er . . .' she says.

'What is it?' I ask.

Valerie might be smiling but it's hard to be sure because she's biting her bottom lip. 'Well . . .'

Ivy's head snaps around to the sonographer. 'What? Is something wr—'

'Everything is perfect,' Valerie says, finally. 'More than,' she adds. 'See this area here . . .?' and an onscreen cursor traces a circular area just beneath my baby's head.

Ivy nods, I nod.

'That,' says the sonographer, 'is the other head.'

'The other . . .?' I manage, after what feels like forever.

'Baby,' says Valerie. 'The other baby.'

I raise my coffee to my mouth, realize my mouth is already hanging open, decide I don't want coffee and return the mug to the table. I feel like my hand should be trembling, but I think I'm too numb, too disengaged from my physical self to do anything as organized as tremble.

Ivy is staring at a small black-and-white photograph, a print-out of our scan, of our *children*.

'Twins,' I say.

Ivy nods.

My coffee is untouched. I pick it up, get it all the way to my mouth this time and take a sip. It's cold – not just lukewarm, but as cold as tap water – and leaves a clag of congealed milk skin on my teeth. I might be hungry, but it's hard to tell. I genuinely can't recall whether or not I ate breakfast this morning. I glance at my watch and see that it's still two hours until anything like lunchtime. This doesn't resolve whether or not I'm hungry, but I do need to get on a train in the next five minutes. The agency has asked me to shoot their toilet roll commercial, and in an hour's time I have to begin casting for a man in a giant rabbit costume.

My sister, Maria, had twins. She is fond of telling anyone who will listen that it was the hardest bloody thing she has ever done. This from a woman who had her first child when she was sixteen and raised the baby without any help from the shit-bag absent father. Since then Maria passed her A levels whilst raising one baby, and gained a degree while raising three. She's run three marathons, all of them in under four hours. She broke her leg skiing and had to crawl out from a copse of trees through four-foot-deep snow dragging a snapped tibia behind her. *Twins?* She'll tell you, *Hardest bloody thing I have ever done.*

'Twins,' Ivy says, not looking up from the grainy evidence in her hands. In the picture, the babies – *plural!* – are facing in the same direction, as if one is sitting on the other's lap. It looks crowded in there.

I sip my coffee again, having already forgotten that it's

cold and tasteless. I take another sip anyway for something to do – something approaching normal.

'Twins,' I say.

'Twins,' says Ivy.

The casting takes place in an upstairs room above a shoe shop on Carnaby Street. Present are: Joe; Suzi, the agency art director; Henry (female), the agency producer; and myself – although to say I'm present is a stretch.

'Fisher?' says Joe.

'Sorry?'

'Would you like to take us through the script?'

The room is white and featureless, maybe eighteen feet wide and long. Also present, standing on an 'X' marked on the floor with black electrical tape, is a middle-aged male actor.

'The script?' I ask.

'That's why we're here,' Joe says, forcing a laugh.

'I can do it, if you like,' says the art director, a pretty girl who looks like she's only a few years out of art college.

'Might be for the best,' says Joe, again with the practised laugh. 'I have to be somewhere in November.'

'So you know loo roll ads, right?' begins Suzi. 'How

they all have cute cats or puppies or bears? Well, we're taking the piss out of that.'

'Gotcha,' says the actor. He's potbellied, unshaven, sounds like he smokes filterless cigarettes and has done since childhood.

'You're going to be a bunny,' says Suzi. 'Mr Hoppity.'

'What, like a rabbit?'

'It's as if we're shooting one of those cliché loo roll adverts,' says Suzi. 'Then the director – in the commercial, another actor – he yells "cut", and you take the head off your costume, revealing yourself to be an actor – not a real bunny.' Suzi laughs at the ridiculousness of what she's saying. 'Sorry, it sounds all a bit . . . God, I dunno . . .'

'Meta?' suggests Joe.

'Post-ironic?' Henry tries.

'Wanky!' says Suzi, and she laughs.

'Wanky,' says the actor. 'Gotcha.'

It's nice to meet advertising people that don't take themselves too seriously. People who have no illusions about what it is they're doing – in this case, selling bog roll. That said, Suzi can't be older than twenty-four; in a couple of years she'll undoubtedly be as arrogant, deluded and precocious as the job requires.

'Point is,' says Henry, 'you're not playing a bunny; you're playing an actor playing a bunny.'

'Gotcha,' says the actor.

'And you hate it,' she says. 'Underneath the suit you're a tough guy.'

'Like a gangster?' he asks hopefully.

'In a bunny suit,' says Joe. 'Exactly.'

'Right-o.'

'Like the loo roll, you see,' says Suzi. 'Soft, but tough.'

'Okey-doke. Tough bunny.'

I'll need two of everything from now on: two cots, two car seats, two great big fluffy bunnies.

'William?' asks Joe, his voice one notch up from normal conversational volume.

Joe only calls me William when he's patronizing, antagonizing or chastising me, so it's a good bet that I've just missed something.

'Excuse me?' I say.

'Anything to add?' says Joe.

'No.' I shake my head. 'No, thank you.'

And so we put the actor through his paces. We give him lines to deliver, ask him to do them in a variety of accents – London, New York, Eastern Bloc. We make him hop like a bunny. And then we do it again with another actor and another and another and I don't know how many more. Throughout the session, people talk to me, ask my opinion, ask if I want things. For the most part, I have no idea what they are saying, so I limit my responses to a series of ambiguous grunts, monosyllables and variations on the classic deferment *I'm not sure, what do you think?* Although I abandoned the latter approach after it became apparent someone had just asked whether I wanted tea or coffee.

'Great day, everybody,' says Joe, and it seems we're finished. 'Got some good bunnies, I think.'

'Spoilt for choice,' says Henry.

'Deffo,' says Suzi.

'William?' asks Joe.

'Couldn't agree more,' I say. 'Let's er . . . you know, sleep on it? Make some decisions next week?'

'Very sensible,' says Henry. 'Best not to rush these things.'

'Cool,' I say.

'But we'll need a decision by nine a.m. Monday morning, 'kay?'

'Monday,' I repeat, because my brain is too preoccupied (*twins twins twins!*) to form a more sophisticated response.

Joe waits until we are on the street and clear of the agency people before he grabs me by the bicep and demands: 'What the fuck is going on with you?'

'Me?'

'Who the fuck else was ac— Suzi,' he says, over my shoulder, switching effortlessly from incandescence to slick affability.

'Excuse me,' Suzi says, 'I wondered . . . I was wondering if you . . .'

Joe is still gripping my upper arm, his fingers digging painfully into my flesh. Suzi holds something towards me. It looks like a pink Lego brick. The only remotely feasible explanation I can come up with is that Suzi is psychic, has sensed I am about to become a father, and is presenting me with a gift for my child. I almost tell her that I'll need two, because I'm having twins. Instead, I just look at her as if she's mental.

'It's a script,' Suzi says. 'I mean it's a memory stick, but there's a, you know, script . . .'

I take the Lego brick and slide it open, confirming that, yes, it is indeed a memory stick.

'Only if you have the time, of course,' she says.

'Time?'

'To read it.'

'Me?'

'I know you know your films,' she says, blushing, 'and I'd really appreciate your . . . you know, opinion.'

I *like* films, but I wouldn't claim to *know* films. What I know is how to drop a movie reference into a commercial treatment so that advertising folk can forget they're working on, oh I dunno, say a toilet roll commercial. But I don't *know* films.

'I'd be honoured,' I say.

Suzi smiles. 'Thank you.' She holds out her hand for me to shake it, then thinks better of it and goes up on tiptoes to kiss my cheek. 'Thank you,' she says again, then walks quickly away.

Joe, still holding my arm, pulls me around so I am facing him. 'We will get to that' – he nods in Suzi's direction – 'in a moment, but first things last: what the fuck is wrong with you? If I didn't know you were too much of a square, I'd swear you were on something.'

'Will you let go of my arm? It's nearly off, you frigging goon.'

Joe releases me one finger at a time.

'And I'm not square, you gob-shite. If anyone's square it's you, you sodding . . . square.'

'What's going on?'

'Can we get a drink?'

'Fuck me inside out,' says Joe. 'You're sure? There's no chance it's a terrible mistake?'

'Well, it wasn't exactly planned.'

'Twins,' he says, rubbing his stubble as if I've just told him I have cancer. 'Fisher, mate, I'm sorry. Are you okay?'

'I think so,' I tell him. 'I think I'm pretty happy, actually. I mean, I am. Happy.'

Joe lays a hand on my shoulder and squeezes, he nods, smiles at my bravery.

'Accident then.'

'Kind of . . . not exactly.'

I think back again to the first time I made love with Ivy, me asking (obliquely but unequivocally) if we needed protection. *Ivy shaking her head, smiling, 'It's okay.'* So what exactly did that 'It's okay' mean? Because I've just seen high-definition evidence that tells a subtly different version of events. Not that I'm saying it's *not* okay, I'm pretty sure it's magnificent, but I can't shake the feeling I've missed a key detail somewhere. Events have happened so fast and out of sequence that sometimes – drifting off to sleep, for example; zoning out in front of a movie; rattling along on the Underground – I find it hard to assemble, order or . . . *how did this happen?* . . . even believe the facts. Once or twice I've come close to asking Ivy what she meant that night, but the timing (nausea, fatigue, quiet intimacy) is always off, and the unasked question feels raw and accusatory.

Joe nods as if he understands. Maybe he does. Maybe he can explain it to me.

'You know what they are?'

I shake my head.

'You wanna pray they're not boys. Take it from me;

they're a fahooking nightmare. You ever been kicked in the sisters by a three year old?'

'Not since I was three, no.'

'Well I have,' he says. 'I'm sitting on the floor doing a four-piece jigsaw, and Sammy just walks up like he's going to hug me, then – Bam! – little bastard hoofs me full tilt in the nadgers. I'm telling you, if I ain't firing blanks by now it'll be a genuine miracle.' He downs the last of his pint. ''nother?'

'In for one, in for two,' I tell him.

As it turns out, I was in for five, and I now have an early hangover. Not how I'd planned on meeting Ivy's parents.

'How's your head?' Ivy asks.

'Fine,' I say.

I don't know why I'm lying; it just feels like the appropriate response. Like I'm honouring tradition. I need sleep but we're in Ivy's Renault Kangoo, driving west on the M4 at eighty-three miles an hour. I tried resting my head against the window, but even with my folded-up jacket as a pillow the vibrations were shaking me sick.

'Now you know how I feel every morning,' she says, a little too smug for my liking.

'Don't blame me, blame . . . your ovaries.'

'You told Joe then?'

The plan was to wait until I had been innocuously introduced to Ivy's family, then – maybe two weeks later – break the news to her parents and mine and then everybody else.

So much for plans.

'Sorry, couldn't really help myself.'

'And? What did he say?'

'He was very happy for us. Said parenthood is a blessing.'

Ivy laughs. 'Right. I'm sure.'

We drive in silence for a while; it's dark and the motorway lights are hypnotically soothing.

'You okay?' Ivy asks. 'You're quiet.'

That's because I was thinking about the first time we made love. Wondering what you meant by 'It's okay'. Do you remember that? Don't get me wrong, I'm deliriously happy and everything, but . . . well, what with you being full of twins now, what exactly did *you mean by,* 'It's okay'? But as ever, the question (redundant anyway in the face of the glaring biological facts) is prickly and the timing stinks. Ivy is radiating happiness after this morning's scan, we're both reeling from the news that our babies are plural, and we're meeting Ivy's parents in a couple of hours where we have to pretend we've been dating for eight months and we're not pregnant.

'Yes,' I say. 'Okay, I mean. It's just . . . it's all just a bit . . . unexpected.'

'You're telling me,' says Ivy. And then, 'Did you ever think about how many you wanted?'

'Kids?'

'No, pints,' she says. 'Of course kids.'

'Less than I just had pints,' I tell her. 'You?'

Ivy doesn't hesitate. 'Three. That's what I always wanted, ever since I was a little girl. But . . . well, I'm not a little girl anymore, am I? I'm forty-one next birthday.'

'You're as young as the man you feel.'

'I suppose I'd let the idea go,' she says. 'But now that we're having two, three wouldn't necessarily be beyond the realm of possibility.'

Out of the corner of my eye I can see Ivy looking at me, waiting for a reaction.

'We didn't find out what they are, did we? The babies?'

'No,' says Ivy. 'Too early.'

'Right, of course, my head's a bit . . .'

'You didn't answer,' Ivy says.

'Answer what?'

'Whether three kids would be beyond the realm of possibility?'

'I didn't realize it was a question.'

'It's a question.'

'We'd need a bigger flat,' I tell her.

'Fine,' she says, and whether she's backing off or closing the deal, I don't know.

After two hours of driving and sitting in traffic, we stop at a Welcome Break services to pee, refuel and buy Skittles. I also buy flowers for Ivy's mother and a bottle of red wine for her father. The final leg of the journey takes a little over an hour, but by the time Ivy rolls the car into her parents' driveway, the flowers have wilted and my hangover has progressed from an idea to the real deal.

In a scene reminiscent of our arrival at my dad's house two months ago, Ivy's parents are out of their front door before either of us has released our seatbelt. Ivy's father is a bear of a man, standing half a head taller than my six-three; a head that's as large, uneven and pockmarked as a month-old Halloween pumpkin. It's the sort of head that would give children – and some adults – bad dreams. They say women grow up to look like their mothers, and I'd worry about that if the discrepancy between Ivy and her mum wasn't so profound as to be practically unfeasible. Mrs Lee is a small, plump woman with bulbous eyes and mad, haystack hair that begins far back on her large, domed forehead. And you have to hand it to Mother Nature for making something as beautiful as Ivy from such interesting genetic ingredients. What the Lees lack in photogenicity, however, they make up for in enthusiasm. Despite being at least twenty years older than my own father, they are both alarmingly energetic.

'Baby girl,' says Mrs Lee, kissing her daughter. She turns to me, looks me up and down and nods as if appraising a pair of curtains. 'And you must be William. Now come on,' she says, patting my bottom, 'give us a twirl so we can get a proper look at you.'

'Eva! Leave the lad alone,' says Ivy's dad as I turn unsteadily on the spot, a bottle of wine in one hand, a bunch of wilted flowers in the other. 'You're like a shrew, woman.' He takes his daughter's head in his giant hands and kisses her on the forehead, the tip of the nose and then the lips. 'Hello, Flower,' he says, and Ivy hugs him around the neck, lifting her feet from the ground and dangling from his shoulders like a child.

And if I have a daughter, I'm calling her Flower, too.

'These for me?' says Mrs Lee, taking the drooping roses before I have a chance to answer. 'Oo, you must have been naughty. Ha ha, only joking. Come on, let's get 'em in some water, they look worse'n you, lad. You all right, William? You look a little queasy.'

I haven't said a word so far, and I'm afraid to try in case

I let slip that I am the father of their lime-sized twin grandchildren.

'Inside, woman,' says Ivy's father. 'You'll scare him off. I'm Ken, by the way,' and he slaps me on the back so hard I nearly drop the wine on his driveway.

'Wine,' I finally manage, holding the bottle out to him.

'Looks like a good 'un,' he says. 'Let's get her open.'

We cross the threshold of the Lee residence, and I'm beginning to entertain the idea of relaxing, when another inflated male specimen charges towards us across the expansive hallway. I brace myself for a crippling impact but the guy – he must weigh close to eighteen stone – swerves past me, and lifts Ivy off her feet. 'Sis,' he says, swinging her around in a full three-sixty that makes me wince for the safety of our secret unborn babies. 'Crikey,' he says, 'you put on weight?'

'If you don't want a family pack of Skittle puke in your ear,' says Ivy, 'you'd better put me down right now.'

Ivy's brother laughs and hoists her even higher.

'Frank!' Ivy says, thumping him hard on the shoulder. 'I'm not kidding, put me down, you gibbon.'

'All right,' he says, lowering her to the ground. 'Chillamena Willamena.'

'Honestly. And you wonder why I never brought him home before.'

Did they? Did they wonder?

'Thought it was 'cos he was ugly or something,' says Frank.

You'd think Ivy's parents would be above (or beyond, but definitely not behind) lookist humour, but the pair of them laugh, snort and slap their thighs as Ivy all but melts with embarrassment.

'Only kidding,' says Frank, slapping me on the exact same spot his father did. 'Pleased to meet you.' He extends his hand and then shakes mine with surprising tenderness. 'Frank,' he says. 'Little brother.'

'Little?' I say, 'God, I'd hate to meet the big ones.'

'*Big ones!*' Frank repeats, laughing as if I were the king of wit. 'Well, you can relax for today. Big bruv number one's in Australia, and number two's in Edinburgh, which amounts to the same thing for all we see of him. Come on, let's get that bottle open,' and he snatches the wine from his father and disappears into another room.

Whilst it's true that, before Ivy, I had never taken a girl-friend home to meet my family, this isn't the first time I've been the romantic novelty. Before I was with Ivy, I lived with Kate – the only other girlfriend I've held onto for more than a week – and after about three months together she insisted (ultimatums were made) I meet her parents.

They were fine, but Kate turned into a posturing caricature of 'successful daughter in grown-up relationship'. It was excruciating – she perched on the edge of any chair I sat on, running her fingers through my hair, kissing me at every opportunity and displaying more affection than she ever did in our own flat. She catalogued every restaurant and wine bar we'd been to, replayed snippets of witty conversation and even seemed to articulate her words more precisely. More than showing me off, it was as if she were making a point about herself. The whole three-day performance was reminiscent of the way my young nieces would breathlessly recount a victory in the egg-and-spoon race or stand to attention in the living room singing the words to a song from the school play. Ivy does none of that. She is the same here as she is when we're alone, and watching her talk, joke and relax with her family in the same way she does with me, makes me feel like I belong here and reinforces how much Ivy and I belong together. It's all I can do not to perch on the arm of her chair and run my fingers through her hair.

Even so, it takes around thirty minutes and a full glass of wine before my nerves begin to settle. Sitting in the Lees' living room, I allow the conversation to wash over me, interjecting only when I am expressly called upon to do so. And as the family catch up on domestic gossip, I sip my drink and take in my surroundings. The house is full of photographs of Ivy, her brothers, Ken and Eva. There are pictures hanging from the walls, standing on shelves and lining the stairway up to the bathroom on the first floor. I'm mesmerized by one in particular, standing in a small frame on the mantelpiece. According to Ivy's mum, her daughter was six when the picture was taken; she is freckled and her teeth look gappy and wonky inside her smile. I feel a surge of love – and there's no question, that's what it is – for this child who is now, thirty-five-years later, carrying my own children inside her. It's a separate affection from the one I hold for the Ivy sitting opposite me, pretending to drink her wine; it's for the child in this photograph as she was the day she sat in front of the camera. There are no scars on the Ivy in this picture; and once I've realized this, I realize there are – as far as I can see – no pictures of Ivy in the years immediately after the accident. There are pictures of baby Ivy, toddler Ivy, 6- and 7-year-old Ivy . . . then nothing until the Ivy in the photographs is maybe twelve years old and then beyond. In these later pictures, Ivy is visibly uncomfortable in front of the camera, generally angling the scarred side of her face away from the lens. This was the room where it happened; where Ivy tap-danced her way through a glass coffee table and tore her face open. And looking at the child in the photograph, I wish I could warn her. But then where would that leave me and my twin babies? I have no time for the platitude that 'everything happens for a reason', but the fact remains – if Ivy hadn't crashed through that table, she would have been a different woman from the one she is today. And maybe that woman would already be married by now, a mother to someone else's children.

'William?' says Eva.

'I'm sorry,' I say, turning to Ivy's mother, 'I . . . I was . . .'

'Boring you, were we?' says Frank, laughing.

'Sorry,' I repeat, 'long day.'

'I was asking where you live, love?' says Ivy's mother.

I wasn't prepared for this. And the thought of lying to this simple question throws a great big spanner into my speech centre.

'In . . . a flat?' I try.

'Blimey,' says Ivy's dad. 'Must've been a very bloody long day.'

'Kenneth!' chides Eva.

'We moved in together,' blurts Ivy, which is a departure from the agreed script.

Everyone goes quiet.

I avoid all eyes and stare into space with an inane smile glued onto my face.

'That was quick,' says Ken.

I take a large gulp of my wine.

The carriage clock on the mantelpiece ticks.

'Well,' says Ivy, 'we thought we might as well, seeing as . . .'

I snap my head around, staring directly at Ivy: *No!*

'. . . seeing as how I'm pregnant!' and she says these last five words in about nought-point-five seconds, on an ascending scale with each syllable twice as loud as the last, so that by the time she hits 'pregnant', she's shrieking.

And now, so is her mother. 'Pregnant! With a baby?'

'Twins!' Ivy says.

'Twins?' shout Ken and Frank and Eva.

'Twins,' I say. And I pull the kind of face you might make if you were admitting some minor *faux pas* like walking mud into the hallway or breaking a garden gnome.

'Blimey,' says Ken, getting up and leaving the room.

Eva is crying, kissing Ivy and rubbing her belly.

'Fast worker,' says Frank, winking at me with what I hope is a form of fraternal affection.

I give him an imbecilic thumbs up.

When Ken returns he's carrying five champagne glasses in one huge hand and a bottle of cava in the other.

'You can have a teensy splash, can't you, Flower?' he says to Ivy.

'Of course she can't,' Eva says, putting her arm around Ivy as if to protect her. 'Silly.'

Ivy scrunches up her face. 'I'll pass.'

Ken rolls his eyes and pours for the rest of us. 'To the twins,' he says.

'Needn't have bothered making up the spare bed, hey?' says Eva.

'No use shutting the stable door after the horse has shot his bolt,' says Ken, and whether it's a slip of the tongue or the world's worst joke, the effect is the same on my complexion.

'So, William,' says Frank, 'how long have you two been together?'

'Oh, gosh, it must be . . . let me . . .'

'Long enough, nosy-bonk,' says Ivy.

'Clearly,' says Frank.

'What do your mum and dad make of it all?' asks Eva.

'It's only my dad, I'm afraid, but—'

'Oh, darling, I am sorry, I—' Eva puts a hand to her mouth.

'It was a long time ago,' I say. 'It's okay, honestly.'

'Oh, William,' she says. Then, after a pause where it looks like she's trying to eat her own bottom lip: 'So, what about your dad? What does he make of . . .' she mimes a big pregnant belly.

'He doesn't know yet,' I tell her. 'You're pretty much the first.'

'Right,' says Ken, levering himself off the sofa. 'We'll put that straight right away.' He picks up a cordless phone from its cradle. 'What's your dad's number?'

'Excuse me?'

Frank grins, enjoying my discomfort.

'Oh, Kenneth, put that thing down,' says Eva half-heartedly.

I look to Ivy for help. She smiles, shrugs.

'Number,' demands Ken.

And that's how Dad hears the news that he has two new grandchildren on the way – over speakerphone with three perfect strangers shouting excitedly in the background. And to give the old man credit, he takes it like a champ. Unlike the Lees, Dad knows exactly how long Ivy and I have been together, but he doesn't comment, doesn't blow my cover. Once the euphoria and crossfire has died down, once two-dozen kisses have been blown down the telephone line, Ken and Eva start the business of getting acquainted with Dad, asking what I was like as a boy, do I have sisters or brothers, how many grandchildren does he have, where does he work, and all the other stuff that's so important to parents of grown-up children. Once we realize we've become surplus to requirements, Frank, Ivy and I move through to the kitchen.

Frank opens another bottle of wine, despite me assuring him I don't want anything else to drink.

'Not going to let me drink alone, are you?' he says. 'We're family now.' And he pours two glasses.

'So,' Ivy says to Frank. 'What's going on?'

Frank sighs heavily, and it's as if someone has opened a valve in the side of him. His shoulders sag, his head drops, he appears to shrink in his seat.

Frank, it turns out, is married, but not happily. The reasons why aren't gone into; Ivy knows the story and it's been going on for a long time. Frank and his wife, Lois, have talked, fought, sought counselling and currently sleep under the same roof but in separate rooms. It seems that they both know the marriage is irreconcilable, but – mainly because of their 3-year-old son – they haven't yet constructively discussed the next phase. Ken and Eva know nothing about this. Frank, a dentist, has told his parents he's in Bristol to attend a conference on a new type of ceramic implant. And so, while Frank and Lois grope about for the courage to do what needs to be done, they spend alternate weekends visiting family or friends, telling lies, and leaving their unhappy spouse in the marital home to think of new ways of becoming their child's favourite parent.

It's been a hell of a day – I'm drunk, hungover, tired, wired, happy, freaked and wrung out all at the same time.

'Never get married,' says Frank, heavy-eyed now with drink.

I look at Ivy; Ivy looks away. 'How's Freddy?' she asks.

Frank nods: *fine*. 'You two are lucky,' he says.

'Thanks,' I say. 'I know.'

'Twins,' he says, prodding his sister's tummy. 'At least if it goes tits up you get to keep one each. Ha ha!'

Chapter 11

Peach.
Lemon.
Apple.
Avocado.
Onion.
Sweet potato . . .

Chapter 12

'How's your better half?' asks Joe.

At eighteen weeks, the babies are about the size of a pair of small sweet potatoes. Big enough that Ivy is now visibly pregnant. Two weeks ago she was offered a seat on the tube; telling me about it that evening, she feigned all manner of offence, but her smile told me she had taken great pleasure in this small rite of passage.

The babies have distinct fingers and toes, their muscles are strengthening. They have taste buds and eyelashes. Fingernails. Three weeks ago, Ivy and I went to a bonfire on Wimbledon Common; the twins have functioning ears now and they would have heard the fireworks exploding overhead. A normal – single baby – pregnancy tends to last thirty-nine weeks; twins come around two weeks earlier, meaning we are now very nearly halfway to our April 11th due date.

'All good,' I say to Joe. 'They're the size of a pair of sweet potatoes.'

'What?' says Joe, miming a pair of breasts. 'Her ... thingummies?'

'The twins, you pillock. The twins are the size of a couple of ... *Christ.*'

'And how about her ... you know?' and again with the cupped hands in front of his chest.

'Bigger than a pair of sweet potatoes,' I tell him.

Actually, they're huge – well past the honeydew-melon stage. It was Ivy's birthday one month ago, and I bought her underwear – a 36DD maternity bra that's sexier than I would previously have thought possible. But every time I try to get anywhere near her new and improved boobs, Ivy fends me off, complaining they're too sore to touch. We haven't had sex since the day before we visited my dad more than three months ago – it's torture.

But now isn't the time and here isn't the place. We're in a darkened edit suite in Soho, working on the final cut of our loo roll commercial. Henry and Suzi from the agency are sitting behind me somewhere in the gloom. Onscreen Mr Hoppity is dancing around a maypole with six children, each trailing a different coloured roll of Softex toilet tissue.

'What do you think, Suzi?' I ask.

'What? About your girlfriend's jubblies?'

'No,' I say, pointing at the monitor, 'the edit.'

'Joke,' says Suzi.

'Durr,' says Joe.

'I think it's awesome,' Suzi says. 'Nothing else to add.'

'Henry?' I ask.

Henry looks up from her iPhone. 'I was happy with it yesterday,' she says a little tetchily. These places cost upwards of seven hundred quid a day, so of course she was happy with it yesterday.

'In that case,' says Joe, clapping his hands together, 'I declare this edit closed. Now, who's going to buy me a pint? Fisher?'

'Got to be somewhere, mate. Sorry.'

'Where? Who with?'

'Just somewhere.'

'You're meant to be my best man.'

'This is an edit, Joseph, not your wedding.'

'Fine,' he says. 'Ladies?'

'Sorry,' says Suzi. 'Got to be somewhere, too.'

Henry shrugs. 'Twenty-two shopping days till Christmas,' she says, stepping out of the room. 'I like anything Chanel, by the way.'

'Later,' Suzi says, following Henry out of the room.

She gives me a knowing smile, and then she, too, is gone.

'Why do I bother?' Joe asks. 'Advertising? Might as well work in a bloody bank.'

'I'll see you on Friday,' I say. 'We'll have a pint then.'

'Here,' he says, handing me a brown envelope. 'Was going to give it you later, but seeing as how you have more important things to do.'

'What is it?' I say.

'Your next mission.'

'Script?'

Joe nods, and I take the envelope and transfer it directly into my bag.

'Not going to read it, pull a face, kick up a stink?'

'What's it for?'

'Cheese,' says Joe.

'Love it,' I say. 'When are we meeting the agency?'

'A-S-A fucking P, buddy. Got to be in the can by Christmas.'

Which means another five-to-ten grand in my bank account shortly thereafter. And that's got to be good for a few packets of nappies.

'Set it up then.'

Joe looks at me incredulously. 'Serious?'

'I never joke about cheese,' I tell him.

'I'll tell you what, William Fisher,' he says, ruffling my hair. 'Being up the duff suits you. Suits you very well indeed.'

The meeting isn't exactly clandestine, but we are nevertheless in a bar that charges more for a small glass of wine than Joe would ever dream of paying for a bottle – so it's unlikely he'll wander in and discover us. Also, it's the first Monday of the month, which means Ivy will be at her book club until around nine, so I can get half drunk with impunity.

'So?' says Suzi. 'You read it?' She fidgets nervously with her ring, a chunky silver band holding an oval turquoise stone, rotating it half a turn clockwise then back the other way.

'I have,' I say, and I catch myself mirroring Suzi's nervous fingerplay, swivelling my wine glass through half-turns on the table top.

'And . . .?'

Suzi's screenplay is a collection of nine interconnected stories. Three of them involve sex, and one of those involves a female protagonist with a penchant for autoerotic asphyxiation. It's not my thing, but each to her own, whatever floats your boat, blows your skirt up, or, as the case may be, turns your face blue. Far from being gratuitous, the sex in general and fetish in particular do serve a purpose within the grand scheme of the plot. The problem I have with these scenes is how damned good they are – how inventive, how erotic, how ... well, sexy. And as I read these scenes, I couldn't help picturing Suzi slap bang in the middle of them. After all, 'write what you know', don't they always say? Take the character with a thing for asphyxiation: when she clenches her slender hands around the throat of whomever it is she is simultaneously choking and fucking, the camera lingers on a ring she wears on the little finger of her right hand. We see it when she's throttling her lover, and we see it again when she is working, holding a stethoscope to one of her patients. It's a device to connect and contrast the different facets of this complex, unreliable, paradoxical character. Which is all fine and filmic. But the ring itself – a fat gold band holding an oval onyx stone – it sounds a lot like the one Suzi can't stop fidgeting with in the right here and now. And it's making it extraordinarily difficult for me to not imagine her naked and gyrating on top of some lucky guy's lap.

'I like it,' I say. 'I like it a lot.'

And even though I don't intend any subtext, I blush.

'The plot,' I qualify. 'Good stories, good characters.'

'Only good?' Suzi says, teasing, but she's nowhere near as convincing as Ivy.

'Good's good,' I tell her, and I wink involuntarily, reflexively.

'Thank you,' Suzi says, revolving the turquoise ring around her finger.

'But ...' I say, and Suzi's brow creases in a minuscule wince. She placed a good deal of trust in me when she asked for my opinion, and to lavish disingenuous praise on her script now would be unfair. Cowardly, even. So I press on, '... it's uneven,' I tell her.

Suzi's wince deepens, but I get the impression I'm not telling her anything she doesn't know.

After a little more wine and waffling, I manage to articulate my criticism in more constructive terms. I mean it when I tell Suzi that a couple of her stories are outstanding. I mean it literally, and explain that these standouts make the remaining plotlines feel flat or inconsequential by comparison.

'What's your favourite?' Suzi asks.

'Probably the one with the art student.'

Suzi nods in agreement, smiles. 'Why?'

'Well, good story,' I tick this point off on one finger.

'Always helps,' Suzi says, and laughs. She holds eye contact while she sips her wine.

I move on to my second finger. 'Interesting characters – I mean, the girl's a bit of a bitch, but she's a good character.'

Suzi nods as if waiting for me to get to the point.

Finger number three: 'Rooftop scene – very cinematic, dramatic.'

'*Two* rooftop scenes,' Suzi corrects, with just a hint of coy.

'Yes,' I say, moving on to finger number four, 'which brings me to . . .'

Suzi raises her eyebrows. 'Sex.'

You read my mind, is what I very nearly say, but I catch myself before I let this unintended insinuation slip past my teeth. If I were single and not expecting twins, I may well have let it fly. But I'm not, and I am – and very happily. Even so, I can't help wondering if Suzi, like her protagonist, has ever made love on the rooftop of a Student Union building.

'Yes,' I laugh. 'We don't get to shoot too many sex scenes in advertising.'

'No,' says Suzi. 'We don't, do we?'

'Poor us,' I say, pulling a stupid face and taking a glug of wine.

Suzi seems to hesitate before saying, 'So . . . want to do it?'

'Excuse me?'

Suzi laughs. 'Shoot it. Shoot the art student.'

The question catches me flat-footed. 'I'd love to, honestly, but you might need a bit of a reality check on what a thing like this costs. You're going to need crew, equipment, actors.'

Suzi smiles indulgently. 'You sound like Joe.'

'Is that an insult?'

'I've got some money,' she says.

'Maybe so, but this isn't some two-header around a kitchen table.' She's right; I do sound like Joe. 'You've got, what? Two leads, a bunch of extras, three or four locations, a rooftop, a night shoot. Even with favours and freebies it's going to run to ... God, I don't know. A lot. You'll need a producer, too – a bloody good one.'

'I've got ten grand.'

'Suzi, that's a lot of money. But even so ... I dunno.'

'My dad died this year,' she says, and all her bravado and flirtation and whimsy are gone.

'I'm sorry. I ... I know what that's like. My mum died when I was fourteen.'

Suzi puts her hand on mine, smiles sadly. Then just like that she lets my hand go, takes a sip of her wine and seems to snap back into herself. 'Thing is,' she says, 'I inherited enough to put a deposit on a flat. That's what Mum wants me to do with it. But a flat's a flat; one day I'll sell it and move out and it'll be gone. If I make this film, whether it's shit, fabulous or somewhere in the middle ...' Suzi takes a sip of her wine. 'People always say *Oh it's what he would have wanted,* don't they?'

'Is it? What he would have wanted?'

'Honestly, I think he'd rather I bought the flat.' And she just loses it laughing. It's infectious and for a moment we must be the most annoying people in the bar.

'Anyway,' says Suzi, 'it's what I want. I don't want to write bog roll ads forever, you know what I mean?'

I nod. *Yes, I know what you mean.*

Ivy and I are in bed, Nina Simone playing at a low volume, a honeysuckle-scented candle flickering on Ivy's bedside table next to an open bottle of baby oil. My choice of music; my choice of lighting.

'This is very sweet of you, baby, but I can do it myself, you know.'

'Relax,' I say, 'lie back.' And I continue massaging the oil into Ivy's drum-tight bump. The sheen highlights a scar that skitters across her belly, and this, I'm sure, plays a large part in her fear of getting stretchmarks.

'How about Henry?' she says.

We still have no idea what genders our twins are. 'For a boy or a girl?' I ask.

'Girl.'

'I'm working with a Henry, she's a bit of a knob.'

'Can you call a girl a knob?'

'If you can call her Henry, why not? Anyway, she says *ciao* on the phone.'

'Where's she from?'

'Wigan, I think.'

'Fair enough,' says Ivy. 'So that's a no to Henry.'

I change direction, moving my hand in slow, gradually widening clockwise circles. 'How about Zara?' I suggest.

'I went to school with a Zara; she used to call me Beef.'

'What, where you . . .?' I blow out my cheeks, hold my hands around an invisible gut, waddle my shoulders from side to side.

Ivy slaps my hand. 'No, it evolved from B.F., short for Bride of Frankenstein,' she indicates the scar on her cheek.

'Bitch.'

Ivy shrugs. 'I had worse. And I gave as good as I got. She had really wide-spaced eyes and a super retroussé nose, so I called her Bizzara. And it stuck a damn sight longer than Beef.'

'*Touché*,' I say, resuming my massage and widening the orbit of my hand just enough that my fingers brush against the waistband of Ivy's knickers.

'So,' says Ivy, stretching the single seductive syllable, 'what's your porn-star name?'

Of course the massage, the music and the candles were

all designed to create a mood, but I hadn't anticipated such a direct reaction.

'My . . . what?'

'You know,' says Ivy, 'you take the name of your first pet, add your mother's maiden name and that's your porn-star name.'

'Oh, right, I see. So my pet's name and . . .?'

'Mother's maiden name.'

'Okay . . . Catch MacCluskey.'

Ivy claps her hands together in delight. 'That's brilliant! You're not kidding me, are you? Are you pulling my leg?'

I shake my head. 'Goldfish and a Catholic.'

'I love it! *Catch MacCluskey.*'

'Go on then, what's yours?'

'Mine's rubbish.'

'Come on . . . you brought it up.'

Ivy sighs. 'Fine – Margaret Smith.'

'Oh, that really is rubbish.'

'I *know.*'

'I mean, who has a pet called Margaret?'

Ivy points to herself. 'That would be me. I wanted a dog or a cat – we'd never had pets, rest of the family weren't interested – and I nagged and nagged and nagged until finally, to shut me up, they fobbed me off with a rabbit.'

'Which you called Margaret.'

'I was four! We'd never had a pet before and no one told me that pets have names like Fido or Fluffy or . . . *Catch*. And what's that all about while we're at it? Way to give a fish a complex.'

'We're Fishers, he's a Catch. And if we're critiquing goldfish names, it's better than Ernest.'

'Shut up!'

'You must have figured the rules out by now, you're forty-*one*, that's ancien—'

'Careful, *Catch*. I could kick you in an extremely painful place from here.' I hold up my hands in submission. 'If you must know, he's named after Hemingway.'

'The writer chappy?'

'He wrote *The Old Man and The Sea*, and he was mad for fishing so it works on two . . . are you laughing at me?'

'Only a little. With you mostly.'

Ivy pouts at me sulkily. 'It's still better than Catch.'

Two of the tealights have guttered out now and Nina is approaching the end of her album, so I pour more oil into my hands and begin massaging Ivy's right thigh.

'Do pregnant women get stretchmarks there?' Ivy asks.

'Depends how huge you get. Relax.' And Ivy does.

When Ivy returned from book club three hours ago, I was asleep and, apparently, snoring like a hog on the sofa.

It was gone ten o'clock but I was starving hungry, so I cooked spaghetti with pesto and grated cheese and we sat up eating a late supper. We talked about our days, and I felt a pinching guilt for having spent the end of the afternoon and the start of the evening in a wine bar with an attractive woman. Nothing happened to feel guilty about, of course – no overlong contact, no lingering kisses, no nascent infidelity. We flirted, probably, a little, but with no objective in mind. But even so, I experience that irritating itch of having misbehaved. I slide my hands down Ivy's thigh, over her knee and calf and take her foot in my hand, push my thumbs into the sole. She takes a deep breath, lets it slowly out. In Suzi's screenplay, there is a scene where a man ties his lover's ankles to opposite corners of the wrought-iron bed frame with silk ties. I push it out of my mind and pour more oil into my palm.

'Ellie?' Ivy suggests.

I slept with a girl called Ellie, but now is hardly the time to divulge.

'Had a Smelly Ellie in sixth form,' I tell her. Which isn't a million miles from the truth.

'Kids,' says Ivy, 'so cr— Oh!' her eyes go wide as her hands move reflexively to her belly.

'What's up? Are you . . . is everything okay?'

Ivy smiles. 'Someone,' she says, stroking her bump as if

154

it were a puppy or a kitten or ... well, a baby, 'someone's restless.'

'Really, which one?'

'Hard to tell.' Then, directed at her bump, 'Who's fidgeting, hmm?'

'First time?' I ask.

Ivy nods. 'No one owning up, hey?' She pushes a hand into her tummy, attempting to elicit some response.

'Anything?' I ask.

Ivy shakes her head sadly. 'Show's over, I think.'

I don't actually say the words: *That's what you think,* but I do raise my eyebrows as I resume massaging Ivy's legs.

Ivy groans.

'Does that feel good?' I say.

But as I look into her face, all the colour drains from Ivy's cheeks. 'I ... I don't think all that jiggling was such a good idea,' she says, and then she holds a hand to her mouth and scampers off to the bathroom to barf.

When I wake the following morning Ivy is not beside me. We've been living together for almost eight weeks now, and it's not unusual for me to wake in an otherwise empty bed. Ivy used to enjoy starting the day with what she euphemistically calls (*called*) a 'wriggle', but now that she has a pair of sweet potatoes using her bladder as a bouncy castle, it seems the only thing on her waking mind is a pee and a cup of tea.

My old neighbour, Esther, has a theory about pebbles in a jar:

If you place a pebble in a jar every time you make love in the first year of a relationship, then remove a pebble every time you make love thereafter, you will never empty the jar. I get it, and I don't doubt it contains a grain (or a pebble) of truth. I just hope, like so much else in our short relationship, this early burst of sexual industriousness isn't a phenomenon Ivy and I have managed to tick off in a condensed time frame i.e. in nineteen days instead of twelve months. There are, of course, extenuating factors. In the seven and a half weeks since I moved to Wimbledon, we've both been working, and it would have been hard to arrange schedules that were less aligned. Added to that, on the nights when we are together, Ivy is usually asleep on the sofa within seconds of nine o'clock ticking over. Even at weekends we're out of synch. I run and Ivy practises yoga, but we never manage to co-ordi-nate these things, which equates to around two hours spent apart on both Saturday and Sunday. She reads, I watch *Columbo*; I walk to the shops, she takes an afternoon nap. And it's not unpleasant; in fact, it's cosy. But too much cosy can get a little . . . well, boring. I like the life we share together; it just feels like we're living it about twenty years too soon.

This morning I find Ivy in the living room, moving through a yoga routine. Dressed in a pair of sky-blue leggings and a pink vest top, she is currently balanced in Downward Dog. Hinged at the waist with her hands and feet on the yoga mat and her limbs locked straight, Ivy's body describes a perfect A-frame.

'Morning, sweet cheeks,' I say to her elevated bottom.

Neither Ivy nor her elevated bottom answer.

I pat her on the backside as I walk through to the kitchen, where I flick on the kettle.

'We should get some full-fat,' I say.

Ivy can't see the bottle of skimmed milk I'm brandishing because her head is now squashed between her knees, but she knows what I'm talking about. We have discussed the fat-content of our milk several times. If I want it, Ivy says, then I should buy it. Problem is, Ivy takes care of the online shop and the only time I think about milk is when I'm standing in front of an open fridge, holding a carton of what amounts to little more than white water. I mean, is a little milk in my milk really too much to ask?

'For coffee,' I say.

Ivy transitions into Cat.

The kettle boils and I make a full cafetiere of coffee.

Into Cow, into Modified Cobra.

'Want one?' I ask.

Ivy grunts – through exertion or as an answer, I can't tell.

'I'll take that as a no,' I say.

'Kind of doing something,' she says from between her legs.

Skinny coffee in hand, I take a seat on the sofa and spectate. I have seen Ivy move through these poses many times now. In the first few weeks of our relationship she encouraged me to join in, which I did; and on more than one occasion our final position was one you don't perform in public. Ivy transitions into Caterpillar – head on the mat, back arched, bum in the air.

'Remember when we used to do yoga together?' I say.

'Unnh hmm.'

'Seems like a long time ago.'

'Uh huh.'

Ivy shifts her weight backward so that she is on all fours. She rotates her hips one way then the other. I doubt it's actually called Sexy Fox, but that's the name which comes to mind.

'What's that one called?'

'Dunno,' says Ivy.

'Funny name.'

Ivy doesn't answer.

'I could join you if you like?'

'Haven't you got things to do?' says Ivy.

'All right,' I say, a little stung. And then, remembering something her brother Frank said when we visited Ivy's parents: 'Chillamena Willamena.'

'Christ, that's annoying,' she says, and I don't remember her reacting the same way when Frank said it.

I leave my unfinished coffee on the arm of the sofa, knowing it will piss Ivy off even further, and go through to the bedroom to change into my running gear. I strap on my iPod and fold a tenner into my trainer so I can buy a bacon sandwich and a carton of full-fucking-fat milk on the way back.

For the first mile I run angry. And with no clear destination in mind, I run not towards Wimbledon Common, but away from it. Instead of the open spaces, the trees, the pond and the bridle path, I pound the hard pavements, running beside busy roads and filling my lungs with car fumes. It takes me less than an hour to arrive at my old street in Brixton.

As I approach Esther's flat, I see that her 'For Sale' sign now bears a glued-on panel saying 'Sold'. This shouldn't come as a surprise; her flat has been on the market for several weeks and she and Nino have been planning their escape to Italy since the summer. But it makes me sad, nevertheless.

'Morning, love,' Esther says, as if she were expecting me. 'You lost?'

'Something like that. Can I use your shower?'

Because I hadn't thought this through in any way whatsoever, I have to borrow a set of clothes from Nino, who stands a foot shorter than I do, but more than makes up for it in circumference. The clothes Esther has laid out on the spare bed are simple enough, but you'd be surprised just how ridiculous you can look in a pair of jeans and a woolly jumper. The jeans hang halfway down my shins, exposing a pair of beige socks that would be awful even if the ankle elastic wasn't shot (Esther has also provided a pair of Nino's now-grey Y-fronts, but I can't bring myself to wear them so I fold them up and stuff them into a pocket in my denim clown trousers). The jumper Esther has selected to complete this ensemble is a loose-knit, purple and green striped article that fits as snugly as a sack on a scarecrow. I look like a mental patient. But needs must when you're a stupid sodding idiot.

Esther cooks me a full English breakfast and probes not-so-subtly into the nature of my surprise visit. I consider lying and telling her that I'm here to check on my tenants in the upstairs flat, but that would involve a) lying; b) checking on the tenants; and c) stepping inside my former residence which, I suddenly realize, I don't want to do ever again. Yes, I had a leather recliner and an HD TV, and yes, the fridge was always replete with full-fat milk, but I also did a lot of stupid things while I lived above Esther. Looking back, it seems the only good thing that happened during that time was meeting Ivy, and the only good decision I made in that flat was to move out.

'Tiff,' I say.

Esther laughs. 'First one?'

'Second maybe.'

'Anything serious?'

'Just me being annoying.'

'If I had a penny ...' Esther says, shaking her head. 'We'd have moved out of this place a long time ago. *Tiff*,' she says, laughing.

'You sold it then?' I say, gesturing at the room around me.

Esther's face morphs from chuckling joviality to sobbing tears, the sound of her laughter transitioning seamlessly into a hitching whimper. I pull my chair around to her side and hug her while she sobs into my shoulder.

'What's up?' I ask. 'I thought this was a good thing?'

'It is, love,' she says, bringing on a fresh deluge. 'Of course it is.'

'So why the tears, hey?'

Esther sits upright, wipes her eyes with a sleeve and sniffs like a dockworker. 'You,' she says, her composure returning, 'you're like a son to me.'

Inside my head, I say the words, *And you're like a mother to me*, but even unarticulated, the phrase catches in my throat and I feel a wet pressure behind my eyes. I smile instead, and I hope that the way I do it speaks for me.

Esther makes more toast, even though I haven't finished the first serving, and fills me in on the remaining logistics of her and Nino's move – the packing, the flights, the new cottage in the Italian countryside. After a family Christmas in Exeter with her daughter, two sons and eight grand-children, she and Nino will leave for Urbino.

'Where's Nino now?'

'After forty-odd years you stop asking,' she says. 'Want some free advice?'

I nod.

'Don't trip over yourselves trying to be a perfect couple, love. Get out of each other's way; don't be afraid of falling out, shutting up, or telling little porky pies; do your share of the cleaning; don't leave your dirty undies inside out on the carpet; leave the seat down; buy her flowers once a month and pinch her bum once a week – the rest's up to you.'

I consider telling Esther bum-pinching (well, patting)

was involved in the build-up to today's tiff, but I know it would be missing the point. 'Works for you, does it?'

'Me and all my babies, love. All had kids, had every kind of problem there is between 'em, but they're all still married.' And she says this with no small amount of pride.

'You should write a book,' I tell her.

'I bloody should, love,' she says, topping up her tea from the pot. 'Not to say me and him haven't thrown our fair share of pots and pans. My word, love, we had some ding-dongs. Came close to falling apart more than a few times, too.' She laughs gently, a philosophical mixture of fond nostalgia and pragmatic regret. Or maybe it's nothing more complicated than simple amusement. 'Just remember you love each other,' she says. 'Easier said than done, sometimes, I know. But that's the trick, sweetheart – just remember you love each other.' Esther gives me a hard look. 'You do love her?'

I nod. 'With all I've got.'

'Well stop moping, you silly boy.'

It takes longer to get to Wimbledon by bus than it did to run the outward journey, not because I ran particularly fast but because London traffic is particularly slow. As the bus crawls onward, I doze, head lolling, vision fuzzing, thoughts turning to nonsense. When I go to bed drunk – like I did last night – I sleep all the way through, but wake up exhausted nevertheless. As if I shut down so completely that even my restorative mechanisms crash. On the number 57 to Wimbledon, I snap awake periodically with my mouth open, drool on my chin and the echo of a snore inside my skull. This, coupled with my escaped mental patient wardrobe and Lidl carrier bag full of sweaty running gear, ensures no one sits next to me. And so I doze some more. By the time we arrive in The Village, I feel like a new man (even if I am dressed like an old tramp).

When I walk onto our street I spot Harold, Ivy's awkward teenaged neighbour, sitting on the front step of his flat. Unlike my flat in Brixton – which at some point in history was simply the upstairs of a bigger, single residence – these maisonettes were purpose built. Even so, we share a gate and a path and our front doors stand adjacent to each other like conjoined twins. Harold is holding half a deck of cards, the rest spread out on the path between his feet. I nod good morning to him and he looks up briefly, grunting a response. We're a few days into December now and although the temperature is mild for the time of year, it's still a little cold for sitting on the doorstep in a T-shirt.

'You not cold?'

Harold shakes his head.

'Waiting for someone?'

He glances over his shoulder. 'Not exactly.'

I sit on the step beside him. 'Patience?' I say, nodding at the cards arranged at his feet.

Harold laughs, a single mirthless note. 'What's with the stupid clothes?'

'Fashion,' I tell him. 'All the cool kids are wearing it.'

Harold's expression tells me he's not buying, but neither is he interested in pursuing the subject. Since our initial encounter (fighting over a set of keys on Ivy's doorstep) Harold has continued to regard me with a mixture of suspicion and disdain. His hostile jealousy, however, seems to have mellowed since it became apparent Ivy is pregnant. His mother, Maureen, is civil but not overtly friendly. As if she's permanently distracted, worried or exhausted. There is a boyfriend, but I've never been introduced. Ivy has invited Maureen for coffee, supper and wine on separate occasions – not because she felt a pressing desire to befriend this shy, bespectacled, harried-looking woman, but because not inviting her was becoming an embarrassment. And every time, Maureen has declined politely with a feasible but flimsy excuse – paperwork, ironing, whatever. And so Ivy has stopped asking and that seems to suit us all just fine.

'Whatsisname in?' I ask.

'Lol,' Harold says.

'Sorry,' I say. 'I wasn't trying to be funny, I . . .'

Harold looks at me as if I really am as stupid as my outfit suggests. 'Not *lol*, Lol. Not *laugh-out-loud*, lol. Lol as in Laurence.'

'Lol? Really?'

Harold shrugs.

'I never knew,' I tell him. 'My best mate's called Laurence, but we call him El. Never heard of *Lol*.' I pronounce the last word with exaggerated playground derision, leaning heavily on both Ls.

Harold laughs at this, repeats it.

'Seems like a nice guy,' I say.

'He's a perv.'

I look at Harold. *Are you sure?*

'Always pinching Mum's bum,' he says, avoiding eye contact.

'There's a lot of it about,' I say.

'What?'

'Never mind, give me those cards.' And I scoop them up before Harold has a chance to answer.

'I was playing with those!'

I shuffle, cut, shuffle again. 'Pick a card.'

Harold does so, silently and with a total absence of enthusiasm. I do all the business of looking away, shuffling, furrowing my brow, etc. before locating his card, which is now – yes, miraculously – upside down within the deck.

Harold shrugs, says he's seen David Blaine do it hanging from a helicopter. It takes two more tricks before the bastard cracks a smile, and by now my bum is numb from sitting on the cold hard step.

'So, Harold,' I say. 'Any chance you could nip inside and get me the spare key?'

'Wondered when you were going to ask,' he says, the smile broadening.

'Lol,' I say, and Harold laughs again.

As I ascend the stairs to the flat, I am welcomed by the aroma of bacon, sausages and eggs. Ivy is reclined on the sofa, reading a novel, and I flop down beside her.

'Afternoon,' she says. 'How's Esther?'

'Who says I've been to Esther's? Maybe I've got a fancy woman stashed away somewhere.'

'Likes you dressing up as a 68-year-old, does she, this fancy woman? And what does she wear, curlers and a housecoat?'

'It's hobo chic.'

'Suits you.'

Ivy puts her book down and pads through to the kitchen area. She takes a heaped plate of full English and places it in the microwave. 'Toast?'

I'm still carrying a bellyful of Esther's fry-up, so I

decline. While Ivy waits for the microwave, she busies herself making coffee. The microwave pings and Ivy replaces the first plate with a second. That she made me breakfast is wonderful; that she waited for me before eating her own is an act of love. Finding space inside my stomach for two sausages, double bacon, half a tomato, beans and a good dollop of scrambled egg is by far the most impressive magic trick I have performed all morning. And the process of reheating has made it no easier – the eggs are rubbery, the bacon tough, the sausages hard, the tomato soggy and the beans congealed – but I get through the entire plate with a great big crazy grin on my face. David Blaine, eat your heart out.

Ivy has clearly decided to sweep the last few hours under the carpet, and I'm happy to be complicit. We were both present at the scene of the squabble, both culpable (some, obviously, more culpable than others), and there is nothing to be gained from a post-mortem. My previous girlfriend and I would fight, then apologize, then backtrack through the incident, deconstructing and apportioning blame, more often than not leading to a repeat performance of the original débâcle. I like Ivy's way better. Particularly when I've been acting like a berk.

Ivy washes the dishes and I dry.

'What are you doing on Thursday?' she asks.

'Nothing as far as I know. Why?'

'Good,' says Ivy. 'We're going on a date.'

'Brilliant. Where?'

Ivy taps the side of her nose with a sudsy finger. 'You'll have to wait and see.'

Chapter 13

Seventeen and a half years ago, whilst driving to collect El and me from the cinema, my mother was killed in a car crash. A supermarket wagon sideswiped her yellow Datsun and spun it into the path of an oncoming motorcycle. A million events and circumstances proceeded, followed, coincided and aligned with each other to bring all the elements – lorry, motorcycle, my mother – together. It wasn't my fault that I went to the cinema and I don't blame myself for my mother's death, but if I hadn't been there then there's a damn good chance my mother would still be alive today.

There is still so much Ivy and I don't know about each other – things you don't drop into conversation, but discover piece by piece as your relationship develops and moves forward. Our relationship proper is only four months old, so there are many pieces left to uncover. Ivy knows that my mother died in a traffic accident, but she doesn't know Mum was driving to collect me from the cinema, and she doesn't know that I haven't been to the movies since.

But as I wait for Ivy outside the train station, I have a dreadful feeling – emphasis on *dread* – that this is where my surprise date is scheduled to happen. The Wimbledon Odeon is visible from where I'm standing, and the thought of going inside is affecting me physically. I can feel my heart thumping, my stomach is knotted and, despite the cold, my head and back are prickled with sweat. But I'm okay with it, I think. I can't live the rest of my life not taking my children to the pictures, and if not tonight then at some point soon I will be forced to man up, bite the bullet and grasp the popcorn. And on some level, I'll be disappointed if we're not going to the flicks tonight. After all, it's not like there's anyone driving here to pick me up afterwards.

I turn away from the cinema to scan the throng pouring through the ticket barriers. It's dark already and there must be hundreds of people pushing and jostling through the gates.

'Looking for anyone in particular?' a voice whispers behind me, and her breath is warm against my ear.

Ivy's hair is tucked up inside a white, knitted hat that might look nerdy on anyone else but her. 'Excited?' she asks.

'Depends where we're going.'

'Well, as it's our first official date night, I thought we should have a traditional date.'

'Does it involve popcorn?'

'You bet your sweet butt it involves popcorn.'

'In that case, I'm excited.'

And we walk arm in arm to the cinema.

The movie is Oscar nominated, apparently. Ivy tells me this as we walk up Wimbledon Hill on the way home, not linking arms now, but holding hands. When she asks what I thought of the film, I tell her I can see why it was nominated, but this is something of a white lie – a 'porky pie', as Esther would say. Not that I didn't enjoy the movie; when I paid attention I thought it was well worth the price of admission. Unfortunately, for the majority of the two hours, my mind was elsewhere.

I thought about Mum and the day she died. I remembered being confused when El's dad collected us from the cinema – how he told me she'd been in an accident and how there was a police car in the driveway when he dropped me at home. I thought about how precious and precarious life is, how easy to take for granted. On

Tuesday, Suzi emailed me the fifteen-page script for her short film. When it's finished she will send it to agents and producers to generate interest in her feature-length script. And while Ivy and I sat in the Wimbledon Odeon, I fantasized about what it would be like to direct a movie instead of a commercial for toilet roll. But it's not just about me anymore, is it? My obligation now is to my children and their mother. To put cash in the bank and food on the table. And my thoughts went round again: remembering, fantasizing, fretting, imagining.

As we walk up the hill towards The Village, Ivy asks: 'What do you think that guy – the priest – what do you think he meant when he said, "Never is a lot longer than forever"?'

'There was a priest?' I ask.

Ivy stops walking. 'You were in the same movie as me, right?'

'Kind of,' I tell her, and then I tell her about the day my mother died.

It's a Friday afternoon and Christmas is less than three weeks away, so the pub is as tightly packed as Santa's sack. Nevertheless, Joe and I have a table to ourselves, tucked away in the corner. For the second time in a week I have managed to surround myself with a force field of unapproachability.

Last Tuesday it was a mental-patient wardrobe, today it is four kilos of Limburger. This afternoon we attended the pre-production meeting for the cheese commercial, where the client presented everybody with a whopping great lump of product. As he distributed the cheese, the marketing manager proudly informed us that this particular cheese has been voted the 'seventh most pungent' in the world. And the knowledge that there are six cheeses more foul-smelling than this one is enough to give anyone some very weird nightmares. It took two hours to finalize the details for the shoot; two hours in a small room with eight head-sized hunks of the seventh-most-stinky cheese in the world and the radiators turned up full blast. And although the script stank only slightly less than its object, I smiled and paid attention and laughed and told everybody what a special privilege it was to be working with them. And not simply because I'm a consummate professional, but because Joe loves all that bullshit and I need Joe.

It would appear that my obsequiousness has paid off, because as well as smelling of cheese, Joe is positively reeking of bonhomie. He returns to our table carrying two pints and wearing an elf cap at a jaunty angle.

'Good elf,' he says, raising his glass.

'Very funny,' I tell him, and even though it isn't, I can't help but laugh.

'Right, now as we're in the festive spirit, I've got a present for you ...' Joe reaches into his bag and produces a brown A4 envelope. He slides it across the table.

'You shouldn't have,' I say, and I take the envelope and place it in my own bag.

'Okay,' says Joe, 'I'll bite, it's for—'

'How much?'

'Fine, fuck it,' says Joe, his festive spirit evaporating rapidly. 'I'll give it to someone else. Someone with a scrap of gratitude.'

'Why're you being all uppity? You don't care what I think of the script, just whether I say yes or not.'

Joe inhales, sighs. 'Listen, I get that you have a new agenda all of a sudden, and I'm glad you're being all *can do*. But I like what I do; I enjoy it. And when you get all fucking supercilious on me' – I raise my eyebrows – 'yeah,' Joe says, 'I know what supercilious means; it means to act like a smug wanker. And when you act like a smug wanker, well, it wears a bit fucking thin. Know what I mean?'

I've known Joe for years, and I know him well enough not to take this lambasting too personally. Particularly when he's started on his third pint. Even so, it's never nice being called a smug wanker.

'Whoa, hold on! I was having a joke. It was a fucking *joke*, all right.'

'Yeah, well, not a very funny one.'

'Really? Unlike *good elf*?'

Joe goes to say something then decides to take a good glug of his pint instead.

I hold up my hands in surrender. 'I'm sorry. What's it for? The script.'

'Tampax.'

I close my eyes and count to three inside my head. When I open them again, Joe is staring at me, arms crossed and impassive. 'How much?' I say.

'Six.'

I say nothing.

'Six is fucking good,' Joe says. 'For a one-day shoot.'

'One condition.'

'What? More games, now, is it?'

I pull an envelope of my own from my bag. Inside is Suzi's script, which has a title now: *Reinterpreting Jackson Pollock* – or simply *Pollock*, as we now refer to it after several emails, phone calls and script revisions. I pass the envelope to Joe.

'What's this?'

'Open it.'

Joe does. He glances at the title on the front page, nods to himself and turns to page one. By the time he's finished reading – in silence and without looking up once – I have finished my pint while Joe has barely touched his.

'And?' he says, finally.

So I tell him; I tell him about Suzi, about her screenplay, and about her ten thousand pounds. Joe slides the manuscript back into its envelope and takes a measured sip of his pint.

I look at the envelope, then at Joe. 'So?'

'It's all right. Title's a bit shit.'

'Is that it?' I ask.

'What are you asking me, William? Do I like it? Will I invest in it? Am I happy about you working for a different bloody production company? What?'

'Would you like to produce it?'

Joe likes to pretend he's above sentiment, but he's a big soft bastard at his core, and an involuntary smile ripples across his face. 'Me?' he says, pointing a finger at his chest.

'You,' I say.

Joe downs his pint in one long gulp, belches and recomposes his world-weary façade. 'All right,' he says. 'Might as well.'

By the time I leave the Goose, Friday afternoon has given way to Friday evening. I'm not staggering drunk, but I'd have a hard time walking a tightrope. Ivy has been working on a perfume commercial today, so she could be back anywhere between an hour ago and three hours hence. I call but her phone goes straight to voicemail. It's not quite seven o'clock when my train arrives in Wimbledon, but the sun set some time ago and it feels later. My legs are heavy and my bladder full as I trudge up to The Village, and the walk is a long one tonight. As I crest Wimbledon Hill, the extortionate butcher is beginning to shut up shop. I've sobered up considerably, but there's enough booze in my system that I walk in of my own free will and allow them to extort more than forty pounds out of me for a fillet of beef, a few slices of pancetta and a string of sausages.

Ivy isn't back so I turn the radio up loud, open the wine and get cooking. The place is beginning to feel like home and while the food bubbles, I plump up the cushions, feed the goldfish and browse the bookshelves, flicking through a selection of Ivy's unfinished novels and reading the paragraphs where she left off.

I set two places at the table, improvise a candlestick holder from an eggcup and line up something acoustic on the iPod. Ivy has been a significant part of my life for four months now and our babies are halfway to being born, to being tiny humans curled up between us on the bed. And still, neither of us has said those three significant words. Or at least not without a mouthful of cashmere.

When I lived with Kate we used to tell each other 'I love you' every night before turning out the lights. Except when we didn't. On the nights – and there were several – when we took an argument to the bed with us, the three little words went unuttered. Which was exactly like telling each other: I *don't* love you – not tonight. So I like that Ivy and I don't trot the words out by rote, turning them into a platitude on the nights we say them and a weapon on the nights we don't. But I do love her, and I'm going to tell her tonight.

I'm dozing on the sofa when I hear Ivy knocking hard on the front door and it takes me a moment to remember where I am. According to the mantelpiece clock it's nearly nine. There's another knock, and the extra iron in Ivy's diet must be working because it sounds like she's about to knock the door off its hinges. I shout that I'm coming, light the candle, check my hair and, because I'm a crazy, whacky, funny kind of guy, I unbutton my shirt to my navel, take a flower from its vase and place it between my teeth. Ivy hammers again.

'Coming,' I shout. Except, with the flower between my teeth it sounds more like *Kerning*.

It doesn't cross my mind to wonder why Ivy is knocking and not using her key. She often knocks when she returns from a shoot – her van is full of expensive make-up and equipment, and it's getting increasingly difficult for her to carry the boxes up to the flat.

So it's a heck of a shock to find her brother, Frank, standing on the doorstep.

'You shouldn't have,' he says.

'Frank,' I reply around a mouthful of gerbera.

'But since you did . . .' and Frank hugs me tight enough to make my head throb. 'Blimey,' he says, releasing me, 'what's that smell?'

'Limburger,' I say, rebuttoning my shirt.

'Jaysus! Whose limb, and how long have they been dead!'

'It's a cheese.'

'Er, durr? You going to invite me in or what?'

Once I get Frank and his suitcase inside the flat proper, I ask what he's doing in London, and he rambles vaguely about friends, work, his sister and spontaneity.

'So when was this . . . arranged?'

Frank shrugs and blows air through his lips in a loose raspberry. 'Oh, I dunno, couple of hours ago? Lunchtime, maybe.' He spots the table set for two, the candle flickering in its eggcup, and he grimaces apologetically. 'Ooops.'

'Don't worry,' I tell him, 'I cooked plenty.'

'What we having?'

'Boeuf bourguignon.'

'Fancy pantsy!'

'Drink?'

'Tell you what; you jump in the shower, and I'll get this open,' he says, producing a bottle of Merlot from a carrier bag. 'Red! I must be psychic.'

And I am so dumbfounded that I do exactly as I'm told. When I return to the living room – clean, dry and wearing clothes that don't reek of cheese – Ivy is back and all the windows are open, letting in the cold winter air.

'Hey, hon,' she says from the sofa. 'Guess who's coming to supper!' And despite feeling just a little shanghaied, I laugh.

I kiss Ivy on the forehead. 'You hot?'

'What? No, why?'

'The windows.'

'I opened 'em,' Frank says, wafting a hand in front of his nose. 'Get the pong of that *fromage* out.'

'*Fromage*?' asks Ivy.

I explain about the cheese; and once we've ascertained that Ivy can't eat it and Frank wouldn't if his life depended on it, I wrap the reeking, sweating hunk of Limburger inside three carrier bags and dump it in the bin outside the flat. If nothing else it should keep the foxes away.

While Frank and Ivy catch up and share old in-jokes, I

unset the table and salvage the boeuf bourguignon with a good glug of Frank's wine. We eat off our laps, in front of the TV and squashed three-abreast on the sofa. Frank, at one end, is as wide across the shoulders as a supervillain, so I'm crammed onto two-thirds of a cushion at the other end, with the hard arm of the sofa digging into my ribs. Ivy's baby brother is in a drinking mood and he's dragging me with him. Approximately every five minutes he commands, 'William. Glass,' and reaches across Ivy to ensure my glass is sloshingly full.

'So,' I say, as nonchalantly as possible, 'you're staying the night?'

'If that's all right, William?'

'Fisher.'

'Yeah, Fisher.'

'Plans for the rest of the weekend?' I ask, trying not to sound too eager to get rid of him.

It's not that I don't like Frank; he's the archetypal 'lovely bloke' – big, cuddly, daft-hearted and amusing in a loud, lummoxing kind of way. It's not hard to imagine us being friends (or, getting a little ahead of myself, being the kind of brothers-in-law that can spend an afternoon in the pub unaccompanied by their spouses – if, that is, Frank still has one). Imagining us spending a quiet weekend together three abreast on this couch, however, that's a little trickier to get my head around. I had plans for this evening, and they didn't involve an eighteen-stone dentist.

'We thought we'd just hang out,' Ivy says, which clarifies nothing.

'Fair enough,' I say. And when I go to put my arm around Ivy's shoulders, I find Frank's already there.

'William! Glass.'

And before I can object, the spout of our second bottle is thrust in front of my face. Frank begins to pour, but the bottle is practically empty and he only manages to fill my glass to within a finger's width of the rim.

'Ooops! I'll open another, shall I?' And as he rises from the sofa, Ivy and I expand sideways into the suddenly available space.

While Frank is selecting another bottle of my wine, I turn to Ivy and send her a subtle shrug: shoulders lifting, wrists rotating outward, head tilting to the right, eyes widening, every movement measured in millimetres. *What's going on?* Ivy scrunches up her brow: *What do you mean?* I raise my eyebrows, point my chin over my shoulder to where Frank is rattling around for a corkscrew: *Your brother!* Ivy bites her bottom lip, gives a minute shake of her head: *Not now.* I turn down one corner of my mouth and sigh: *Fine.*

'Not interrupting anything, am I?' says Frank, wedging himself back into place.

I begin to answer but the air is forced from my lungs as I am once again compressed into the corner of the sofa.

'Glass,' he says, reaching across Ivy and topping my Merlot with Pinot Noir until the meniscus bulges over the rim.

There wasn't as much sex on TV when I was a young boy living with my parents, but whenever there was, Dad would jump up as if his chair had been electrified and change the channel. Later, when I reached my teens, he would simply leave the room, tutting and muttering and not returning until the filthy business was completed. And awkward as it was, it has nothing on watching a movie romp in the company of my pregnant girlfriend and her hulking great brother. Frank's strategy for dealing with embarrassing sex scenes is to deliver a running commentary in a variety of comedy voices and regional accents.

Hello! Someone's feeling frisky! Is that a banana in your pocket or are you just pleased to see me? Ha ha ha. Allow me to help you with those, love . . . Oo, pink lacy ones, saucy. And they're off! Badddoinggg! Shall we adjourn to the kitchen table? Never mind the dishes, we'll pop to Ikea tomorrow. Get a hotdog, ha ha. Look at his face! Looks like he's struggling with a cross-word. One up, four letters, begins with a B, ends in K . . . B-O-N-K! Cheers, darling, how was it for you? Ha ha ha ha!

And all the way through this excruciating one-man show, I'm waiting, *praying*, for Ivy to tell him to just shut the hell up, but she says not a word. And now, as I sneak a sideways glance at her, I see why. Squashed between us like a wilted flower, Ivy is still sitting but her chin has dropped onto her chest. I lift her head as gently as possible and see that her eyes are fully closed. A delicate snore escapes her open mouth.

Frank has the remote and I ask him to turn down the volume, drawing his attention to his sleeping sister.

'Ah, bless,' he says, stroking Ivy's cheek with the back of his index finger. 'Right,' he says, pointing the remote at the TV. 'Shall we turn this shit off?'

I assume Frank means the TV, and that he is ready to call it a night. But instead he speed-flips through umpteen programmes until he finds a Chuck Norris movie on some obscure satellite channel.

'Bit of Chuck?' he asks.

Living with a pregnant girlfriend, it's not often (in the way it's not often that Hell holds a snowman-making competition) that I get to drink too much and watch old action flicks on the telly. So why not? I let Frank refill my glass, then I take hold of Ivy's sleeping hand and settle back into my tiny corner of the sofa. It's not what I planned (what is?), but as cold Friday nights go, it could be a whole lot worse. Even so, I was up at six thirty this morning, and after this afternoon's meeting, beer with Joe and wine with Frank, the day has had its way with me. Chuck Norris has kicked, punched, knifed and choked to death barely fifty villains before my own eyes begin to close. I tell Frank I'm calling it a day, and rouse Ivy on the third attempt. Frank volunteers to wash the dishes; Ivy dries and I – determined not to be outdone – insist on putting everything away. There really isn't room for three people behind the breakfast bar (particularly when one of them is the size of Frank), and it's a miracle that nothing gets broken during the entire awkward routine.

Dishes cleaned, dried and stowed, we say our good nights. Frank gives me a buddy punch on the shoulder before giving Ivy a protracted bear hug. He kisses his big sister on the side of her head and tells her he loves her. Ivy tells Frank she loves him too before reaching up on tiptoes to give him a final bedtime smacker. Which is all very coochy-coo for the pair of them, but it's kind of taken the wind from the sails of my own love boat. If I tell Ivy I love her now, it's going to look like I'm simply joining in for fear of being left out.

Friday nights have become baby-book nights. The book is snappily titled *Countdown to Your Baby: A week-by-week guide to your changing body and your little one's development.* Every week we read a new chapter; this week it's chapter 19 and it's Ivy's turn to read. She tells me that nerves are forming, connecting our babies' brains to their muscles and organs. The babies have as many nerves as an adult now, and our newly wired-up babies might jump in response to a shock.

'Like their uncle turning up unexpectedly?'

'Shut up and listen,' says Ivy.

'I had a flower in my teeth,' I tell her. 'And a candle. Not in my teeth, on the table.'

Ivy holds a shushing finger to her lips. 'Frank told me.'

She continues reading. The placenta is fully formed but still growing. Tooth buds are forming inside the babies' gums. They have tongues. The babies are covered in downy hairs and a waxy substance, which keeps their skin supple. Our babies will be with us in just eighteen weeks, and whilst they are doing just fine for fur, wax and tooth buds, they still don't have names.

'How about Angus?'

'Bit Scottish,' says Ivy.

'Hamish, then.'

Ivy laughs. 'I like Agatha.'

'And if it's a boy?'

'How about Dashiell?'

187

'That's a name?'

'He wrote *The Maltese Falcon*.'

'Aggy and Dash,' I say. 'I actually like it.'

Ivy grimaces. 'I think I hate it.'

'What's Frank's boy called again?'

'Freddy,' she says, sighing. And that's that moment killed.

'What's going on with him and . . .?'

'Lois. Frank's moved out.'

'What happened?'

'Nothing, just . . . stuff.'

'Did he cheat on her?'

'No.'

'She cheated on him?'

'Shh, will you. He's in the other room.'

'I'm just asking who did the dirty,' I say in a stage whisper.

'You don't have to look so *amused*. It's just really sad. You should have seen them when they met . . . they were . . . made for each other. Everyone said so.' Ivy exhales slowly, shaking her head. 'It's tragic, just . . . just tragic.'

'I'm sorry, I didn't mean to . . . you know.'

Ivy smiles at me. 'I guess that's just how life goes sometimes. Things change, people change.' And she says it with such sincerity and apparent introspection that I experience a tickle of paranoia, as if, at some level, the sentiment also applies to us. I make a note to (paraphrasing Esther) fart less and buy flowers more.

'How long is he going to be here?' I ask.

'Not for long.'

'How long is that, then?'

Ivy shrugs. 'He's my brother.'

'He's a nice guy, don't get me wrong, but that sofa ain't big enough for the three of us.' It's meant to sound jocular, but I'm a bit pissed and it comes out with too much spin on it. 'We're going to need a bigger boat,' I say, trying to lighten the mood.

'You can always sit in the armchair,' Ivy says.

Not in my own, I can't.

It's true, Ivy does have an armchair. A piece of junkshop thrift that she personally sanded, glued, filled, varnished and reupholstered with rose-printed velvet. None of which make it any more comfortable – it's like trying to relax on a skeleton draped with a floral blanket. My armchair on the other hand, is a chocolate-brown recliner with magazine pouch, and it's stuffed with enough padding to stop a runaway train. You could drop a baby from a third-floor window onto that chair and the little bundle of joy would bounce once then drift off to sleep. We've discussed this, of course, but according to

Ivy my chair clashes with her rug, curtains and sofa. 'Leather goes with everything,' I told her. And – thinking she was being cute, I'm sure – Ivy said, 'Then it'll go just fine in the spare room, won't it?' I let it go, because that's what you do, isn't it. You compromise, bend, accommodate, let stuff go. Which is what I should do now, but (blame Frank) I've drunk too much wine for that.

'Not in my own,' I say out loud

Ivy looks at me – *this again* – as if I've just disappointed her.

The spare room is next to ours, and through the thin walls we can hear Frank stumbling and clattering about. Judging by the sudden cacophony of gunfire, explosions and screaming, Frank has just switched on my 42-inch HD TV. So now it's my turn to do the look of exasperation.

Ivy gets out of bed, thumps on the wall and shouts, 'Volume!' The sound halves, leaving it merely loud. Ivy hits the wall a second time. 'More!'

'Sorry!' bellows Frank.

The volume drops again so that it's now nothing more than an irritating bass rumble through the plasterboard.

'You didn't answer my question,' I say. 'How long is not long?'

Ivy climbs back into bed. 'I don't know. A week, a couple of weeks, maybe.'

'It's Christmas in three sodding weeks.'

'Fine, he'll be out before Christmas.'

'Fine,' I say.

Ivy turns out her light. And neither of us says *I love you*.

After the Chuck Norris film finished, I heard Frank get out of bed and begin rummaging around. It sounded like he was assembling flat-pack furniture, and it was only when I heard more gunfire and the throb of a familiar, muscular engine, that I realized he had found and plugged in my Xbox and was playing *Grand Theft Auto*. Ivy, of course, was deep asleep and sawing wood. After *Grand Theft Auto*, Frank plugged in a shoot 'em up I couldn't identify, and after that I'm pretty sure it was *Resident Evil*. I don't know what time I fell asleep but it wasn't before two, and as I eventually drifted off my mind was stuck in a scratchy, nagging loop: Ivy and surprise guests, first the babies (*it's okay*) and now Frank. My sleep was infested with banal stress dreams (locked doors, lost keys, a squeaking chair), and when I wake a little before seven a.m., it's almost a relief. It's still dark beyond the curtains, but the clock on Ivy's side of the bed casts enough light to illuminate her face. She looks like she's smiling in her sleep, but it might just be that her face is squashed against the pillow. I kiss her cheek, slide out of bed, pull on a pair of jogging bottoms and a T-shirt and creep out of the room.

I'm sitting on the sofa, sipping a coffee and reading the chapter where Ivy abandoned *Catch-22*, when Frank shambles into the room in his boxer shorts. And he really is a specimen: heavy bones, thickly muscled, coated in a layer of hard fat and thick fur. When we visited the Lees in Bristol, Ivy called her brother a gibbon, and the half-naked reality is only a small evolutionary step forward – as he stands before me now, yawning and scratching his armpit, Frank looks like something that's just rolled out of a cave instead of a bedroom.

'Morning, matey,' he says loudly, and I hold a finger to my lips, point down the corridor to where Ivy is, hopefully, still sleeping.

Frank makes a *silly me* shrug-and-grimace, and goes about fixing himself a coffee from the cafetiere. He plods over to the sofa and plonks himself down beside me, crossing his legs underneath himself, one big hairy knee pressed firmly against my thigh. His boxer shorts are agape at the fly and I can see more than I want to through the parted material.

'Morning,' he says again in a stage whisper. 'Sleep well?'

'Not entirely,' I tell him.

Frank nods as if this is of no real interest to him. 'What you reading?' he says, reaching across me to pick up the novel from the arm of the sofa. I close my eyes as his torso fills my vision, and a hair of some description tickles my cheek.

When I open my eyes again, Frank is inspecting the cover of *Catch-22*. 'Classic,' he says, laughing. 'Major Major Major Major.' But I don't get the joke.

Frank sips his coffee, scratches his belly, stretches expansively.

'You not cold?' I ask him. Hopefully.

'Never feel it,' he says, rubbing a hand over his thatched chest. 'Tell you what, though, I am Hank Marvin.'

My mind flashes onto the four expensive sausages I bought last night, for breakfast this morning. 'There's cereal in the cupboard,' I tell him. 'Help yourself.'

'Might just do that,' he says, jumping up from the sofa and landing with a thud on the floorboards.

'Cupboard above the sink,' I tell him. 'Bowls to the left, spoons in the drawer to your right.'

Frank selects a box of Bran Flakes and pours a gigantic pile into a bowl. He farts, doesn't comment.

'Want some?' he asks, rattling the Bran Flakes at me.

'Not hungry,' I tell him, which is only partially true. I'm

waiting for Ivy to get up so I can make very-expensive-sausage sandwiches.

Frank pulls open the fridge. 'Milk, milk, milk,' he says. 'Got any full-fat?'

'Only skimmed, I'm afraid.'

Frank sighs. 'Fair enou— hold on, snags! Now we're talking; do you mind?' he says, slapping the sausages down on the counter.

'Actu—'

Ivy walks into the room, yawning, rubbing her eyes. 'Morning, boys.'

'Morning, sis. Fancy a couple of sausages?'

'Amazing,' says Ivy. 'Frying pan's in the cupboard next to the dishwasher.'

'Dishwasher? Would have been useful information last night, don't you think?'

'It's more of a dish smasher, these days. Stopped using it after it broke my favourite mug.'

'There's coffee in the thing,' I say.

'Not any more there isn't,' says Frank. 'Shall I make more?'

'You're a star,' Ivy says to her brother.

I nearly say something to put the record straight, but the words taste petty in my mouth and I turn them into a long, noisy yawn. Ivy joins me on the sofa. She kisses me on the cheek and winks – a small thing just between us, and it says she is sorry and she forgives me and aren't we both silly and I'm still her number-one guy. 'Not eating?' she says.

I shake my head. 'Going for a run.'

'If you can wait half an hour, I'll come with,' says Frank.

He's cooking the sausages now and the smell of them sizzling in the pan is maddening. I look at Ivy with a conspiratorial, pleading expression and she returns it with a complicit smile and nods her head towards the door.

'I would,' I say, 'but if I don't go now I won't go at all.'

'Another time,' Frank says.

'You bet,' I tell him, but I wouldn't advise him to bet much.

I don't know how long I run for but I've covered a heck of a lot of Wimbledon Common, and I am exhausted and breathless when I trot back down our street. I've certainly been gone long enough for Frank to finish his breakfast – *my breakfast* – get a shower and cover his hairy barrel with some clothes. Or so you'd think. I hear a loud *thunk* as I enter the flat, the sound – it transpires – of the bathroom door closing behind Frank. As if the big hairy brute was peeping through the blinds, waiting for me to stick my key in the lock before running, giggling, to the bathroom. Ivy is lying on the sofa, reading.

'Hey, babe,' she says, heaving herself into a sitting position and resting *Catch-22* on the arm of the sofa.

While I lean against the doorjamb, stretching, Ivy swings her legs off the sofa and shuffles over to the kitchen area where she picks up a tea towel and fills a pint glass with water. At nineteen weeks pregnant with twins, she looks alarmingly large and moves with corresponding ponderousness.

'Here.' She hands me the water.

I drink half of the water in one gulp and use the tea towel to mop the sweat off my face and neck.

'Sorry about the sausages,' she says, falling back into the sofa. 'And the boeuf bourguignon.'

'It's fine,' I say, going to sit in the armchair.

'Uh huh,' Ivy says, and she points at the floor in front of the sofa.

'Don't know why you're worried about a little sweat,' I say. 'It'll be covered in sick and pee and poo in a few months. Everything will be.'

'Wonderful, isn't it,' says Ivy, and she places her hands on my shoulders and begins massaging the muscles. I relax into her hands, and she kisses the back of my neck. In the distance I can hear Frank singing under the shower. I can't make out the song, but it sounds as if he can at least hold a tune.

'Someone sounds happy,' I say.

'Bear with him,' Ivy says. 'It's been hard for him. I know he can be a bit of a galoot − *a lot* of a galoot actually.'

'A galooteus maximus?'

'Yes. Very clever.' Ivy presses her thumbs into the meat of my neck, working upwards from my shoulders to the base of my skull. 'Anyway,' she says, '. . . I know you're not meant to have favourites − brothers and whatnot − but, well, Frank's mine. Closest in age, and he always stood up for me in school.'

My scalp and temples tingle under Ivy's fingers and I emit a low moan, which I hope communicates both that I am listening and that I appreciate what Ivy is doing to my head.

'It was worse in secondary school,' she says. 'My scars, you know. In little school, I don't know, maybe the kids were too innocent, or maybe they were just too afraid of getting in trouble. But when I went to secondary . . . Scarface, Freak Face, Bride of Frankenstein . . .'

The commercial production Ivy and I met on was called 'Little Monsters' − four commercials featuring kids transformed into various horror staples: vampire, werewolf, zombie and, of course, Frankenstein's monster. Not for the first time, I wonder how awkward that must have been for her.

'There was one bastard,' Ivy continues, 'Aaron Harding. He used to call me Humpty – as in, couldn't be put back together again. And of all the names, that one stuck the longest. He'd hum the nursery rhyme in class and the other kids would start laughing. And when I blush, my scars stand out like streaks on bacon . . . no, like . . . sorry, I'm rubbish at similes.'

'At least you know what one is.' I begin to stand, but Ivy pushes down on my shoulders and continues to manipulate the muscles of my back. 'We'll ban it,' I say.

'What, similes?'

'No, Humpty Dumpty. You numpty.'

'Very poetic.'

'It's your literary influence,' I say.

'What, numpty?'

'Sure. As in numptious, numpacity, numpate.'

'I'd quit while you're ahead, if I were you. So, this was in my third year, and Frank, because of how our birthdays work, he was only one year behind me. And he's always been a whopper – he was ten pounds something when he was born, God help my poor mum. Anyway, by the second year Frank was playing rugby for the third year first team. Same as horrible Harding.

'Excellent,' I say. 'So he smashed him?'

Ivy laughs. 'Frank? He's a softy, he's never hit anyone in

his life. No, it was better than that. He started a rumour that Harding had a tiny penis.'

'And did he?'

'Not according to Frank. But it wasn't big enough for the rumour not to take, either. Frank started calling him Acorn instead of Aaron, then the rest of the team are calling him Acorn, then everyone in his class and then everyone in school. Funny thing is, by the end of the fourth form no one was calling me Humpty anymore; in fact the whole name-calling thing in general had pretty much stopped. But they called Harding Acorn until the day he left.'

'All thanks to Frank.'

'All thanks to Frank.'

Ivy's favourite brother is still in the shower, gargling the chorus to 'Bohemian Rhapsody'.

'So he's a softy?'

'As a kitten.'

'Do you reckon I could take him in a fight, then?'

Ivy laughs so loudly and abruptly that I feel her spit, snot or both splash onto the back of my neck. 'God, sorry!' she says. 'It's just . . . remember in *Tom and Jerry*, how the bulldog would slam Tom from side to side like a ragdoll?'

'Before my time,' I say. 'Was it in colour?'

Ivy flicks me on the ear. 'Any more of that and I'll set my bulldog on you.'

In a variation on the previous evening, Frank falls asleep in front of the TV, whereas Ivy is as lively as a 5-year-old full of chocolate cake – telling me about her day, asking about mine, fidgeting in her seat and offering thoughts and opinions on everything from the Saturday-night movie to the colour of my socks. After Frank comes abruptly awake (his sister's wet finger in his ear), he takes himself to bed and Ivy announces that we are going for a walk.

'It's almost eleven,' I tell her.

'So?'

'And it's winter.'

'Yes?'

'And you're nineteen weeks pregnant. With twins.'

'I know,' says Ivy, 'second trimester, baby! Now get your coat.'

To say she jumps up from the sofa would be an exaggeration, but she is on her feet in under a minute, which, under the circumstances (approximately twenty extra pounds of bodyweight) is pretty impressive.

It's past chucking-out time, and the open expanse of mulchy grass is quiet as we circle the duck pond and head towards the denser woodland of Wimbledon Common proper.

'Spooky,' says Ivy. 'Are you scared? I bet you are.'

'Bloody freezing is what I am.'

Ivy's arm is looped through mine and she pulls me tight against her side. 'I've got heat to spare,' she says. 'Snuggle in.'

'I hope you're not planning on making a habit of this.'

'Shh, don't ruin it. I'll be crashed out on the sofa for the next seventeen weeks. Enjoy it while you can.'

'Doesn't sound long, does it? Seventeen weeks.'

'Nuh huh; four of us soon.'

'I expect we'll spend a lot of time up here, with the twins. Picnics, bikes, kites.'

'Treasure hunts.'

'Paper boats.'

'See those trees?' Ivy says.

'I can't see anything.'

'They are *teeming* with conkers in the autumn. Hundreds and hundreds of them.'

'Better hope we have boys, then.'

Ivy shoves me with her shoulder. 'I was conker champion of our house, thank you very much. Trick is to soak them in vinegar and bake them.'

'Isn't that cheating?'

'That attitude is why you will ne—' Ivy stops walking. 'Shh, look . . .'

'What, where?' Ivy takes my chin in her hand and points my head towards a stand of thin sparse trees. Something moves and a pair of eyes glint out from the tangled undergrowth. My heart quickens. 'The fuck is that?'

'Womble.'

'Can you eat Womble?'

'Yes, but they make better slippers.'

I laugh under my breath.

'Hang on, what happened to those slippers I bought you?'

'They made my feet hot, and Uncle Bulgaria's fur made my ankles itch.'

Ivy sighs. 'I should take them back.'

'God no, I love them. Just not . . . on my feet.'

The Womble darts out from the bushes as if it's going to attack.

'Jesus Christ!' This from me.

'Calm down, it's only a fox.'

The fox is maybe twenty yards away now, facing us down, challenging us. I'm acutely aware of my own breathing as the three of us stand regarding each other in the thumping silence.

'How fast can foxes run, do you think?'

'Don't be such a wuss,' Ivy says. 'It's more afraid of you than you are of it.'

'Debatable. I hate foxes.'

'What have foxes ever done to you?' Ivy says.

'What have they ever done *for* me?'

'Well, they eat rats, for a start. No foxes and you'd be tripping over rats the size of babies.'

'Nice image. Can we go home now, please?'

Ivy claps her hands together. 'Go on! Scoot!'

The fox stares at her disdainfully for a second, before turning and walking casually away.

'See?' I say. 'Attitude problem.'

'The problem with foxes is bad PR,' says Ivy.

'What?'

'Did you know, for example, that foxes form strong family units?'

'Can't say that I did.'

'Well, they do,' says Ivy as she sets off walking again. 'And they breed like crazy.'

'Lucky foxes.'

'And when all the cubs come along, the aunties and big sister foxes all pitch in and help to raise them. Put some human families to shame.'

'When did you become an authority on foxes?'

Ivy hums all the syllables of *I don't know*. 'Must have read it somewhere.'

'Okay, I take it back. Foxes are amazing.'

'Fox is a good name,' says Ivy.

'Not on my watch.'

'Or Vixen.'

'Only if we have one with superpowers.'

'What would be your favourite superpower?' says Ivy, tugging on my arm and dragging me further into the deep dark woods. 'For me it would have to be mind control. Or time travel.'

'How about night vision?'

Ivy begins on a long, tangential riff about the pros and perils of time travel. It's been four months since we went on our impromptu road trip from London to the Northwest. Ivy would have been pregnant at the time, but we were blissfully ignorant of the double miracle unfolding behind her belly button. It feels like a lifetime ago now, and in a way it was – *two lifetimes*, in fact. When we weren't in bed, the car or a pub, we were rambling through late-summer countryside, walking nowhere and talking about nothing. Not unlike we are now. It will be roughly eighteen years before we have that kind of extravagant liberty again, but in return we get picnics and kites and treasure hunts and Wombles and all the conkers a kid could wish for. From where I'm standing – in cold mud while Ivy talks nonsensically about quantum cause and effect – it sounds like a pretty good deal. As Ivy expounds on the inherent dilemmas of meddling with history (assassinating Hitler, saving Hendrix) I know one thing for certain – if I could go back in time to the day Ivy became pregnant, I wouldn't change a single thing.

Chapter 14

I normally see El on a Tuesday, but Ivy is working tomorrow, so here we are – me, El and Ivy – at the Natural History Museum on a fresh Monday morning in December.

The last time I saw El – six days ago, now – it followed a similar pattern to every other Tuesday: we ate pizza, drank alcohol-free beer and El fell asleep in front of a DVD. What was different was Phil; he was more drunk than usual when he got back from the pub, and correspondingly more tearful and maudlin. Part of it, I'm sure, is the ADRT sitting in a drawer in Phil's office – a signed four-page testament to the fact that El is not simply ill, but dying at an indeterminate speed. The other part, Phil only hinted at, but I think loneliness has a lot to do with it. He spends practically every waking moment with El, but it's not the El he fell in love with. Instead, Phil is left with a bad copy of the original that can only serve as a constant reminder of what and who he is living without. When he came back from the pub that night, Phil was so drunk he was afraid to carry El upstairs, and asked me to do it for him. El is in a separate room now, and sleeping in a form of cot. Sitting on top of his single mattress is an inflatable, four-sided cocoon called a SafeSides. This protects El from falling out of bed or bashing himself against the wooden bed frame, both of which are a significant risk since his tics and twitches have become more exaggerated.

'Poor soul doesn't even get a break while he's sleeping,' Phil told me through more tears.

Phil is taking antidepressants now, but it's as clear as the bags under his eyes that they aren't proving entirely effective. I offered again to take El out for the day, and again Phil demurred.

When I told Ivy about it on Saturday night, she said we should 'kidnap El' and take him to the Natural History Museum for a day. And these are the kinds of things love is made of, I suppose, because I have never (in our long four months together) felt closer to Ivy than I did at that moment. There have been other moments, of course – the first time we made love, the day we first saw our babies on the sonographer's screen, the night she asked me to move in with her – and while they have been both wonderful and profound, they were also, to an extent, inevitable: a million couples do these things every single day. But this empathy and understanding towards both El and Phil, the desire to be involved, it just reminded me how much I love her.

I phoned Phil this morning to check he and El were home, saying little more than I needed to 'collect something'. Neither Phil nor El has met Ivy before and her unannounced visit provided enough shock and laughter that Phil put up no resistance when we announced our intention to take El out for the day. We ordered a taxi and it arrived before we'd finished our first cup of coffee. I just hope Phil uses his day well.

For El's part, I haven't seen him happier or more excited in a long long time. El has a wheelchair now; he can still walk, but he tires quickly and stairs are practically impossible. Ivy is slower moving, too, and she takes some of the weight off her feet by leaning on the handles of El's chair as she pushes him into the central hall of the museum.

Much of El's excitement has been the prospect of a day at the museum, but he is also beside himself at having finally met Ivy, and hasn't stopped talking at her since we loaded him into the taxi. He's even managed to get her name right. But as we cross the threshold of the museum, even El falls silent. The word that springs to mind is cavernous, but no cavern was ever this expansive or flooded with light. The wide tiled floor is enclosed on either side by two tiers of stacked, terracotta arches, each one maybe twenty feet high and leading the eye upward to a vaulted ceiling, composed of decorative panels and broad glass panes. At the far end of the hall a row of tall stained-glass windows boom with rose-tinted sunshine. Majestic, ethereal, magnificent, opulent – they all come close. You could almost miss the museum's most famous exhibit, but of course nobody does. It's early in the day and the schools are still in term time, so there are fewer visitors than there might be; even so, there are a couple of hundred people in the main hall. And, of course, they are entirely preoccupied with the twenty-six-metre dinosaur skeleton that has pride of place.

'J... Jesus!' El points at the giant pile of mahogany-coloured bones. 'L... look the s... size o' that f... fuckig diosonour!' he says, his voice echoing around the glorious space. 'R... right, l... less go ex... explorin'.'

Without El we might be tempted to flow with the crowd, but both his wheelchair and his unselfconscious awe force us to amble at a slower, more considered pace.

After graduating from Bristol University with a degree in Biology, El came to London to do a Ph.D. in something involving bugs and DNA. Maybe this is why he is so uncharacteristically quiet – reverential, even – as we stand mute before the fossils, models and stuffed specimens of beasts prehistoric, extinct and – you could be convinced – simply imagined. We examine glass cases displaying shells and minerals and teeth and petrified dung ('Dino poo!'). We linger over glass cases of butterflies, skulls and preserved footprints from one hundred million years ago. An archaeopteryx fossil in a square slab of rock looks like some prehistoric fairy-tale book, and a decorated dolphin skull makes the hairs stand up at the nape of my neck. We stare open-mouthed at a woolly mammoth, a sabre-toothed tiger, a duck-billed platypus and a gorilla that bears an uncanny resemblance to Ivy's brother Frank.

'Want me to push?' I ask Ivy, and she accepts the offer.

'Practice for you,' says El. 'For when b... baba c... comes along.'

We stop to look at a Neanderthal skull. The yellowed bone is broken and incomplete, as if it's been dropped and shattered at some point in the last couple of hundred thousand years. After pondering the exhibit for a minute, El turns to Ivy and stares at her face. He holds a shaking hand to his cheek as if checking to see if his own face is scarred like Ivy's.

'F... Fisher din't tell me,' he says. 'W... w...'

'What happened?' Ivy asks.

El nods.

Ivy smiles, squats down beside the chair so that her face is level with El's. 'When I was eight, I decided to try and tap dance on top of a glass coffee table.'

El's head wobbles on top of his shoulders; he pulls a face that suggests he doesn't believe this.

''s true,' she says. 'The table was toughened glass, so I thought it'd be okay. Although it's so long ago now, I'm not really sure if I was thinking anything at all.'

'B... blimey,' says El, 'b... bet you w... won' do th... that again.'

Ivy laughs and shakes her head. I've been worried about El meeting Ivy — worried that he'd say something to offend her, or incriminate me. But seeing them together now, I feel myself relax and I regret not introducing them to each other sooner.

Before we leave, we stop at a glass case containing a first edition of Charles Darwin's *On the Origin of Species*. And (with the exception of the dino poo) this captures El's attention more than anything else we have seen today.

'Old Ch... Charlie,' El says. 'He's my h... h...'

'Hero?'

El dismisses the word with a frustrated flick of his hand, as if it irritates him, but he nods to himself nevertheless. The ancient copy of Darwin's book is displayed alongside an imposing marble statue of the great man himself sitting in a hefty chair, beard rolling down his chest, coat draped across his knees. The symmetry between my friend in his wheelchair and Charles Darwin on his white marble throne is impossible to miss.

'F... fuckig g... g'netics.'

And seeing El sitting before his idol, twitching and jerking and diminished ... with the right soundtrack it could move me to tears.

'R... right,' says El, 'I need a p... pee, and one of y... you two is going to h... hold my imp... impressive exhibit.' He grins up at us, enjoying the effects of his hard-earned words.

Charles Darwin may well have developed the theory of natural selection, but I'll bet everything I have he wasn't as funny as my friend El.

We eat a late lunch at a posh restaurant in South Kensington. El struggles to grip cutlery now, so we have brought his own – a knife and fork with bicycle handgrips fitted over the handles to make it easier for him to hold.

Every time the waiter brings something to our table, El raises his knife and dings an imaginary bicycle bell. Far from being offended by this behaviour in a Michelin-starred restaurant, our waiter appears to be highly entertained by it. A lot of rich and famous people live around here, so maybe he's used to eccentrics. Either way, I tip him heavily, but this, too, seems to be nothing extraordinary – at least not to the waiter.

'You sh... should be s... savin'.' El points a shaking finger at Ivy's bump.

'He's right,' says Ivy, smiling. 'You're a family man now.'

'C... can I touch it?' El asks, and he has the expression of a child asking to stroke a puppy.

Ivy moves her chair so that it's alongside El's, takes his hand and places it inside her shirt on the bare skin of her bump. I'm expecting some lewd comment or innuendo from El, but he simply closes his eyes and sits very still (as still as he can) with his hand against Ivy's tummy.

'Did you feel them move?' asks Ivy, once El has removed his hand.

El nods, and when he opens his eyes they are shiny with tears. He turns to me: 'So y... you goin' p... pr... propose or w... what?'

Ivy laughs awkwardly and I excuse myself to the loo.

In the taxi back to Earl's Court, El sits on the back seat

next to Ivy, holding her hand and, after only a few minutes, falling asleep with his head resting against her arm. Ivy strokes his head absent-mindedly.

It's close to five o'clock when we drop El at home, and I help him up the steps to his front door as the driver removes El's wheelchair from the boot. Phil invites us in for wine, but Ivy and I are both exhausted and the taxi is waiting to take us on to Wimbledon. With El safely installed in front of the TV, Phil comes to the taxi to say goodbye.

'Same time next week?' he says, and then, seeing our expressions, he laughs. 'Your faces!' he says, and his laughter catches until he is wiping tears from his eyes. It's the most relaxed I've seen Phil in months, and I feel pretty good about myself for it. Not good enough to take the bait, though.

'You know there are places,' Ivy says, 'where you can put El into daycare?'

Phil looks up at the clouds, puts his hands in his pockets then immediately removes them.

'It might be good for you,' Ivy says. 'Both of you.'

Phil sighs and it feels like a gesture of acquiescence, or the step towards it. He leans in to the cab, kisses Ivy on the cheek, then turns to me.

'If I were you, William, I'd put a ring on this girl's finger and quick.' And then, of course, he bursts into tears.

Ivy sleeps in the taxi back to Wimbledon, and if there's a happier man stuck in slow-moving rush-hour traffic this evening, then I'd like to shake his hand.

When Frank gets back from work a little before eight, I'm dozing in front of a property show and Ivy is reading her book club assignment. Frank is carrying four bags full of groceries, and after a cursory hello, he changes out of his work clothes and starts cooking a spaghetti bolognese for the three of us. It's a nice gesture, of course, but to me it feels a little too much like he's moving in.

This is only his fourth night staying with us so it's too soon to have formed a concrete impression of the guy, but he seems unusually quiet as we eat our supper. Maybe he's tired – it's the first day of his working week, after all. Frank divides his professional time between St Mary's Hospital in Paddington and a private practice in North London. Where he was today, I don't know, but both are an awkward commute from Wimbledon, and he is surely earning enough to rent a flat of his own somewhere more convenient. As a prelude to sewing this seed, I ask how long it took him to travel to work this morning, but he merely shrugs and grunts. I comment on how unreliable the District Line is, and Frank collects the dirty supper dishes, takes them to the sink and washes up.

I flick on the TV and we watch a smug couple convert

an abandoned brewery into a million-pound, eco-friendly, context-sympathetic mansion with a swimming pool. Ivy is asleep within five minutes, but tired as I am, one-minute to nine is too early for me to turn in. I begin flicking through the channels and Frank drops onto the sofa at the exact moment I land on the opening sequence of an Arnold Schwarzenegger movie.

'Beer,' he says, handing me an open bottle of Asahi.

I make idle chit-chat throughout the movie, not because I want to know how Frank's day was, or how many bedrooms his house in Bushey has, or whether he plays for the local rugby team … I ask these things because I'm hoping to make the bugger homesick. I ask about Christmas, because Christmas is a time for children and I want to establish whether or not Frank is interested in salvaging his marriage so he can remain a part of his son's life. Frank doesn't answer any of my questions with more than the minimum number of syllables, but he answers my overarching line of enquiry very eloquently just after Mr Schwarzenegger shoots Sharon Stone, his duplicitous wife, in the head.

'Consider dat a divowce,' says Arnie.

'You fucking tell her, mate,' says Frank.

And that, it seems, is that for Frank and Lois.

*

According to the bedside clock, it's 2.58 a.m. when Frank gets up to piss out four bottles of Asahi, then turns on the Xbox and starts shooting shit. And however sorry I feel for myself, at least I'm not the unfortunate patient scheduled to have his fillings drilled out by a tired, depressed and hungover gorilla in approximately six hours' time.

Chapter 15

Friday night is a bad night for a stag do. But needs must when you have twelve men to marshal; all but one are married or living with someone and the majority have children, which effectively means I have to accommodate the plans and demands of more than thirty individuals. It's December and there are presents to buy, decorations to dust off, parties to attend, family to visit, displaced children to take to the panto ... and this is the single day this month on which all of Joe's buddies are available. Ivy and I have our twenty-week scan tomorrow morning – the unambiguously named 'anomaly scan' – and it's caused no small amount of friction that I'll be attending with a honking great hangover. But the best man's priorities (and those of his girlfriend and unborn twins) are last on the list, apparently. Joe isn't getting married until the middle of

February, so January would make more sense. However, the average age of the stags is closer to forty than thirty, and for a depressing number of them January is a month of voluntary or enforced abstinence. February is too close to the big day for approval by Jen, Joe's fiancée, so here we are in a central London strip bar on the penultimate Friday before Christmas.

The reason most stag dos happen on a Saturday is that it gives you the option to distract yourself during the day with go-karts, clay-pigeon shooting, basket weaving or whatever. You get a chance to ease into the day and pace the drinking. On Friday nights, though, it's straight out of the office and into the pub. You've been thinking about it all day, watching the clock, hating your job and already tasting that first drink. By six thirty we were three pints in, by seven thirty we hit the tequila, and by eight we were a seething, braying, back-slapping mob. By nine we were fading with terminal velocity and Joe – eyes simultaneously drooping with drink and flashing with maniacal zeal – insisted we 'hit the tits'.

We are surrounded – literally *surrounded* – by aggressively beautiful, filthily athletic, over cosmeticized, underdressed women. It's all your teenage dreams come true, but to look at the faces (disdain, despair, fear, shame, regret) of the dozen drunken men in attendance, you'd think we were watching breaking news of some brutal, unfathomable atrocity.

'I mean, look at that. Just … Look. At. *That!*' says Malcolm, indicating the balloon-tight buttocks of the stripper rotating her hips just inches in front of his face. He sighs as he places his head in his hands.

'Tell me about it,' says Tom, laying a comforting hand on Malcolm's shoulder.

'Before she had kids, my missus had an arse like a Chinese swimmer,' says Finn, slicing a shallow curve through the air with the blade of his hand. 'Now …' He stares at his cupped hands, weighing their imagined contents and frowning as if trying to ascertain just what the hell he is holding. 'Tits, I understand,' he says. 'Breastfeeding, and all that. But how does having a baby make your arse fall off the back of your legs? Explain that to me, someone.'

The collective tuts, shakes its head, blows air through its lips and sips its beer.

And these are your victims, these old stags, the middle managers, school teachers, lawyers, husbands and fathers who can't accept that they are no longer 18-year-old bucks. And this – life and time and reality – is the atrocity.

'Show some fucking tact, you bell end,' says Steve. He flicks his eyes in my direction.

'Sorry,' says Finn, slapping my back. 'No offence. Some birds get away with it, don't they. How many has Posh Spice squeezed out?'

'A lot,' says Tom.

'Exactly,' says Finn. 'And you still would. I know I would.'

'Two times,' says Malcolm.

'Yeah, so maybe your bird ...' Finn snaps his fingers in the air.

'Ivy,' I say.

'Grows on you,' says someone, possibly Dave.

'So maybe Ivy,' continues Finn, 'maybe she won't get wrecked. Maybe she'll be lucky, yeah.'

'Thanks, mate,' I say, clinking my pint of overpriced watered-down lager against Finn's. 'That means a lot.'

'Welcome,' he says, entirely missing the sarcasm.

'Mind you,' says Steve, 'she's having twins, isn't she?'

'Two of them,' I say.

'Hmm,' says Finn, shaking his head, apparently deciding that Ivy has as much chance of getting lucky with pregnancy as he does of getting lucky with Destiny the stripper.

Last night was date night. Ivy and I went to the cinema again, this time to watch a pregnancy-themed rom-com that managed to miss all its beats. The only halfway decent scene was the one we'd already seen in the trailer. I sat in the dark, eating my popcorn and pre-producing Suzi's script inside my head. Ivy got up to pee twice, and she yawned so deeply and often it was infectious. We should have walked out but this was only our second date night and I guess neither of us wanted to be the one to end it. After the movie I just wanted to go home and flake out on the sofa, and I'm sure Ivy (sore back, swollen ankles, indigestion) did, too. But we have a Frank on our sofa, so flaking out ain't what it used to be. We went for a late supper in The Village and spent the majority of the meal in a tired, disengaged silence. Ivy worked on a commercial earlier in the week, and when I asked how it went she told me, 'It was okay. You know how it is . . . it was fine.' Ivy asked how the cheese commercial was shaping up, but what is there to say? *I hate it; It's junk; I feel like a prostitute . . .* I said it was shaping up fine.

I started to tell Ivy about Suzi's script and found myself suddenly animated; I told her the plot of *Reinterpreting Jackson Pollock* and she told me she hated the title. I agreed and asked her to help me come up with an alternative, but Ivy didn't come up with much; didn't even try, it seemed to me. Ivy has agreed to do the hair and make-up on the production, and I asked if she'd had any thoughts about it.

She hadn't. I told her I was nervous about shooting a sex scene, and laughed. Ivy made a small harrumphing sound, but it wasn't a laugh.

Christmas is eleven days away and we have yet to discuss where we will spend the break. Whenever I've been in the country, I've always gone back to Dad's, but then again, I've never had anywhere else to go. I ask Ivy if she's bought my present yet and she tells me, 'No, not yet.' I tell her she'll need to get two because my birthday is on Christmas Day, and Ivy tells me, yes, she knows.

'Jesus,' I say, 'you could at least pretend to be interested.'

And I take myself quite by surprise. The outburst, as contained, timid and frankly justifiable as it is, goes down about as well as the steak, which, while we're on the subject, is a little disappointing.

'What do you want me to say?' Ivy asks.

'I don't know. Anything?'

'You've hardly taken a breath.'

'And you've hardly said a word.'

'I'm tired.'

'I know,' I tell her. 'You've been tired for the last twenty weeks.'

Ivy doesn't respond. Cuts a piece of broccoli in half then doesn't eat it, just sets her knife and fork down on her plate. This should be my cue to back off, but I have another point to make.

'I'm sorry if I'm excited about it,' I say. 'It's the only thing I've got right now.'

I don't mean it the way it comes out, and I think Ivy knows this, but we're in the heat of bicker and the rules state that Ivy cannot let this go.

'The only thing?' she says.

'The only thing I have to myself, I mean. The only thing I'm doing just for me.'

'Fine. Maybe you should find another make-up artist, then.'

'Don't be like that.'

'Like what?'

Ivy's default setting is relaxed and playful. Frank and her parents are the same, so nature and nurture obviously shook hands on this one. It's one of the first things that drew me to Ivy and one of the best things about living with her. Like the way she sets me up, then smiles and paints a number 1 in the air every time I take the bait. But there is no mischief in the question she has just asked: *Like what?* So maybe I should ask myself why she's acting so out of character, but then it's not in my nature to not be an idiot. It's in my nature to swim towards the worm – fake, fat or fearsome – and swallow it whole.

'Petty,' I say.

'Petty?'

I shrug, take a mouthful of tough steak.

'Do you know what the day after tomorrow is?' Ivy asks.

'Saturday?'

'It's our twenty-week scan.'

'I know. You must have reminded me five times this week.'

'Someone has to.'

'Why, because I'm going to my best mate's stag do? I thought we'd had this conversation.'

'That's not what I'm saying. I told you, I don't mind.'

'Well, you weren't very convincing.'

A waiter asks if we've finished, we tell him yes. He goes to ask if we would like desserts, but I cut him short and ask for the bill.

'You know what they call tomorrow's scan?' Ivy asks, and I have to admit that I don't.

'If you'd bothered to read a book or spend five minutes online, you'd know it's called an anomaly scan.' And she articulates the word *anomaly* as if for a moron.

'So now I know, don't I.' And it's unlikely that the face I pulled made me any more endearing.

'You could at least pretend to be interested,' Ivy says,

playing my own words back to me. But coming from her mouth, in response to my childish expression, they carried approximately ten times the weight.

I paid the bill and we walked home together, side by side but to all intents and purposes apart. We spoke in abstractions – talking about the cold, the quiet, the dark – and it seemed to me that it took twice as long to walk home as it should have done.

While Ivy washed her face and brushed her teeth, I sat on the edge of the bed and thought of ways to apologize. And at the same time I wondered whether I should. I didn't ask for any of this, no one asked me if I was ready to start a family, and in light of the way things have worked out I think I've been astonishingly magnanimous. *It's okay*, Ivy said the first time we made love. But is it? Is this really okay? If anyone should be apologizing, surely it should be Ivy. I replayed the night's conflict over and over in my head as I tried to fall asleep, analysing the words, gestures and inflections. On a rational level I just about managed to convince myself that I didn't do anything wrong, but on every other level I knew that I could have handled the whole thing with a heck of a lot more grace, sympathy, empathy, compassion and all that other grown-up good stuff. When I finally drifted off to sleep last night I had resolved to make Ivy breakfast in bed and, time permitting, run down to the shops and (as per Esther's instructions) buy flowers. But by the time I woke, both Ivy and Frank were already up and I was already running late.

This morning Ivy, Frank and me all had different places to be before nine thirty, and we rotated between bathroom, bedrooms and kitchen, squeezing past each other in the hallway, sleepy-eyed and wet-haired, coffee and toast in hand, muttering good mornings and after yous. In an attempt to find five (or even two) minutes alone with Ivy, I ended up making three cups of coffee and brushing my teeth twice, but all for nothing. Whenever I contrived to put myself in the same space as the mother of my foetal children, she was either leaving that space with a full mouth (breakfast, toothbrush, coffee), or the space was simultaneously occupied by Frank.

We left the flat as a threesome, clean, dressed and miraculously unscolded, but the whiff of last night's spat (*Row? Fight? Surely more than a tiff*) lingered. Smiles had been exchanged, elbows squeezed and enquiries made into the quality of each other's sleep, but there was still a lingering tension that would only dissipate with a kiss, a *sorry* and a bloody big hug. We walked together down the hill to the tube station, talking about our plans for the night and the weekend. After work Frank was heading to Watford to spend the weekend with a friend; I, of course, had a stag-do to coordinate; and Ivy has an old friend, Sophie, coming to stay for a girly night in.

I bought coffees for everyone at Wimbledon station, and we boarded the same train managing to find three seats together. I made a quick calculation that the seat opposite Ivy would provide me with a better vantage point from which to broker reconciliation – blown kisses, funny faces, a mouthed apology – but before I could sit, Frank had volunteered me into the seat beside her. So as we trundled north and east, I made do with a hand on the knee, leaning into Ivy, attempting to send love and contrition via the gentle pressure of my shoulder. I left the train first, and when I kissed Ivy goodbye she pressed her hand against my cheek and it felt as if we'd repaired some of the rift. Frank gave me a hearty hug, patted my back as if to say, *it'll be fine*, and I dived through the closing doors and into the sea of Friday morning commuters.

Joe and I had cheese meetings with the location direc-tor, art department and DP, and I spent what was left of the day working in a Sprocket Hole office, making final preps for Monday's shoot. By five thirty I'd worked a full day on a bad night's sleep and was ready for the sofa and an early night. One of the very last things I wanted to do was drink too much and hit a strip club with twelve, mostly miserable men.

Not everyone is so appalled, however. Gaz, a junior director from the Sprocket Hole, couldn't grin any wider or concentrate more completely on the woman straddling his lap. I know what the guy earns; it's not much, and he must have deposited an entire week's wages into G-strings tonight. Bob, a recent divorcé, is leering with such cartoon intensity (you get the unsettling impression that his bugged-out eyes will at any moment eject themselves from his skull and into the cleavage of the dancer) that he has drawn the scrutiny of a square-headed bouncer. Even Joe appears to be having a small amount of fun. And say of me what you will, but if a beautiful 19-year-old wants to take her clothes off for me, I'm more than happy to watch.

Stan, an old school friend of Joe's, held forth with the idea that stripping is the ultimate feminist act. 'Who's got the power? Tell me that? They *choose* to do this. Half of them are sodding students, they could be working in a bar, restaurant or whatever, but they *choose* to work here. And why?' Stan rubs his finger against his thumb. 'Yes, exactly. Money, *our* money. This isn't human trafficking; these girls earn more than we do. You want to talk about power? Look at Bob – he look like he's in control to you? No, exactly, he's the one being exploited. Stripping? It's the ultimate feminist act, I'm telling you. Burning your bra's all well and good, but getting your growler out for cash – that's fucking feminism, mate.'

Impassioned as Stan's rhetoric is, I'm not sure it would carry much truck with Germaine Greer. Or maybe it would; you never know with feminists. For my part, I simply think it's rude not to show your appreciation. These women work hard, stay in shape, eat right, practise their routines (you try a backflip into inverted no-hands pole slide wearing high heels) and their make-up is immaculate if not exactly subtle. They are professionals, and the least you can do is smile. Joe, apparently, agrees.

'For fuck's sake!' he says, slamming his pint down. 'I'm trying to fucking enjoy this.'

'Sorry,' says Malcolm.

'Yeah,' chimes in Finn, 'sorry, mate.'

'Take a leaf out the nipper's book,' says Joe, slapping Gaz so hard on the back that the youngster's nose comes within a downy hair of getting wedged between a dancer's buttocks.

'Phwoarr!' says Tom, unconvincingly.

'Get 'em off,' says Stan, somewhat redundantly.

And just as everyone is warming to the agenda, it all goes rapidly and grotesquely wrong.

'Gnnurghafffkkkk!' says Bob, drawing the attention of

everyone within earshot, including his dancer (Mercedes) and the bouncer.

His jaws are clamped and the cables at the side of his neck are standing out now, as if he's attempting to lift a car off a 2-year-old. And even in the club's low blue-tinted light, you can see that his face is red with the effort of self-restraint. Mercedes takes a half-step backward, glances uncertainly at the bouncer and – to her eternal credit – continues dancing.

Bob's lips part, revealing his teeth in an ugly, feral grimace that alone should be grounds for confinement in the secure wing of Wandsworth prison. 'Struffnprrngnang,' he manages, shaking his head with apparent loathing.

I too glance at the bouncer and his posture brings to mind a cage-fighter waiting for the bell.

'What the fuck are you on about, Bob?' says Joe, forcing a laugh.

The whole party is looking at Bob now, drinks halfway to mouths, the other dancers momentarily forgotten.

Mercedes – naked except for a tiara and a thimbleful of glitter – smiles uncertainly, lifts her arms above her head and undulates like a snake rising from a basket. And this, it would appear, is the final straw for Bob.

He lunges forward, one hand extended, fingers splayed as if waiting to receive a basketball, the other making a grab between his own legs. The bouncer is a blur, descending on Bob before he is halfway off his stool and wrapping one mitt around his neck and the other around his outstretched wrist. Bob's mouth comes suddenly unhinged and he lets out a cry – no, a scream – of such anguish that the goon releases his grip and Bob drops to the floor as if shot.

The ambulance driver calls it an inguinal hernia. 'Not uncommon and not life-threatening,' apparently. 'Excruciatingly painful, mind,' he says. Although anyone with eyes and ears doesn't need telling. Worried, perhaps, that a writhing screaming man might dampen the ardour of the other punters, two bouncers attempted to remove Bob from the floor, but Bob reached for a new octave and instead, someone brought a blanket. Mercedes (a student nurse, 'call me Sharron') stroked Bob's forehead and administered sips of water until the paramedics arrived.

'A good way of thinking about it,' says the paramedic, Carlo, a handsome man who looks like his uniform has been tailored with the sole purpose of dramatizing his biceps, 'is he's basically blown a gasket.' He turns to Sharron. 'And let's be honest, who can blame him.'

'Blown a gasket?' says Stan.

Carlo addresses his answer to Sharron, the two having established a professional camaraderie and maybe something more. 'You know where the inguinal cavity is?'

Sharron shakes her head. 'I don't think we've done that yet.'

'Here,' says Carlo, placing two fingers on his groin. 'The membrane, yeah? – it's basically ruptured, torn open, and a chunk of his lower intestine – a big one from the looks of it – has popped through the rip. Nasty business.'

'Jesus bloody wept,' says Joe, inflating his cheeks and holding a hand to his mouth.

'Intestines?' says Stan.

'Think about it like this,' says Carlo. 'You know when you get your sausages from the butcher, and he puts them in a plastic bag? Now, imagine exerting pressure on the bag ...' he clenches his fists, flexing his biceps as he mimes bending an iron bar or tearing a phone book in half. 'If the bag's weak, like those small white ones you get in the market ... well, something's got to give.' Carlo releases the tension in his arms and makes a sharp echoing *Pop!* with his full, wet lips.

'Fascinating,' says Sharron.

'I think I'm going to puke,' says Joe.

The entire stag party is outside, coats on, to see Bob into the ambulance. And the relief is palpable, with Gaz being the only one in any way reluctant to call it a night. I suggested we all relocate to a restaurant, but Joe (who never regained control over his gorge after learning that

233

Bob had begun the process of turning himself inside out) wasn't the only one who couldn't face the thought of food. Besides, everyone has something to do tomorrow, something that will be considerably less painful without a hangover: visiting in-laws, buying a turkey, fixing the toilet seat. Sharron accompanies us to the door (numbers have been exchanged between her and Carlo); dressed in Ugg boots, jogging bottoms and a baggy jumper, she looks small and timid. We hold an impromptu whip-round and (the fathers notably more generous) tip her in excess of a hundred pounds. Not a bad night for Sharron and Carlo, less so for Bob.

Joe and I hang back, bear-hugging and handshaking everyone onto the tube or into a taxi until it is just the two of us left.

'Right then,' he says, rubbing his hands together. 'Burger King?'

'I thought you were sick.'

'Sick of that lot of old women. It's like trying to enjoy veal with a convention of fucking vegans, know what I mean?'

'Serious?'

'Come on,' Joe says, steering me across the street. 'I'll buy you a Whopper. Oh, and I'm sleeping at yours tonight.'

'You are?'

'I am. And if Jen asks, we were out till four, did a shit-load of coke, got vomitingly drunk, kicked out a nightclub and Malcolm had a fight with a taxi driver.'

We're back at the flat before eleven.

'You're back early,' Ivy says as we walk into the living room. She and Sophie are huddled under a blanket, a bowl of popcorn balanced between them, a blurred freeze-frame (Rowan Atkinson, it looks like) on the paused DVD player.

'Not a word to Jen,' says Joe. 'She'll go fucking potty; accuse me of not taking it seriously. Joe, by the way,' he says, extending a hand to Sophie.

'Sophie, pleased to meet you.'

'And how you doing, gorgeous?' Joe says to Ivy, kissing her on the cheek.

'It's going,' she says, rubbing her stomach and scooching up to make room.

Joe squeezes onto the sofa between the girls, pulls the blanket up over his legs and rests the popcorn on his thighs. 'What's this?' he says, pointing his chin at the TV. '*Mr Bean?*'

'*Love Actually*, actually,' says Ivy, glancing towards me.

'Great film,' says Joe.

235

'Can I quote you on that?'

'Can you, fuck. This is a stag do – what goes on tour, stays on tour.'

I still have my coat on, still haven't said a word. 'About last night,' I say, and Sophie and Joe snap their attention from the popcorn to me. 'I'm sorry.'

Joe turns to Sophie, raises his eyebrows: *Ooh, interesting.*

'I'm sorry too,' says Ivy, and it looks like there's a film of tears on her eyes. She beckons me with two hands. I go to her, kiss her, give her the bloody big hug I've been holding onto since nine o'clock this morning.

'I could murder a cup of tea,' says Joe.

'Milk no sugar,' says Sophie.

'Raspberry leaf,' says Ivy.

'Ooh, second thoughts,' says Joe. 'One of those.'

'So, no strippers?' says Ivy, as I go about fixing everybody's drink order.

'Obviously,' says Joe. 'Chucked it in after half an hour, though.'

'Seems a shame,' says Sophie.

'Bob had a funny turn,' I say.

'Didn't have the stomach for it,' says Joe, and he laughs so hard Sophie has to rescue the popcorn.

'Care to share?' says Ivy.

'Another time,' Joe says. 'It'll put you off your popcorn.'

I administer various teas, and take a seat in Ivy's uncomfortable armchair.

'Ready?' she says, pointing the remote at the DVD player.

'Ready,' we say, and Rowan begins the business of gift-wrapping Alan Rickman's necklace.

Sophie left shortly after the film finished, and Joe is now tucked up in the spare room, vacated by Frank for the weekend. I'd hoped to wake up in a quiet house tomorrow morning, but I really should know better by now. After I've brushed my teeth and texted Jen (*Joe in bit of a state. Sorry. Staying with me, don't wait up x*), I find Ivy propped up in bed, waiting.

'Everything okay?' I say, climbing in beside her.

'I was going to give you this tomorrow,' Ivy whispers. 'But, seeing as you're home early.'

'It's almost one.'

'Okay, seeing as you're not trolleyed, then.' She reaches under her pillow and produces a small gift-wrapped box.

I experience a sudden, gut-squeezing panic. Christmas is more than a week away; we still haven't agreed on our plans, but the sight of this small package suggests that Ivy might be heading to her parents even earlier than planned. When I got back to the flat with Joe tonight, it appeared that all was forgiven, but now, confronted with a Christmas gift at one in the morning, it seems that I might have misjudged the situation.

'What's up?' says Ivy, holding the damned thing out towards me. 'It's not going to explode.'

'I'm sorry,' I say. 'About yesterday. I've been stressed. Stressed with work, and the stag do and the babies; and I know it's hard for you, harder than it is for me, obviously, but I've just go—'

'Fisher.'

'What?'

'I'm trying to give you a present.'

'Are you leaving?'

'What? Where?'

'Are you going back to Bristol?'

Ivy looks at me as if I'm high. 'Not right now, no.'

'So why are you giving me my Christmas present? I don't . . .'

'It's not a Christmas present,' Ivy says. 'Just take it before my arm drops off.'

I take the present; turn it over in my hands, inspecting it as if it's some kind of test I'm failing. 'What is it?'

'It's an apology. Will you just open it?' She's smiling.

Cautiously, I begin tearing the paper. 'You don't need to apologize, babes.'

'I'm a lot more fun when I'm not pregnant, honest.' Her smile is sincere but playful.

'I'll have to take your word for that, won't I.'

'Ouch.'

'Sorry, joke.'

Ivy sighs. 'This isn't easy, you know. I'm baring my soul here and—'

'Babes, seriously, I didn't mean it like that. Come on ...' I go to hold Ivy's hand but she pulls it away from me.

'I ... call me an idiot, but I thought you might be a bit more gracious about it.'

'Ivy, please ...' she shakes her head as a grin spreads across her face '... oh, you're kidding. You're *kidding*.'

Ivy shrugs. 'Never let your guard down, mister.'

'Seriously, babes, you're all the fun I can handle.' I kiss Ivy and she kisses me back.

'I know,' she says, smiling. 'Now open your present.'

Behind the paper is a small jeweller's box. Inside is a pair of black and silver clapperboard cufflinks.

'They're amazing,' I say. 'Thank you.'

Ivy kisses me. 'You're welcome.'

'You know, I don't actually have one of those ...' I indicate my wrists '... one of those shirts.'

'Really?' says Ivy, unconvincingly. She takes the cufflinks from me. 'Well how about I look after them for you until you do?'

'That's very kind of you.'

'Yes,' says Ivy. 'And I'll think of you every time I put them on.'

Chapter 16

The babies are more distinct on the monitor, they are moving and their hearts are beating; they look perfect. But we are tense, nevertheless. The sonographer measures our babies' heads, abdomens and spines, muttering under her breath as she punches numbers into a spreadsheet. She counts their legs, arms, fingers and toes. She checks for cleft lip, spina bifida, heart defects, brain abnormalities, misplaced organs and short limbs. And whilst, of course, it is possible any one of these things could be anomalous, I never thought they would be. Call it dumb optimism or subconscious denial, but ever since our twelve-week scan showed no evidence of Down's syndrome, not once have I worried that our children might have malformed hearts or misshapen limbs. I realize now that I have been guilty of gross complacency, and I can feel my own heart thump behind my ribs as the sonographer confirms that the twins' bowels, intestines and livers are inside their bodies, their spines are covered in skin and the valves of their hearts are present and functioning. And as the sonographer moves her cursor and squints at the monitor, I hold my breath and squeeze Ivy's hand.

Again we are in the Tooting café that serves bad coffee. Only this time I'm in a state of relief rather than shock, so I'm actually drinking the beige, lukewarm liquid that passes for a latte. If anything, it's worse than I remember.

Joe left this morning after eight hours' sleep and a full English breakfast; fresh, rested and ready to face the traditional post-stag berating. Today and tonight we have the flat to ourselves for the first time in a long time – just me, Ivy and our two perfect twins.

As she stares at the most recent photograph of our babies, Ivy's smile is so broad and involves so much of her face that her scars are pulled into deep crinkles. I've never seen her look more beautiful.

'What?' she says. 'What are you grinning at?'

'You,' I tell her, and I lean across the table and kiss her. 'I love you.'

And this greasy spoon is not the mountaintop, meadow or Michelin-starred restaurant I had in mind when I'd imagined saying these three words. I didn't think Ivy had any more smile in her, but it turns out that she does – just one more increment, and it lights me up.

'You took your time,' she says, blushing.

I nearly tell Ivy that I have, in fact, told her this once before, through a mouthful of jumper. But I'll save it for another time – when we're old and grey, perhaps.

Ivy leans across the table and kisses me lightly on the forehead, the nose and the lips – one, two, three. 'I love you, too.'

Mount Everest, Niagara Falls, the Hanging Gardens of Babylon . . . who needs 'em? This moment, at this stained and wonky table in south-west London, is absolutely perfect.

Chapter 17

Yesterday I shot the cheese commercial. For thirty seconds of old shtick, it took a lot of time and effort and we didn't wrap until after ten in the evening. That's fourteen hours under hot studio lights with a trolley-full of the world's seventh stinkiest cheese. I stood under the shower for twenty minutes when I got back to the flat and washed my hair three times. And in the morning I could still smell Limburger on my pillow. I'll probably have to throw out the clothes I wore. Ivy's morning sickness stopped several weeks ago, but she came close to a relapse this morning when she got a whiff of my cheesy carcass. I soaked in a steaming hot bath for a further thirty minutes before breakfast, and once again before leaving for Phil and El's two hours ago.

We're having an early Christmas dinner. The big day is

has trouble chewing and swallowing, so it can take him well over an hour to get through an average meal. I've learned to eat slowly when I eat with El, so he doesn't end up finishing his meal on his own. As a result, I am now sitting in front of a large plate of cold food in congealing gravy.

El oinks again. 'Piggies!' he says, and Phil, sighing, deposits a pair of bacon-wrapped sausages onto El's bright pink plastic plate. We are all, in fact, eating from plastic plates out of solidarity. El, however, is the only one drinking his meagre splash of champagne from a double-handled plastic sippy cup. We look like gate-crashers at a toddlers' party.

'Turkey's delicious,' I say.

'Yes,' says Craig. 'Very moist.' He articulates the last word with a good serving of camp. 'It can be a dry old bird, can't it.'

'Fisher works in advertising,' says Phil. 'He's a director.'

Craig raises his eyebrows. 'Très glam.'

'H... h... hardly.'

'Took the words from my mouth,' I say.

'Working on anything interesting?' Craig asks.

'Actually, I'm working on a short film.'

'Get you,' says Phil. 'What's it about?'

'Love, I suppose.'

'Aren't they all?' says Craig.

'T. . . title?'

I sigh a little. '*Reinterpreting Jackson Pollock.*'

There is a beat of silence.

'Interesting,' says Craig.

'Pollock,' says Phil.

'B. . . b. . . bollocks!' says El, as I imagined he would.

'You could be right,' I admit. 'I'm not crazy about it.'

Phil asks me to describe the plot, so I give a rundown of the story: art student meets girl; art student and girl make love on roof of library beneath a skyful of stars; girl dumps art student; art student decides to throw himself from library roof; art student thinks better of it.

'Ki. . . ki. . . killing himself 'c. . . 'cos he got d. . . dumped?'

'There's more to it than that.'

''cos he g. . . got f. . . f. . . dumped!' El seems offended by the idea.

'He doesn't go through with it.'

'F. . . f. . . fuckig fuckig s. . . stupid!' El's brow is knotted in frustration. He goes to put his knife and fork down, his arms not twitching now, but moving as if in slow motion. Even so, as he sets his cutlery down, he inadvertently knocks his cup to the floor. 'F. . . cunt!'

'Elly, darling,' says Phil. 'Settle down.'

Craig picks up the cup and places it back on the table.

'F... f... stupid s... story,' El says, and no one corrects him.

Val Doonican sings 'Chestnuts Roasting on an Open Fire' into the silence.

'I'm also shooting a Tampax commercial,' I say.

El goes still for a second, the tension seeming to drain from his small, failing body. Phil, Craig and El look at me as if they are assessing my sanity.

'T... T... Tapax!'

Craig laughs first, then Phil, then, after another few seconds, El. By the time I join in, we are all laughing so hard that Phil has to get up from the table to stop El falling from his chair, Craig has tears rolling down his cheeks and the back of my head feels like it's in a vice.

After Christmas pudding we pull crackers, then move through to the living room to exchange presents. I give El a box set of 'Allo 'Allo, and Phil a gift box full of assorted moisturizers and gels and creams. They give me a cookery book for Christmas and a book on parenting for my birthday. El falls asleep halfway through the first episode of 'Allo 'Allo, with his head resting on Phil's thigh.

'How's he been?' I ask.

Phil shrugs. 'He's not getting any better,' he says with a sad smile.

Craig is sitting in an armchair beside the sofa, and he reaches across now, placing his hand on Phil's wrist and squeezing it. And still no one has said anything to shed any light on who he is or how he fits into this picture. If there is something between Phil and Craig, I won't be offended and neither will El. Phil knows this (or should) because we have discussed it at excruciating length. El isn't who he used to be, and Phil deserves romantic companionship as much as anyone else. None of which makes me feel any more comfortable in the middle of whatever this is.

'His tics seem better,' I say.

'It's something else,' Phil says. 'Begins with a B. B . . . br . . . God, I'm beginning to sound like him now.'

'Bradykinesia,' says Craig, and how the hell does Craig know about it?

'What's brady . . . '

'Bradykinesia. It's when his muscles sort of freeze,' Craig explains, clenching his fists in front of his chest. 'The twitches haven't gone away entirely, but sometimes they're replaced with these incredibly slow movements.'

I look to Phil for confirmation of this. 'Both arms,' Phil says. 'For now.'

'And how are you?' I ask him.

'Okay,' he says. He flicks a glance towards Craig and then inspects his fingernails – what's left of them. 'In the

New Year . . . I'm going to put him in daycare. One day a week.'

'To start with,' Craig adds, and he nods at Phil as if to say: *Isn't that right?*

Phil doesn't say anything.

'That's good,' I say. 'About bloody time.' And Phil smiles.

The awkwardness from earlier is still present, and I don't think it will clear until Phil tells me what is or isn't going on with Craig. It's close to ten o'clock, so I make my excuses, hug Phil and shake Craig's hand.

As I stand to leave, El wakes up. 'Happy Christmas,' he says, sleepily and surprisingly easily. 'G . . . give my love to y' mum 'n' d . . . dad.'

Phil looks at me, slightly aghast, wondering perhaps if I am going to correct El and remind him that my mother died when we were teenagers. That I was in the cinema with him at the moment her car collided with the lorry.

'I'll do that,' I tell him, and El lowers his head back onto the cushion and falls back to sleep.

Ivy and Frank are curled up on the sofa when I get back to the flat, some movie on the crappy TV. Ivy has her head on Frank's shoulder; Frank has his huge sweaty feet on the coffee table, next to a greasy pizza box.

'Nice night?' asks Ivy.

I sigh. 'Sort of.'

'Blimey,' says Frank, 'I'd hate to see your face after a bad night.' He laughs, and Ivy gives me a small, apologetic smile.

I pick up the pizza box and take it to the kitchen bin, which, I discover, is too full to take one more item. I remove the heaving bag from the pedal bin and several cans, packets and wet tea bags clatter and splat to the floor.

'Fucking hell!'

'What's up?' Ivy asks.

'The bin,' I say. 'Did no one think to empty the bin?'

'Fine,' says Ivy, and she begins the process of levering herself out of the sofa.

'Whoa, whoa, whoa,' says Frank, putting a hand on Ivy's shoulder and getting up himself. But I'll be fucked if I'm going to let the bastard play the good guy now.

'I've got it,' I say. 'Watch your film.'

'Suit yourself,' Frank says, and I visualize myself throwing a dirty tomato can at the back of his fat head.

I take the bag downstairs to the bin in the front garden, and the temperature has dropped to somewhere in the region of freezing. When I get back upstairs my nose is running, my head aches and it seems I'm coming down with a sore throat. I must have had my chin on my chest when I came back from El's, because it's not until I walk into the flat for the second time this evening that I notice the decorations. Spray-can snowdrifts on the windows; loops of tinsel drooping from the underside of the break-fast bar; silver stars hanging from the light fittings.

'Squidge in?' says Ivy, patting the cushion beside her.

But I'm too tired and jaded to squash onto two-thirds of a cushion and watch the arse-end of whatever movie is on the box.

'I'll see you in bed,' I tell her.

'Don't let the bed bugs bite,' says Frank, and it annoys me more than it probably should.

I must have been more tired than I realized, because the next thing I know it's thirteen minutes past one in the morning and I think Ivy is in labour.

In my dream she was grunting and panting and pushing and shouting all manner of profanities, but as I come to with my pulse racing, she is as still and silent as a rock. Someone, though, is still moaning and gasping and it's get-ting louder and more insistent by the second.

I slip out of bed and pull on a pair of boxer shorts.

Frank is in what I now think of as his room. He is passed out in my expensive leather armchair in front of my HD TV and a still-playing porn film. From my horrified

vantage point in the doorway, I can see a toilet roll balanced on the arm of the chair and enough skin to ascertain
that Frank is almost certainly naked.

The room is small and there is scant passing space as I
creep to the TV, keeping my eyes pointed away from
Frank and whatever mess he's made on himself and my
beautiful recliner. As I turn the TV off, a split-second
before the room is dropped into darkness, I spot the DVD
case on the floor. And even in the dark I flush with embarrassment. The film is titled *Cocktopussy* – multi-armed,
megaboobed femme stood behind tuxedoed porn star, one
hand on his chest, one in his hair, another in his pants. As
is often the way with pornography, I'm not entirely sure
how this piece came into my possession, and I'm shocked
that it still is. I had – or so I thought – a thorough porn
clear-out when my last girlfriend, Kate, moved into the
Brixton flat last spring. Evidently, this DVD somehow survived that cull, and I'm only glad Frank found it rather
than Ivy. I think. I eject the disk, return it to the case and
slide it behind the wardrobe, making a mental note in red
ink and bloody big letters to retrieve and dispose of it at
the next opportunity.

Sneaking back out of the room is even more precarious
now that the room is entirely dark, and it's not made any
easier by my fear of stumbling into Frank's no-doubt sticky

lap. It takes two minutes and all of my skill to escape the room, but I make it undetected and unviolated. I creep back into my own bedroom avoiding all the creaky floorboards, remove my shorts with barely a whisper and lower myself to the mattress like a feather dropping to soft ground.

'Woke me up,' says Ivy, and she huffs and puffs as she hauls herself out of bed and off to the bathroom.

By the time she gets back into bed it's just about one thirty.

'You were up ages,' she whispers.

I consider telling Ivy that Frank was watching porn, but decide against it. It's a bastard thing to do, and it was, after all, my porn.

'Frank left the TV on. I had to turn it off.'

Ivy sighs. I kiss the back of her neck.

'How was El?'

'No better, no worse. There was some guy there – Craig – I've never seen him before. I think . . . I dunno, it was weird.'

'Weird how?'

'I think there might be something going on with him and Phil.'

'Awkward.'

'Yup.'

Ivy knows the history, and although she hasn't explicitly said as much, I get the impression she likes – or at least understands – the idea of Phil having a relationship with someone else.

'Was he fit?'

And despite the hour and clinging funk, I laugh, albeit very quietly. 'Not my type.'

'Sleep well, babes.'

'Christmas in a week,' I say.

Ivy *ha-hums*.

'We still haven't talked about where we're going?'

Ivy says nothing.

'You awake?'

'Not by choice.'

'That makes two of us,' I say. 'And we both know whose fault that is.'

Nothing.

'Do you know where he's going to be for Christmas?' I ask.

'Frank? Here, probably. On his own, poor thing.'

'He won't go to your folks' house?'

'Not without Lois and Freddy; Mum and Dad are funny about all that stuff.'

'What stuff?'

'Divorce.'

'Funny how?'

'Just funny.'

I turn on the light.

Ivy pulls the duvet up over her head. 'Christ, what are you doing?'

I pull the duvet down, revealing Ivy's scrunched-up and pillow-creased face. 'We haven't talked about Christmas.' Ivy opens her eyes with what appears to be great reluctance. 'Where we're going.'

'I was planning on going to my parents',' she says.

'I was planning the same. I mean, planning on staying with Dad.'

'Okay.'

'What? Okay, you'll come with me?'

Another sigh. 'Okay, you go to your dad's.'

'On my own?'

Ivy props herself up on her elbows, picks up a glass of water from the bedside table and takes a sip. 'You're welcome to come with me.'

'Does that mean you *want* me to come with you?'

'Yes. But I don't mind if you don't.'

'Well, I'd *really* like you to come with me,' I say.

'Mum and Dad'll be on their own.'

'They have each other.'

'You know what I mean.'

'What about your other brothers?'

Ivy shakes her head. 'Long flights, big families. It's only for a couple of days.'

'One of them's my birthday.'

'I know, I'm sorry, but ... this is the last Christmas before we have the babies. I want to be with my parents. I want to be where I'm comfortable.'

'As opposed to my dad's, where you won't be comfortable?'

Ivy shrugs. *Yes.*

'Charming.'

'It's not meant to be charming. I'm not making a big deal about you coming with me, am I?'

'No.' And maybe that's half the problem, maybe I'd be happier if Ivy did make a big deal about it – at least then I'd know she gave a shit about spending some time with me.

'We can do your birthday when we get back,' Ivy says. 'Just me and ...' she trails off.

'What? Just the two of us? What are we going to do with Frank? Lock him in his room with a bottle of wine and a packet of pretzels?'

'Shush.' Ivy frowns, flicks her eyes at the wall separating Frank's room from ours.

'Really? Shush? Me shush?'

'If it's not too much to ask.'

'Fine,' I say, and I turn out the light and drop to my pillow like a sack of dirty laundry.

Approximately thirty seconds later Ivy is breathing the deep slow breaths of someone heavily asleep, and the fact that she can do this while I'm lying here stewing only aggravates me further. In the next room, Frank creaks out of bed and bumbles into the bathroom for a two-minute piss, straight at the water and with the door wide open. And Ivy has the audacity to shush me. My dad described being in love as feeling like you're running as fast as you can. I felt that way with Ivy when we met, and for about two weeks immediately after. But if I'm honest with myself, lately it feels more like I'm tripping over my feet and that any minute now I might just fall and smash my face into the pavement.

Chapter 18

Before this winter, I hadn't been to the cinema in seventeen years. And here I am for the third time in three weeks. Suzi dips her hand into my popcorn, and I feel an entirely unjustified pang of guilt.

Yesterday a van arrived from John Lewis, carrying two flat-pack cots, two baby bouncers, two car seats, two Moses baskets, a double buggy, two cuddly elephants and a big box of nipple shields. The corridor of our flat is now an obstacle course; the utility cupboard is packed to capacity and ready to explode like something from a slapstick comedy. This morning I stubbed my toe on the boxed buggy underneath the dining table. In a perverse kind of way, I like the clutter; it's a great big visual reminder that there's a great big Frank in the room we should be transforming into a nursery. I stacked the Moses baskets on Ivy's side of the bed, to make it a little more difficult for her to get to the bathroom in the middle of the night. And when she stage-whispered 'bloody baskets' at six thirty this morning, I saw bright white subtitles reading 'Bloody Frank'. I probably should have felt guilty, but beside the cuddly elephants in the utility cupboard, there is still a big bloody elephant in the room – Christmas is just four days away now, and I still don't know where I'll be unwrapping my presents. And it's unlikely to get cleared up this evening.

It should be date night tonight, but Ivy is having Christmas drinks with her book club buddies while I eat popcorn in the dark with Suzi.

We met to talk about *Pollock* over lunch. So far Joe has found a director of photography and a soundman, we've looked at a couple of locations, briefed a casting director and it looks like this thing is actually going to happen. Over lunch we talked about the sex scene. It's going to be tricky for a few reasons. We'll be shooting on the roof of a four-storey building in the middle of the night. It will be cold and dark and logistically demanding. Suzi and I discussed in what position, or positions, the lovemaking should happen. Unavoidably perhaps, subjectivity coloured the conversation with phrases like 'If it was me ...' 'The way I would ...' and 'I always find ...' And then, once we'd finished our expensive lunch and vicarious sex, Suzi told me we were going 'on a date'. She said it ironically, but the reality of the afternoon is a little close to the joke and I don't plan on telling Ivy about it.

The movie Suzi has taken us to see features almost as much sex and nudity as the DVD behind the wardrobe in Frank's room. We've seen three different couples going at it in a variety of moods, modes and tempos from slow and tender to fast and nasty, and I'm more than a tiny bit turned on. Take the couple presently banging each other's brains out of their skulls, for example. They have worked together for years and they do not like each other; they despise each other, in fact. They have lied, cheated and connived to undermine each other in the workplace and they are both in line for the same promotion. As the animosity and the stakes rise, the antagonists have each decided they will not leave the office before the other. And so these beautiful lawyers find themselves alone in an otherwise deserted office at three thirty in the morning. They call a temporary truce, find a couple of cold beers and drink them in front of a huge plate-glass window overlooking downtown New York. Before the beers are drunk, however, it's skirt up, trousers down and the duelling lawyers are screwing up against the window eight storeys above the sidewalk. An exterior shot looking in shows the actress's buttocks squashed against the glass like a couple of pickled eggs in a jar. The man thrusts with measured, violent strokes, and the impact of the two bodies against glass reverberates around the empty office like a drum on a Viking longship. The scene is erotic and terrifying in equal measure, delivering a fifty-fifty mixture of arousal and vertigo. I like it.

Suzi leans towards me and when she whispers in my ear she is close enough that I can smell beer and popcorn on her breath. 'I don't know whether to cover my eyes or sit on my hands.'

I fake a quiet laugh, because I'm not sure how to interpret the comment. Suzi and I met around ten weeks ago and we've spent a lot of time together – not all of it talking about toilet paper or Jackson Pollock. We are amused, entertained and annoyed by the same things, we make each other laugh, and talk about our lives. This afternoon over lunch, Suzi told me she had split up with her boyfriend. He dumped her, it seems, and I couldn't help but feel a pang – entirely unbidden – of happiness about it. I've never met the guy and know nothing about him, but the knowledge that Suzi is available appeals to something in my genetic code. She asked how Ivy and the twins were and I told her about our unresolved argument over where to spend Christmas. I told Suzi about Frank and the strain it's placing on our domestic bliss.

In the movie, the lawyers are somehow still fucking. They relocate onto a desk – as couples screwing in offices are wont to do – scattering Post-it notes and paperclips all over the carpet.

I lean across to Suzi. 'Sit on your hands,' I tell her, and a twang of something primal thrums between my legs.

Chapter 19

Tonight is the Sprocket Hole Christmas party. I don't want to be here, but Joe insisted. As well as being a chance to get stinking drunk and tell each other how wonderful we all are, the Christmas party is attended by numerous clients, and the more I schmooze the more I earn in the New Year. It's past eleven now and the party is showing no signs of slowing down. I'm all out of schmooze and the drink is turning my stomach.

Yesterday afternoon, after we left the cinema, Suzi and I went on to a wine bar and drank too much. Even so, I was home and in bed before Ivy came back from book club. I don't know what time she came home, but she was sleeping beside me when I woke at five thirty with a hangover. I kissed her on the cheek, crept — as I so often do these days — out of bed, dressed in the hallway, then drove (probably still over the limit) across London to spend the next twelve hours shooting a commercial for tampons. It still took me six Panadol Extra, four Nurofen Express, one Lemsip and four litres of skinny latte to get me to the final shot and 'it's a wrap'. That was three hours ago now, and all I wanted to do was crawl home and pull a pillow over my head. But instead, I'm trapped inside a Christmas party. I'm hot with fatigue, my headache is still antagonizing me, I have a cloud of mizzly non-specific booze-induced guilt hovering over me and I miss Ivy.

I summon my final grain of energy, haul myself to my feet and begin the long journey to the exit. Weaving a path of least resistance, detouring away from anyone I recognize, I'm three feet from the door when Suzi appears before me.

I knew she was here, but Suzi is one of the last people I want to see tonight. We had a great time at the cinema and in the bar yesterday, we laughed, drank and flirted. And although I feel a little grubby about it, I can live with it. It's more than that, though. I told Suzi things about Ivy I ought to have kept to myself – I bitched again about Frank and about Christmas, I told Suzi that Ivy is ten years older than me, I told her Ivy used the toilet with the door open and I told her we hadn't had sex in four months. And that – these intimate revelations – feel like a betrayal. I woke up this morning with the memory of that indiscreet tittle-tattle fresh in my mind and it hurt more than my not insignificant hangover. Last night's revelation that I had been chaste for four months tugged the conversation into dangerous waters. Sex, albeit in script format, has become a key theme between Suzi and me, and, inevitably, our exploration of the topic moved from speculation to revelation. We talked about our first times, our best times and worst times. We discussed appetites and skirted around preferences, and in the not uncomfortable silences in between we regarded each other appraisingly, a raised eyebrow, a pursed smile. I've been around enough to know when I'm getting a green light, and at any other time in my life last night would have ended with me and Suzi in bed or up against a wall in some dark alley. And that knowledge doesn't make me feel particularly great about myself. We live at opposite ends of London, but I walked Suzi to her tube stop. Before we kissed good night, we looked at each other for a split second longer than necessary, assessing, maybe, just what kind of kiss we were puckering up for. Suzi initiated, landing a closed-mouthed kiss on my lips. Not a snog nor anything resembling one, but it was more than a kiss on the cheek. At several points during the day, as Suzi and I had regarded each other like kittens eyeing balls of wool, or like cats sizing up mice, I wondered not so much what Suzi would be like in bed (I'm confident she'd be a lot of fun), but what she might be like the morning after, and the morning after that and the day after that. When Suzi laughed and blushed and asked what was I thinking, I said 'nothing' in a way that suggested something. What I was thinking – the process influenced by alcohol and lust – was that Suzi and I would be great together.

But as my own tube travelled south, I knew I was wrong. We would throw ourselves into each other, go to bars, meet the friends, maybe spend a weekend away near the sea. And then the novelty would fade. We would irritate each other, ignore the phone, make excuses and – after one too many goodbye-fucks – move on, with the manner of our break-up vandalizing all the good stuff that went before. I don't know how I know, but I do; I've been there before and my (smarter) subconscious mind has recognized the signs: the forced laughter, perhaps; the tendency to egocentricity; the asymmetric ears. Whatever it is, it's there, under the surface like a nascent zit. As the train approached Wimbledon, my thoughts veered into animosity. Suzi knows very fucking well that Ivy is pregnant with my twins, and for her to flirt with me the way she undeniably does, to waft the suggestion of sex under my nose . . . well, what does that really say about her? And the way I lapped it up and played the game and flirted back, what does that say about me?

Ivy and I are squabbling more frequently and with, it seems, deeper irritation. More often than not the catalyst is trivial, and I can't work out whether that diminishes or compounds the issue. Everything is out of sequence and it's skewed my perspective. The business about where to spend Christmas, for example. It's possible that if Ivy weren't twenty-one weeks pregnant, I'd have no problem spending the holiday apart. But, like it or not, we're a family now and how can you honestly know if you're meant to be together when circumstance is dictating terms? And being with Suzi only seems to blur the distinction. So, yeah, she's pretty much the last person I want to talk to tonight. But here she is, standing before me and blocking my exit from this festive free-for-all.

'Sneaking off?' she says.

'Long day,' I say.

'How was the shoot?'

'Uninspiring.' And I'm not being truculent on purpose, but really, what else is there to say about it?

Suzi looks a little unsettled by my demeanour. 'Fair enough,' she says, and passes me a small present wrapped in Jackson Pollock-style wrapping paper. 'Happy Christmas.'

And don't I feel like a dick.

'I didn't get you anything. I'm sorry. I've been . . . you know.'

'Don't worry about it,' Suzi says. 'It's only a book.' And she balances on tiptoes and kisses me on the cheek. 'Happy Christmas, yeah.'

'Yeah. I'll see you in the New Year.' But she's already gone.

The cab ride costs forty-six pounds, and by the time I arrive at the flat it's past midnight and only three days until Christmas. Even so, I make no move to get out of the cab as the driver goes through the act of looking for four pound coins to give me my change.

'Cheer up, pal,' he says, shoving the small change through the partition. 'It might never happen.'

'It already has,' I tell him.

And as he drives away, I realize that I've left my present from Suzi on the back seat, unopened.

The flat is quiet and clean, and I remove my shoes at the top of the stairs and undress in the bathroom to avoid disturbing Ivy. I brush my teeth gently and am careful to piss against the porcelain, not into the water. I've drunk, but I'm not *drunk*, so I manage to avoid all the creaky floorboards *en route* to the bedroom. The bedside clock says it's 12:18 and I can see the ghost of Ivy's face in the green glow of the digits. I haven't seen her face in daylight since

Thursday morning, almost two days ago. I get into bed silently, but as I turn onto my side, the duvet shifting on top of me sounds like an avalanche in the stillness of Saturday morning.

Ivy turns over and kisses me. 'Hey.'

'Hey,' I say.

She levers herself up onto her elbows. 'Give me a push,' she says. And as I do, she makes it all the way into a sit and swings her legs from the bed. She's nearly made it to the door when some part of her bashes into stacked Moses baskets. 'Ow! Jesus.'

And I descend one more notch in my own estimation.

'How was your day?' I ask when Ivy shuffles back into the room. I've relocated the Moses baskets to my side of the bed, so she avoids further injury.

'Good,' she says behind a yawn. 'You? How was the shoot?'

'Could have been worse. Maybe.'

Ivy pulls the duvet over her shoulders and nestles herself comfortable.

'I was thinking we could read the baby book,' I whisper.

'I read it with Frank already.'

'What? What about me? Friday's baby-book day.'

'Well, it's Saturday now.'

'You're joking, right.'

'No. It's gone midnight, I'm exhausted and I want to go back to sleep.'

And that's the end of that conversation.

I'm wide awake now and vibrating with impotent anger. If there was a spare room to sleep in, I'd take myself there right now. But the spare room is full of Frank, as is this flat, as is my life. I'd sleep on the sofa but there are no curtains in that room and I don't know where Ivy keeps the spare blankets. I have a flat in Brixton but it's full of tenants. And lying here in the dark, in this room, it's hard to imagine feeling any more trapped inside of a cell.

Chapter 20

Nino has cooked pizza, we have paper party hats and Esther has laid out napkins printed with a robin perched on a snow-coated log. Most of Esther and Nino's possessions are packed ready for their move to Italy, and they have adorned the boxes and crates with tinsel, glitter and blinking fairy lights. Ho ho ho.

Since I got home from the Sprocket Hole Christmas party last night, Ivy and I have done a pretty good job of avoiding each other. I slept until after ten, got up, pulled on my running kit, realized my cold had solidified and spread to my legs, made a Lemsip and went back to bed for another hour and a half. Ivy went shopping, then out to lunch with Frank and Frank's son, Freddy. I was invited but I declined. And not out of petulance. A trip to the cinema, McDonald's and the Wimbledon shopping arcade is the sum total of Frank's family Christmas this year, and I didn't want to crash it. I just want him out of our fucking flat. Ivy and Frank returned home sometime around six, and Ivy slept on the sofa under a novel while I made apple pie then played *Grand Theft Auto* with Frank. She showered, I showered and then a taxi came and took us to Brixton.

On the way over, Ivy and I talked around the last couple of days and the conversation had an air of cautious civility. We talked about the weather, about Frank's son, about my shoot and the book Ivy was reading. We didn't talk about Christmas, about Frank moving out, about holiday arrangements, about arguing last night. But all of these things are at the forefront of my mind and I'm finding it difficult to contain them.

Esther tops up my wine glass. My head is thick with cold and I should be taking it easy, but I also have a strong urge to get thoroughly drunk.

'More apple juice?' she says to Ivy.

'I'm good, thank you.'

'We have our own apple trees now,' Nino says.

'In Italy?' Ivy asks.

Nino nods. 'Apple, lemon, orange.'

'Sounds amazing.'

'Is amazing.'

'You'll come and visit?' says Esther.

'Try and stop us,' Ivy says, and she flicks her eyes towards me and then away, as if the 'us' is still in debate. Or maybe I'm imagining it.

'You're quiet, love,' says Esther.

'Tired,' I say. 'I had a shoot yesterday, then a party.'

'Shooting what, love?'

'Nothing interesting.'

'Good God, love,' says Esther. 'This is our last night, make an effort.'

'Sorry. Tampax.'

'*Gesù Cristo.*' Nino gets up from the table and checks the oven.

'That's nice,' says Esther, going to top up my glass, then realizing it's already full.

'So . . .' says Ivy. 'Italy.'

'Italy,' says Esther.

'Nervous?'

Esther glances at Nino's back as he fusses about at the oven. She nods conspiratorially to Ivy. 'A little,' she says, quietly.

'It'll be fine,' I say.

'Besides,' says Esther, 'he's done so much for me. Lived in a strange country, given me three children and always put food on the table. It's his turn now, innit.'

275

Nino sits back at the table and Esther leans across and kisses him on the jowl. Nino smiles at his wife and love flickers in his normally impassive eyes. 'Pie in five minutes,' he says.

We travel halfway home in silence. It's past midnight now, which means – technically speaking – it's Christmas Eve. And although Ivy and I still haven't made our plans official, it seems pretty clear that she's going her way and I'm going mine. Ivy's head is resting on my shoulder, people are singing in the streets and festive lights are reflected in the taxi's windows. It should be a beautiful scene, but Ivy's head is heavy and it's making my neck ache. I am biting my bottom lip, and if I don't say something soon I'm in danger of drawing blood. I shrug my shoulder out from under her.

Ivy makes a sound as if she may have been dozing.

'Sweet, isn't it,' I say.

'What's sweet?'

'Esther and Nino.'

'Uh huh.'

'Esther uprooting herself for Nino like that. Going all the way to a foreign country where she doesn't know anyone and can't speak the language.' My voice sounds slurred, skidding a little on the s's.

276

'She'll have a great time,' Ivy says, completely missing my point. 'I'd love to live in Italy.'

'I wouldn't.'

Ivy doesn't answer.

'Would you go without me?'

'What?'

'To Italy?'

'Don't,' Ivy says. 'Not tonight.'

'It's Christmas Eve,' I say.

Ivy says nothing.

'I just don't understand how . . . how Esther is prepared to move all the way to Italy for Nino. To live. And you won't even go to North Wales for Christmas.'

'And you won't go to Bristol.'

'I might if you asked like you meant it.'

'Fine, come, then.'

'Very convincing. Anyway, it's my birthday.'

'And I'm pregnant.'

'With my babies.'

The cab ride is twenty-three pounds and I tell the guy to keep the change from thirty, but I don't know who I'm trying to impress – Ivy is already halfway up the stairs to the flat before I get out of the cab. Frank is in his room, and we resume our argument in the bathroom, sitting on the toilet, washing our faces, with mouths full of toothpaste.

'Your mum and dad have each other,' I remind Ivy. 'We can drive over on Boxing Day.'

'Your dad will have a house full. And I don't want to drive two hundred miles on Boxing Day.'

'Jesus. Why are you being so fucking . . . stubborn?'

Ivy's eyes widen, she pulls her head back as if recoiling from some awful vision. 'Stubborn?'

I gesture at her as if this should be patently evident.

Ivy shakes her head and spits a gob of toothpaste foam into the sink and walks out, slamming the door.

When I get to the bedroom Ivy is already under the covers.

I walk round to her side of the bed and sit beside her. 'I feel like I haven't seen you since I moved in,' I say, reasonably.

'I'm not the one who's working on a screenplay in my spare time.'

'Is that what this is about?'

'It's not *about* anything. No. I—'

'That screenplay,' I say, 'is the one thing I do for me. You have book club.'

'I just want to go and see my family for Christmas.'

'Ivy, we're living with your fucking family. Th—'

'My "fucking family"?' There are tears in Ivy's eyes and I feel terrible, but my blood is up and I'm not the bad guy here.

'Your brother has been under our feet for *two weeks*.'

Ivy holds a finger to her lips, scowls, points at the wall between our room and Frank's.

'Are you serious? You want *me* to be quiet?'

'Can you manage?'

'I wouldn't have to if we didn't have a frigging lodger.'

'It's my flat.'

'What?'

'Nothing, I . . . I didn't . . .'

'*Your flat?*'

Ivy closes her eyes.

'Fine.' I stand up. 'Do you have any spare blankets any-where in *your flat*?'

'Fisher . . . there's no need.' She reaches a hand out to me. 'Come here.'

I almost go to her, visualize myself doing it, *want* to do it . . . but my feet feel nailed down.

'Please,' Ivy says, 'let's not do this.'

'I'm pissed,' I say. 'You'll sleep better without me in the bed.'

'It's okay,' Ivy says.

And something snaps. 'That's your answer to every-thing, isn't it?'

'What?' says Ivy, genuinely bemused.

'*It's okay*. Do you remember the first time you said that?'

'Fisher, I—'

'The first time we . . . made love. The very first time we made love, I asked if you had condoms.'

'I don't rememb—'

'And you said, *It's okay*. And I've thought about that – *a lot* – and . . .'

Ivy looks at me like I'm some mad stranger. I hold out my hands and shake my head, trying to find the words or drum up the courage to spit them out.

I turn away from Ivy and open the cupboard above the wardrobe. 'I just need a blanket. I need sleep.'

'Fine,' she says. 'Have it your way; there's one in the hallway cupboard.'

I don't exactly slam the bedroom door, but I make damn sure the bastard thing is closed.

I have to empty the hallway cupboard of several boxes, many of them containing items for our babies, before finding a single, thin blanket. It's grubby and partially covered with blades of dried grass.

It's cold in the living room, so I don't undress. I make a nest of pillows and cocoon myself under the picnic blanket, but I can't sleep. There is a streetlight outside the window and amber light washes into the room through the venetian blinds. From where I lie I can see the boxed pram beneath the table. A door opens and a few seconds later I hear Frank's muffled bass. I don't hear Ivy reply and a couple of seconds later a door closes. My mouth is dry, so I pull the blanket tight around my shoulders and shuffle to the sink to get a glass of water.

Sitting on the counter top is the baby book.

At twenty-one weeks the babies' circulatory system is complete, their ears are in position on the sides of their heads and they can be soothed by calming music or disturbed by an argument. They may have recognizable family features; perhaps they have Ivy's eyes, or my red hair. Their eyes move, they have discernible eyebrows and eyelashes. They may play with the umbilical cord, gripping and pulling it. Much like their father, my babies' brains are still developing. Some experts believe this is the time when memories begin to form, and if so, I hope they don't remember me shouting at their mother. At twenty-one weeks the mother will feel increasingly heavy and awkward. Her ankles may swell and she might develop haemorrhoids. It is not uncommon to be struck by fear in the middle of the night, anticipating the pain and trauma of labour and the associated risks for the babies. At thirty-one years, fifty-one weeks and six days old, the father is still a very long way from fully developed. His priorities are not yet aligned; his ego is fragile; his timing, tact, empathy and restraint are entirely absent. He still has a great deal of growing up to do.

According to my phone, it's 7:43 when Ivy gets into the shower on the morning of Christmas Eve. I didn't think I'd drunk a great deal last night, but I have a hangover that permeates every cell of me when I wake up clothed and shivering beneath a thin picnic blanket. My head hurts, my stomach is in revolt, I ache from sleeping on an old sofa that's approximately eight inches shorter than I am, and my pride is throbbing like a bastard.

I need a pee but I'm not ready to face Ivy, so I hobble into the kitchen to expel one and a half pints of urine into the sink. Judging by its contents – plates, pans, colander, cheese grater – it looks like Frank and Ivy ate burnt bolognese last night and the sight of the aftermath makes my stomach turn.

Normally, Frank moves around the house with all the stealth of a baboon on a pogo stick, so I nearly jump out of my skin when I hear his voice behind me.

'Morning, Fish.'

I'm only halfway through my piss and stopping isn't an option, so I continue to pee on last night's dishes.

'Oops,' Frank laughs. 'Didn't realize this one was taken. Ha ha.'

I finish, zip myself up and start running hot water into the sink.

Ivy's voice is shrill from the bathroom. 'Water!'

And here is one of life's very modern dilemmas: turn off the tap so your pregnant girlfriend can continue her hot shower on a winter morning, or continue filling the sink so you can wash the piss off her kitchenware. Ignoring Ivy's increasingly loud shouts of 'Water!' and Frank's running commentary, it feels as if it takes two weeks to half fill the sink.

'Christmas, hey?' says Frank. 'Shall I dry?'

'I'll be fine.'

Frank picks up a tea towel and starts drying a plate while I use my thumbnail to scrape congealed meat sauce off the bottom of a pan.

'You okay?' he asks.

'Been better.'

'You going back to your dad's then?'

'Looks that way.'

'Ivy's very close to Mum,' Frank says.

'That's nice for her.'

I focus my attention on the pan.

'You heading off today?' he asks.

'Mind if I use your room?'

'Hey?'

'I need some sleep.'

'Oh, right, sure. I mean, it's your flat.'

'Your sister's actually, but . . . whatever.'

Frank grabs a pair of jeans and a shirt, and I crawl into his bed and shut the door. The sheets are still warm and the pillow smells of Frank's primate musk, but I'm asleep before I have a chance to worry about it.

If anything my hangover has put on some muscle and developed an attitude by the time Ivy slips into Frank's room. I'm disorientated and confused, first that I'm not in our room, and then that I'm not on the sofa; as if my consciousness is running along behind me, like a toddler struggling to keep pace with his daddy.

Ivy sits on the edge of the bed and strokes my hair. 'Morning.'

'Hey. What's the time?'

'Little after ten. How's your head?'

'Stinks. How's your . . . everything?'

Last night, whenever I woke up cold or dehydrated or with a sofa spring in my liver, I also had a question lodged in my mind. Does Ivy want babies more than she wants me? Of course she does, is the glaringly obvious answer. They are my children, too, and, putting my tiny ego aside, I want her to want them more than she wants me. That's how it ought to be, that's how life works. I suppose. The more difficult question originates twenty-one weeks ago: *Did* Ivy want children more than she wanted me? Was my most appealing feature the biological material in my underpants? The answer is less clear, and if that answer is in the affirmative, it's less easy to live with.

I do love Ivy; I think she's smart and funny and beautiful … but as much as I don't want to acknowledge the thought, I don't feel as if I'm running as fast as I can. I keep turning away from the thought, but it pursues me like a belligerent doomsayer – is this the woman you should spend the rest of your life with? Is she The One? Or are you simply sticking around out of a sense of duty and the hope that everything will turn out okay in the end?

And the truth is, I don't know. It certainly didn't work out that way for Frank.

'Are you getting up?'

'I feel lousy,' I say.

'If I go now-ish I can get ahead of the traffic,' Ivy says. 'Maybe.'

'Okay.'

'Do you want me to wait?'

'No, you go, it's a long drive.'

'Your present's under the bed,' Ivy says.

Despite everything, I laugh. 'Yours too.'

'Great minds,' says Ivy. 'Shall I get them?'

'My head's banging.'

'Shall I get you some tablets?'

'Had some a couple of hours ago.'

'We'll do presents when we get back?' says Ivy.

I nod, close my eyes and I feel like crying. This is not how it's meant to happen. We should be wearing matching jumpers with gaudy reindeers embroidered on the fronts, we should be walking on the Common, playing Bing Crosby on the stereo, roasting chestnuts at gas mark seven. Not this; not Ivy trying to force a smile while I lie in her brother's pungent bed, incapacitated with cold, doubt and a hard-edged hangover.

'Hey,' Ivy says; she rubs my aching head, whispers in my ear: 'Cheer up, baby, Christmas is overrated, anyway.'

She raises her eyebrows, broadens her smile, waiting for a reaction. But I don't know how to react. Ivy goes to kiss me on the lips, but I turn my head to the side.

'The babies . . . you'll get my cold.'

Ivy twists my face around and kisses me on the mouth.

'I'll see you on Wednesday,' she says.

I don't even know what day today is, I don't know if Ivy is going away for one, two or three days. 'I'll see you on Wednesday.'

Ivy stops at the doorway, places a hand on her stomach. 'I didn't know,' she says. 'Please believe me.'

And I do. Whatever the explanation, I know she is telling the truth. 'I believe you.'

Ivy nods, mouths the words *thank you*.

As she leaves, pulling the door closed behind her, something glints at Ivy's wrist. And as her footsteps move down the corridor, I realize she is wearing the clapperboard cufflinks that she gave me just over one week ago.

When I next wake it's after twelve and the house is as quiet as a monastery. I can't even hear the neighbours. I go through to the main bedroom, lie on Ivy's side of the bed and doze again. I spend a long time in the shower, and by the time I'm dry and dressed I'm so hungry I feel nauseous.

Frank is sitting on the sofa, reading quietly.

'Sausage sandwich for you,' he says, pointing *Catch-22* at the breakfast counter. 'And there's coffee.'

The coffee and the sandwich are hot.

'Thank you,' I say, plonking myself down beside him on the sofa. 'This is amazing.'

'Got some of those posh sausages from The Village.'

'How's your wallet?'

'Let's just say it's a good job I don't have to buy a Christmas present for Lois this year.'

'Every cloud, hey?'

'You know she's crazy about you, don't you?' Frank

nods at the hallway door when he says this; the one Ivy left through about two hours ago.

And the truth is, I don't know that I do.

'Well, she is,' Frank says, as if reading my mind. 'Trust me, she is.'

'You staying here, then?'

Frank sighs. 'Looks that way. Can't really go home solo.'

'Why not?'

'Mum and Dad are funny about divorce.'

I remember Ivy saying the same thing. 'Funny how?'

Frank shrugs. 'Just funny.'

I turn on the TV and eat my sausage sandwich in front of a daytime panel show full of mid-alphabet celebrities in party hats. Topics discussed include: the best way to cook a turkey, the best Christmas movies, the best Christmas songs, what's on TV over Christmas and a segment about a crazy bastard from Wigan who eats turkey with all the trimmings 365 days a year – 366 on a leap year. Normally I drive down to Dad's with a carful of ingredients to cook Christmas dinner for him and Maria's family, but because I didn't know (or refused to accept) what I was doing this year, I am woefully underprovisioned. I'll have to visit the expensive butcher before I head off, and take whatever extortionate fare he has left, festive or not.

'What time you off?' asks Frank, who is uncharacteristically sedate this morning.

The clock on the mantelpiece says it's twelve twenty-three. 'Any minute,' I tell him.

'Before you go . . .' Frank springs up from the sofa and thunders down the hallway corridor.

He returns maybe nine seconds later, holding a small gift-wrapped package and a card. 'Happy Christmas, happy birthday,' he says, pulling me into an awkward bear hug.

'Frank, thank you. I'm afraid I haven't . . .' I shrug, showing Frank my empty hands.

Under the bed next to Ivy's (and my own) present, is a book on card tricks and a marked deck, already wrapped and ready to give to Harold on my way out. And I briefly consider redirecting the present to Frank – he would probably appreciate it more than my surly teenage neighbour – but it seems a little wrong-spirited.

Frank dismisses my empty-handed gesturing with a wave of his paw. 'Don't be daft. I really appreciate you putting me up, man.'

'It's nothing.'

'Well . . .' Frank glances at the hallway door again, an involuntary flick of the eyes, 'it's not nothing to me. And I know things are . . . I know it's . . . anyway, thanks.'

'Thank you,' I say, holding up the clumsily wrapped

present. And if it's not a DVD box set behind the snowflake paper, I'll be very surprised.

I'm not big on Christmas, but even so, I don't like opening presents prematurely. Maybe it's because December 25th is also my birthday and I'm trying to squeeze the most possible enjoyment out of the single day. So I'm not being coy when I place Frank's present on the coffee table unopened. It's simply force of habit.

'You not going to open it?'

'I thought I'd save it for the big day,' I say.

'Open it, open it.'

In the time Frank has been staying in this flat, he and I have watched an eye-aching amount of TV with Ivy squashed between us on the sofa. And invariably, within five minutes of Ivy falling asleep, Frank flicks through the channels until he lands on some old action movie from the eighties or nineties – *Highlander*, *First Blood*, *Delta Force*, *Cyborg*. So although it's been less than three weeks, it has the feel of an old in-joke when I unwrap an Arnold Schwarzenegger box set of *The Terminator*, *Predator*, *Commando* and *Conan the Barbarian*.

'You shouldn't have.'

'Well, if I hadn't I'd probably end up watching *Home Alone* or something. Have you seen the shit that's on over Christmas?'

I affect an expression that, I hope, projects equal parts hurt and disappointment. 'You mean . . .' I point at the DVDs, then at Frank. 'You bought these . . . you bought them for yourself?'

'What? No, I mean . . . not exactly, I thought . . . I thought we could watch them tog—' Frank catches the amusement in my eyes. 'Oh, you bastard.'

'Got you.'

'Damn! Ivy does the same exact thing.'

'Yes,' I say, 'she does.'

'Listen,' Frank says, suddenly serious, as if he hadn't been taken in by my ham routine at all, and was, in fact, simply setting me up for his own pay-off. 'I know I've been in the way, and I know things have been a bit . . .' he wavers his hand, palm down '. . . a bit wonky with you and Ivy.'

'I appr—'

'But . . . me and Lois . . . we never had what you and Ivy have.'

'Ivy said you were made for each other.'

Frank sighs, shakes his head. 'We were good friends, made each other laugh, fancied each other. Ha, we even look like each other.'

'She sounds . . . nice.'

Frank manages a smile. 'Dark hair,' he says. 'And yes,

she was nice. Is nice, I suppose. But it was all . . .' the smile fades '. . . trust me, we never had what you and Ivy have. We just didn't. So don't fuck it up, okay?'

I nod.

'Or I'll fucking kill you.'

And although Frank laughs when he hugs me, I can't help picturing the muscular bulldog from *Tom and Jerry*, and the way he would hammer the indestructible cat through the floorboards.

Chapter 21

The roads are as busy as you'd expect them to be at two o'clock on Christmas Eve. I have close to two hundred quid's worth of glazed ham, turkey sausages, and free-range organic lamb in the boot, and the smell of all that blood and meat within the confines of this tiny car is nauseating. Despite the cold and billowing exhaust fumes I have my window wound down to its full extent, but at an average of three miles per hour, it's not helping to clear the air.

All three lanes of the M25 are moving at walking pace, the cars' back windows packed with cuddly toys, wrapped presents and gurning children. Miles of families crammed into their cars, some of them no doubt singing, talking, playing silly games; others will be arguing, shouting or sitting in silence and wishing with all their hearts that they were anywhere else with anybody else. At this rate it will take me about five days to get home, but I'm in no hurry; I need time to think and it looks like I've got all I can eat. Frank said he never had with Lois what I have with Ivy. It's a nice sentiment, but neither of us is in a position to know its validity. Frank doesn't know what I have with Ivy any more than I know what went wrong with him and his soon-to-be ex-wife.

Reasons why I'm annoyed with Ivy:

1) She invited her brother to live in our flat.

2) Which Ivy still views as her own.

3) Making me a glorified lodger.

4) She has more sympathy for her brother's situation than mine. Which, now that I think about it, is probably fair enough considering he's getting divorced and is semi-estranged from his son.

5) Not enough sex. Mitigating circumstances, I agree, but it's been four bloody months, for God's sake.

6) She would rather spend Christmas with her family than mine.

7) She doesn't buy full-fat milk.

There is a short-lived surge in the traffic and I cover maybe half a mile, getting all the way up into third gear before we settle back to a steady four miles an hour. It starts to rain, fat drops bouncing off the windscreen. Ivy and I had our first kiss in this car; parked outside the fourth lamppost on the left. It was raining then, too.

It seems only fair to make the case for the defence: I love that Ivy goes to book club with a bunch of people twice her age; I love that she is a make-up artist and wears no make-up; I love that she is wise and thoughtful and confident and maternal and playful. I love that she believes in the Wish Fairy, can't whistle and has a goldfish named Ernest. I love that it was her idea to take El to the Natural History Museum. I love the way she makes scrambled eggs. And I love that she loves me and I love (however it happened) that she is pregnant with my twins. And I don't need to make a list; I just know, in my heart, in my gut, that she is the one for me.

It's all so obvious sitting in stationary traffic on the M25. Maybe I should have driven out here a week ago, rather than brooding and sulking like a stupid sodding teenager.

In the movie version of my life, the rain would turn to snow now and the traffic would open up, I would turn on the radio to 'Driving Home for Christmas', and sing all the way to Dad's house.

The traffic doesn't move and the rain does not relent, but I'm okay. I'm happy.

I pick up my phone from the passenger seat and text Ivy.

Xx

I put the phone back on the seat and wait for it to ping Ivy's love straight back to me.

It doesn't ping.

It takes seven hours and forty-five minutes to cover the two hundred miles from Ivy's flat to Dad's house and my phone doesn't ping one single time. By the time I arrive it's close to ten o'clock at night. Dad must have heard the car approaching because he opens the front door as I pull up to the kerb in front of his house. I kill the headlights and he waves from the doorway before stepping out into the December night in his socks and a short-sleeved shirt. Not long after bonfire night I told Dad that Ivy and I would visit for Christmas and, optimist, idiot, mule-headed fool that I am, I haven't once suggested otherwise.

Dad frowns and looks past my shoulder as I walk up the driveway to meet him. He whispers, 'Sleeping?'

I shake my head and let my expression do the talking.

'Not here?'

'At her folks'.'

Dad hugs me. 'Son,' he says. 'What went wrong?'

Dad turns up the flame on the gas fire, refills my whisky and lowers himself into the sofa. It would be a perfect scene if the mother of my unborn children were sitting between us. On the other hand, it's nice to have room to spread out for a change.

'Did you call her?' he says.

After arriving, I gave Dad the abridged version of the last couple of months, culminating with me sleeping on the sofa last night. And while I confessed, Dad tutted, shook his head, made tea and told me I should talk to Ivy. He handled it, in other words, perfectly.

'Texted,' I say.

Dad rolls his eyes as if this — texting — is simultaneously baffling and risible, like dyeing your hair green, or listening to minimal techno.

'Did she *text* back?'

I shake my head again.

'Maybe you should call?'

'She'll be in bed by now. I'll call tomorrow.'

'So, what's the plan?'

'The usual: grovel and apologize.'

Dad laughs. 'Don't be too hard on yourself.' He takes a sip of his drink.

'I love her,' I say, and I don't know why I say it. Maybe to remind myself.

Dad nods. 'I know.'

And I nearly choke on my whisky, laughing.

'What?'

'You reminded me of someone.'

'Who?'

'Han Solo.' Dad frowns. 'From *Star Wars*. He . . . he's a cool guy,' I say, and this seems to satisfy my old man.

'What do you love most about her?' Dad asks.

I shrug. 'No one thing, you know . . . just lots of silly things.'

Dad smiles. 'Best that way,' he says.

'I take it back, you remind me of Yoda.'

Dad swats at my leg. 'Cheek.'

We sit for a while, not talking, just listening to the hiss and flicker of the fire.

'Your mum and I . . .' Dad begins '. . . it wasn't all plain sailing.'

'No?'

'She threatened to leave me once, you know?'

'No.'

Dad nods. 'After you came along.'

'Sorry,' I say.

Dad smiles at me with love. 'It wasn't your fault. It's just . . . life, you know.'

'What happened?'

Dad shakes his head. 'I was being selfish, is all. It was all the rage in those days. Your lot are better, I think.'

'And . . .'

Dad smiles at the memory. 'I bought flowers, washed the dishes, learnt to change a nappy.'

'Sounds like a big sacrifice.'

Dad drains his glass, picks up the bottle from the side table and points it in my direction.

I shake my head. 'I'm shattered.'

Dad looks disappointed; he hesitates, unsure whether to pour himself another drink.

'You go ahead,' I say. 'I'm good for another twenty minutes.'

Dad doesn't need asking twice. 'Your mother used to say I looked like Robert Redford,' he says. He raises his eyebrows, as if daring me to contradict him.

I indulge him with a look.

'A woman like that,' he says, 'she's worth all the sacrifice in the world.'

Before I go to sleep, I text Ivy one last time.

I love you.

Chapter 22

I hate Christmas.

The first thing I do when I wake up is check my phone, but there are no messages.

I can't have grown since last year, but my old single bed feels smaller than I remember it. Last year I'd just ruined my relationship with Kate. This year I've ruined my relationship with Ivy. It's becoming something of a tradition.

Traditionally I lie in bed until I hear Dad leave the house for Mass, then I go for a long run. But fuck tradition and fuck it hard, I'm going to church. I even shower first. When I wake Dad with a mug of tea and the news that I'm forgoing my festive run to accompany him to mass, his face lights up like it's, well, Christmas.

I honestly don't know why I've decided to do this – whether it's my first step towards becoming a less selfish man, or if it's an act of abject desperation. I don't believe in God, and the only thing we have in common is that me and his boy share a birthday, but when the rest of the congregation kneels for silent prayer, I screw my eyes tight and offer up my missive with all the others. I pray that Ivy still loves me. But it's impossible to stop at just one: I pray that my babies will be born healthy, I pray they will grow up happy. I pray for Dad, Maria, my nieces, Hector, Frank, Esther, Nino, El, Phil, Joe and Joe's family – because to leave anyone out feels equivalent to asking God *not* to look out for them. I'm just starting in on a petition for crispy roast potatoes and a good movie this afternoon when the priest stands us all up. And this must be how they get you – this prayer lark is addictive, you can't fit it all in in one session so you come back the week after. Very crafty.

Despite my devout atheism, I enjoy the service. The hymns are rousing, the priest (possibly drunk) is surprisingly entertaining, and the sherry and mince pies in the Church Hall don't make a half-bad breakfast.

When we get back to Dad's, though, Ivy still hasn't returned my text. I call, but her phone goes straight to voicemail. And so much for the power of prayer.

I'm thirty-two today, although no one has said happy birthday to me yet. It is traditional in the Fisher household to wait until three fifty-five in the afternoon, the exact time of my birth, before acknowledging my birthday. It started as a way of giving me a piece of the day that was all my own, and evolved over the years into a piece of pantomime at my expense; everyone pointedly not wishing me happy birthday, or discussing plans for their own, months hence, celebrations. And in the last thirty-two years, I've only spent one away from this house – the year I went travelling, which seemed to provide a valid form of exemption.

Maria and her family descend on Dad's a little after midday, and after they have made a point of wishing me Happy Christmas and nothing more, Maria and I take three glasses of wine into the garden – another tradition. The summer after Mum died we placed a stone birdbath in the garden as a memorial, and every year for the last ten, Maria and I have come out here on Christmas Day to spend five minutes with her. Some years Maria gets teary, others she almost seems embarrassed by the mawkishness of it. But as long as we're here, this is what we do.

We sip our wine in silence, and in my peripheral vision I watch my sister brush at a tear. I go to hold her hand but she pulls away from me.

'You okay?'

'No,' she says.

I turn to face her, and rather than looking sad, Maria is visibly angry.

'What's up?'

'So how did you fuck it up this time?'

I gesture towards Mum's birdbath, frown. 'Do you have to?'

Maria shakes her head, irritated. 'You're having twins!'

'I know.'

'Do you know how hard that is?'

'I know what a fuss you made.'

Maria punches me on the arm, hard enough to slosh half the wine out of my glass. 'So?'

'It's complicated.'

'Dad said you've been sleeping on the sofa.'

'Oh, did he? Well, why don't you go and ask him all about it?'

'You're such a dickhead.'

'I slept on the sofa once. One time.'

'You said you loved her, she was the one, your soul mate and all that blah.' Maria affects a simpering playground sing-song as she says this.

'I remember.'

'And . . .?'

'And what?'

'And grow the fuck up, William. Happy Christmas,

Mum,' and Maria downs her wine and walks back into the kitchen, leaving me out in the cold with my glass half empty.

'So,' says Hector. 'Sleeping on the sofa?'

'Once. I slept on the sofa once.'

Hector reaches across the table with a bottle of wine. 'Top up?'

I place my hand over my glass. 'I'm fine.'

'Ahem,' says Maria, tilting her own glass towards her husband.

'Why did you sleep on the sofa?' asks Rosalind.

'Because he's a wally,' says Maria.

Rosalind giggles and whispers something into her twin sister's ear. 'Why is he a wally?' asks Imogen.

'Because he's a man,' says Hermione, and she and her mother clink glasses.

I scowl an ironic *thank you* at Dad and the old bugger just laughs. Then Hector laughs, then Hermione, then everyone else joins in.

We're most of the way through a family-sized tub of Celebrations and halfway through *Back to the Future Part II* when my mobile rings. Someone pauses the TV while I squirm out of the armchair and take my phone from my back pocket. I don't recognize the number.

'Who is it?' asks Hermione.

'That's for me to know.'

'If it's Ivy I want to talk to her.'

'And say what?'

'*That's for me to know,*' my niece parrots, then pokes her tongue at me for emphasis.

It's unlikely that Hermione is any more difficult or wayward than any other very-nearly-18-year-old girl. But she and her mother have a thorough falling out at least a few times a year. And when they stop talking to each other, they get on the phone to me – blowing off steam, making threats and, more often than not, crying. Although in the last few months (and I'm not sure how the transition occurred) Ivy has become Hermione's preferred confidante. And far from feeling usurped, it's just another item on the list of things I love about the woman I was mean to on Christmas Eve.

'Watch your film,' I say to everyone, and I go through to the hallway to answer the call.

'Hello?'

'Happy Christmas, babes.'

'Ivy?'

'You don't recognize me?'

'Yes, of course, absolutely. Just didn't recognize the number.'

'Who were you expecting?' There's an edge on Ivy's voice, but I'm not falling for it. Not today.

'Happy Christmas, gorgeous. I take it this is your mum and dad's phone?'

'Yes, I fo—'

'Hold on a moment.' Hermione's head pops around the doorway and I shoe her away and trot up the stairs to my room. 'I texted,' I say to Ivy. 'You didn't reply.'

'Phone ran out of charge. And I left my plug in London. I left in a . . . in a bit of a muddle, I suppose. I'm sorry.'

'No,' I say, 'I'm sorry.'

'Yeah, well, so you should be.'

'I miss you.'

'Don't be soppy, you'll start me . . . '

But whatever Ivy says next I don't catch because Hermione, Imogen and Rosalind come barrelling into the room. Hermione tries to take the phone from my hand, but I palm her off as Imogen and Rosalind circle around me reaching for the device.

'Give it,' says Hermione, making another grab. I stand up on the bed to keep the phone from my nieces' evil clutches. 'Ivy, I'll have to be qu—'

'What's going on? What's that noise?'

'Goblins,' I say, kicking Rosalind a little harder than intended and knocking her from the bed.

'Goblins?'

'Nieces.'

Imogen bites my ankle and Hermione clambers onto the bed and starts jumping for the phone.

'I love you,' I say, a second before Hermione grabs my wrist.

And like lions on a giraffe, they take me down.

Lord only knows what the mother of my children and my nieces have to talk about, but whatever it is takes approximately thirty minutes.

'Ivy says Happy Christmas,' says Rosalind, returning my phone.

'That it?'

'She said to give you a big kiss, too,' says Imogen, wrinkling up her nose.

'Well? Who's giving me my kiss?' I half rise from the sofa and my three nieces scatter.

'So,' says Dad to Hermione, 'it'll be your birthday soon?'

'Eighteen,' says Hector.

'God help us,' says Maria.

I check the time on my phone and see that is now ten minutes until my birthday.

The twins laugh behind their hands. 'I like birthdays,' says Imogen.

And this is my cue to affect disgruntlement and leave

the room. I sigh heavily as I traipse up the stairs. When I come back at three fifty-four, I'm carrying a packed bag. If the roads are clear and if I leave soon, I might just make it to Ivy's parents' house in time for turkey sandwiches. But first I have to get through a birthday cake.

It's an almighty effort not to bolt my slice of Victoria sponge and tear at my presents like a 2-year-old. But I take my time, chew with my mouth closed, and make a fuss over every gift. I even stick around for the end of the movie because, who knows, this may be the last year I get to go through this ridiculous, awful, wonderful charade.

Dad doesn't appear surprised when I tell him I'm about to get in the car and drive nearly two hundred miles to Bristol. And in a way, I think I've been planning on doing this since I opened my eyes this morning.

'Surprised you stayed as long as you did,' he says, kissing my cheek and hugging me tightly.

The whole family have come to the front door to wave goodbye. Hector takes my bag and places it in the boot of the Fiat.

'Drive safe,' says Maria. Then she punches me on the arm again, hard. 'Dickhead.'

'Love you, too,' I say, climbing into the car.

On the apocalyptically empty roads, with my foot hard

to the floor, leaning forward in the driver's seat, the Fiat has a top speed of eighty-two m.p.h. Two police cars pass me as I head south, exceeding the speed limit by a full twelve m.p.h., but all they do is wave and grin and honk their horns. 'Honk if you're horny', says one of the bumper stickers on El's 'battymobile'; and though I can't say that I am – I am happy and frantic and eager, which, perhaps, amounts to the same thing – I honk and grin and wave back to the speeding coppers.

Door-to-door, the trip takes two hours and fifty-seven minutes. I ring the Lees' doorbell at four minutes past eight on Christmas evening, and my heart is banging as if I've run the entire journey.

Frank answers the door. 'What the fuck are you doing here?'

'Happy Christmas, and right back at you, shit-bag.'

Frank puts a hand to his temple as if he's just been struck with a migraine. He shakes his head. 'For fuck's sake.' And then he laughs.

'Is everything okay?'

Ivy's mother shouts from inside: 'You're letting the cold in. Who is it?'

Frank shouts back into the house: 'Fisher!'

'Arseholes!' This bellowed welcome from Ivy's dad, followed by an explosion of booming laughter.

'Frank, are you going to ask me in, or what? What's going on? Where's Ivy?'

Frank looks at his bare wrist as if checking a watch. 'Somewhere on the M6, I imagine. My guess is she'll be arriving at your dad's gaff in about . . . twenty minutes.'

As I travel towards London on the M4 on Christmas evening, attempting to push the accelerator through the footwell, El's Fiat reaches a terrifying, teeth-rattling eighty-six m.p.h. The wind must be blowing east. Or maybe it's the force of my will.

Frank was ten minutes out and it wasn't until after eight thirty that Ivy called her parents' house from my dad's. Thirty not unpleasant minutes in the company of Ivy's mum, dad and Frank, me drinking tea and eating a turkey sandwich, them drinking wine, whisky and advocaat respectively. Frank, it transpires, managed less than twenty-four hours of festive solitude before deciding he was in danger of going mad or drinking himself into oblivion. Following a Christmas breakfast of burnt bacon sandwiches, he spent an hour watching kids' TV, agonizing over whether or not to open the Cointreau. Halfway through *The Muppet Christmas Carol*, he threw a bag into the boot of his Audi and set off for Bristol. He arrived at his folks' in time for Christmas dinner. He revealed all this while we were in the kitchen, making another round of drinks. I asked whether he'd told his parents about the Lois situation, but before Frank could answer Eva came into the room to fetch the Quality Street.

Despite vocal protestations from her son and her husband, Mrs Lee insisted on a round of charades (*It's a Wonderful Life; You Only Live Twice, Bridge Over the River . . . sounds like mince pie*). Ken wanted me to have a drink and Eva wanted me to stay the night, but I resisted both offers because I was still holding out hope.

The motorway is quiet, but there is still more traffic at ten thirty in the evening than I would have guessed, and it makes me sad. Many of the cars contain single drivers – people who should be with other people. Maybe they are returning from days well spent with friends and family, but in my imagination they are alone and adrift. Perhaps they're thinking the same thing about me. No one honks on the motorway at ten thirty on Christmas Night.

Ivy called at eight forty, as Frank was miming the act of throwing up (*'Out of breath? Dodgy tummy? Retch? Sick? Spew? Wallace and Vomit!*). Maria and her brood had gone home by then, so it was just Dad and Ivy on the other end of our six-way Christmas conference call. The consensus was that Ivy and I should spend the night at our respective 'in-laws", but foolishness prevailed and Ivy

311

squeezed herself back into her van and I squashed myself behind the wheel of the Fiat.

Even travelling in excess of a hundred miles an hour (speeds neither of our vehicles is capable of) it was extraordinarily unlikely that both Ivy and I could make it back to Wimbledon before midnight. But we calculated that, with luck, faith and a good tailwind, we could both get to the Oxford services while there is still some Christmas left in the day. It's not exactly *en route*, but when have I ever done anything the easy way?

The car park at Oxford services is practically deserted, and I immediately spot a white van with the words 'Glamour Squad', stencilled onto the side. Ivy is perched on the bonnet, her breath forming white clouds in the air. I pull up alongside and unfold myself from the tiny car at six minutes and a bunch of seconds to midnight.

'You made it,' Ivy says, managing to communicate with a quiet smile that this is a moment I should resist cheapening with any kind of glibness.

I put my arms around Ivy and hug her as tightly as I can without crushing her or my babies. 'Happy Christmas.'

Ivy kisses me, softly at first, increasing the pressure and tension by increments until we're engaged in the kind of kiss that would be embarrassing if there was another soul around to witness it. 'Happy Christmas,' she says, and we sit side by side on the bonnet of her white van, holding hands and saying nothing else until midnight ticks over, and then Ivy kisses me again.

'Right,' she says, 'if I don't pee in the next two minutes, I think my bladder might explode.'

If I had expected any kind of festive atmosphere in Oxford services in the early hours of Boxing Day morning, then I would have been an idiot. The skeleton staff (Santa hats drooping over their eyes) regard us with indifference as we gaze into each other's eyes across a Formica table and two steaming cups of burnt coffee.

'Do you think we passed on the way?' Ivy asks.

'Are you being metaphoric?'

'Too late at night for that. Or is it early in the morning? I can never decide.'

'I think we must have done,' I say. 'I'm sorry.'

Ivy shrugs. 'It'll make a good story to tell our children.' She smiles, and it's a smile I'll remember until I lose my hair, teeth and mind.

'Shall we go home now?'

We pull up outside our flat at a little after two a.m. Ivy is dead on her feet, and with her arm around my shoulders, I all but drag her up the stairs. I've driven a six-hundred-mile triangle in thirty-six hours to get here, but it's been worth the trip.

'Shall I put the kettle on?' I ask as Ivy curls up on the sofa, still in her coat and shoes.

'Do we have any sherry?'

I open cupboard doors and rummage through the tins and packets. 'No sherry. Cointreau or port?'

'Hmm, tricky. Cointreau might be a little pokey, d'you think?'

'You could have a small one.'

'Surprise me.'

I pour two ports and take them to the sofa.

'Happy Boxing Day, baby,' I say, going to clink my glass against Ivy's.

Ivy pulls her glass out of clinking range. 'I'm pretty sure it doesn't stop being Christmas till we go to bed.'

'Really?'

'Totally.'

'So ... if we stayed up for the next two days?'

'Still Christmas.'

'In that case, Happy Christmas, baby.'

And now we clink. Ivy sips her port, closes her eyes and savours the sweet liquid. 'First drink I've had in twenty weeks.'

'How is it?'

She purses her lips. 'Bloody good.' And she takes another sip.

'I'm sorry, you know. About . . . everything.'

Ivy shrugs a minuscule shrug. 'Me too,' she says. 'I'm sorry too.'

'I forgive you.'

Ivy goes to kick me in the leg. I grab her foot and hold it in my lap, massaging the heel, sole and toes. And that, it seems, is that. We could have said these words two days ago, of course; but I don't think they would have carried the same weight and value without a six-hundred-mile, two-day road trip behind them.

'You must be exhausted,' I say.

Ivy nods. 'Don't think I'll be staying up for the next two days, I'm afraid.'

'Can you manage ten minutes for presents?'

My parcel is about the size of a packet of crisps; Ivy's is roughly the size of a signed first edition copy of *A Prayer for Owen Meany*.

'You first,' Ivy says with a sly smile.

I tear open the snowman paper to reveal a pack of ten picture hooks.

As well as deferring my birthday until three fifty-five on the afternoon of December 25th, my family has always (for the last fifteen years, at least) found it highly amusing to give me a feeble, disappointing 'joke' gift for Christmas, only to follow it up with a present proper at five minutes to four in the afternoon. I have never told Ivy about this tradition, but it appears someone (Hermione, is my bet) has, and it seems I am doomed to suffer this festive farce for as long as I have the strength to tear paper.

'Hooks,' I say, with my traditional routine of forced enthusiasm and poorly concealed disappointment. 'Just what I always wanted.'

Ivy smiles, picks up her own parcel and picks at a corner of Sellotape with her nail.

'Be careful,' I advise.

Ivy regards me suspiciously. What she is holding is obviously a hardback book. What she doesn't know, though, is that this particular bunch of pages cost me over four hundred pounds. Worse still, she has read it before.

Ivy frees the tape from one end of the package and starts working on the other.

'*Owen Meany*,' Ivy says, clutching the book to her chest.

'You were reading it the first time we met.'

'I remember,' Ivy says, laughing.

'It's a first edition.'

And then she melts into tears. 'Thank you,' she says, wiping her eyes on her sleeve. 'It's ...'

The tears come harder now, and I'm terrified that one of them is going to land on the book and do about a hundred quid's worth of damage. Carefully, I take the book from Ivy's hands and place it on the coffee table.

I pull Ivy into a hug and kiss the top of her head.

'I love you,' she says. And if that's it, if those three words and a packet of picture hooks are all I get this year, then it will still be the best Christmas of my life.

'It's only a book,' I say. 'Pull yourself together.'

Ivy sniffs, wipes her eyes again. 'Phew,' she says, 'must be my hormones.'

She picks up the book from the coffee table, holds it reverentially and opens the cover, revealing John Irving's rather clumsy signature. She turns to the first page of the story, and starts reading. 'So good,' she says under her breath. 'Do you think it's safe to read?'

'Now?'

Ivy laughs, closes the book. 'Probably not, hey.'

I shake my head. 'I'd keep it well out of the reach of little fingers, too.'

Ivy's hands go reflexively to her belly.

'How are they?' I say.

'Great. Moving all the time.'

I lean forward and kiss her bump. 'Happy Christmas, babies.'

Ivy strokes my head. 'I almost forgot,' she says.

'Hmm?'

'It's your birthday, isn't it?'

'Thirty-two today.'

'Wait here.' Ivy begins hauling herself from the sofa.

'Shall I?'

She shakes her head and disappears into the hallway. When she returns, she is holding a flat package almost an arm span high and wide.

'Happy birthday,' she says, propping the article up against the sofa.

The very first day I met Ivy, we were discussing the make-up for the *Little Monsters* commercials I was shooting. Ivy made the comment that the scripts were 'horror in fancy dress', citing the old movie *Abbott and Costello Meet Frankenstein*.

And it is these three faces that adorn the framed poster Ivy has bought me for my birthday. *The laughs are monsterous*, according to the headline.

'I love it.'

'First day we met,' Ivy says, kissing me, and it sends a red-hot impulse straight to the centre of me.

'I remember. Where will I hang it?'

'Anywhere you like. It's your house, too.' And she leans forward and kisses me hard on the lips.

'So is it Christmas until we go to bed, or until we go to sleep?' I ask.

Ivy grins. 'Not sure what you're getting at.'

'Well, I thought that, as we've got the place to ourselves for a night . . .'

'A bit more than a night, actually.'

'Why, when's he coming back?'

Ivy shakes her head. 'He isn't.'

'They got back together?'

Another shake of the head. 'No. Frank and Lois are done. I told Frank it was time to move on. To move out, actually.'

I force myself not to grin too expansively. It's not easy. 'What did Frank say?'

'I told him we, me and you . . .' She kisses me on the forehead, the tip of the nose, the lips. 'I told him we needed our own space. He's fine, he gets it.'

'Do your folks know?'

Ivy nods.

'Wow, that must have been fun around the Christmas pudding.'

Ivy winces. 'Anyway,' she says. 'You taking me to bed or what?'

I fell asleep – with an idiot smile on my face – attempting to resolve a calculation . . . we last made love on the last weekend in August, the day before we visited Dad. Thirty days has September, April, June and November ... all the rest have thirty-one ... but every time I close in on a figure, I drift into sleep ...

Whatever the number, it had been well in excess of one hundred days since Ivy and I made love. Until last night. Until this morning.

When I wake several hours later, Ivy is not beside me. The sheets on her side of the bed are cool, but the physical memory of her still clings to me under the heavy blanket. Like the imprint of a sheet on my cheek and the smell of port on my breath. I'm hungry and need to pee, but I want to stay here, wrapped in the echo of Ivy's heavy breath, the residual heat from her body, the smell of her hair, the ghost of her back pressed against my chest ...

Today is the twenty-sixth day in December ...

I love Christmas.

Chapter 23

Papaya.

Mango.

Courgette.

Broccoli.

Aubergine.

Cantaloupe.

Cauliflower.

Acorn Squash . . .

Chapter 24

Ivy is twenty-nine weeks pregnant, and if you didn't know she was expecting twins you'd assume she was due in approximately ten seconds. Climbing the stairs is a feat of epic determination now; getting off the sofa is a two-man job; and standing, Ivy appears to defy the laws of physics – remaining somehow upright, despite her asymmetric planetary mass. She appears to be twice the size of the other women in the room.

There are eight couples in this chilly church hall, the men looking awkward as the women sit cowboy-style on their chairs. The instructor is teaching us how to massage our partners during labour, pushing our thumbs into the hollows at the tops of their buttocks – the instructor, Julie, calls them the 'Nodes of Venus'. Ivy's bump is too big for her to sit astride a chair like the other seven women, so she is kneeling on the floor, leaning forward over an inflatable gym ball.

After Ivy the person furthest along is a woman called Kath, who isn't due until mid-May – a full five weeks after the twins have made their entrance. Kath, like every woman here besides Ivy, is expecting a single baby, and there is a general sentiment of awe, fear, sympathy and admiration directed at my girlfriend and her stupendous bump. I'm fairly confident Ivy is the oldest mum-to-be by a good half-dozen years, and she is the only one not wearing a wedding ring.

I push my thumbs into Ivy's nodes, and resist the urge to kiss the back of her neck.

'If you can't get comfortable sitting on the chair,' says Julie, 'try leaning on a ball like Ivy. Or stand in front of a chair and lean on the back, like this.'

One of the women tries this, bending at the waist and gripping the back of the chair. From behind, her husband puts his hands on her hips and thrusts up against her.

'Get it while you still can, boys,' he guffaws, and a couple of the more polite guys laugh with him awkwardly.

Another guy, Steve, catches my attention and rolls his eyes; I nod subtly – *tosser.* Steve laughs. His wife and Ivy gravitated (in every sense) towards each other during the coffee break, leaving Steve and me to make not entirely awkward small talk – *What team do you support? What do you drive? What did you do last night?*

Last night was Valentine's Night. Our first together. And the most expensive date of my life. We went to a drive-in at Alexandra Palace and watched *The Princess Bride*. It's not a sexy movie, but I'm pretty sure the couple in the adjacent car were doing more than just kissing. Tickets, popcorn and drinks came in at over fifty quid. Which is a drop in the ocean compared to the eighteen grand we spent four hours earlier on a second-hand Volvo XC90. There is no question we need something more family friendly than Ivy's two-seater van or El's tiny Fiat, but this thing is the size of a small tank. It's very Wimbledon, though, and there's enough room in the back to deliver twins should the necessity arise.

They do antenatal courses for couples expecting twins, but the next one is too close to our due date and too far from our front door; so here we are, the odd ones out with one extra baby and two months fewer until our due date on April 11th. The course consists of two seven-hour sessions, of which this is the second, and after we leave today, we are, in theory, as prepared as we will ever be for the arrival of our babies. We have covered breathing, breastfeeding, nappies, sleep, forceps, suction cups and Caesarean sections. We have talked about emergency scenarios, and what are the best types of snacks to power us through labour. We have a list of items to pack in our hospital bag and a shopping list of essentials to buy from Boots.

It's informative and exciting and scary, and I have four pages of notes and a laminated wallet-sized checklist to consult during labour. But if anything, I feel more nervous than I did one week and seven hours ago. After the course we adjourn to a local pub for eight pints of beer and eight soft drinks. Squashed around three pushed-together tables, we form a large and conspicuous group, and the other drinkers are amused by our presence, nudging their friends and glancing in our direction as if we are some novelty act due to start performing at any moment.

Apart from learning how to change a nappy, the other reason anyone goes to antenatal classes is to make friends that won't be irritated by their incessant 'they did the funniest thing' anecdotes. It's a lottery and, looking around our group, I'm not planning on buying too many extra Christmas cards this year. The guy who was thrusting up against his wife just two hours ago is called Keith, and he has appointed himself social secretary.

'So,' he says, addressing the group as if we were guests

on his show. 'What does everybody do? I'll start, shall I? Lawyer, I'm afraid.'

There are, it transpires, three lawyers around the table, plus a wine importer, a property developer and two City types. Listening to the job descriptions, looking at the shoes, watches and lethal engagement rings, it's pretty clear that Ivy and I are the paupers in this group.

'Hair and make-up,' says Ivy, and all the women lean forward in their seats.

'Work with anyone famous?' asks Steve's wife, a pretty woman called Carrie.

'A few,' says Ivy, smiling.

'Who was the worst?'

'Hmm, I don't know about the worst, but . . . someone farted on me once.'

Carrie's hands go to her cheeks in horror. 'No!'

Ivy nods. ''fraid so. I was making a bite mark on his bum.'

'She suffers for her art,' I say.

Ivy shoots me a faux-withering glance. 'Funny. It was a vampire film. I used a pair of false teeth and some red eye-liner.'

'That's her story,' someone says.

Ivy winks. 'And I'm sticking to it.'

'Come on,' says Steve, 'we're going to need a name.'

'He . . . he was in *The Talented Mr Ripley*,' says Ivy. 'And that's all I'm saying.'

'Jude Law?' says Kath. 'I bet it was him.'

'What's that other one?' says Keith, flapping his hand in mid-air. 'Damon! Yeah, he looks like a farter. Definitely Damon.'

Ivy shakes her head. 'My lips are sealed.'

'I should hope so,' says Steve, laughing.

'So,' says Keith, slapping his hands together and signalling the end of that story. 'Fisher? How'd you earn your wonga?'

'I'm a director,' I say.

'Of?'

'Commercials.'

'What, like adverts?'

I nod.

'I like that one with the drumming gorilla,' says Keith. 'Did you do that one?'

'Afraid not,' I say, shaking my head.

Keith seems disappointed. 'Or them meerkats? They're funny.'

'Nope,' I admit.

'What's the last thing you did?' asks one of the City types.

I wince involuntarily. 'Nothing exciting.'

'Come on, spill the beans.'

The irony of this last piece of phrasing is horribly appropriate. 'Fastlax,' I say.

'What's that? Laxatives?'

I nod. 'Laxatives.'

'With the woman in the courtroom? The judge?'

Again I nod, and it practically echoes in the deflated silence.

'He did *Mr Bogeyman*,' says Ivy. 'Didn't you, babes?'

'I saw that!' says Carrie. 'When he goes to the funfair?'

'Yes,' I say, feeling an unexpected flush of pride.

'Won an award,' says Ivy, rubbing my shoulder.

'Is that how you met?' asks Steve.

'Never seen it,' says Keith, his bottom lip curling downward, dismissively.

'Yes,' I say to Steve. 'But not on *Mr Bogeyman*. On a Wine Gums shoot.'

'The one with the little vampire?' says someone else.

'I loved that,' says Carrie. 'The little girl was *soo* cute.'

I glance at Ivy and see that she, too, knows what's coming next. And, wouldn't you know it, it's coming from Keith.

'Hold on,' he says. 'They were on recently, weren't they?'

'Last summer,' I say.

Keith looks at me through narrowed eyes, like a TV detective closing in on the killer. He looks at Ivy, at her enormous bump. 'So . . . how long have you two been together?'

'About twenty-nine weeks,' says Ivy.

The background chatter amongst the group has died away. All eyes are on Ivy. She is blushing and it's making her scars stand out against her cheek, neck and lips. Ivy's hand goes to the left side of her face, but she catches herself and continues the motion of her arm, brushing her hand over her hair.

'And how pregnant are you?' pushes Keith.

'About twenty-nine weeks,' says Ivy.

There is a beat of silence before everybody laughs. It's good-natured laughter, though, and if anything it feels like our cachet has just risen.

'You dirty dog,' says Keith, slapping me on the shoulder. 'You dirty, dirty dog.'

After the clamour and questions and awe die down, the group fragments and we find ourselves in a cosy foursome with Steve and Carrie.

'Plans for the weekend?' asks Steve.

'Wedding,' I say.

Carrie's eyes widen.

'I'm the best man,' I say.

Carrie glances at Ivy's naked ring finger.

'Keep your eye on that bouquet,' says Steve, winking.

And again, Ivy blushes to her hairline.

Week twenty-nine in the baby book marks the start of a new section: 'Late Pregnancy'. The chapter opens with a description of the increasing physical discomfort the mother may be experiencing. Her organs are pushed out of place by the growing babies. Her bladder is compressed, her stomach forced upward, she will feel increasingly tired and fatigued. As per the book's description, Ivy's feet, ankles and hands are swollen with retained fluid. The book advises removing any rings and, not for the first time today, I am acutely aware of our unmarried status.

We drive to the New Forest tomorrow for Joe's wedding; I have polished my shoes, ironed my shirt, and – perks of living with a hair and make-up artist – Ivy has given me a haircut. My best-man's speech is written, rehearsed and reduced to five cue cards, now sitting on the bedside table. Ivy must have suffered through the three-minute monologue ten times or more. There is a paragraph about love and soul mates, and whilst I'm sure Joe and Jen are indeed 'made for each other', I describe a passion and romance that I can't in any honesty claim to have witnessed first-hand. Ivy smiles whenever I read these sentences, she looks me in the eye and I am speaking these words directly to her. Twice, it has made her cry. And then I move on to a bawdy anecdote, compliment the bride and invite the guests to raise their glasses. Ivy raises her invisible champagne flute, claps a small theatre clap and gives me notes on where I can tighten the speech. And every time we do this, I feel one increment sadder that Ivy and I are not married, and one degree more convinced that we should be. But at least Ivy doesn't have any rings she needs to remove due to her ballooning fingers.

The book says we should have started attending antenatal classes by now, and I laugh a little because this must be the first time we have done anything with conventional timing. Ivy swapped phone numbers with Carrie, and we both agree that she and Steve are the top candidates for the position of new best friends. They aren't due until five weeks after us, but they live nearby and don't seem to be insurmountably more affluent than the Fisher-Lees.

An acorn squash is around 16 inches long and looks like a cross between a pepper and a pumpkin. I have never heard of an acorn squash before today, but the twins are now the size of this strange-looking vegetable. Our babies are still active, the book informs us, but they will turn less frequently now as the womb becomes more cramped. Our babies' eyes can focus, they can blink, make out

331

shapes and silhouettes through the membranes and skin and fat of Ivy's stomach. If I fly a shadow bird across Ivy's belly, the babies can see it. The babies are growing by as much as one centimetre a week, laying down fat and flexing their muscles. *You may already have names for your new baby*, the book speculates. But all we have is a list of rejects.

'I like Evan,' says Ivy. 'I think.'

'Bit Welsh?'

'That's Evans, isn't it?'

'Both probably. What will they be – the twins – Fishers or Lees?'

'Well, if we have an Evan it'll need to be a Fisher.'

'Why?'

Ivy looks at me as if this should be obvious. 'Evan Lee?'

'Wh— ah . . . as in all the Evan Lee angels, I see.'

'Exactly,' says Ivy. 'Which, by the way, is another one.'

'Another what?'

'Lee, Zack Lee.'

'God, I'm slow, so your mother is—'

'Eva Lee, and my brother is Frank Lee.'

'That's mean. The other two don't have daft names, do they?'

Ivy shakes her head. 'Dad wanted to call Peter, Brock—'

'Brock Lee . . .'

'But Mum wouldn't let him. Then Geoff was nearly a Sylvester.'

'Don't get it.'

'Sly, Sly Lee. He wanted to call me Belle but, again, Mum with the veto. And then when poor old Frank came along, I think Mum either threw in the towel or was simply too distracted to notice.'

'So if they're Fishers, can we have Brock?'

'No.'

'Sylvester? I like Sylvester.'

'How about Dan, Danny?'

'I like it. Good boy's name.'

'Or Danielle.'

I cup my hands against Ivy's belly. 'What do we think about Danny in there? Any take—'

'Quick, look!' Ivy lifts her T-shirt, revealing the bare dome of her stomach. For a moment nothing happens. Then the most weird and wonderful thing I have ever witnessed: a smooth protrusion forms on the surface of Ivy's belly. The blunt point – which I'm hoping is the knee or elbow of a twenty-nine-week-old baby – travels from north-west to south-east on a curving trajectory then vanishes like a seal beneath the surface.

'That's Topsy,' says Ivy.

'Topsy?'

'Yeah, the one on the bottom's called Turvy. Here ...' She takes my hand, holds it against her bump and something ripples beneath my palm. My baby – no more than two centimetres away – pressing against my hand.

'Are you a Danny?' I say to the bump and, boy or girl, it moves again.

Chapter 25

Not that I've been to more than five or six, but I have never yet failed to enjoy a wedding. I'm a sucker for the romance, the vows, the ceremony, the dress, the tears, the free-flowing booze, the flowers, the silly dancing, the cake and the uncoupled bridesmaids. But this is the first time I've been on the staff, and it's a different story when you have a speech to deliver, taxis to coordinate and a dipsomaniacal photographer to marshal.

'Brilliant speech,' says Joe, patting me on the back. Although he's had a good deal to drink, and it comes out more like *Brilyanspeesh*.

My speech was fine, I remembered my lines, got everyone's name right and the guests laughed in most of the right places (Bob popping a hernia in a strip club, for example). But it's never going viral on YouTube. I've been carrying a small deck of index cards in my back pocket all day, a constant reminder that at some fast-approaching moment I would have to stand up in front of two hundred guests – half of them boozed-up advertising wankers – and deliver five hundred words on love, life, hurried sex and the effects of depilatory cream on the male nipple. The prospect was terrifying enough, but made all the more ominous by the fact that I have one current and two former girlfriends at this wedding (although the term 'girl-friend' is a woefully inadequate one for the mother of my babies, and a spectacularly glorified one in regard to my former squeezes: Pippa and I slept together half a dozen times over the course of a few weeks; Fiona and I screwed once, over the course of her sofa).

I had neither the time nor the nerve for a drink until I finished my speech, but Joe has been knocking them back since eleven this morning. It's now something past eight and he is running his words together and having difficulty walking in a straight line. Three times during the first dance (The Carpenters' 'Top of the World'), Joe came close to falling and dragging his new bride to the ground, and every time he did, the guests brayed and clapped and stamped their feet. You might be tempted to describe the whole day as 'Bacchanalian', but I'm not sure the Romans had access to as much cocaine and Ecstasy.

At a guess, there are one hundred and ninety-six people dancing to 'Agadoo' on and around the dance floor. Jen's centenarian grandmother is slumped – dead or asleep – at a table in the corner, Bob (propping up the bar) is off dancing duty under medical advice, and Joe and I are taking a breather at a table on the periphery of the action. Periodically, someone (friend, colleague, mother of the groom) attempts to drag us into the fracas, only to be told to 'fuck the fuck off' by Joe. Jen or Joe thought it would be cute to give the guests jars of old-fashioned penny sweets as wedding favours and – among my many other chores – I had to place two hundred of them on the tables this morning. Joe is holding one now, rummaging around inside until he finds a sherbet lemon. He holds it towards me. I decline and Joe pops it into his own mouth.

'Did I tell you, you're my best fucking mate?' he says.

'About ten times, and twice, using those exact words, during the speech.'

'Good, 'cos you are. Best. Fucking. Mate.'

'Thank you,' I say, as Joe kisses me wetly on the ear.

'Here,' he says, sliding his closed fist across the table-top.

'What's that?'

'Take it.'

'What is it?'

'Fuck's sake, Fisher, just take it.'

Joe places something into my hand. I assume it's some sort of sweet, but when I look at my palm I'm holding a blue, diamond-shaped pill.

'Viagra,' says Joe, loud enough to wake Jen's granny from whichever variety of slumber is dragging her head inexorably towards the table top.

'What the hell is this for?'

'Stupid question,' says Joe.

'I don't want it!' And I slide the pill across the table to Joe. 'And what the hell are you doing with Viagra?'

Joe shrugs. 'Wedding night, innit. Didn't want to take any chances. Take it.' He pushes the pill back to me.

'No, thank you.'

'Oh, I suppose *you* don't need it.' Suddenly Joe looks mortally offended.

'No. I mean … well, as it happens, I almost certainly don't need it. You've seen Ivy, right?'

'Course I have; she looks amazing.'

'I know she does. Thank you.'

'I'd do it in a heartbeat,' says Joe.

And before I have a chance to be offended, Ivy drops into the seat next to Joe.

'Do what?' she says.

'Beg pardon,' says Joe, visibly flustered.

The Viagra tablet is sitting on the table, hidden from

Ivy's view behind my wineglass. Very slowly, I place my hand on top of it.

'You said you'd "do it in a heartbeat",' pushes Ivy.

'Did I?'

Ivy nods. Today is the first time I have seen her in a dress, and despite the beach ball shoved up the front of it, Joe is right – she does look amazing. Her hair is coiffed onto the top of her head, and – another first for me – she is wearing full make-up. The funny thing is, though, she doesn't look like Ivy. I prefer the version with no make-up, no hairspray and a man's shirt. But it seems impolite, foolish even, to say so.

'Can't remember,' says Joe with a shrug. 'Right, I need a drink, see you two later.' And he gets up and leaves me hanging.

Ivy slides across into Joe's chair and places her hand on top of mine on top of the little blue pill.

'I just had a very interesting conversation with someone called Fiona,' she says.

'That's nice.'

Ivy looks me in the eye. 'She was very interested in me and you – when we met, how long we've been together, how far pregnant I am.'

'Some people,' I say, shaking my head.

'One of your conquests, I take it?'

'Wh ... me? I ...'

Ivy raises one eyebrow, purses her lips. I shrug.

'God help that poor bloke she's with,' Ivy says, smiling.

'You look beautiful,' I tell her.

'You scrub up okay, too. Want to dance?'

'You bet.'

'And you'd better bring that Viagra,' Ivy says. 'There are unattended children running around.'

Ivy is a terrible dancer, but, as with so much in our life together, I have no idea whether this is a product of her pregnancy or a fundamental truth. Shuffling about the dance floor, though, stepping on each other's feet and rebounding off the other careening guests, with our arms around one another and our two babies between us, I can't remember feeling happier in my life.

For whatever reason – oversight, most likely – the throwing of the wedding bouquet doesn't happen until early evening. And as such, the jockeying women waiting to receive the hurled flowers, are drunk, excited and utterly without shame as they elbow, bump and jostle each other for position. They are so frantic, in fact, that I'm genuinely concerned for Ivy and the twins' safety. From the centre of the mêlée Ivy glances over her shoulder and grins at me with an expression that's hard to read. I flash her a pair of crossed fingers and goofy smile that could be ironic or encouraging depending on what you're looking for.

'Scary, isn't it,' says a man beside me.

'Yours in there?' I ask.

The man points at Fiona, at the front of the pack. She rolls her shoulders and shakes out her fingers, loosening up. Pippa, standing beside Fiona, bounces nervously on the balls of her feet.

'Nice girl,' I say.

The man glances at me sideways and smiles. 'You're old friends, I believe.'

'Something like that.'

Eight stilettoed strides from the scrum, Jen braces herself to launch the fateful flowers. Ivy takes a deep breath, bellows her cheeks outward then exhales. Fiona removes her high-heels and tosses them aside.

'Good luck,' I say to Fiona's fella.

'Something tells me I'm going to need it,' he says, not taking his eyes off his girlfriend. 'I'm Hugh, by the way.'

'Pleased to meet you, Hugh.'

Hugh is drinking beer from a small brown bottle. He's holding it in his left hand, dangling at his side between us, and I wonder if it would be possible to drop the Viagra into the neck of his bottle undetected.

'You'll be fine,' I say.

And it's a lightning-fast, alcohol-assisted decision, involving none of my brain's higher departments. And as the pill drops silently into Hugh's beer, I feel exhilaration at my audacious panache, followed immediately by guilt and panic and, *what the fuck are you thinking, Fisher!*

'Let me get you a fresh beer,' I say, reaching for his bottle.

'I'm fine, thanks.'

'Here,' I say, grabbing the bottle.

Hugh pulls against me. 'I'm *fine.*'

I'm still holding the bottle, but then Hugh yanks it from my grasp, looking at me like I'm some kind of moron.

Fair enough.

And Jen swings the flowers between her legs and up and over her head. From where I'm standing, their trajectory looks to be carrying them directly to Ivy. Pippa jumps first. Fiona waits until her adversary is airborne before initiating her own leap and driving her shoulder into Pippa's midriff. As Pippa is knocked violently off course, Fiona rises like a prop forward, takes the bouquet with both hands and immediately draws it to her chest before landing neatly on her feet. The crowd goes wild.

'Cheers,' I say to Hugh, raising both my eyebrows and my gin and tonic.

Hugh smiles at me graciously. 'Cheers,' he says, tapping the neck of his bottle against the rim of my glass.

And what the hell.

A hand drops onto my shoulder and I turn to see Pippa's boyfriend, Gaz.

'Hey, Fish,' he says. 'Brilliant speech.'

I roll my eyes. 'Well, no one threw anything.'

Gaz laughs.

'Lucky escape,' I say, nodding towards the huddle of disappointed women pretending to be happy for Fiona.

'Yeah,' says Gaz, but his smile isn't very convincing.

It's another couple of hours before Ivy and I finally get back to our room. In the intervening time, I've broken up a fight and seen three different women and one guy in various degrees of tears. There are more drugs floating around the place than there are in an old lady's bathroom cabinet, and I'm glad to be out of it. Or not, as the case may be. I must have consumed close to my blood volume in beer, and it's a toss-up between who's unsteadier on their feet – me, or my heavily pregnant, high-heeled girlfriend.

And it's that damned word again – 'girlfriend' – growing increasingly inadequate as the twins continue to grow inside Ivy's belly. She is the mother of my children, we live in the same flat, we are connected at the chromosomes, and 'girlfriend' seems a little insipid for the situation. 'Partner' is the word people default to, but I hate it – too practical and pragmatic, too much like an arrangement.

While Ivy goes to the bathroom to remove her make-up, I sit on the bed and kick off my brogues. In one hand I'm holding the hipflask Joe gave me as a present for being best man, and in the other I have a glass jar full of penny sweets. I take the lid off the jar and dig among the flying saucers, white mice and vampire's teeth until I find a fizzy cola bottle.

After the flower throwing, I think I recognized the disappointment on Gaz's face because I felt it too. Yes I'm drunk, yes I'm high on the fumes of today's occasion, and yes there's nothing like the sight of a maniacal ex to enamour you of your current – *that word again* – girlfriend. But none of that changes the simple fact that Ivy is my 'one', and I intend to be with her until one of us (me, I hope) dies peacefully in our sleep. In amidst the pineapple chunks and jawbreakers and jelly babies is a single jelly ring. The toilet flushes and Ivy's ponderous footsteps thump along the corridor. I take the jelly ring from the jar and get down on one knee.

'Oh my God,' says Ivy as she rounds the corner. Her hands go to her face and she stops so abruptly she almost topples forward.

'Ivy . . .' I begin.

'Fisher, wait, no, I . . .'

'. . . will you marry me?'

Did she just say 'no'?

Ivy is frozen.

I offer up the ring and wobble a little on my knee.

Ivy winces.

'I know it's only a sweetie,' I say, 'but I'm serious. We can go shopping for the real thing tomorrow. Selfridges, Harrods, anywhere you want.'

Ivy still hasn't moved.

'I love you, Ivy. Completely and utterly and . . . well, completely.'

Ivy's hands drop from her face. She smiles . . . yes, apologetically. 'Babe,' she says, 'I love you, too. Completely and utterly and completely. But . . .' she shakes her head.

'But I thought . . . I don't . . . why?'

Ivy sighs, looks at me with a combination smile and grimace. 'Been there, done that,' she says. 'Sorry.'

I realize I'm still kneeling, still holding the stupid bloody jelly ring out towards Ivy. She sits on the bed and pats the space beside her.

It takes maybe half an hour for Ivy to get from the day she met a guy called Sebastian until the day her divorce came through. It shouldn't take thirty minutes to tell, but I interrupt her narrative every three minutes with indignant outbursts, elaborate compound insults and trips to the minibar. The salient details involve Sebastian and Ivy's inability to conceive and Ivy's assumption that the problem lay within her. For his part, Sebastian appeared to be entirely untouched by the disappointment that left Ivy sleepless with tears and nausea and heartbreak. More than this, though; not only did he – her fucking *husband* – fail to share Ivy's sadness, he failed to care about it. When she asked him to go with her to see a fertility specialist, Sebastian all but laughed. The marriage continued with sporadic sex and occasional highlights, but nothing changed except a gradual erosion of any affection. Before their first wedding anniversary Ivy had cheated on Sebastian twice (one-night flings on two-day shoots), and was reasonably certain he had returned or pre-empted the favour at least as many times. They spent a happy, romantic, perfectly civil week in Alicante to mark their first wedding anniversary and then, maybe three weeks later, sitting on the sofa with bowls of pasta on their knees, Sebastian turned to Ivy and said, 'This isn't working.' Ivy didn't correct him; she washed the dishes, went to bed, and in the morning she phoned a friend who happened to be a solicitor. Within a year Sebastian was living with another woman and their brand-new baby boy, further confirming Ivy's fears that she was unable to have children. Ivy got the flat.

And now I understand what Ivy meant by 'It's okay',

about contraception and I feel horrible for haranguing her about it on Christmas Eve.

'And you never thought to tell me this sooner?' I ask.

Ivy gives me a look that all girls learn when they are about three years old – chin down, eyes wide and an aren't-I-just-adorable smile. It's the look they give you when they want something, broke something, or forgot something.

'Just waiting for the right moment,' says Ivy, still beaming that look at me.

Ivy shrugs, holds up her right hand, fingers extended. 'Couldn't tell you the first time we met, obviously. *Oh, by the way, did I mention, I used to be married.*' And she folds down her thumb as good-reason-for-not-admitting-to-being-a-divorcée number one. She moves on to her index finger. 'Then we spent most of a week in bed. Then we went on holiday; then we went to your dad's. Then—'

'You got pregnant.'

'Then I found out you had got me pregnant. So, again, not good timing.' Ivy moves on to the fingers of her left hand. 'Then you moved in, then we had a scan, then we went to Mum and Dad's, then Frank moved in, then you got all stroppy on Christmas Eve.'

'Sorry about that.'

'It's okay – *ha!* My "answer to everything"!'

I shake my head at the memory.

'I don't blame you, babes, honestly I don't. But it certainly wasn't the time to bring up a failed marriage. Just . . . never a good moment.'

'Until now?'

Ivy nods. 'Until now.'

It's a bloody shock, for sure, but I'm less perturbed than I might have imagined. Maybe the signs were there all along. Maybe fatigue and alcohol have anaesthetized me. Maybe I'm immune to shock after the events of the last twenty-nine weeks.

'Who's better looking?' I ask. 'Me or *Sebastian*?'

Ivy punches me on the shoulder, but doesn't answer.

'Sorry. I . . . I'm just getting my . . .' I gesture at the invisible imps, elephants, tweeting sodding birds circling my head.

'It's why I was so . . . I don't know . . . protective, I suppose, of Frank.'

'Because you'd "been there, done that"?'

Ivy nods. 'I'm sorry. Are you okay? Are we . . .?'

I look at Ivy and only now register the anxiety on her face. I've been so wrapped up in my own insecurities that it hadn't occurred to me she might be wrestling with her own.

'Are you kidding? Yes, I just bloody proposed, didn't I?'

'That was before you knew I'd . . . you know. You don't

think I'm damaged goods?' There is a hint of a smile.

'Well, yes, obviously, but . . .' I place my hand on Ivy's stomach '. . . well, I'm stuck with you now.'

Ivy's head is down, her eyes on my hands on her belly. There is a tear on her cheek. As I watch, a drop forms in the corner of her eye, swelling, catching the light then spilling over and chasing its predecessor down Ivy's face.

Keeping one hand on her belly, I put my free arm around her shoulders. 'Baby, what's the matter?'

Ivy puts her hands to her face, her shoulders begin to shake and her breathing comes in hitching gasps as the quiet tears progress into full-on sobbing. I have never seen her like this and it's alarming.

'Babes, I was joking, you know that, right?'

Ivy nods. 'I love you so much,' she says, the short sentence punctuated by shuddering intakes of breath. 'I love you.'

'Marry me then.'

It's not until the words are out of my mouth that I realize how belligerent and ungracious they sound. I would take it back if I could, but instead I hug Ivy tightly as she shakes her head. The sound of shouting and screaming and music and laughing and two hundred drunken wedding guests rumbles down the corridor as if piped through cheap speakers at a low volume.

'I thought I couldn't have babies,' Ivy says. She sits up and wipes her eyes on the shoulder of my shirt. 'I thought I couldn't have babies, and then I could, then I thought I was going to lose you and I'd only just found you.'

'I'm still here,' I say.

'Stuck with me,' says Ivy. 'Aren't you?'

'I'd be stuck with you even if you weren't up the duff,' I tell her, and Ivy starts crying all over again.

We're sitting up in bed, talking baby names, when the couple in the next room crash through their door. More accurately, Ivy is talking baby names and I'm using all my willpower to stay awake. I'm drunk and tired and emotionally baffled, but I'm also horny as hell, and if nothing else I'm an optimist. Ivy has a book, *5001 Baby Names*, and as she reads through the D's – Declan, Dedalus, Deepak – I nuzzle into her neck, plant kisses on her shoulder, stroke her knee. Whether she's oblivious or determinedly ignoring me, I don't know.

And then the couple next door clatter into their room and thump up against the dividing wall. From the muffled groans and growls, it's immediately apparent that whatever pheromones are absent in this room, they are present in great sloshing bucketfuls in the next.

'Love is in the air,' I say, letting my eyebrows add a suggestive inflection.

Ivy closes the book, puts it down on the bedside table, rummages through her bag of toiletries.

'If you can't beat 'em . . .' I say to Ivy's back.

Ivy turns to me, holding something in her closed fist.

'Earplugs,' she says, dropping a pair of yellow foam bullets into my hand.

'I love you,' Ivy says, and I can feel the honesty of it when she kisses me.

She turns out the light.

The earplugs, it turns out, are effective enough at muting the vocal manifestations of sex, but aren't quite up to blocking out the noise of a headboard banging against a bedroom wall. When the guy next door starts testing the construction of the bed for the fifth time, it's gone four a.m. and I've given up hope of getting any sleep. Maybe Ivy kept the best pair for herself, because she sleeps as peacefully as if we were in a soundproof chamber. And I'm grateful for this mercy, because whoever the hell is in the next room, he's making me feel woefully inadequate. Who knows, maybe someone spiked his beer with Viagra.

Chapter 26

For the first year of our friendship El was half a head taller than me. In the twenty-two years since, I have grown by around a foot and a half, and El by approximately three inches, but I have always looked up to him. He is almost fourteen months older than me, so he went to big school a year before I did. That kind of profound class distinction could kill a friendship, but we went to different schools and weren't put in a situation where El was forced to ignore or patronize me. He lived a short walk from my house so we played together most days, El bringing information and artefacts from the future: pornography, cigarettes, sherry, dirty jokes, new bands, details of sexual mechanics and anatomy. El is a year older than me, always was. But as I look at him now, I can't ignore the knowledge that soon his clock will stop; his age will reach its limit the same way his stature did twenty years ago.

With hindsight it was always apparent that El was gay, but as a young boy I was as ignorant of the signs as of the possibility ('gay' being nothing more than a slur or a far-fetched rumour). Take the pornography, for example.

''member wh... wh... what y'used t'call me?'

'El Tittymonger,' I say.

'T... t... tittymonger tittymonger!' El says, throwing his head backward and barking a harsh, gasping laugh that sounds worrying, like he's choking on his pizza. I go to stand, but El shakes his head and waves me away.

Through some intermediary or other, El would come home from school with his bag straps straining under the weight of *Men Only*, *Penthouse*, *Club* and *Razzle*. El would sell these to the frothing teenage boys in the village, but I didn't question why he never kept any material for his own perusal.

The mention of El Tittymonger appears to have swerved El's train of thought from things past to things pending. 'A... a... are y... you h... havin a...' his lips come together and his cheeks bellow outward as he struggles to find or eject the right word.

'Can you spell it?' I ask.

El's face creases with effort. 'B... f... b...'

'What does it sound like?'

'S. . . sound. . . sounds like fuck off!'

'Sorry.'

El scowls as he raises his hands, twitching less now, instead moving with hypnotic slowness — as if bound in elastic — as his disease advances. His hands come to rest in front of his belly, hugging an invisible bump.

'Baby,' he says. 'Are y. . . having a baby?'

'Two,' I tell him. 'Twins.'

El smiles. It's genuine but transient; dropping from his face as quickly as it formed. 'K. . . kill for a d. . . f. . . d. . . drink,' he says.

I reach for El's pink sippy cup of orange squash.

'Bollocks!' he shouts, startling me. 'R. . . r. . . real drink.'

Reflexively, I look over my shoulder, which is a stupid thing to do as we are on our own in the house. I don't intend giving El any alcohol, but it appears that some subconscious part of me would.

'You know it's bad for you,' I say, hating the sound of my own voice.

'L. . . life's f. . . fukig b. . . bad f'me.' And he laughs genuinely.

El doesn't eat much now; the bulk of his calories coming from fortified drinks and powders. Always slight, he looks angular and fragile. His beard, though, is magnificent – thick and glossy, lending him the look of a guru, perhaps, or a junkie rockstar.

'Wh. . . when?' he says. 'Th. . . th. . . the b. . . baby?'

'Babies,' I remind him, holding up two fingers. 'April the 11th – seven weeks and two days away.'

El nods. 'Good.' He smiles. 'Y. . . you'll be good,' he says. 'G. . . d. . . g. . . good dad.'

'We'll see.'

'Goin' m. . . marry that g. . . gir?'

'Ivy,' I tell him, smiling at the memory of my clumsy and unsuccessful proposal at Joe's wedding. 'Yes,' I say, because the real story is too difficult to tell, and anyway, it's as good as the truth – love, honour, obey; to have and to hold; for better for worse . . . yes to all of that; I will and I do, and as much as I'd like it, I don't need a certificate to stay with Ivy until death do us part.

'More pizza?'

El shakes his head and flops backward into the sofa. 'I. . . I'm . . . done,' he says.

'Not even one more slice?'

El shakes his head violently; his face is screwed up in annoyance. 'D. . . done!' he says, bringing his hands slowly but deliberately to his head. 'T. . . tired of th. . . this,' he says, and there are tears running down his checks.

'El, hey.' I sit next to him and put my arm around his shoulders.

'Wish I was d... d...'

He's still struggling to end his sentence, and I hug him to me, stroking his long hair and pressing his face against my chest to stifle the final word. He's crying so hard I can feel the wetness of his tears through my T-shirt.

After a minute or maybe two, El pushes away from me, sniffing.

'Wh... wh... w...'

'What? ... When? ... W—'

El nods. 'When... when's Phil's b... b...'

'His birthday? May. Start of May.'

'S... soon then,' El says.

'A few months still.'

Phil went to the pub tonight, as he always does when I visit El. Tonight, though, is the first time he's openly admitted to meeting Craig there. He hasn't yet suggested they are anything more than drinking buddies, but I have my very strong suspicions. Last week Craig was already here when I came to see El, and there was something in Phil and Craig's body language, tone of voice and eye contact that felt more than platonic.

'A... after Phil's b... birthday h...' El takes a deep breath, steels himself and presses on with scowling, dogged determination, 'he's t... takin me t'that place. W... wh... wh...'

'What?... When?... Why?... Where?'

El nods. 'Wh... where th... they k... m... k... kill you.'

'What? Pardon?'

'Th... they kill you,' he says, smiling as if describing a trip to Disneyland. 'D... D... Diggitas.'

'Dignitas?'

El nod, nod, nods. 'T' get killed!' he says, chuckling and letting his eyes close and his tongue loll out onto his chin.

'El, wh— shut up! Phil hasn't ...'

El grins and nods, and as much as he is prone to inventing scenarios and bending the truth, his sincerity shines through. 'Wh... what I want,' he says. 'B... birdy present for E... El.'

'But ...'

But what? El struggles to speak and think, he can't walk without help, climb the stairs, or get up to pour a glass of water. He can barely operate a remote control. He can't eat curry or drink beer; he can't follow a plot. He needs Phil to wipe his backside and he sleeps alone in a padded cot. And this disease is progressive; there is no remission, no cure, no hope for anything other than decline. And death. And as much as I don't want to hear it, I get it.

'Your birthday isn't until November,' I remind him.

El shakes his head. 'Can't w... can't wait t... till Nember.' And he shakes his head again. The devilment slips from his eyes and when he smiles, it's a composite of sadness, fatigue and silent appeal. There is no bravado or insincerity, and it's the most present and lucid I've seen El in many months.

'How about that drink?' I ask him.

El's eyes go wide. 'Really?'

'Really,' I tell him.

When Phil gets back from the pub an hour later, El is sleeping with his head in my lap. And when Phil walks into the room, the first thing he does is notice the half-empty whisky glass on the table in front of El. Mine is full, for the third time.

'He told you, then,' says Phil, dropping into his favourite armchair.

I nod.

'And ...?'

I raise my glass. 'Join me?'

Phil reaches across the table and picks up El's unfinished drink, he clinks the glass against mine and takes a sip. 'How much did he have?'

'That was his first and last glass. Had about three sips.'

Phil smiles, nods.

'How's Craig?' I ask, and maybe there is a little edge, a little snide on the question.

Phil hesitates a second before answering. 'He's fine,' he says. 'We're . . . good, you know.'

I nod and smile.

'Nothing happens,' Phil says. 'Not really, not . . . not often.' He puts a finger to the corner of his eye.

'Don't you start crying,' I tell him. 'Had plenty of that for one night.'

Phil starts crying.

'Does El know?'

Phil nods, shakes his head, shrugs. 'I don't know, Fisher. We . . . Craig stays over sometimes.' This sets Phil off on a full-on, shoulder-shaking, head-in-hands crying jag – he goes from nothing to sobbing in a single second, then after half a minute of histrionics, he somehow pulls himself together at about the same speed. It's exhausting to witness. Phil takes a deep breath, swallows the last of El's whisky and refills both of our glasses. 'El sleeping in that . . . fucking cot,' he says, 'and me and Craig in the next room. It's so . . . I'm a fucking mess. It's a fucking mess.'

'It's okay,' I tell him. 'You're allowed to be happy.'

'Easier said than done,' Phil says.

'How long have you been seeing him?'

'On and off since November.'

'Going well?'

'Yes. I think so, I mean ... yes,' Phil allows himself a smile. 'He's good to me, makes me feel ...' Phil shrugs and dabs his tears with a handkerchief. He glances at El. 'And then there's my baby boy here.'

I don't know what to say, so I don't say anything.

Phil is crying again. 'It's like the worst thing and the best thing happening at the same time, and I ... God, I sound so selfish.'

'El would be happy for you, you know.'

'I wish I could be.'

'Give it a try,' I tell him, and the triteness of it embarrasses me to the point where I feel myself blush. 'I mean, he'll act up, shout, call you names, throw things ...'

Phil laughs. 'At least he can't throw things very far, hey?'

'There is that. But you should – you should tell him.'

Phil nods. 'I know.'

'So,' I say. 'After your birthday?'

'July, August, maybe. In about six months.'

'Best make them a fucking good six months, then.'

I empty my glass and immediately refill it.

Phil swallows the last of his. 'Pass the bottle.'

Chapter 27

Three times in two months.

Twice in one day.

I am a sex god, a bedroom legend, a mattress master. Oh, yes and make no mistake, I am a non-stop love machine.

This year is a leap year, and today is the last day in February – the 29th, if you please. It's Ivy's turn to read the baby book, which is a good thing because I'm too fuzzed-out and soft around the edges on my post-coital comedown. On my post-*day* comedown, for that matter. At thirty-one weeks our babies are at least as long as a stick of celery. Which may not sound particularly impressive, but at thirty-one weeks Ivy looks like she is full term, and it's the limit of my reach to wrap my arm around her waist and pull her against me as we lie on our sides making love. At thirty-one weeks, the twins can hear us singing, talking, laughing, they can feel my hands on their mother's stomach. They can – although the book doesn't mention this explicitly – hear Ivy saying, 'That's it . . . like that, yes, yes, oh my God yes,' and so on. It doesn't do to think about it too deeply.

The babies' lungs have secreted a surfactant that will enable them to breathe independently outside of the womb. Their cheeks are chubby, their bottoms are soft and plump. Ivy's uterus undergoes involuntary Braxton Hicks contractions – practice contractions for the real thing just six weeks away. There is less space than ever inside Ivy's womb, but even so the babies will make noticeable movements around ten times a day.

As I lie beside Ivy, still tingling with the afterglow of our lovemaking, drifting in and out of that surreal pre-sleep state, my hand rests at the top of Ivy's bump and (always the more active of the two) baby Danny, or Danni if it's a girl, kicks against my hand. Turvy is still without a proper name, but Owen is on the shortlist for a boy and Juliet, my mother's name, is the front-runner for a girl.

'Did you have a nice honeymoon?' Ivy asks.

I nuzzle my face into the side of Ivy's neck and nibble at the soft flesh. 'Is it over already?' I ask.

Ivy strokes the top of my head and it sends a shiver across my skull, and down my nape and spine.

This morning Ivy brought me breakfast (toast and coffee) in bed.

'Do you know what day it is?' she asked.

'Friday?'

'The . . .'

'I don't know . . . is it pinch punch first of the month?' I say, pinching then punching Ivy on the bicep.

'Ouch! No,' she slaps my hand. 'It's the 29th of February, doofus.'

'Leap year,' I say, sitting up suddenly and very nearly spilling a full mug of coffee all over myself.

'Yes,' Ivy puts her hand on top of mine, 'and before you get excited, I'm not proposing.'

I lower myself back into my pillows. 'Oh.'

'Want to know what the best thing is about getting married?'

'The presents?'

Ivy shakes her head. 'The honeymoon.'

'Where did you go?'

'Botswana, Tongabezi, Uganda, Mozambique, Madagascar.'

'What?'

Ivy shrugs apologetically. 'He was a banker.'

'You said it.'

'Anyway,' says Ivy, and she leans in and kisses me very

delicately, her tongue brushing against my lips, 'we're going to the zoo.'

'The zoo? Today?'

Ivy nods. 'Remember when we met in the café, the day I told you about …' and she places a hand on her belly. 'You said we should go to the zoo?'

I smile at the memory; me clumsily trying to stave off what I thought was an imminent dumping.

Ivy kisses me again. 'Happy honeymoon, baby.'

I pick up the tray of coffee and toast, place it gently on the floor and then help Ivy remove her T-shirt.

After the gorillas and tigers, the giraffes, penguins, lions, zebras, long-snouted seahorses and ice creams in the freezing cold, Ivy took me to a Michelin-starred restaurant. And after the vichyssoise of asparagus and the pressed-duck-liver pâté; the caramelized halibut, heirloom tomatoes and slow-cooked rump of lamb; the Valrhona chocolate hotpot with confit orange and poppy-seed sorbet; the Muscadet, cappuccino and hand-rolled truffles, after all of that Ivy put me in a taxi, brought me home and made love to me for the second time in one day.

And there is not one single thing, animal, ingredient, nuance or whispered word that could have made this day any more perfect. My face is still pressed into that place where her neck joins her body and my face seems to fit so well. I lick a trail up to the tip of her chin, kiss her mouth, take her bottom lip between my teeth.

'Are you serious?' asks Ivy, me still biting her lip.

'You only get one honeymoon,' I tell her.

'Speak for yourself,' she says, removing my hand from her thigh. 'But this was definitely in my top two.'

The First Monday Reading Circle is seven people around, and the youngest person after Ivy is probably Agnes, who I have pegged in the low-to-mid sixties. At the other end of the loop is Cora, surely well into her eighties and who seems permanently bewildered to the extent that I'm surprised she can even hold a novel the right way up. Today they are assembled in our living room, eating biscuits and discussing a chap I've never heard of called Paul Auster. Listening to the racket coming through the walls, it sounds like a bunch of angry men arguing about football, rather than a group of pensioners discussing fiction; and it's making it remarkably difficult to concentrate on the task in hand.

I'm kneeling in the centre of a fairy-tale forest, staring at an inaccurate map and feeling more than a little lost. The recently cleared spare bedroom (my chair and TV have been granted admission to the living room,

Cocktopussy has been disposed of and everything else is wrapped in polythene and wedged into the tiny loft space) is now a nursery. The walls are painted blue and green and adorned with vinyl transfers of trees, birds, squirrels, a castle, a knight, a princess and a dragon that, if you ask me, is a touch too scary for a baby's bedroom. In the middle of this make-believe wilderness, I am surrounded by screws and bolts of various sizes, nubs of dowelling and assorted pieces of wood that, according to the instructions, are a mere ten steps away from becoming a cot. And when I've assembled this one there is another, still in its box, propped up against the radiator. The race is on to see if I can make sense of four pages of Ikea instructions before the pensioners (and Ivy) dissect four hundred pages of contemporary American literature. At thirty-two years old I have of course 'done flat-pack' before, with modest, if imperfect, success; but the stakes are so much higher now. Panel A is virtually indistinguishable from Panel B, and neither looks very much like its diagram, so I check again, because this construction will be holding babies, not books, and there is zero margin for error.

There is a knock on the other side of the forest door.

'Hello?' says a gentle, plummy voice.

'Come in.'

Jim, the only male member of the First Monday

Reading Circle, is somewhere in his mid-sixties and married to Agnes. His bald head appears around the door jamb. 'Golly,' he says, taking in the scattered components. 'Looks complicated.'

'Just a little,' I say, holding up the useless instructions.

Jim's arm snakes around the doorway. 'Thought you might need refreshing,' he says, presenting a large glass of wine.

'Jim, you're a legend. A knight in shining armour, in fact. Come in, please.'

Jim steps into the room and tiptoes with surprising nimbleness around the strewn pieces of my flat-pack cot.

'Cheers,' he says, passing me the wine then clinking his glass against mine.

'I'd invite you to sit down,' I say, gesturing apologetically at the absence of any furniture. 'But . . .'

Jim waves this away and sits cross-legged on the carpet beside me. '*Dim problem*, as they say in Wales. Aggy makes me do yoga three times a week; I can manage a few minutes on my bottom.'

'You Welsh?' I ask.

Jim shakes his head. 'The in-laws were, so you pick up the odd phrase.' He laughs. 'Well, I had to; they didn't speak a word of English the first three times I met them. Or rather, they chose not to.'

'Odd.'

'I think they were rather suspicious of my intentions towards their daughter,' he says, waggling his bushy eyebrows in what is probably meant to be a lascivious fashion. 'Being a parent does funny things to you,' he says. 'You'll discover that for yourself soon enough.'

'You have kids?' I ask.

Jim holds up three fingers. 'All girls,' he says, beaming. 'Delores, Florence and Myfanwy – all grown up now, all mummies in their own right.'

'Wow.'

Jim nods. 'Most wonderful thing in the world, being a daddy, but . . .' and he clicks his fingers in the air '. . . it goes fast,' he says. 'Very, very fast.'

Jim picks up a piece of dowelling and rolls it between his fingers.

'Any words of wisdom?'

Jim laughs again. 'You're asking the wrong chap,' he says. 'I don't know, just . . . just enjoy it. Do the best you can and don't be too hard on yourself when you get it wrong.'

'I'm sure I will. Get it wrong, I mean.'

Jim puts a hand on my shoulder. 'You'll be fine. I mean, yes, you'll get it wrong, but you'll be fine. Ivy is a wonderful girl, wonderful, wonderful girl.'

'Yes. Yes, she is.'

'You know,' Jim says, setting his glass down carefully, 'I always rather enjoyed a bit of flat-pack. Need a hand?'

I nod at the wall, in the direction of the chatter coming from the book club. 'Aren't you meant to be . . .?'

Jim shrugs. 'I didn't care much for the book, to be honest. Skimmed most of it.' He winks, holding a finger to his lips in an arch gesture of conspiracy.

I pass the assembly instructions to him. 'Please, be my guest.'

Jim ignores the instructions and instead dives straight in, sliding the piece of dowel into what I hope is the correct hole.

'Have you been in the book club long?' I ask.

'Must be more than ten years,' he says, selecting a screw and attaching a leg to what might be Panel B. 'Funny thing is, I'm not really much of a reader.'

'So why join a book club?'

'It's what you do, isn't it. For each other, I mean. Aggy liked the idea but was too shy to go on her own. So I went along for moral support more than anything else.' Jim hunts through the various pieces of pine until he finds the one he wants. 'I was only going to attend the first one or two, to get her started, but the girls had left home, and . . .' Jim balances a piece of cot between his feet, holding it in place with his knees '. . . pass me that leg, would you. It's just a nice thing to do together. The book's the least part of it, if I'm honest. For me, anyway . . . that screw, there, if you will . . . thank you. Going somewhere on the bus, meeting friends, having a glass of wine.'

'Is that a hint?'

'I beg your pardon?'

I hold up my wine glass, which is now empty.

Jim grins mischievously. 'Don't mind if I do, young man. Do not mind if I do.'

By the time Jim leaves, my new friend has assembled two cots, two mobiles, two baby bouncers and drunk (an indulgent, admonishing look from Agnes for her husband, and a smack on the bottom for me) the best part of a bottle of wine.

'Just remember,' he says, the words coming a little more thickly now, 'it goes like that . . .' and once again, he clicks his fingers in the air. 'Enjoy every moment.'

'And change your share of nappies,' says Agnes. 'Honestly, James, you'll be up half the night now.'

'Blame this one,' says Ivy, putting her arm around my shoulders. 'He's a bad influence.'

'Yes,' says Agnes, and she kisses me on the cheek before steering Jim out of the door.

*

'How about Agnes?' I ask.

'How about her?'

'As a name, I mean.'

'You're drunker than I thought,' Ivy says. 'Ouch! Easy ...'

I have three fingers inserted deep into her vagina. 'Sorry. Want me to take a finger out?'

'No, just ... slow it down a little.'

'How's that? Better?'

Ivy winces. 'A little.'

Depending on which website you get your information from, approximately one in three women will suffer a vaginal tear during childbirth. Which isn't surprising when you consider the dimensions of the various elements – try pulling a sock over your head, for example; just make sure it's a sock you don't mind destroying. These rips and tears tend to happen in the no-man's land between anus and vagina – the perineum. One way to protect against this kind of trauma is to pre-stretch the perineum beforehand. Long live romance.

'Poppy?'

'My neighbours had a dog called— Jesus!'

'Maybe I should stop?'

Ivy shakes her head. 'Did you cut your nails?'

I nod. 'So, your neighbours ... they had a dog called Jesus?'

'Little yappy thing,' says Ivy, grimacing. 'And a cat called Satan.'

'You sure you're okay?'

'Just keep going.'

With my fingers hooked into Ivy's vagina, I stretch the flesh outward, rotating my hand at the wrist the way a potter might open the neck of a vase. Ivy screws her eyes tight and takes a sharp intake of breath.

'Rose?' I try.

'Whatever,' says Ivy.

'You don't like Rose?'

'Seriously, you can call it Cinderfuckingrella if they can get it out without ripping me in half.'

'Actually,' I say, 'I quite like Cinderfuckingrella; it's . . . I dunno, classic.'

'Romantic?'

'Romantic!' I say clicking the fingers on my free hand. 'Cinderfuckingrella. And if it's a boy, we can call it Rumplebastardstiltskin.'

'Perfect,' says Ivy. 'We cracked it!'

I rotate my hand anticlockwise and back again. There is nothing remotely pleasant, pretty or sexy about it. Nevertheless, it does cross my mind that whilst I'm here, whilst we have this intimate contact, we might as well . . .

'Don't even think about it,' says Ivy.

'What! Think about what?'

'It's written all over your bloody face,' she says. 'And just to be clear, you've got more chance of seeing Cinderfuckingrella on a birth certificate than having a wriggle tonight.'

'So tomorrow?'

'I'll think ab— Bastard!'

'Sorry.'

'Sod this,' says Ivy, scooching her bum backwards so that my fingers snap out of her with a wet pop. 'Whatever happens, happens. It's going to be bad enough on the night without going through this now. Sod it.'

'Sure?'

'Positive.'

'Cup of tea?'

Ivy nods. 'And don't forget to wash your hands.'

Chapter 28

Coconut.
Pineapple.
Butternut squash . . .

Chapter 29

If there's a day I dislike more than Christmas, it's Mother's Day. And the entire four weeks leading up to it, with every other shop window and TV advert reminding me that my own mother is no longer with me. Maybe that's why I went so overboard on Ivy.

When we woke on Saturday morning, I informed Ivy that it was exactly nineteen days to our due date. To celebrate, we ate our toast and drank our coffee in the fairy-tale forest. The nursery is now complete: two cots, two mobiles, two Moses baskets, two baby bouncers plus a small sofa bed for bottle-feeds and bedtime stories. There is barely space on the ground for a teddy bear, and my feet rested against one of the cots while we sat on the sofa and ate our breakfast in the quiet of the small anticipant room. In the afternoon we bought flowers and a card for Ivy's mother. And while Ivy took an afternoon nap, I bought flowers, a card, chocolates, wine and two balloons for Ivy from baby DannyorDanni and baby Julietorsomethingelseifitsaboy. I stowed the goods in the Volvo's vast boot and went for a long run through the Common. I went to sleep imagining the look of joy, gratitude and unvarnished love on Ivy's face when I surprised her with my Mother's Day bonanza.

Ten hours later, I wake in an empty bed to the gentle sound of a teaspoon stirring milk into a mug of coffee. Ivy is sitting at the living room window, reading a novel, sunlight blowing out through her bed-tousled hair.

I fetch a mug and sit opposite her. 'Hey, you.'

Ivy reads on for a few seconds while I pour myself a coffee. She glances up from her book. 'Hey.'

'Do you know what today is?' I ask.

Ivy nods, smiles. 'Sunday.'

'Not just any Sunday, it's Mother—'

'Don't say it.'

'What? I'm just saying i—'

'Please! Sorry ... I'm nervous enough, babes, I don't want to tempt ... let's just let it happen, yeah?'

I feel stupid sitting there in my underpants, squinting against the sunlight. My instinct is to say something smart and petulant, but the smart part eludes me so I say nothing and sip my coffee.

'Sorry,' Ivy says.

'No, I'm sorry, I wasn't thinking.' My mind flashes to the car boot full of premature, fate-tempting Mother's Day paraphernalia. 'What time we leaving?'

'As soon as you get out of the shower.'

Driving the width of the country to give Ivy's mum her flowers, and heading straight back after lunch, takes around ten hours and puts four hundred miles on the Volvo's clock. We could have stayed the night but Ivy is thirty-four weeks pregnant, and determined to have the baby in 'her own' hospital. Ivy's sense of practicality is marginally stronger than her fear of fate, so her 'birth bag' is now packed and standing by the hallway door and we have installed the twin car seats into the rear of the Volvo. I keep catching the seats' reflection in the rear-view mirror, and their presence gives me a pleasant sensation of butterflies in my stomach. It feels real now, and frighteningly imminent.

As we pull into our street my eyes sting, my brain is fuzzy and my legs ache from a day behind the wheel. I turn off the engine, kill the lights, crick my neck and go to open the door.

'Babes?' says Ivy.

'What is it?'

'Can we go to the hospital?'

Panic!

'You're not . . .'

'No no no' – a hand on my shoulder – 'I just want to check the route, see how long it takes.'

'Like a test run?'

'Do you mind?'

'Well, I am kind of completely, utterly and thoroughly exhausted.'

She does the look. '*Please?* Just a couple more miles?'

It takes twenty-three minutes to drive from our front door to the hospital.

It's past ten on Sunday evening, the sky is clear and dark and the car park is largely empty. We're too tired to talk, so we relax in the warmth of the large car, listen to the radio at a low volume and soak up the surprising calm of St George's Hospital.

'Soon,' I say.

'Soon,' says Ivy.

As well as her scheduled appointment with the midwife, Ivy had a check-up with a paediatrician last week and everything is 'perfect', the twins are healthy and in a good position and Ivy, despite her swollen ankles, is in great shape. In less than three weeks we will be a family of four and this car will be full of noise and the smell of dirty nappies.

I'm debating how to dispose of the Mother's Day contraband in the boot, when a battered Ford Focus pulls into the car park. Approximately three-quarters of a second after the car comes to a stop, a man practically falls out of the driver's-side door and sprints around the vehicle to the passenger's side.

Ivy reaches across and takes hold of my hand.

The man pulls open the passenger's door and leans inside. After maybe a full minute, but it feels like five times that, a heavily pregnant woman emerges. She is no sooner out of the car than she drops to her hands and kneels on the tarmac. The guy turns around in a full clockwise circle then rotates back the other way before crouching down beside the woman. He places his hand on the small of her back, and although they are fifty or sixty metres away, we hear her bellow at him to 'Get off me!' The guy stands, rotates another one and a half circles and crouches again. Despite myself, I laugh, and Ivy squeezes my hand hard enough to make my fingers throb.

The man helps the woman to her feet and they begin shuffling towards the hospital entrance.

'Should I go and help?'

'And do what?' Ivy says.

After only four or five steps the couple stop again and the woman bends double at what was once her waist. Even from this distance, you can see the man struggling to support her. She shouts out in pain and the man lowers her to a kneeling position. He looks around as if for assistance, and suddenly sprints into the distance leaving the woman alone, kneeling on the pavement.

'Maybe you should go,' Ivy says.

'Yeah, but you're going to have to let go of my hand first.'

'What?' Ivy looks at my hand; her expression suggests she is surprised to discover her own wrapped around it. 'Oh, right, yes.'

But as she releases her grip the man comes sprinting back into view, pushing a wheelchair he has acquired from God knows where. He eases the woman to her feet, manoeuvres her carefully into the wheelchair, and hurries off in the direction of the hospital building.

And all of a sudden, the car park is quiet again.

'Did that just happen?' Ivy says after a minute.

'I think so.'

'Fuck!'

'My thoughts exactly.'

'Take me home,' says Ivy.

The engine starts with a reassuring, confident rumble; I put it into gear, and begin reversing out of the parking space.

'Blimey,' says Ivy.

And as she hits the second syllable there is a loud, heart-jolting *Bang!*

Ivy screams.

'What was that? Did we hit something? Did so—*ooh* . . .' She puts both hands to her bump.

At thirty-four weeks, our babies are the size of a pair of butternut squashes, around eighteen inches in length and weigh approximately five pounds each. Their brains and nervous systems are fully developed; our babies will dream when sleeping, and they may even have developed a preference for certain flavours (although I struggle to believe that amniotic fluid comes in more than a single variety). Their lungs are almost completely developed, and if the twins were born now, in the front seat of an XC90, there is a good chance they could breathe for themselves.

'Are you okay?' I ask, my nerves vibrating like power cables in a high wind.

'I think so, just had a bit of a Braxton Hicks thingy. What was that bang?'

'I have no id—'

Unless . . .

'What?' says Ivy.

I look at Ivy, bite my bottom lip and widen my eyes

in what I hope is an expression of lovable incorrigibil-
ity.

'What! I'm freaking out here.'

'It might . . . have been a balloon.'

'A what?'

'Promise not to get mad?'

'No!'

I shrug, get out of the car and walk around to Ivy's side
and open her door.

'Fisher, will you just tell me what's going on?'

'Easier to show you,' I say, helping her from the car.
'Come on.'

Reluctantly, Ivy follows me to the boot, which I click
open revealing a card, chocolates, wine, a bunch of
thorny roses, one inflated balloon and various fragments
of one burst balloon. Ivy retrieves the remaining balloon;
printed across its surface are the words 'Happy Mother's
Day'.

'You shouldn't have,' Ivy says. 'Really.'

'I know . . . I bought them yesterday, while you were
sleeping. Didn't have a chance to dispose of them. Sorry.'

'I'll keep the flowers,' she says. 'And the chocolates.'

'Can I have the wine?'

'Only if you give me a sip.'

'Only if you give me a chocolate.'

'Only if you get rid of the card.'

'It's a deal,' I say, leaning in to kiss Ivy.

She lets go of the balloon and we stand watching as it floats away into the night sky.

Chapter 30

We're shooting on a rooftop overlooking an industrial estate in south-east London. We're miles away from any residential properties, but when I shout, 'That's a wrap,' I shout it quietly; and the applause that follows is restrained. Standing here with Suzi, Joe, two actors and eleven crew, I should feel exhilarated. But the sun is still several hours away from rising and my predominant feeling is one of deep, cellular fatigue.

We have tweaked, re-tweaked, finessed and polished the script, but still I'm not convinced it's as good as it can be. There is an inbuilt distance with commercial shoots: you are given the script and you do the best you can, knowing you can blame the agency if the finished product stinks. Not so with this, it's all on us, which is scary and exciting all at the same time. The schedule is erratic and protracted to accommodate everyone's schedules and day jobs, and it will take us another four weeks to get through the remaining two shoot days.

Two runners do as their job title dictates and run towards our naked actors, draping them with thick blankets. I'm sure my phone could give me an accurate assessment of the temperature, but going by the chill in my neck and knees, I'd guess it's in single digits. As with so much else in my life, the narrative is out of sequence, and we are – for logistical reasons – shooting the rooftop lovemaking scene before the couple, Mike and Jenny, have been introduced in story-time. In real time, of course, the actors have met and we have rehearsed this scene a few times. They work well together in front of the camera, projecting a sexual chemistry between the characters that doesn't appear to exist between the actors themselves. On the other hand, there does appear to be something between Chris, our male lead, and Suzi, and I can't help but wonder whether they will now go to one or the other's home and make love for real, in a bed and without a dozen crew watching from the wings.

'Good job, buddy.' Joe puts a hand on my shoulder.

'Woohoo!' says Suzi, going up on tiptoes to kiss me. 'Amazing.'

I force a smile.

I don't know why I'm not more excited. I've wanted and planned this for a long time and everything went perfectly. The actors were brilliant, so was the cameraman, and – the big worry – it didn't rain. But even so, where I should feel buoyed, I simply feel deflated. Maybe it's the story. On paper it looked good, but now, committed to film, I don't feel so confident.

We aren't scheduled to shoot again until late April. Watching the film, viewers will see seamless chronological continuity, but in the space between this scene and the next, I will have become a father. Maybe that's why I feel so disorientated.

'Next time I see you . . .' says Suzi, widening her eyes. 'Here,' and she hands me a large yellow Selfridges bag. Poking their heads from the top of the bag are two teddy bears, each one surely (I hope, for Ivy's sake) twice the size of my soon-to-be babies.

'Good luck,' Suzi says, and something about it makes my stomach clench.

Chapter 31

Ivy is awake when I get back to the flat.

She is sitting on the sofa, an open book splayed face down on the floor.

'Hey, babe,' I say, going to her and kissing her on the forehead. 'What you doing up?'

'Couldn't sleep,' she says, and as she looks at me her expression collapses as if she has been holding back an enormous weight of emotion and can contain it no longer. She screws her eyes tight and starts weeping in great racking sobs.

'Honey, what's up? Are you okay?'

'The baby hasn't moved all day,' she says in between the tears.

I pull Ivy to me and hug her gently. 'Are you sure?'

'Tops,' she says, putting her hands to the top of her bump.

'Tops never moves much.'

'That's the other one, this one's always wriggling.'

'Have you seen any blood?'

Ivy shakes her head and seems to regain a little composure. 'No.'

'Maybe he . . . she . . . maybe it's asleep?'

'Not all day.'

'Are you sure it hasn't moved?'

'I don't think so; I mean . . . sometimes it's hard to tell with both of them. But . . .' she starts crying afresh.

'What do you want to do?'

We drive slowly and in silence but the air in the car is dense with a kind of deliberate, determined non-thought. Ivy, slumped sideways in her seat, stares straight ahead, and I focus my attention on the road and the steering wheel and the lights and the hairs on the back of my fingers. The doctors will talk in facts, but before they do we exist in a small cocoon of will, denial, hope and fear. While we are inside this silent bubble, the world is on pause and there is a chance that, when it starts again, everything will be as it should. Until then, it feels that by speaking, or even thinking about . . . *it* . . . we risk breaking the fragile barrier and letting something terrible inside. And so I stare straight ahead, and try to control my pulse and my breath.

We pull into the hospital car park at seven minutes past one on Saturday morning. Ivy waits in the car while I go around to the boot to collect her overnight bag. Ivy is thirty-five weeks and one day pregnant; she is not in labour and not due to give birth for another thirteen days, and I hesitate before removing her bag because it feels like the kind of presumption that might provoke fate. Standing in the cold, my eyes adjusting to the weak light, I notice several spots inside the boot that look like dark spilt liquid – like blood. I go to touch one and realize it's a fragment of burst Mother's Day balloon. Unwittingly I have parked in the same spot, beneath the same lamppost where – just six days ago – Ivy let the remaining balloon drift into the night sky.

'What are you doing?' Ivy says from the front seat.

'Nothing,' I tell her, gathering up the scraps of burst balloon and slipping them into my pocket.

The hospital is still and quiet; the fluorescent-lit corridors all but empty. We pass a man polishing the floor with a whirring machine. He stands aside and nods at us with a small smile, which I can't return. There is more noise in the delivery ward. Not the howling and crying and cursing that I had been fearing, but the calm conversation and efficient bustle of staff reading notes, making phone calls and going about their work. There is one other couple in the waiting room – the woman appears to be in early labour, measuring her breath, wincing, gasping periodically. Her partner is playing a game on his iPhone.

Ivy sits with one hand over her eyes and the other resting on her bump. I put my arm around her shoulders but she doesn't seem to notice. I pull her towards me and she resists, leaning away. It's almost an hour before one of the midwives takes us through to a small room.

She asks questions: has Ivy had a fall, has she been in pain, has there been any blood? Ivy answers no. She says nothing has happened, she tells the midwife she is expecting twins and one of her babies has stopped moving. The woman asks when is Ivy's due date and is this her first pregnancy. April, Ivy says. Yes, she says. The midwife asks have Ivy's waters broken, has she had cramps, has labour started. I already told you, Ivy says, nothing has happened, my baby is not moving. The woman asks when was the last time your little one moved and Ivy shakes her head and breaks down crying.

The midwife lies Ivy down on an examination table and asks her to lift her top. She presses her hands against Ivy's stomach, working methodically around the bump. Next she uses a hand-held device to listen to the babies' hearts. It emits a clear fluid beat when she holds it to the bottom of Ivy's belly, but when she slides the device to the top of the bump, all I can hear is white noise and static.

I ask, 'Can you hear anything?'

'Something,' the midwife says, but her tone does nothing to reassure me. 'I'll be right back,' she says. 'I'm just going to find the doctor.'

I hold Ivy's hand and she squeezes it back. I open my mouth to ask if she is okay, then close it again and make a silent wish.

The midwife returns with a young woman who she introduces as Dr Edwards. Dr Edwards asks Ivy all the same questions she already answered. She listens to Ivy's abdomen. She pushes on her belly, shifting the bump to either side. Something – maybe a knee or a fist or an elbow – moves inside Ivy's stomach. The doctor pushes the bump again, the top this time, kneading the flesh with the heel of her hand.

'The baby at the top doesn't appear to be moving,' she says. 'I can't hear a heartbeat there.'

'That's what I've been telling you,' Ivy all but shouts. 'I told you this. Why isn't anybody listening to me?'

'Try and stay calm,' the doctor says. 'The other one is responding well.'

'Is my baby dead?' Ivy says. 'Please tell me. Please. Is my baby dead?'

The midwife puts her hand on Ivy's forehead.

'I don't know,' says the doctor. Her tone is neutral and I hate her for it.

The doctor turns on a monitor, picks up a tube of gel and tells Ivy, 'This might be a little cold.'

We've been here before: the monitor, the white crescent of light, the image of two babies cuddled together inside their mother's womb. Ivy looks away from the screen, staring straight up at the ceiling.

The doctor pushes on the bump, there is a shift onscreen and it looks as if both babies move. A small fist clenches, opens and closes again and I realize that my own hand is doing the same thing inside my coat pocket. A small white shape beats rapidly in the centre of the screen. I look at the doctor and her expression is unreadable. Again she moves the probe, pushes Ivy's stomach and I can see red marks on her skin. The doctor scans again, using a vaginal probe this time. She tries for several minutes before she turns off the monitor.

'I'm sorry,' she says.

Ivy pulls her hand from mine, and rolls onto her side. Her back shakes convulsively, and the way she cries, it sounds as if she's in physical pain. In between the tears she repeats the same words over and over: 'My baby, my baby, my baby.'

The doctor and midwife leave us on our own.

I watch impotently, searching my mind for comforting words, but what can I say that isn't shallow or dishonest or fucking trivial? Ivy cries so hard that I almost tell her to control herself out of fear for the remaining baby. My face feels pulled out of shape by sadness and I feel as if I should cry too. I could force (or allow; I don't know which) the tears to come, but it would be deliberate and disingenuous and offensive against Ivy's raw, reflexive outpouring. So I don't cry and I don't speak. I stroke Ivy's back and kiss the top of her head and when she cries herself into silence, it is a huge and shameful relief.

At around three a.m. the midwife returns. She takes Ivy's blood pressure and examines her cervix, and all the while Ivy lies mute and impassive as if in some kind of trance. The midwife tells us that they will need to induce labour for the safety of the surviving twin. She asks if Ivy understands and Ivy nods. The midwife says we can stay in the hospital, or go home for one last night. What do you want to do? she asks, and Ivy shakes her head and wraps her arms around her belly. The midwife says it might be a good idea to go home, get some sleep and have some final time together 'just the four of you'.

'What do you want to do?' I ask Ivy.

She looks at me blankly, then sits up and climbs down

off the bed. She walks to the door, and I pick up our hospital bag and follow her out of the room.

We drive home with the radio on. But the awful suffocating truth is riding with us, drowning out the music and filling all the space inside the car, inside our heads, inside our hearts. When we get back to the flat I am sick with hunger. I ask Ivy if she wants anything to eat, but she shakes her head and I feel guilty for having an appetite. I make toast, spread it thinly with butter and every bite feels dry and dreadful inside my mouth.

Ivy says she is going to the bathroom. The flat – the street, the whole of London – is silent, and whatever Ivy is doing in the bathroom it makes no sound. After five minutes I get up from the sofa and find her lying on our bed, fully clothed.

'Do you want anything?'

'Could you turn off the light?' she says.

Ivy doesn't protest when I remove her shoes and jeans. She lies quietly, staring at the ceiling as I take off her socks and cardigan and manoeuvre her underneath the duvet. I turn out the light, undress and slide under the covers. I wrap my arms around Ivy's waist and rest my hand on the top of her bump.

*

When I wake a little before six in the morning, I find Ivy sitting on the sofa bed in the nursery. Her eyes are red and swollen, and if she's slept it can't have been for more than a handful of minutes.

'How are you?'

'Is it . . . was it a boy or a girl?' Ivy asks. 'Did they say if it was a boy or a girl?'

I shake my head and Ivy turns away from me, disappointed.

'Sorry,' I say. 'Have you eaten?' Ivy shakes her head, and I feel a sudden urge to shout at her. I clench my teeth and take a deep breath through my nose. 'You have to eat,' I say.

'Okay.'

'For the other one,' I say.

'Okay!' Ivy shouts. 'I said okay!'

We eat bowls of cereal and drink coffee at the kitchen table.

'Did you sleep?' I ask.

Ivy shakes her head.

'You should sleep.'

Ivy puts down her spoon and walks through to the bedroom. She shuts the door behind her. When I look in thirty minutes later, she at least appears to be sleeping.

I phone her parents; I phone my dad and my sister. I have three terrible conversations and listen to people cry down the phone. I go through Ivy's phone and send texts and ask people to leave us alone while we try to get through this. And as I sit on the floor, typing messages, the replies begin pinging in, and after the first few I delete the rest without reading because they all say the same thing and none of them changes anything. I text Joe and Esther and ask them both not to reply. By the time I put Ivy's phone down I need painkillers for the pounding in my temples.

Ivy wakes after one in the afternoon. She takes a shower and changes her clothes, then comes and sits next to me on the sofa. She kisses me on the cheek, strokes my hair then rests her head in my lap where she lies still and silent for close to an hour. I doze sporadically, slipping in and out of pre-sleep scenes where I am lost in some place that is at once familiar and alien.

It's almost three in the afternoon when Ivy sits up, brushes her hair off her face and says, 'I suppose we should go.'

'I spoke to your parents,' I tell her. 'Your mum said she'd come up.'

Ivy shakes her head and fresh tears roll down her cheeks. 'Not now. Not yet.'

And all I can think is: *this is not the way it is supposed to happen.*

Chapter 32

The hospital car park is full and we have to drive two circuits before we find a space. There are visitors carrying flowers, fruit, sweets, magazines. I see one young man holding a balloon printed with the words: 'It's a girl!!!'

I shoulder Ivy's hospital bag, still packed with enough clothes for two babies, and we hold hands as we walk quietly into the hospital. People nudge each other and smile and try to catch our eyes, the expectant couple, as we make our way through the corridors and ride the lift to the delivery suite. I push the buzzer on the intercom and squeeze Ivy's hand while we wait. I don't remember there being a buzzer last night. It is just fifteen hours since I came home from the shoot on Friday night, and in that time – less than a day – the entire shape of our world has changed forever.

A doctor examines Ivy and confirms again that one of our twins – Danny if he's a boy, Danni if she's a girl – is dead. The doctor explains what is going to happen and connects Ivy to a drip. They attach a monitor to her bump, and another to the scalp of the baby we have yet to find a name for. A bedside monitor beeps with a single, rapid pulse. Our midwife tells us it will take several hours for the drugs to induce labour and suggests we try and rest.

There is a television mounted to the wall, and we watch films and old detective shows and cookery programmes and panel shows and commercials, not changing channels but staring through the box, passing occasional comments to fill the silence on this side of the screen. I fetch food from a supermarket concession in the hospital foyer, and we eat pre-packed sandwiches and crisps and drink bottles of juice and water. The food makes me feel sick.

Ivy sleeps for maybe two hours in the late afternoon. I turn the TV off and close my eyes, but sleep doesn't come. Without the background drone of Saturday daytime television, the steady beep of the monitor fills the room. Does our baby know its twin is dead? Is he or she distressed, sad, lonely?

Inside my wallet is a laminated card, given to us at our antenatal class. Printed on one side is an acronym to help dads ask the right questions and make the right decisions while the mums go through labour. If anything goes wrong, you consult the card and work though the word: BRAIN: What are the *Benefits* to going ahead with this decision or procedure? What are the *Risks*? What are the *Alternatives*? What does your *Intuition* tell you? What happens if you do *Nothing*?

None of it helps.

The baby's heart beats at between 120 and 130 beats a minute. I count in time with the monitor: *one, two, three, four* . . . all the way up to one hundred and twenty, or one hundred and twenty-four, or one hundred and thirty-two . . . over and over and over.

The sun sets between six and seven, and the sky – streaked gold and rose and purple – is beautiful. And I count to 124, and 122 and 127.

When Ivy wakes it is completely dark outside our window.

'I think it's happening,' she says.

The midwife is called Phoebe; her shift finished an hour ago but she is staying to see this through to the end. She tells me they will attempt to deliver both babies naturally. Even so, there are another four medical staff in attendance, their mute bodies seeming to amplify the silence, making it palpable and ominous.

Phoebe is the one who takes charge of the situation, everybody else apparently here only on standby – despite her professional demeanour, Phoebe's eyes are wet with tears. Ivy is offered an epidural to help her deal with any pain. The midwife says it will make it difficult for Ivy to feel the contractions and know when to push, possibly prolonging labour. Ivy asks for the injection. The tension in the room ebbs and flows with the contractions, and Phoebe – her voice soft and Irish accented – tells Ivy when to breathe and when to push. Ivy is passive and expressionless throughout. She stares straight up at the ceiling and closes her eyes for minutes at a time. Phoebe stares at me, grimaces, and mouths the words: *Help her!*

I hold Ivy's hand but I don't know what to say. I form words in my head: *you can do this; nearly there; well done –* but they're all inadequate; all inappropriate; all wrong.

The first baby is born at fourteen minutes past one on Sunday morning, March 30th. He's a boy. The less active of the twins, we used to call this baby Turvy, but the nickname sounds shamefully frivolous now.

The midwife asks if I want to cut the umbilical cord, but I shake my head.

Ivy holds her son to her chest and cries and kisses his thin, wet, dirty hair.

This is supposed to be the happiest day, the happiest moment of my life. And maybe – as I look at my perfect baby boy, loose purple skin covered in wax and blood and gunk, eyes screwed tight against the world – maybe for a split second it is. And then it's gone, because – and everybody in the room knows this – Ivy still has one dead child to deliver. Even our new baby is quiet, as if he too understands that his big moment has happened in shadow.

Phoebe asks if he has a name and we say no.

Time passes in the hard, conflicted silence of the room; me sitting beside the bed, Ivy pulling our boy against her as if, having just given birth to him, she is trying to reabsorb him into her. Phoebe busies herself, arranging equipment, checking Ivy's pulse, taking the baby's temperature. She says our boy is healthy and doing fine, but he is colder than he should be and needs to go to the special care unit. When she goes to take him from Ivy, Ivy becomes hysterical.

'Don't take him. Please. Please! Don't take my baby!'

I put one hand on Ivy's forehead, another on her hand, and she pulls the baby tight to her chest.

'Your boy is doing fine,' says Phoebe. 'He's doing great. But he needs a little extra attention. Just for a short while.' As she speaks, Phoebe takes hold of the boy and pulls him gently from Ivy's grip. Ivy's face is a mask of sadness and fear, and she holds onto her child until her arms are fully extended. When, finally, she lets go of her son, her hands fall limply to the bed and her expression glazes over as if she has become suddenly catatonic.

Our boy is placed in a plastic-sided cot that I hadn't noticed until now, and he is taken from the room. As the doors swing closed he starts to cry – the sound echoing and fading down the corridor.

Danny – he is a boy, too – is born 'sleeping' at two twenty-eight. Identical twins. The doctors had to cut Ivy and use forceps to facilitate the delivery, and Danny is slick with blood when he emerges. The midwife does not ask if I want to cut the cord and she wipes the baby before placing his still body in my hands. Like his older brother, Danny's eyes are closed. Whereas his brother was tensed against the cold brightness of the delivery room, Danny is relaxed and peaceful.

Ivy's face is turned away. 'Is it . . . is it okay?' she asks.

'He's beautiful,' I say, 'here.' And I hold the baby out to her.

Ivy turns to me and smiles, but only with her mouth. She takes Danny. 'Hey,' she whispers into his neck, and she kisses the top of his head, his nose and his lips. 'Hey there, baby.'

We are transferred into a private room where Phoebe helps Ivy express a small amount of breast milk, which will then be given to our boy in the special care unit. Phoebe says I can stay, but Ivy encourages me to go home and sleep in our own bed. She asks me to call her mother and father but to keep them away for the time being. She wants to be alone with Danny, she says.

In the corridor, Phoebe hugs me and we cry together. I ask her what went wrong and she says that sometimes it 'just happens'. There is no obvious cause, no immediately apparent reason why one of our boys survived and the other died inside his mother. She tells me they will keep Ivy in for a day or so, and that Danny will be able to stay with his mother. The idea sounds macabre, and I say as much to Phoebe, but she assures me that it will help Ivy deal with her grief and say goodbye to our boy. She explains that they will put a cold cot in the room, and when Ivy is not holding him, this is where he will stay.

It is after six in the morning when I get back to the flat, and the sun is rising above the silhouetted trees and houses on our street. The flat feels unnaturally quiet and empty – it feels today as if it is missing not only Ivy, but the two babies she has been carrying since the middle of last summer. Since forever ago.

I feed the goldfish, clean yesterday's dishes, make coffee and take it into the nursery, where I begin dismantling one cot, one mobile, one baby bouncer. I take the disassembled parts down to the car along with the extra, unneeded Moses basket. I remove the second car seat from the back of the car and transfer it into the boot with the rest of the stuff baby Danny will never get to sit, sleep and bounce in. When I go to open the front door of the flat, my hands are shaking so much that I can barely fit the key into the lock.

And now, finally, the tears come. Angry, hysterical tears, and I'm so grateful for them that I shout at the walls like a drunk, and grind my knuckles into my temples until white spots crackle across my vision.

At one minute past nine o'clock I drive to the charity shop, but I've forgotten it's a Sunday and everything is closed. I'm tempted to leave the stuff on the pavement, but it feels disrespectful to Danny. I drive to Earl's Court and pull up outside El and Phil's flat. But as I sit behind the wheel, listening to the engine cool, it occurs to me what a bad idea this is. El can't be relied upon not to say something crass and stupid; and the state I'm in, I couldn't be relied upon not to slap him. And even the thought of some imagined facetious comment has me gripping the steering wheel tight enough to make my knuckles pop. So as much as I want to talk to Phil and sit with El, I put the car into gear and drive back to the flat.

I haven't slept more than half a dozen hours in the last forty-eight and I feel sick. I make more coffee and call my dad. We don't say much. I tell him what happened, and while I sob down the phone Dad says things that are supposed to comfort me. You'll get through it, son, he says, eventually you'll get through it.

He repeats this phrase to me as I sit in the fairy-tale nursery, crying, staring at the indents in the carpet where baby Danny's cot stood only one hour ago.

Chapter 33

When I walk into Ivy's hospital room on Sunday evening, she is lying in bed with Danny, caressing our boy's head with her cheek. Pink, peaceful and beautiful – he looks alive. Perfect fingers curled into tiny fists, fat cheek resting against his mother's chest. Ivy's eyes, too, are closed.

I sit in the chair beside the bed and stroke Ivy's head. I run my hand over her brown hair, following the line and flow of it to where it falls against Danny's shoulder. I let my hand drift onto Danny's head and it's as cold as a stone. When Ivy opens her eyes, I flinch.

'Hey,' I say.

Ivy looks through me, expressionless.

A new mother and her baby should be a beautiful

image, the most beautiful image in the world. Ivy looks like hell; like she hasn't slept and hasn't stopped crying since I left this morning.

Inside my skull I say: *Are you okay? Did you sleep? I'm sorry.*

I say, 'Have you seen baby . . . the other baby?'

Ivy shakes her head. A tear forms in the corner of her eye, thinning as it travels across her cheek and down her chin, disappearing into Danny's sparse brown hair. He's been cleaned since yesterday, but his head is damp and sticky with accumulated tears.

'Can I hold him?'

Ivy's bottom lip trembles, she holds Danny closer to her chest, closes her eyes, presses her cheek against the top of his head. And then she relaxes, opens her eyes and passes my son to me. He weighs nothing at all; born five weeks premature, Danny fits comfortably into my cupped hands and he weighs . . . nothing. He is dressed in a white cotton onesy and his chest is warm with absorbed heat from Ivy. One side of his face, too, is warm, his cheek soft against my neck. The other side of his face, though, like his back and bottom, is cold through the thin material. I push my index finger into his curled palm and it feels as if his tiny fingers, his perfect fingers, grip back.

'We should go and see his brother,' I say. 'He doesn't even have a name.'

Ivy's chin dimples and I wonder how many tears a person can physically make.

'We can't call him Turvy forever,' I say, forcing a smile. But it's too soon, and Ivy turns away from me.

'Have you seen him?' Ivy says.

'I thought we could go together.'

Ivy turns her head to face me. 'Is he . . .?'

'He's fine,' I say. 'The midwife says he's strong, drinking his milk, keeping them busy.'

Ivy extends her arms, asking for Daniel, and I pass him back to her. She settles him on her chest, kisses his hair, rubs his back as if trying to warm him. 'I can't,' she says. 'Not today.'

'Just for five minutes?'

Ivy shakes her head. 'After this' – she strokes Daniel's head – 'after this there's nothing. This is it . . . this is all I have with him.' She kisses Daniel's head. 'This is it.'

After an hour, Ivy falls asleep and I cuddle Daniel for as long as I can bear before placing him in his cold cot. While Ivy sleeps I visit our boy in the special care unit.

He too is sleeping, curled up inside a sealed incubator. Two blue pads trailing wires are attached to his chest, and another wire is strapped to his foot via a Velcro cuff.

'Nothing to worry about,' I am instantly reassured, he is breathing well but needs a little help maintaining his temperature.

Two babies who can't keep themselves warm – one lying still inside a cold cot; the other sleeping in a heated incubator, his belly rising and falling as he draws breath. There is a circular hatch in the side of the incubator, and after I have washed and disinfected my hands I am allowed to touch my boy through the narrow aperture.

'Hello, baby,' I whisper. 'Hello, Baby T.'

Baby T straightens both legs in a long stretch and yawns, before relaxing back into a loose bundle. I place my finger in his hand, and when he squeezes it is strong and unequivocal. I feel myself smile as if it is something happening to another person. The smile sits clumsily on my face – the first one I haven't forced in almost two days.

On Monday morning I arrive at the hospital a little after nine and go straight to the special care unit. Baby T – just thirty hours old – is still inside his cot, but the midwife says I can take him out and cuddle him. It's the last day in March and warm outside; even so, Baby T is dressed in a onesy, cardigan, booties and tiny woollen cap. He makes a small sound and it moves me more than any words could. After this, when I go to see Ivy and Daniel, everything will change again; I'll be in a different world, one where our baby is dead and smiles are not allowed. So I carry a chair across to the window and sit with Baby T where he can feel the sun on his face. I watch him sleep and watch his eyes flicker briefly open, I watch his fists clench and uncurl, I watch him breathe. When he starts crying a mid-wife brings a bottle of milk and I feed my baby boy. I rub his back until he brings up wind and I change his nappy, seeing for the first time his tummy, thin legs and wrinkled bottom. He sleeps in my arms for one still quiet hour before the midwife puts him back inside his incubator.

Daniel is in his cot when I go to see Ivy. She smiles when she sees me, a thin polite smile, and asks have I 'seen him' yet.

'Just been,' I say. 'He's amazing.'

Ivy nods, the same resigned smile still on her lips.

'I brought pictures,' I say, passing my phone to Ivy.

She swipes through the pictures, zooming in on his face and hands. Her smile begins its journey towards her eyes (not quite making it all the way, not yet) as she looks at her boy and touches her fingers to the screen, touching his face.

'Baby T,' I tell her.

Ivy frowns. 'What?'

'Baby T. That's what I've been calling him.'

Ivy nods. 'T for Turvy,' she says, and she hands the phone back to me.

'Did you sleep?'

'A little.'

'How are you?'

What little smile was on Ivy's face, it dissolves now as she turns to look at Danny.

'I gave T his bottle,' I say. 'Changed his nappy.'

Ivy nods, makes a small *humph* of a laugh.

'They said we can take him home tomorrow.'

Ivy swings her legs out of the bed, climbs down and goes over to the cold cot and picks up Daniel. We listen to the radio, eat sandwiches, cuddle our baby and doze until, at around six in the evening, Ivy tells me she's tired and needs to be alone. On the way out I spend another hour with my boy in the special care unit.

Two minutes after I get back to the flat, someone rings my doorbell. After they ring for the third time, I go downstairs to open the door.

'Hi, Harold.'

'Flowers came,' says my next-door neighbour, fidgeting with his hands, apparently reluctant to meet my eyes.

'Right.'

Still looking at his feet, Harold asks, 'What happened?'

I take a deep breath. 'We had two boys,' I tell him.

'Twins. But one of them was ... they call it *stillborn* – he was born ...'

Harold nods. 'I'm sorry.'

If I thought it wouldn't terrify him, I'd hug him. Not for his sake, but for mine. Harold is the first person I've spoken to in the flesh outside of the hospital since Friday.

'I'll get them,' Harold says, and he disappears into his flat, leaving me alone. After a minute Harold arrives with a large bunch of white lilies. He goes back into the house as I read the card: 'Sending love at this time, Joe & Jen'. Harold returns with flowers from Phil and El: 'All our love at this sad time'. Harold brings flowers from Maria, Eva and Ken, Esther and Nino, all of them sending me their love at this tragic fucking time.

'Can I do anything?' Harold asks.

I consider asking him to take all these flowers and throw them in the nearest skip, but instead I ask him to help me bring them up to the flat. I offer him a drink, but Harold says he has to do his homework.

We now have more bunches of flowers than things to contain them, so I drive to the department store in Wimbledon and buy three new vases. On the way home I stop at the supermarket and buy fresh milk, bread, fruit, ready meals and wine. Back at the flat I pull the supermarket receipt from my jeans pocket and find a small scrap of burst red balloon. I put the receipt in the bin and the scrap of balloon into a compartment inside my wallet.

After I've sorted out the flowers, I eat a frozen lasagne for two and finish an entire bottle of Shiraz. When the wine is finished, I open another bottle and get almost halfway through before I fall asleep on the sofa.

On Tuesday I take Baby T to see his mother.

I hold Daniel while Ivy cradles her live baby and sobs. We introduce the brothers to each other, and although two days have passed since Daniel was born sleeping, the boys still look identical. On the midwife's advice I have brought our camera and we take photos of Daniel on his own and with his mother. Phoebe is on duty today, and she takes pictures of Ivy and myself with Daniel, but we take no pictures of the two boys together. Phoebe brings a plaster kit into the room and takes impressions of Daniel's hands and feet. As the moulds set, she cleans him gently with cotton balls and water. She asks if we would like to keep a lock of his hair but Ivy says no. Ivy changes his clothes. Naked, Daniel's skin has less colour than his brother's, his still chest and tummy have a faintly blue tinge to them, and it's an overwhelming relief when she re-dresses him in a clean white babygrow.

With all the ceremony and formalities finished, with the

casts of Daniel's hands and feet dry and wrapped inside a towel, it still takes over an hour of crying and cuddling to say goodbye to our baby boy. Dressed now, and with our bags packed, Ivy sits in a chair by the window, holding Daniel against her chest and stroking his hair while I perch on the bed cuddling Baby T. And as ashamed as I am for feeling this way, I want this to be over now. I want to go home and move on with our son.

Just as I'm considering saying something, Ivy stands up. 'Okay,' she says. 'Let's go.'

Chapter 34

A week after we bring our son home, he still doesn't have a name.

Ivy has tried breastfeeding him but – possibly because he spent his first three days apart from his mother, taking his milk from a bottle – Baby T can't or won't latch onto Ivy's breast. Ivy expresses milk, but she has no desire to give our baby his bottle. So instead, I give him his bottles and Ivy spends large parts of the day uncommunicative, curled into the corner of the sofa (as if trying to disappear behind the cushions) lost in a daze or the pages of a book. Baby T doesn't cry often, but more than once I have watched Ivy wince at the sound as if she resents him for disturbing her. In spite of this, she now sleeps in the nursery where she can watch over him throughout the night. Originally we had planned to have the twins sleep in Moses baskets in our room, but as he spent his first days in an incubator, the least we can do, Ivy says, is let our son sleep in his own nursery. And so, while Baby T sleeps in his basket, inside his cot, Ivy sleeps on an uncomfortable sofa bed that isn't long enough to stretch out on. I sleep alone in our double bed.

In the evenings we sit in front of the TV. We eat our supper off our knees and make innocuous small talk while Ivy expresses milk and I drink anywhere between most and all of a bottle of wine (this on top of the two or three beers I drink during the day). I have tried bringing up the subject of Baby T's name, but whenever I do, Ivy retreats and cries and asks – irritated – what is the rush?

On a cold but sunny Thursday, one day before he was due to be born, we bury baby Daniel. His twin sleeps impassively in the double buggy as the casket is lowered into a small hole in the ground. We haven't seen Daniel since we said goodbye in the hospital eight days ago, and now, as he disappears from sight, I wish with all my heart that we had visited him one last time and given him a teddy bear to keep him company. A man asks would we like to scatter earth, but neither of us does. Ivy turns to the buggy, and with tears rolling down her cheeks she very carefully lifts Baby T into her arms. With one hand under his bottom and one cradling the back of his head, she kisses him on his forehead, nose and both cheeks and says, 'Come on, baby, let's take you home.'

Chapter 35

On Easter Sunday, Ivy says she is going to church. Ivy and I have been together for eight months and one week and this is the first time she has mentioned church. She doesn't ask if I want to go, but simply announces she is taking Baby T to Easter Mass. I pull on my coat nevertheless, and as the three of us sit at the back of the church, I wonder if there is any way back for me and Ivy. She hasn't been hostile towards me, but neither has she shown any interest or affection. And whilst I have enjoyed watching her bond with our son – reading him stories, singing to him, making silly faces – I have watched as an outsider. Also, Baby T is latching on now and takes the majority of his milk from the breast; and whilst this is good – better than good – for mother and baby, feeding our son is something I am now excluded from. Ivy sleeps and dozes throughout the day, and when she does she curls up with Baby T beside her. So while the three of us sit together in the Church of Christ the King, I don't feel like we are here as a family.

On Thursday Ivy's parents came to visit, and Ivy emerged a little further. She smiled on occasion and even managed a small laugh at her parents as they made a fuss over their grandson. We cried, of course, but the simple fact and presence of Baby T kept us all anchored to the present. Ken shared a bottle of wine with me, and at the end of the night I bedded down on the sofa while the Lees took our room and Ivy slept in the nursery. Even with pillows and a new blanket, I tossed and turned for more than an hour before giving up on the idea of sleep. The house was too still and quiet for me to turn on the TV or even the kettle, so I turned my attention to the bookshelves, looking for something soporific. I picked up and replaced maybe half a dozen books before I noticed ... all Ivy's half-read books – *Catch-22*, *Crime and Punishment*, *Lord of the Rings* and twenty more besides – are gone. When or where, I don't know, but the discovery unsettles me. Maybe our story, incomplete as it is, maybe she has abandoned that, too.

The next day we walked on the Common and Ken and Eva bought us all lunch in The Village. Strangers approach you when you have a new baby; they will walk up to your table uninvited, stroke your baby's cheek, tell you he's gorgeous and ask his name. And you grit your teeth and smile politely and say thank you, and you laugh when you tell them he doesn't have a name yet. And when they look at you with that hint of disbelief, you turn away, call the waiter and order another large glass of wine.

As we said our goodbyes in the early evening, Eva hugged me and told me to be patient. Ken kissed me on the neck, something he has never done before, and it is the most affection anyone has shown me in almost two weeks. My own dad still hasn't met his first grandson; I'm not sure Ivy is ready yet, and I'm not sure I want my dad to see us like this.

On Friday, Eunice, our big exuberant midwife, came to check on mother and baby. She went through her own version of the routine that is now becoming familiar to me: hugs, kisses, tears, congratulations and apologies. Eunice suggested Ivy might want to get a prescription for antidepressants. She explained that Ivy would need to stop breastfeeding, and Ivy simply shook her head. Eunice told us that Daniel was 'with Jesus now', and I had to leave the room. I don't know if I was angry with Eunice for this blithe dismissal, or angry with myself for not believing her. It occurred to me that maybe I need antidepressants, too, but the thought frightened me and I turned away from it.

Now, sitting in the cold church on the border of Wimbledon Village, I wish that I had the refuge of faith. A place where I could find reason or solace; a place where I could offer up a prayer or a message to my dead baby boy. But wishing doesn't make it so. This thought reminds me of Ivy's purported belief in the Wish Fairy – these things that seemed so cute and wonderful just two weeks ago, they are revealed now as hollow and fatuous.

'Today,' the vicar tells us, 'we celebrate the day Jesus came back from the dead.'

I glance sideways at Ivy, but she has her eyes closed and her head bowed.

And so, in the absence of faith, I, too, close my eyes and make a wish: I wish Daniel was sitting here on my lap, cooing and crying and breathing, and I wish that I could have Ivy back the way she was when we fell in love.

Chapter 36

I'm standing on a rooftop, staring down at a love heart chalked onto the concrete fifty feet below. We've been here since five a.m., to shoot the sun rising over the rooftops of the sleeping city.

Ivy is out there, and my son, thirty-one days old now and still without a name. It's the last day in April and we are shooting the second rooftop scene for *Reinterpreting Jackson Pollock*. And whilst I'm here in person, my thoughts are elsewhere. I was going to cancel the shoot, but Ivy wanted me to do it. She said it would be good for me, but more and more I'm forming the idea that she is happier when I'm not around.

This is the scene where our heartbroke hero – depressed, alone – considers throwing himself to his death. When I read it on paper, the scene felt poignant. Now, with all that has happened, as I lean over the parapet wall and feel the cold brick digging into my hips, now it seems trite and insincere. When I explained the plot to El he called it 'fuckig stupid'. I get the impression that our actor and the assembled crew feel the same way. Or maybe I'm simply projecting. When I arrived on set I could sense their emotional machinery trying to find the balance between normalcy and compassion, sympathy and restraint. I watched their expressions flicker and distort as they attempted to smile just enough but not too much. Only Suzi cried. 'I promised myself I wouldn't do this,' she said, 'but … I'm so sorry. I'm so so sorry.' I feel bad for her, because this is her script, this is her baby, and it should be amazing. Instead, we move through the shots in a perfunctory manner, crossing them off and moving on to the next, embarrassed by the contrived sentimentality of it in the face of real life. How could a jilted lover ever contemplate suicide in a world where babies are delivered stillborn?

I'm getting through a bottle and a half of wine a night now, and I experience a wave of nausea and vertigo as I look down on the gaudy chalk heart. I'm tired.

Joe is standing behind me. I can hear him breathe through his nose, and every so often I catch the smell of coffee and bacon on his breath. We shot yesterday and the day before, too, covering all the interior scenes. In the story, this is where it starts going right again for our hero. When we wrap, that will be all our filming completed. Then we'll edit, add sound, grade the film and move on to the next thing. What the next thing is for me, I don't know. I don't think it involves me and Ivy together. We are different people now.

Ivy still sleeps in Baby T's room, while I sleep alone in our double bed. I run most days and Ivy has started doing yoga again. She reads in the nursery; I watch TV on the sofa. Because we are on different schedules we tend not to eat together any more. We occupy the same space, but we interact less and less. Sometimes we go for walks, pushing Baby T across the Common or into The Village for coffee. But even then it feels to me like we are strangers sharing nothing more than proximity.

On the nights when I don't pass out drunk, I take over-the-counter sleeping tablets. The packet says they are one-a-night, but I take them two at a time. And even so, most nights I have nightmares. Some mornings I wake up and for a few seconds I have forgotten that Daniel died in his mother's womb. And then I remember.

Joe's hand comes to rest on my shoulder. He hugs me tight against his side, whether out of camaraderie, or sympathy or fear that I might just throw myself off this fucking roof . . . who knows?

'Ready to go?' he asks.

'Yeah,' I tell him.

We shoot the final take of the final scene at around ten thirty. It was cold and dark when we set up almost six hours ago, but the sun is already warm now and the sky is a clear, cloudless blue. I watch the final shot on the play-back monitor and it looks fine. Whether it's poignant, melodramatic, filmic or flat, I honestly can't tell; I don't have the perspective to view it objectively.

'It's a wrap,' I shout, and everybody claps and slaps each other on the back.

I start clapping too, I whoop and whistle and cheer like a lunatic, and the crew have no option but to join in. The last time I was here, when I went home, Ivy was waiting up for me with the news that our baby had stopped moving. Exactly one month ago now, and yet it feels like it was only a day and over a lifetime ago all at the same time.

'So,' I say to Joe and Suzi. 'Is someone going to buy me a drink, or are you going to let me drink alone?'

'At ten thirty on a Wednesday morning?' says Joe. 'What the fuck else am I going to do?'

Suzi glances over her shoulder to where our actor (her boyfriend?) is having his make-up removed.

'Just the three of us, hey?' I say.

Suzi nods. 'Sure. But I'm buying.'

It's closer to eleven thirty by the time we say goodbye to everybody and finally hit the pub. It's deserted except for two staff and a scattering of grey alcoholics. True to her word, Suzi buys the first round. She and Joe sip their pints slowly, and I've finished mine before they're halfway through.

'We should be drinking champagne,' I say. 'You can't celebrate a wrap without champagne.'

Suzi looks at her watch and Joe's expression flickers.

'What?' I say, a little aggressively. 'What?'

'Nothing,' Joe says. 'You're absolutely right. Let's get some food with it, yeah?'

'I'm not hungry. Thanks all the s—'

'We'll get some food,' Joe says. 'You sit tight, and I'll go to the bar. Okay, Suzi?'

'Sure,' Suzi says. 'Of course.'

'Three burgers, okay?'

'Burger and bubbles!' I shout, drawing the attention of the resident winos.

Halfway through the food, and about the same amount through the champagne, all the energy drains out of me. My stomach is in knots and the drink tastes sour to me now. The last time I saw El I poured him a drink against Phil's instructions, medical advice and common sense because . . . well, why the fuck not? But as drunk and self-pitying as I am, I'm sober enough to know the same blasé answer can't apply to me. I'm a father now. Whatever happens to me and Ivy, I'm a father.

'Sorry to be a party pooper,' I say, putting my glass down, 'but I should be going.'

'Cab's waiting outside,' says Joe.

'Think you're pretty clever, don't you?'

'Here,' he says, passing me three twenty-pound notes. 'And get Ivy some fucking flowers.'

The shoot took place in Islington, north London, so it's a good cab ride back to Wimbledon Village. Long enough to sober up a little, to calm down, to think. It's a sunny spring day and the streets are full of people living their lives: workmen, students, tourists, mothers pushing prams. The cab driver must think there's something wrong with me as I watch London pass by with my forehead pressed against the glass, crying intermittently. We cross the river at Waterloo Bridge and I am still holding the three twenties Joe pressed into my hand half an hour ago. 'Buy Ivy some fucking flowers,' he said, and maybe Joe was being even more direct than I gave him credit for. I took it as nothing more than male bluff and bravado – a cool thing to say to diffuse an awkward situation. But the more I think about it, the more I think Joe was telling me, in his own sweet and subtle way – to pull myself together and start thinking about Ivy instead of feeling sorry for myself. And he makes a good point. Ivy and I both lost a child when Danny was born, but she's the one who had to sleep with a dead child inside her, who went through labour to deliver one live and one stillborn baby. And as sick, sad, lonely and depressed as I feel; as much as I want to wipe it all out with drink and sleeping tablets . . . it's worse, infinitely worse, for Ivy. And if she needs to retreat inside her head and her heart to get through this, then the least I can do is act like a grown man about it. Or, as Joe so succinctly put it: *Buy her some fucking flowers.*

I ask the taxi driver to drop me outside the florist, and after I buy twenty-four yellow roses, I pay a visit to the extortionate grocer and the criminal butcher.

Chapter 37

It's around five o'clock on Friday morning when Dad's snoring wakes me for what must be the sixth time. He came to visit yesterday so, once again, I'm sleeping (or trying to) on the sofa. The sun is beginning to show itself and there is enough light coming through the living room blinds to illuminate the two dozen roses in a vase above the fireplace. Several of the stems are beginning to droop after only two days, which is disappointing considering how much I spent on them. There's been no shortage of flowers in the flat in the last month, but Ivy cried all the same when I presented her with these twenty-four blooms – I didn't say as much, but I think she understood these were for her and not for our dead baby boy. I cooked spaghetti bolognese and we ate it at the table. I had resolved not to drink, but Ivy suggested we open a bottle of wine and it seemed churlish to say no. I had one glass and made it last. I told Ivy I was sorry and she asked, 'What for?'

'I'm just sorry,' I told her and that set us both off crying.

It was okay, though. We ate our supper, sipped our wine and watched most of a movie before Baby T woke up crying for his milk. Ivy asked me if I'd like to give him a bottle seeing as she'd had wine. And so I gave him five ounces of formula milk, sitting on the sofa with Ivy curled up beside me. Like a family.

Even so, Ivy slept on the sofa bed in the nursery and I went to our bed (*my* bed?) alone. We kissed each other good night – a chaste touching of lips – and I realized it had been weeks since we'd done that. I had nightmares again – indistinct, harrowing, confusing – and needed to take a sleeping tablet to get back under in the early hours.

I had no nightmares on Thursday, but woke instead to the sound of Ivy shuffling about in the nursery. It was before six in the morning, but I got up and made toast and coffee and we ate it together in the living room while Baby T slept in the nursery. I asked Ivy about the half-read books and she shrugged and shook her head. I was hoping she might tell me it was about moving on, starting afresh, putting the past behind us, but she said none of those things. It rained all day, so we stayed in our pyjamas and watched TV and dozed on the sofa and played cards and rolled around on the floor with our baby.

What the future holds for me and Ivy, I still don't know. We've been together nine months now, but ninety per cent of what you might call our 'romantic life' happened in the first two weeks – before Ivy became pregnant. There have been high points since then – me moving in, my failed proposal, our 'honeymoon' – but so much else has happened that I'm not sure either of us knows the way back to the way we were. But the last two days have been good days and whatever happens I will always love Ivy and will always have her and my son in my life, one way or another.

Dad is still snoring like an old sailor with a whelk in his throat, and I'm worried he's going to wake the baby. The sleep of the just, maybe. Or just a happy granddad. Of everyone that has visited – the midwife, Eva, Ken, Frank, Phil – Dad has been the least coy on the subject of Daniel's death. I don't know (*don't think*) that the death of a spouse is as profound a shock as the death of a baby, but Dad has displayed a naked uncontrived empathy that felt like cold air blowing through the flat. He talked about the pain of loss from a personal perspective, and how my mother's death affected him when he was a similar age to that which Ivy is now. He cried at the memory and smiled at the same time as he remembered everything he loved about my mum. I have only a hazy recall of my own grief and bereavement, partly, I think, because I was too immature to fully embrace and experience those emotions, and partly because, like the cliché says, time really does heal. 'I don't know exactly how you feel,' my dad said, 'I can't. But it does lose its edge, slowly. I don't think you ever fully recover, but . . . that grief, I think it's a part of the person you lost. In a funny way . . . a silly way, I suppose . . . it's almost a comfort. Don't be afraid to hold on to that.'

Ivy went to my dad then, put her arms around his neck and cried like a child. And he just held her and stroked her hair. I put the kettle on and went to the bathroom where I sat on the toilet and cried on my own – not out of self-pity, but because that was their moment, and it would be more powerful and more healing between just the two of them. Obviously Dad spent the rest of the day annoying the hell out of me, getting down on his knees and braying like a donkey, roaring like a lion, playing peek-a-boo for a bloody eternity, spilling his tea, repeating old anecdotes about my own infancy and generally carrying on like he was demented. But Baby T loved it.

And now he has woken his grandson. I hear muffled

sounds as Ivy creaks out of the sofa bed and lifts Baby T from his cot. I listen to her making soothing sounds – a steady loop of *shush, baby, shushhh . . . Mummy's here . . . shush, baby, shushhh . . .*

I must have drifted off again, because I wake with a start to find Ivy sitting on the edge of the sofa.

'Hey,' I say, shifting back into the sofa to make room.

Ivy lies down beside me, her back against my chest, and pulls the blanket over her shoulders.

'Sorry about Dad.'

'Why?'

'The snoring.'

'You think you don't snore?'

'Do I?'

'Like a tramp,' Ivy says. 'Anyway, T always wakes up around now for his milk.'

'How is he?'

'Sleeping like a baby,' Ivy says with a small laugh at her own joke.

I drape my arm around her, my hand resting on her still-soft belly. We lie quietly for a while and this is probably the most intimate we've been in the five weeks since the babies were born. I press my face into the back of Ivy's neck and kiss her there.

Ivy moves her head away from me, subtly, but enough

to break the contact between my lips and her neck. 'I think we're done,' she says, matter-of-factly.

So this is it.

'Is that what you want?' I say.

Ivy nods, something I feel rather than see. I hug her tightly and she smells of baby – of milk and heat and musk. I love Ivy in a thousand small and large and trivial and important ways. I want her in my life and in my bed, and I want us to be a family, but I'm not going to try and talk her into it. I only want her if she wants me too. Anything else is un—

I realize that Ivy is still talking.

'Excuse me?'

'Is that okay with you?' Ivy says. 'I want it to be okay with you, too.'

'Well . . . not really, not if I'm honest. But if that's what you want, what can I do about it? What can I say?'

'We'll put all our love into Baby T,' she says.

'I don't . . .'

'I know it sounds selfish but . . . I don't want to share him with anyone else . . . with another baby. Not after everything that's happened.'

'But . . .'

'We'll be a three,' Ivy says. 'Just the three of us.'

'Three?'

'You, me and . . . him.' Ivy rolls over so she's facing me, and her smile is big, true and beautiful. 'We really need to pick a name, don't we.'

The night after we discovered Ivy was expecting twins, we drove to Bristol to see her parents. During the drive she asked how many children I wanted; I prevaricated, but Ivy's answer to her own question was an unambiguous *three*. And now I understand what she is telling me – when she said 'we're done', Ivy meant she doesn't want any more children, she wants us to be a three – and that three includes me.

'Yes,' I tell her. 'We do.'

'This sofa is lumpy,' she says.

'I know.'

Ivy stands up from the sofa and holds her hand out to me. 'Come on,' she says. 'Come and sleep with us in the forest.'

Chapter 38

'Ti... t... t...'

'What does it sound like?' I ask.

'T... t...' El screws his face up in concentration, his skin – clean-shaven now – turns red with effort. Without the beard he looks smaller and frailer than ever.

'Slow down, Elly,' Phil says, 'take a nice slow breath.'

'B... b... breaths!' says El. 'Breaths, breathty dumplings!'

'Breasts?' says Craig.

El nod nod nods and points a trembling finger at Ivy's chest. 'Tits. Y... y'tits're s... still m...' El holds his cupped and shaking hands in front of his chest.

'Massive?' tries Ivy.

'F... f... fuggin huge,' says El, stamping his feet and clapping his hands. And his laughter is rampantly, virulently infectious.

At home we still have our low hours and low days. We sleep in the same bed now, and often Ivy cries in her sleep – not waking, but sobbing gently, tears leaking from behind her closed eyelids. Some days she can't motivate herself to get out of the house, others she struggles to get out of bed. But we have good days, too – we smile, play, cuddle and sometimes we even laugh. Never like this though. But that's El for you. This is the first time I've seen him since before our boy was born, and if it wasn't for Phil's birthday I might have stayed away even longer. The last thing we need is El saying something tactless. Fortunately, the fact that we were expecting twins seems to have slipped his failing memory.

Phil is forty-five today and we are having a quiet bar-becue in his back garden. It's just the six of us: me, Ivy and T; Phil, Craig and El. Two families of three; two babbling dependants; two sets of circumstances that have thrown joy against sadness.

'I wish the sun would come out,' says Phil, shivering.

I turn to Ivy, waiting for her to scold Phil for making a 'shit wish', but she says nothing. She just looks up into the cloudless sky, smiling resignedly. 'Me, too,' she says.

Craig and Phil are no longer concealing their affection for each other – nothing bold or insensitive, but a candid touching hands, a hug, a simple kiss. El mocks, of course, but his pleasure shines through from behind the façade.

Despite it being Phil's birthday, our celebrations are restrained. Because this square on the calendar holds a significance beyond another candle on Phil's cake. Between today and El's birthday, Phil will take my best friend and the love of his life to Switzerland. They will visit Dignitas (or 'Diggitass', as El insists on calling it), and on the return flight Phil will sit on his own – getting smashed on gin and tonic, I hope – while El travels in the cargo hold inside a sealed box. El doesn't want anyone but Phil to know exactly when it's going to happen, but it will be before the end of November.

'H... have tr... f... treat me g... n... nice now. Treat me l... like a p... f... princess. Ha ha!'

'The things you'll do for attention,' I tell him.

'D... d... dyin' f'ttention! Ha ha ha!'

El doesn't know about baby Daniel, but Phil does and he winces at El's outburst, glancing in our direction to check we're not offended by this gleeful raspberry in death's face.

El stamps his feet. 'Dy... dy... dyin' f'rit!'

'El!' says Phil. 'You'll wake the baby.'

El turns to look at Ivy and Baby T. 'C... can I h... hold her?' says El, extending his thin, spasming arms.

'It's a he,' says Phil.

'L... looks like a sh... she.'

'El!'

'M... maybe h... he's a p... puff.'

'Not on my watch,' I say reflexively, and earn a thump on the arm from Phil.

'H... hold her ... hold her.'

'El, I don't th—'

'Here,' says Ivy, carrying Baby T across to where El is sitting in his wheelchair. 'You have to be very careful, okay?'

El nods and a calm settles over him. Ivy places T in his hands, but stays crouched at El's feet like a wicket keeper ready to spring into action.

'Th... that's nice,' says El, holding Baby T gently to his chest.

'Wh... what's her n... name?'

'It's a boy,' says Ivy. 'He doesn't have a name yet.'

'How long has it been?' asks Craig.

'Thirty-seven days,' Ivy and I say in unison.

Legally we have forty-two days from T's birthday to pick a name and register his arrival. I don't know what the punishment is for failing to do so, but if we don't choose a name in the next five days, we'll find out shortly after.

'N... no n... name!'

Ivy shakes her head. 'Can't find a good one.'

'E... El's a good n... name. S... speshly if she's a p... puff.'

'I'll put it on the shortlist,' Ivy tells him.

El frowns as if something is troubling him. He turns to Phil. 'D... din you s... say they're h... havin t... t...'

We hold our collective breaths.

'Twins!' El says. 'T... twins.'

We have alluded to our tragedy today, and talked about it in fragments and oblique references that sail over and around El's head. But this has caught us all with our guards down. I can feel Craig and Phil trying to bore holes into us with their eyes.

Ivy shakes her head. 'Just the one, El,' she says. 'It was just the one.'

'So,' I say to El, 'you got bored of the beard?'

'If I g... go Swissland with a b... beard,' he says. 'I'll have it f... f'rever, won' I? M... m... might go out fash-ion!'

'Maybe you're right, Ivy,' says Craig.

'Excuse me?'

'Maybe he,' Craig nods at the baby in El's lap, 'maybe he was only ever meant to be one baby.'

Phil stares at Craig but his expression is impassive.

'I mean ... that's how they start out, isn't it?' He glances at El who is distracting himself by poking his tongue at Baby T. Craig mouths the words *Twins*. He says, 'When they're identical ... they start out as just the one, don't they? I... I'm sorry, I don't really know what ...'

Ivy gathers Baby T up from El, she holds him above her head, smiling up into his face. The sun turns Baby T's thin spiky hair into a fuzzy halo of light. 'Is Uncle Craig right?' she says in a sing-song baby voice.

Baby T smiles. Then burps.

'Yes. I like that idea, too,' Ivy says. 'Yes I do. *Yes I do*. I like it very much.'

Chapter 39

On Thursday we complete the edit on *Pollock,* although it's now called *The View from Here* (Ivy's idea), which I prefer. The film is good; whether it's good enough, time will tell, but after we watch the twelve-minute and forty-eight-second cut, even without the grade and sound dub, I have a smile on my face and tears in my eyes. But I do tend to cry easily these days.

When I get back to the flat, Ivy is lying on the floor playing with Baby T.

'Hey,' she says, regarding me with a strange expression – a composite of guilt and amusement, it looks like.

'You okay?'

Ivy nods. 'Been out.'

'Where?'

'Oh, you know, just the Town Hall.'

'You ...' I point at Baby T, who is trying to suck the paint off a wooden rattle. 'You gave him a ...'

Ivy nods. 'A name, yes.'

'But we haven't picked ... I thought we were going to go tomorrow. Together.'

Ivy shrugs. *Tough luck, Buster.*

'Well?'

Ivy picks up our baby and carries him over to me.

'Say hello to Daniel,' she says.

And there's nothing I would like to do more, but I'm crying so hard I can't get the words out. Ivy puts her arms around me and Daniel, and we stand that way, hugging and crying in the middle of the living room, for a long time.

Chapter 40

The small brass plaque reads: IN LOVING MEMORY OF ARTHUR. THIS WAS HIS FAVOURITE PLACE IN THE WORLD. I don't know who Arthur was but he had great taste in park benches, and I've spent many hours here over the last handful of weeks. Rain, shine or howling wind, we walk on the Common most days now (we have even taken the occasional late-night ramble, braving the dark, the foxes and the local teenagers), and I've come to think of this bench – set back a pebble's throw from the duck pond – as our bench. We seldom talk on our bench; we simply sit, rock Daniel's pram and let the open space wash over us.

On Sunday, Dan will be fourteen weeks old and we are celebrating by driving to North Wales and introducing him to his aunty and uncle and his frenzied cousins. Four weeks ago, Steve and Carrie, the couple we met at our antenatal group, brought a baby girl, Daisy, into the world. We met them for coffee yesterday and passed two happy hours catching up and passing on parenting advice like the seasoned pros we are. I'd worried that seeing them and their baby might set us back, but if anything it's helped us move on. We have invited them to our flat for supper next week and Ivy is already fussing over what to cook. In a lot of ways it's like dating; discovering and revealing, making plans, hoping they like you as much as you like them. Who knows, maybe Dan and Daisy will get together one day, maybe they'll get drunk on cider in this very Common and get up to things it's best not to think about. I check my watch, stretch my arms overhead and roll the stiffness out of my neck – a signal that it's time to head home. Ivy stands, and while she checks on Daniel, I use my sleeve to polish the fingerprints and dust off Arthur's plaque. Maybe one day there will be a bench here with my name on it.

'What are you grinning at?' says Ivy.

'Oh, nothing. Just thinking how much I like it here.'

Summer started last week and the sweat is rolling down my back as I push our new single buggy across the rough terrain of Wimbledon Common. I'm going into town next week to meet Joe and talk about a couple of pitch-es. Ivy doesn't know it yet (I haven't told her) but the pressure to start earning again is on – in a big way. But no more shit, that's for sure – no toilet roll, no low-cost loans, no cures for constipation. You only live once, after all. And I'm already talking with Suzi about what next. Ivy is undecided as to when – or if – she will return to work, but my bet is she won't. Not for a while, anyway.

We reach the edge of the Common and I steer the buggy off the grass and onto the pavement.

'God, I wish there was just a hint of a breeze, you know.'

Ivy looks at me with an indulgent smile, but says nothing. It's become a little in-joke between us: me baiting Ivy with shit wishes, and Ivy swimming away. It's amusing enough, but I make a silent promise to myself to let it go now. We both know the Wish Fairy doesn't exist, and I sense that the joke is wearing thin.

'Let's go this way,' I say, pointing the buggy at a wide street lined with trees and imposing, double-fronted houses.

'I need to get home,' Ivy says. 'I'm semi-bloody-incontinent since that little monkey popped out of my whatsit.'

I push on down the road all the same. 'It's only a couple of minutes out of our way. We'll walk quickly.'

'If I pee myself it's your fault.'

Maybe twenty yards down the road, we draw level with

a house that has a 'For Sale' sign attached to one of the tall stone gateposts. I stop the buggy.

'Come on!' says Ivy, doing a little cha-cha on the spot. 'I honestly can't hold it much longer.'

I point at the 'For Sale' sign. 'Maybe they'll let you use the loo.'

'Stop messing about.'

'We'll pretend we're house-hunting.'

Ivy is still shuffling from foot to foot like a toddler desperate for the bathroom. 'Fisher! Do you know how much these places cost?'

Thank you!

'Oh, I dunno, a few grand more than yours.'

'Try a few hundred thousand more. Try five or *six* hundred thousand.'

'We could always sell mine.'

Ivy stops dancing; her face relaxes. 'Would you want to?' she says. 'Sell your flat?'

I shrug.

'Well . . . what's it worth, do you think?'

So I tell her.

Ivy's eyebrows creep towards each other as she stares at me. 'That sounds like a very precise number.'

'It includes the furniture, fridge and the washing machine.'

'Are you telling me you put your flat on the market?'

'Yup. Although ... well, it's not *actually* my flat anymore.'

'You ... you *sold it*?'

I nod.

Ivy's stare grows cold, turns sour. 'Why would you do that?'

'I ... I just ... I thought ...'

'No!' Ivy shouts. 'No. You didn't. You didn't think. Because if you had, you might have thought to ask me if *I* wanted to move out of *my* flat.'

'I ...'

All the anger melts off Ivy's face. 'Honestly,' she says. 'It's just too easy.'

'You ...?'

Ivy nods, licks her index finger and paints an invisible number 1 in the air. 'Too easy.'

'I hate you,' I say.

Ivy puts her arms around my neck and kisses me hard on the lips. 'I love you,' she says. 'I love you, I love you, I love you.'

'Nice day for it,' a male voice says behind us.

I turn around to see a man locking a car emblazoned with an estate agent's livery. He walks towards us, hand extended for the shake.

'Mr and Mrs Fisher?' he says.

'Yes,' I say, taking his hand. 'Something like that.'

'Ben,' says the estate agent. 'And who's this little fella?' he asks, crouching down in front of the buggy.

'I don't mean to be rude,' says Ivy, 'but if I don't get to a toilet in thirty seconds, I'm going to pee my pants.'

'Not a problem,' says the estate agent. 'You've got four to choose from.'

And we follow him into the house: me, Ivy and baby Daniel.

Epilogue

It's the last week in August and we still have a lot of unpacking to do. The essentials are in place: a cot in Daniel's room; Ivy's books on the shelves; my leather arm-chair, 42-inch HD TV and Xbox installed in the living room. Ivy's flat sold within a week of going on the market, and after that things moved frighteningly fast. We have lived here for three weeks now, and I still haven't adjusted to our new home (or the scale of our new mortgage). Of all the changes, one of the most trivial is giving me the most pleasure.

Ever since I have lived in London I have never had my own letterbox, I have always shared one in the communal door outside of my own private living space. And the sound of mail dropping through my own front door, onto my own mat in my own hallway . . . even if the mail is predominantly junk . . . it's like a small sonic sting, reminding me how far we've come and how lucky I am.

It's eight thirty in the morning when the melodic clatter wakes me from a shallow drowse. I creep out of bed, leaving Ivy and Daniel – *five months old now* – curled up and sleeping.

On the mat are a few flyers, a bill, a letter from the bank and a local paper. When I scoop them up I almost miss the postcard.

The front shows a log cabin sitting beside a stream in a glade of lush grass dotted with yellow flowers. In the background, snow-capped mountains thrust into perfect white clouds (all the way to heaven, perhaps). There is a single word artlessly printed on the front: 'Switzerland'.

My breath catches and my eyes are already damp as I turn the card over in my hands. The message on the back is written in scratchy, uneven letters.

Wish you were here
  Ha ha ha!
  El

And I find myself laughing and crying at the same time. *The last laugh*, I think, the tears coming harder now. I take the card through to the kitchen, attach it to the fridge with a magnetized cow and put the kettle on for coffee.

Acknowledgements

It's taken a long time to get here – to the acknowledgements page at the back of this book – and I couldn't have done it without the help of several generous, clever, patient and supportive people. Top of that list is my wife, Sarah. Mrs Jones has read just about every word I've written. Besides giving great notes (including a zero-tolerance policy towards bad jokes and self-indulgence), she helps me protect the time I need to write – looking after our girls while I lock myself away. Looking after me while I lock myself away. It's been a long time coming, babes, but we got there together xx. The other woman in my life, my other wise and demanding reader, is the same one who went through twenty hours of labour to bring me into the world. Braving bad language and a severe cataract, she read numerous drafts with good humour and a critical eye (who needs two!). I know it made you blush at times, but at least you learnt some colourful words along the way – thank you, Mum. Stan at Jenny Brown Associates is everything I could hope for in an agent – not only did he sell my book (no small thing), he improved it tremendously with some truly brilliant notes. In typical blokey fashion, he downplays his contribution, but make no mistake it has been huge. And then there is Clare Hey, my editor at Simon & Schuster. No Clare, no book. Clare's input has been significant – with many insightful and sensitive notes on the draft, including a free lesson in words that make women cringe. Who knew? A sincere thank you to the following people for reading drafts and giving me expert advice on midwifery, Huntington's disease and film production: Harriet Jones, Kylie Watson, Sarah Tabrizi, Mike Oughton and Steve Huggins. And finally a massive thank you to the publishing team at Simon & Schuster. Not only for your enthusiasm, dedication, expertise and infectious charm ... but also for making this experience a tremendously exciting and enjoyable one. Kerrie McIlloney, Sara-Jade Virtue, Ally Grant, Rumana Haider, Hayley McMullan, Elinor Fewster, Sarah Cantin, Sarah Birdsey and Emma Capron ... you're all wonderful.